J.E.H

‖‖‖‖‖‖‖‖‖‖‖‖‖‖‖‖‖‖‖‖‖‖

◁ **W9-CSM-014**

IMPRISONED BY PASSION

"Take off your clothes here and now, Lizzie," Galt said firmly. "We bathe together."

"I will *not*," she contradicted indignantly.

"But you will," he disagreed coolly, lifting her up and striding determinedly toward the water with her handcuffed hands beating at his arm and her feet kicking wildly at his legs.

He plunked her down and briskly unlocked one cuff so her hands were free. "It will be my pleasure then," he said in a deceptively ingratiating tone as he pulled her toward him.

"You've got a sassy mouth, Lizzie," he muttered, tilting her face up to him. "I know just how to shut you up."

Her lips parted and he claimed them before she could utter a word. She felt herself being drawn up against him, tighter, and still tighter. Then she was melting against him, her body seeking his closeness, her lips responding to his gentle assault.

It was crazy, she knew it was crazy, her uninhibited reaction to him. It had to be something in her, something about herself that she had never known that allowed her to let this stranger kiss her this way—touch her this way. And she knew she could never get enough of this seductive, wild madness . . .

IDA PARADIS
4502 - 50 STREET
WETASKIWIN, ALBERTA
T9A 1J3   PHONE 352-9397

ZEBRA'S GOT THE ROMANCE
TO SET YOUR HEART AFIRE!

RAGING DESIRE   (2242, $3.75)
by Colleen Faulkner

A wealthy gentleman and officer in General Washington's army,
Devon Marsh wasn't meant for the likes of Cassie O'Flynn, an im-
migrant bond servant. But from the moment their lips first met,
Cassie knew she could love no other . . . even if it meant marching
into the flames of war to make him hers!

TEXAS TWILIGHT   (2241, $3.75)
by Vivian Vaughan

When handsome Trace Garrett stepped onto the porch of the Santa
Clara ranch, he wove a rapturous spell around Clara Ehler's heart.
Though Clara planned to sell the spread and move back East,
Trace was determined to keep her on the wild Western frontier
where she belonged — to share with him the glory and the splendor
of the passion-filled TEXAS TWILIGHT.

RENEGADE HEART   (2244, $3.75)
by Marjorie Price

Strong-willed Hannah Hatch resented her imprisonment by Captain Jake Farnsworth, even after the daring Yankee had rescued her
from bloodthirsty marauders. And though Jake's rock-hard physique made Hannah tremble with desire, the spirited beauty was
nevertheless resolved to exploit her femininity to the fullest and
gain her independence from the virile bluecoat.

LOVING CHALLENGE   (2243, $3.75)
by Carol King

When the notorious Captain Dominic Warbrooke burst into
Laurette Harker's eighteenth birthday ball, the accomplished
beauty challenged the arrogant scoundrel to a duel. But when the
captain named her innocence as his stakes, Laurette was terrified
she'd not only lose the fight, but her heart as well!

*Available wherever paperbacks are sold, or order direct from the
Publisher. Send cover price plus 50¢ per copy for mailing and handling to Zebra Books, Dept. 2522, 475 Park Avenue South, New
York, N.Y. 10016. Residents of New York, New Jersey and Pennsylvania must include sales tax. DO NOT SEND CASH.*

Ecstasy's Hostage

THEA DEVINE

ZEBRA BOOKS
KENSINGTON PUBLISHING CORP.

ZEBRA BOOKS

are published by

Kensington Publishing Corp.
475 Park Avenue South
New York, NY 10016

Copyright © 1988 by Thea Devine

All rights reserved. No part of this book may be reproduced
in any form or by any means without the prior written
consent of the Publisher, excepting brief quotes used in
reviews.

First printing: November, 1988

Printed in the United States of America

Especially dedicated to the memory of Marcia Coury, who taught me about subjunctives and excellence while in the course of the seemingly futile task of trying to teach me French (she did); my gratitude for lessons which have stayed with me to this day.

And for my beloved John, who does everything to give me the freedom to write, and who, in the tradition of all true heroes, always tells me what I don't want to know.

One

He had watched her out of his jail cell window for nearly a month. He knew her walk now, and her stance; the way she held her body and the stubborn set of her shoulders. He knew her intensity when she was involved in something, whether it was tending the little garden she kept to one side of the stone-built jail building or cosseting the covey of stray dogs that always milled around the back door of the jailhouse. Her hands were always gentle, her beautiful oval face reflecting her resigned acceptance and a kind of compromise contentment.

He watched her hands unceasingly. And the line of her slender body, which was invariably dressed in a cotton shirt and dark divided skirt covered by a coarse apron as she strode across the flat arid rear court of the jailhouse, or knelt among her plants or her pets.

He knew the way her tawny hair glinted gold in the sunlight, and he had perceived the scorn flashing in her leaf green eyes when she received out-and-out snubs from passersby, who would then greet the sheriff cordially if he happened to be standing by her side. He would always introduce her to strangers as, "Elizabeth Barnett, who was to have been my daughter-in-law."

He knew the townspeople talked about that nearly as much as they talked about him. Elizabeth Barnett, he had heard, had come west to marry the sheriff's son, who subsequently presented himself at the altar in the form of a terse apologetic letter to his intended bride. The sheriff had immediately surrounded her with the protection of his family. He and his good-natured wife, Martha, had promptly taken her in; to them, she *was* family, in form if not in fact, and if their reprobate son had reneged on his commitment to her, they would not. She had nowhere to go, no way to support herself. She had fully intended to have been married and raising a family by then.

Instead she had become indispensable to Martha, and to the sheriff himself, the gossip said. The whole town had witnessed her humiliation, and not the least of it, he supposed, was being maneuvered into serving as the sheriff's factotum.

He wondered, sometimes, what she had really wanted. He admired what she had done: that in the face of her shame and adversity, she had accepted what fate dealt her, and she had made a life for herself.

She seemed to tackle everything with a kind of amused exuberance; everything seemed to interest her. And he never got tired of watching her. He felt sometimes that his observation of her saved his sanity; that he would have ripped apart the jail cell and the sheriff himself personally were it not for the sight of her calm serene face in his presence twice a day, bringing the fruits of Martha's mediocre culinary labors.

Her tranquil expression never changed, not even when she entered his cell. Only his close observation of her detected the darkening of her eyes to a wary jade, and the covert glance she invariably threw outside the cell where one of the sheriff's two deputies stood guard. The routine was always the same, yet always her mink brown brows would dip into the same concentrated frown as she set the tray down on the one wobbly table with a decided thunk.

Sometimes he would say something to her, something calculated to get a rise out of her, something, he thought later, to make her notice him.

But she had noticed. Her expression, as always, remained calm, but the eyes—she hated him.

He was a killer, and he was locked up where he belonged, and she hated him for killing Buck McCreedy, her eyes said, as she regally swept into the cell and collected yet another day's dismal remnants of a meal he could barely force himself to eat.

8

All to the good, he thought one particular day as their eyes clashed and he saluted her with a sardonic wave of one hand. She should be wary of him. He had been convicted—hadn't Lonita McCreedy testified so convincingly against him?—and he was awaiting transportation to a security prison.

And he was feeling desperate as the days flew by and the hours ticked away and his sentence became a nightmarish reality.

He knew only one thing: Lonita had gone and, with her, his hope of some kind of commutation of his sentence. He had heard the sheriff say so, one anguishing day long ago, with *her* voice following, a placating murmur. And the sheriff's voice, strident, angry: "Damn it all, Elizabeth; *you* don't understand. Lonita McCreedy is totally damn gone, my one witness, mind you, and she done left town without so much as a fare-thee-well, damn her to hell . . ."

He never heard the rest. He knew it was at that moment he began planning his breakout. And watching Elizabeth. How far could an unattached woman have gotten by then? Not bloody damn far from a small town like Greenfields without someone noticing it. No matter; he would get out and he would haul her back, and he would *make* her tell the truth.

The fury and tension in him roiled up once again, and the single-minded iron determination, as he began planning—and watching.

There was something different about him today, Elizabeth thought, as she unlocked the cell door and hesitated. For one thing, he was standing by the window rather than sitting. For another, she sensed an escalation of the rage in him. He was like a caged animal, ready to pounce.

His snappy black eyes grazed her face as she hesitated, and she stiffened. He didn't scare her. His coiled stance, with one muscular shoulder against the whitewashed wall, and his arms folded across his broad chest, did not unnerve her.

She walked briskly into the cell and set the tray down, aware that he was watching her every movement with the intensity of a predator.

9

Something wasn't right. She closed the jail cell door behind her firmly, and stood watching as he moved slowly from the window with the grace of a cat, his coal black eyes still pinned on her, a caustic twist of his firm chiseled lips beneath his gray-streaked mustache denting his lean right cheek.

He reached behind his long rangy body with a sudden movement and dragged forward the rickety chair from its usual place by the window wall, and positioning it in front of the table, he jackknifed himself into it. All the grim humor left his face as he bent his gray-shot-black head over the food, then looked up at her again and smiled unpleasantly.

Menacingly, she thought. She stared steadily back, raising her finely defined brows haughtily. His thick perfectly formed black brows immediately slammed into a forbidding frown.

She retreated then, motioning to Tex, the evening's deputy on guard, to follow her, warned by the latent angry power that emanated from him. The man was a killer and something was not right: calm as he seemed under all that mockery, she sensed he was about ready to explode.

"Galt Saunders isn't going anywhere, Elizabeth. Take my word for it."

"That man is in such a fury, he's capable of tearing that cell apart with his bare hands," Elizabeth contradicted urgently as she braced her body over the sheriff's desk to hammer home her point—no, her feelings.

But the sheriff, kind as he was to her, did not deal in feelings. Saunders was locked away, and guarded, and what could happen with Tex and Happy on the scene, he demanded reasonably, referring to his two bruisingly strong deputies.

Elizabeth straightened up and turned away from him, shoving her hand through her gold-brown curls in frustration. "I don't know. I don't know. There's just such rage in him under that impassivity. I swear, Edgar, you just don't see him every day."

"So he's angry," Edgar Healey agreed, tilting back his chair in almost the same motion and at the same angle as she had seen Galt Saunders do a dozen times. "Lookit, Elizabeth honey; your feelings about him are probably right, but I tell you, there's nothing he can do. He's strung in here until the circuit riders arrive, and that's that. I appreciate your interest and your concern, you hear? But you help me out more by keeping things running smoothly than by trying to make judgments about the mental condition of my prisoners."

Elizabeth backed away, feeling her usual flash of resentful anger at his patronizing tone. "Truly," she murmured, turning to stare out the jail office's one window.

Of course; she was a mere woman: what could *she* know about *male* things like anger and desperation?

The devil take him, she thought, and was startled at herself and how many times that exact same notion had crossed her mind in the past months.

She whirled to look at him, the kind bluff-faced man who would have been her father-in-law. His tall stocky body now fronted the desk, and his fleshy face was immersed in some papers. A strand of his thinning black hair fell over his broad forehead, and his full cheeks were tinted pink with either exertion or anger. She wondered which. His face was jowly, with two bright perceptive chocolate brown eyes, his long nose, and thin pursed mouth centered in the middle. He had a wide hearty smile when things were going his way, and a thick disapproving pout when they didn't.

But he was a good sheriff, kind and caring about the people of Greenfields, quick to act on any misdemeanor, no matter how small, even the matter of his wayward son jilting her at the altar, leaving her vulnerable and humiliated before the whole town. It had been a year and the shame of it, in spite of the sheriff's and Martha's good intentions, had not abated. It had settled in a hard little knot in the pit of her stomach that turned her away from the jockeying cowboys who sought her company to the affectionate horde of strays who demanded attention and love but who gave it back unceasingly.

She had packed away her trust, and her deep-seated need to be loved. She didn't need that. She didn't *need* a family. She needed to be self-sufficient, doing something productive. She needed to be independent.

The Healeys had offered her succor when she needed it, and

11

with it had come an ever-tightening web of their dependence on her because of her gratitude to them for taking her in.

She hadn't even been aware that this was happening until she found herself mentally railing against Edgar time and again for his attitude toward her—almost as though she were a servant—and his cavalier dismissal of her ideas.

She backed out of Edgar's office thoughtfully, not saying another word. *It's time to leave.* The thought bubbled up from nowhere—or somewhere beneath the smooth settled surface of her life with them—and she instantly knew it was the right thing to do. It was time to pack up and go. Time, she thought, to *really* be on her own.

She threw a considering glance down the corridor toward the cell that Galt Saunders occupied.

He was watching her.

But he always watched her.

The notion shocked her. How long had she been aware of it? It wasn't only when she delivered his meals, and his snapping black eyes coursed up and down her body, intent and all-seeing in that particularly *male* way of his. It was also when she was gardening, or feeding the dogs. She was sure she had sensed him at the jail cell window, observing every movement.

As he was doing now, as she signaled Tex to follow her, and she walked slowly along the corridor to his cell to collect his tray, as she did every evening.

His eyes followed her, pitch dark and glittering with jetty lights.

He was still at the table, overwhelming it and his chair by his sheer rangy height. She glanced at the tray, which bore evidence that he had, once again, only picked at its contents.

Tex, as usual, stationed himself on the hinge side of the cell door as she grasped one of the iron bars in preparation to unlocking it.

"You're finished," she said flatly, her expressionless voice not even remotely concealing its husky timbre.

"Oh yes, I'm finished," he answered in kind, and some inflection in his voice startled her for a moment.

But nothing could happen. Tex was right by the door and Edgar right in the next room.

12

She turned the key, swung back the cell door, and entered. He didn't move.

She walked in firmly and approached the table, meeting his cold black killer's eyes defiantly.

A murderer. The word tolled in her brain as she picked up his tray with her usual outward semblance of calm.

He smiled then, a sour menacing grimace. All her senses shot to attention. She faltered, and in that instant, he shoved back the table with his legs and grabbed her arm. The tray flew out of her hands and crashed to the floor as she felt herself hauled backward roughly onto his thighs, his arm gripping her like a vise around her midriff and both arms. His voice grated in her ear, his mustache rasping against her lobe. "Don't scream; I'll cut your throat."

She was struggling already, screaming Tex's name, her legs flailing and her foot stamping blindly for his boot.

He yanked her to his side as he jacked himself upright to face Tex, whose gun was drawn and his burly body dared his prisoner to make one unwarranted move.

"I'll kill her," Saunders growled.

"Oh yeah, cowboy? What with?"

Elizabeth watched Tex's face; she saw something move in his bulgy little pale blue eyes. She felt the scrape of metal against her neck, metal that had been bent and folded, and then honed, on its ragged point, to a fine edge against the stone windowsill. She felt it move cuttingly against her skin, hurtfully, meaningfully, and she stopped struggling at the same instant she saw Tex lower his gun.

"I'll stick it into her throat if you don't move."

The threat was real, uttered in a guttural growl that sounded like death against her ear. Tex moved slowly, but he moved away, as she felt the jagged point against the pulse at the base of her throat.

"Slowly now, woman," he breathed harshly as he moved her out of the cell still wedged against his long hard body with the metal point of his makeshift weapon close against her throat. Too close.

"Don't scream; don't talk. Do what I tell you."

She nodded, paralyzed with fear.

13

"Good." He shoved her forward slowly as Tex backed himself into the sheriff's office, and she could do nothing but let him push her, as though she were a marionette, to the threshold of Edgar's office, where he still sat, reading now the Greenfields newspaper.

"Healey!" Saunders's roar in her ear nearly deafened her.

Edgar looked up, startled, made a move for his gun, and then sank back into his chair as he took in Tex's helplessness and Elizabeth's predicament.

"For goddamned sakes," Edgar muttered, "damn it all, Tex; how the hell did you let this happen?"

"He'll cut her," Tex mumbled. "She could bleed to death."

"I'm glad you appreciate the niceties of the situation," Saunders ground out. "The gun, Sheriff." And Elizabeth was shocked to see the sheriff hesitate. "The gun, man or I'll cut her. This little point could rake her up real bad; you'd be stuck with her for the rest of your life, I could make her so ugly, Sheriff. Or she could die, Sheriff. The gun."

Edgar stared into a killer's eyes. Elizabeth's body turned cold as he did not move, and then hot as in seemingly slow motion Edgar made his decision and in little measured increments took out his gun and threw it across his desk. "And your handcuffs," Saunders added, edging his body and hers to the desk to take the gun and the metal cuffs that Edgar unwillingly slid across the table. "And the keys."

"You all want just about everything," Edgar grumbled, fumbling for the keys, hoping that Tex would make a move. When he looked up, he saw Tex was mesmerized by the sight of a spot of blood on Elizabeth's neck. He threw the keys at Saunders, who caught them deftly in the hand that now held the gun.

In that space of a flat second when his attention was diverted from her and he was momentarily off guard, Elizabeth wrenched her body against the iron bar of his arm. "Let me go now; you've got what you want. He won't stop you. I couldn't . . ."

His muscular arm tightened around her at her hissing words. It was true; he could let her go now, but he knew he wasn't going to. "Shut up, woman; you're coming with me." He pulled

14

her backward, out of the office to the corridor and the outer door, which was ajar. He kicked it open, aware already that Healey was in motion, out of the back door with Tex at his heels.

He dragged Elizabeth into the cool night air, and lifted his gun and shot into the darkness. The jolt of its report rocketed through Elizabeth's limp body and stopped Edgar and Tex in their tracks as they emerged from the shadows around the far corner of the building.

"I'll kill her," Saunders shouted into shadows where they hovered, guns in hand. He jammed the barrel of the gun against her neck.

Icy horror swept over her. The gun barrel was cold and hard, poking at her with a most deathly reality. She was frozen with terror; she couldn't have moved a muscle if he had dropped her right then and told her to run for her life.

He dragged her, still pinned tightly against him, along the broad avenue, which had quickly cleared of loiterers at the sound of gunshots. His eyes darted around quickly, looking for a horse or a wagon to commandeer. At intervals he shot into the air, aware that Healey and Tex were stalking them silently along the plank board sidewalks, under the cover of darkened storefronts, aware that he had little time, and a still more minuscule chance of escaping.

When he spotted the wagon, he had only one shot left. He threw Elizabeth facedown onto the hard surface of the wagon bed, tussling her arms together, wrenching them behind her, and snapping on the handcuffs. In another blurring moment, the wagon jolted into bone-jarring motion.

She heard shots behind him, and shouts. She heard the crack of a whip and the grunting of the team of horses as the jouncing wagon increased its speed.

Pain pounded through her head, behind her eyes, coursed through her awkwardly positioned muscles. She felt her body toss every which way at the mercy of the motion of the wagon, and with great effort, she began rocking back and forth to try to roll onto her back. The effort blocked out thought, blocked out horror. While she concentrated, she couldn't think or assess what was happening to her. But after a while even that strain

15

became unbearable. She felt like an animal, seeking surcease from attack.

She rested for a time, then once again struggled to find a bearable positioning for her aching body.

After a long time, the speed of the wagon decreased slightly, so that when she laid down her head, she did not bounce around so much. The rocking motion comforted her now; her limbs felt heavy with exhaustion, but she felt less desperate. He didn't intend to kill her—yet. She had a chance to plan, to try to escape. They were obviously headed someplace. Certain swerves of the wheels told her he had chosen a particular track, certain veer-offs on the road. She still had a chance.

She was determined to make her chance. She closed her eyes. He could hardly leave Missouri tonight. They would have to stop someplace.

And when they stopped, she would be ready.

The wagon careened around a wide curve and then slanted down a steep incline onto a gravel track on which, after a few hair-raising minutes, it lurched to a shuddering halt.

Elizabeth tensed her body as the wagon tilted and depressed on one side as *he* jumped off the driver's seat. She heard his boots hit gravel and crunch as he walked around to the back of the wagon.

She closed her eyes and waited, an eternity it felt like, and a thousand things sifted through her mind, all pointed, all irrelevant. She had one chance, and it was coming closer and still closer. She heard the sound of metal, and a creak as he unfastened a latch and the rear wagon gate swung down.

She held her breath as she felt herself being pulled forward by her legs, and turned—yes, turned! A lucky break. She gathered all her strength as she felt air beneath her legs, and in one springlike movement, she launched her feet upward—and connected. She felt him fall backward, growling in pain, and she opened her eyes to pitch blackness.

Frantically, she slid down off the wagon and began running. She couldn't even tell where she was going, except that she had passed the horse when he caught up to her. Even in his pain,

16

his strength and stamina surpassed hers. She supposed, in her terror, that she wasn't surprised to feel his large hands grasp her shoulders and pull her down.

"Where the hell did you think you'd get to, woman?" he growled, a terrifying splotch of black before her eyes as she stared up at him from the dirt at his feet.

She couldn't even answer. Nor protest as he hauled her up roughly and pushed her ahead of him.

He knew where they were, she thought, gathering her wits. He knew exactly what he was about. He had to have planned it; it wasn't a spur of the moment break. He *had* been waiting for his chance.

And she had been right.

"There's a step." *His* voice, not so angry now. He nudged her and she lifted one leg, feeling for the up step as he instructed. It was there.

"Where are we?" she had the courage to ask.

"My hideout," he answered promptly, and she did not like the satiric note in his voice.

She heard the rasp of a key in a lock, and the creaking of a long unused hinge; his hand snaked out and pulled her after him into a building that smelled musty. The door closed behind her, and his imperative hand released her. She heard his movements as he groped around the cabin, then smelled the scent of sulphur as he lit a lamp and she was finally able to see where she was, and his deadly intent expression.

"Welcome to my humble abode," he said mockingly, and set the lamp down on a table in the middle of the room.

She looked around. He had brought her to a small crudely built cabin that seemed to consist of two or three rooms and a loft, or at least there were stairs along one side of the room leading somewhere. There was minimal furniture: the table, some chairs around it, a cookstove nearby, a cupboard beside it, a fireplace made of stone on the opposite side of the room, a ragged-looking upholstered sofa some years out of date that still looked incongruous in that rough room, and a rag rug in front of it.

"Where *are* we?" she asked again.

"Sit down," he said brusquely, not answering.

17

"I *won't*," she threw back defiantly. "You know any minute the sheriff will come. You know that. It's useless."

"The sheriff won't find us here," he said with heavy finality, and she recoiled from the hawkish look of his face as the lamplight threw his features into shadowy relief.

"Then let me go. Let me go. Take me back to the road—and I'll walk. By daylight, I couldn't possibly tell anyone where you are. You don't need me," she added desperately.

He looked up at her. "I need you," he said, his words measured. And she wilted. He was implacable. But she couldn't give up; she wouldn't give up. She lifted her head to see him striding across the room to light another lamp and draw the curtains across the windows on the far wall. So he was afraid—afraid the light would draw someone who would be curious about who was in the cabin. But not the sheriff.

He moved to the window on the perpendicular wall, and she backed up against the door and turned the knob before scooting back to the spot where she had been standing.

He saw her movement; the witch, he thought as he came across to her and pulled her farther into the room. Her whole body resisted.

"Sit down," he ordered, pulling out a chair. "I want to look at that wound."

"Such kind concern," she spat, "when you are the one responsible for it. Let me bleed to death then."

"You won't die, woman, even if I do," he said grimly, waiting her out, his hands on his hips.

"What an unsatisfactory end for a killer—to see his victim survive," she tossed back at him—and whirled, racing toward the door, which she could have opened with just a jut of her foot if he hadn't been watching her so closely. He was right at her heels, and he dove against her body just as she reached for the corner of the door.

They fell heavily onto the floor; she landed on her knees and then fell face downward and he lay directly on top of her in such a way that if she flexed her fingers she could grasp him in his most undeniably male place. She didn't move. She didn't have to. The sense of his body on hers, all heat and hard angles, permeated her senses. A killer who had the potential to violate

18

her body as well.

Her fear escalated. She lay stiff as a statue. His living weight, his warmth, and his arousal shocked her. She knew nothing of these things from the tepid, respectful lovemaking of the sheriff's son. The feelings of her body warred with the perceptions of her mind. Fear won out; she couldn't lie there like a stick so he would think he could do anything he wished, or that he could intimidate her.

She began struggling to wriggle out from under him. "Damn it!" Her words were muffled as his large uncompromising hand pushed her face against the wooden floor.

"Now hear me good, woman," he whispered harshly into her ear. "I'm never letting you go, Lizzie, you hear? Never."

She stopped her feverish movements abruptly. She only heard one thing: her name—the corruption of her name. She lifted her head.

"Lizzie?" she shrieked. "Lizzie? How dare you! How—!"

"Hell, woman . . ." He eased himself off her and roughly pulled her up. "Now sit the goddamned hell down and let me look at you."

She threw him a mutinous green glance as she stumbled to her feet and allowed him to push her finally into a chair. "Lizzie," she mumbled. "You have a nerve! Lizzie. How the devil *do* you know my name?"

"I listen good," he grunted, tilting her head sideways with gentle hands so that her neck was exposed, and the tiny cut around which now the blood was congealed. "Damn, I wonder if there's some whiskey."

"Oh no," she protested, struggling to her feet. God, she hated not having the use of her hands; she hated feeling this helpless, this useless.

He pushed her back again, and she was forced to look up at him. His face was set in its usual hard, deeply cut lines. Only his eyes were alive, burning with some kind of emotion she couldn't begin to understand.

"I didn't kill Buck," he said suddenly. "I'm not a murderer."

"Sure," she agreed caustically, "that's why McCreedy's wife testified against you, why the jury convicted you, and why

19

you had to break out of jail."

He turned away from her without a word and began scavenging through a cupboard by the stove, looking up warily from time to time at Elizabeth, who sat calmly—perhaps too calmly, he thought—watching him with equally wary eyes.

"Don't move!" His voice cracked out before she could give action to her thoughts. He rose up slowly, his long fingers encircling a brown bottle, his coal dark eyes holding hers, daring her to move, to twitch, to breathe. He moved toward her, and his height and shadow-darkened features made him seem so menacing that for one instant she feared for her life.

He put the bottle on the table, where, in the dim flickering lamplight, she could see there was about a teaspoon of liquid in it. He knelt in front of her and lifted her skirt. Instinctively she reared backward.

"Well now, Lizzie, I reckon you've got the cleanest clothes of the two of us. I need a piece of your underwear for a swab."

She considered this for a moment, then nodded, thankful that today she had elected to wear a petticoat, something she sometimes omitted if the weather were too oppressively hot. She felt his hands grasp the flimsy material, and the flex of his fingers and shoulders as he pulled and it obligingly ripped apart, and ripped again as he sectioned off a large piece of it, and tore it again, and in half again, before folding it and pouring the odoriferous liquid from the bottle onto it, and applying it to the cut on her neck.

She screamed. The alcohol in the liquor burned and cauterized her skin—she hadn't expected that. She hated him even more. Her legs kicked out as the pain assaulted her, and her feet stamped at his. She cursed him, she had no compunction about it. He was a murderer and a torturer, and he was keeping her for some nefarious purpose he had yet to reveal to her. She didn't know she knew such words. She didn't know there could be such pain.

He held the padded material inexorably against her skin, stepping neatly out of the way of her flailing legs, circling behind her, keeping one hand on her shoulder, the other at her neck, amused at her feisty imprecations. He let her yell a lot before he lifted off the padding and examined the cut.

20

"You made it worse," she accused him. "I'm going to die of whiskey poisoning."

"Calm down, woman. It's clean now and somewhat disinfected. I'm going to wrap you up in a neckband for tonight."

"What? More?" Again she struggled upward, and again he pushed her down. He folded up a fresh piece of the material, liberally sprinkled it with the remainder of the liquor, whipped out his own bandanna, and pressed and tied the two pieces of material around her neck.

"God," she moaned. She didn't know then whether to be scared or laugh. She knew she had believed him when he threatened to jam the point of the tin plate into her neck, and to rake it over her face. She *had* believed him desperate enough to harm her, or to kill her. And now? The opposite side of the coin, and his going out of his way to succor her rather than let the wound fester? How did the two sides mesh? "You're choking me," she snapped as he yanked the knot and spread out the ends over her shoulder.

"A more fitting end for that sassy mouth of yours," he suggested testily, just on the verge of touching her hair, and stopping himself with the greatest effort of will.

"Thank you—even though you caused it in the first place," she said ungraciously, scanning the room furtively. He was still behind her, there was no use trying for the door. She envisioned herself diving through a window. Anything; he'd never let her go . . . not if she had any say in the matter. He was not going to win her over with kindness.

She turned her head and looked over her shoulder at him. His hands still rested on her shoulders, and he was watching her with an interested expression.

"You're coming with me," he said, answering the question in her jade-darkened eyes.

"Where?" she demanded.

"To hell and back, Lizzie, until I clear my name."

Two

"How?" she whispered.

"Never you mind. You hungry?"

She shrugged, trying to shake away his hands, which began to feel like two heavy weights pressing her down. As he most likely intended, she thought wrathfully, making a move to stand up. He wasn't going to tell her anything, she wasn't to be *sure* of anything except that for the time being apparently she was of some use to him and her life did not hang in the balance. There was something else, something she would make him tell her.

"No," she said finally. "I'm thirsty, and tired, and I don't know how you expect I'm going to sleep after what you've done, and with my hands cuffed up behind me like this."

He smiled at her, a slow reluctant smile. "I expect you'll make do, Lizzie; you're going to have to."

She cringed at his use of her name. He obviously intended to address her that way from now on, and she had no way to retaliate. She whipped her head away from him and stared stonily at the decrepit sofa across the room.

"I can offer you some stale coffee," he said, still behind her, "some equally stale, but probably more refreshing water, and some dried meat—at least for tonight. And a bed."

"Beef, water, and bed, in that order," she ordered in the same tone of voice as if she were in a hotel, to needle him.

"Your servant, ma'am," he murmured sardonically. She felt his hands lift from her shoulders, and heard him move away.

22

She had another chance now he was occupied, but she didn't think she had the energy, or the strength, to wrestle with him again. In a few hours it would be daylight; she would be refreshed with sleep and the sketchy meal he was preparing for her. He surely would uncuff her so that she could eat and rest. She still had time.

She looked up as he came around the table and pulled up another chair with his foot. In his hand was a cup of water, and a plate on which he had cut up a slab of dried beef into manageable pieces. He set both on the table, and she waited expectantly for him to release her.

He did not. He had a fork in his shirt pocket, and he removed it and stabbed a piece of the unappetizing-looking meat with it and held it out to her lips.

"You're going to *feed* me?" she asked in disbelief.

"Part of the service, ma'am," he said satirically. "You surely didn't think I'd release you just for this?"

"Funny, I was hoping . . ." she started, staring at the meat.

"It's edible," he prompted, nudging her lips with it.

"I hope you tasted it first," she muttered, still eyeing it as if it were the enemy.

"If your highness would just open her endlessly gabbling mouth . . ." he growled, running out of patience. Yes, he had tasted it, and it was hardly a continental meal, but it filled the stomach, and she needed sustenance, especially for what was to come.

She closed her eyes, opened her mouth, and he thrust the portion onto her tongue. "Ugh."

"Better than anything Martha Healey ever prepared for *me*," he commented, watching her face screw up as she relentlessly chewed the tough meat.

Her eyes flew open. "Pig swill."

"My sentiments exactly." He popped another piece into her mouth. "Drink some water; it won't seem so bad."

"You're too kind. *Killingly* kind," she added spitefully.

"And hasn't her highness a nice way with words," he murmured, pushing a third piece into her mouth. "Just shut up, Lizzie, before I gag your mouth instead of your wound."

She spit out the meat, and it hit him on the chin and fell to

23

the floor. "Oh, if I only had my hands free . . ." she hissed as he lunged to his feet and loomed over her threateningly.

"And what would you do, Lizzie? What *could* you do?" he demanded harshly, pulling her head back by grasping her hair and pulling at its molten weight. "I give the orders here, Lizzie; you do what I tell you. Nothing else, and without one damned more sassy word. Now, eat!"

She could only stare at him rebelliously out of sparking green eyes. The angle of her head constricted her throat, and she wasn't even thinking of the damage her legs could do. She could hardly think at all.

His face had taken on the ruthless expression of the killer, the man desperate enough to maim, to destroy. She mustn't forget that. She mustn't let herself be lulled by kind acts and caustically bantering words.

She moved her head slightly, and he released his grip. His other hand presented her with a fresh piece of the stale beef and she opened her mouth obediently. He pushed it in and she began chewing as he took his seat opposite her again.

His implacable pitch black eyes held hers, watching every movement. She couldn't read anything behind the glittering jetty light in them, nothing in the deeply etched lines of his face. Nothing in the faint twist of his mouth under his bristling mustache. He was a man used to hiding his thoughts, a man who preferred isolation and anonymity. Everyone said so. No one knew much about him, she thought as she chewed and watched his face for some lessening of the taut tension in it.

She swallowed. "That's enough," she whispered, turning her head from his offer of still another piece. "Some water now, please."

He stared at her for a moment, then held up the cup for her to sip. She looked at him pleadingly over the rim. "Can't you let me use my hands?"

"Not likely," he said, and a grim little amused smile flicked across his lips. He stood up, towering over her, it seemed to her, looking no less threatening. "It's time for bed, milady."

She looked around. "I don't understand."

"You don't have to understand."

"But wouldn't it be more pleasant if I did?" she asked

24

flippantly before she could help herself, and then she cringed.

That sardonic little smile skimmed his lips again. "I swear, Lizzie, I never thought you were such a damned chatterbox when I was in jail. There's nothing for you to understand. I call the shots, you come with me."

"Where are you going?" she had the temerity to ask.

"That's not for you to know."

"Is there anything for me to know?" she demanded, thrusting her body up from the chair indignantly.

"I'm not letting you go," he said again, his rich-timbred voice hard now with purpose.

She stopped her movement; what did he mean by that? What? "Uncuff my hands," she commanded. "I promise I won't run."

He considered her arrow-straight body for a moment, his burning gaze sweeping over her like a storm. "Wouldn't that be interesting? No, Lizzie. Good try, though."

"Scared you can't control me, is that it?" she taunted, moving around his tall lean body so that she was behind him. He didn't turn. She backed toward the door.

"I know the perfect way to control *you*," he contradicted harshly. He wheeled toward her with the grace of a panther and grasped at her shirt just as she turned to dash for the door. He caught the collar of her shirt, and her pulling away from him and his inexorable tugging ripped half her shirt right off her back.

She hated the smug crooked smile on his face. "Some fight, *Mr.* Saunders. You've got the height and the strength, and you've stacked the cards by trussing me up like a thrown calf."

His smile widened just a fraction. "All right, Lizzie of the sassy tongue; we'll even the odds." He slipped his hand into his back pocket and removed the key to her cuffs. "There it is." He dangled it in front of her eyes for a moment, then came to her and took her arms in one large hand and unlocked the metal bonds. He dropped her arms and paced around to face her.

Her relief was incalculable and it showed in her face. She couldn't bring herself to move her arms just yet; they felt cramped and bruised. She flexed one experimentally, and a sharp spasm convulsed the muscle. Her lips thinned as she moved the other arm, with the same result. She rubbed each arm briskly, and then her wrists, looking up at Saunders periodically with perfect hate greening her gaze.

He watched her with that trace of smug amusement playing over his mouth. His arms were folded now across his chest, and he looked tall and forbidding in spite of the slip of a smile. It did nothing to soften his features, nothing to reassure her. He was still the predator, and she was still his prey.

I'm not letting you go. She could still hear the words echoing in the room. No matter what she had promised, she had to try to escape. She had to try to defy a killer.

She shot a wary look at him. He was still standing in the same place, in the same way. The torn piece of her shirt still dangled from his long fingers.

"So now, Lizzie . . ." he said softly.

"Damn, *don't* call me Lizzie," she grated, swinging her arms experimentally, slanting another curious look at his face. It gave away nothing. "God," she muttered, seething in frustration. "Aren't they all right about you!"

"Absolutely," he agreed equably, but there was a flicker in his eyes, the faintest shift in his stance. "What are you going to do, Lizzie?"

She took a deep breath and slipped one arm behind her back surreptitiously. "Fight you, with every ounce of my strength," she hissed, making her move.

"I didn't expect anything less," he growled, lunging for her, his powerful long arms reaching her before she could reach the door. The rest of her shirt came off in his hands, and the front of her skirt and petticoat tore off as he brought her down on her back to the floor, then heaved himself onto her body.

And this time it was different. This time she had her hands to grab him, and pinch, to rake his arms and score his face, her hands predatory claws, her desperation fanning his anger and something else.

"So now, Lizzie—we know who is in control," he growled, his dark line-etched face close to hers. "We know you're not to be trusted. We know . . ." He stopped, his body becoming aware of her frenzied struggle beneath him, and her barely clothed writhing limbs. "We know . . ." he whispered.

26

"We know you're a criminal," Elizabeth spat in his dark grim face, her body twisting frantically beneath his lean hard weight, which this time felt shatteringly familiar.

His two large hands slid upward to surround her head. She felt his fingers winding into her hair and his palms press heatedly against her temples. He held her head immobile as his dark-shadowed eyes examined every detail of her face, her flawless skin, her spiky dark lashes that were the same color as her brows, which now veiled the telltale darkening of her leaf green eyes. Her stubborn firmly molded mouth that was set in an obstinate line.

What was she thinking? She had stopped her thrashing and lay quiescent now. Her hands grasped his wrists as if she had the strength to wrench his hands from her hair, but she made no move to do so.

She couldn't move, and she knew he would not and she could not make him. She was truly at his mercy, and she could feel already what her frenetic movements had done to his body. The air between them thickened, heavy with his growing heat and her heightened feelings. She didn't like what she was feeling. Her mind understood the ramifications of challenging this convicted murderer, and yet her body was reacting in a strange, different way.

"Lizzie . . ."

His voice was a mere whisper just above her mouth. She opened her eyes for an unguarded instant.

"I'm not a killer, Lizzie."

"I'd be a fool to believe it," she muttered.

"Wouldn't you?" he agreed softly, his jetty eyes searching hers. She prayed she gave nothing away, not her terror or her resignation, or her warring emotions. She felt as though he might be able to see everything in the dim close light where there were only the two of them and time was at a standstill.

He had a terrible amount of time to play with her, to use her, to do anything he wanted with her. The fear shot through her veins again. This just wasn't the time to challenge him. He had not been thinking of her as a woman. She had been a means of escape for him, and afterward, possibly, a ticket—somehow—
to someplace else.

27

"I'm not a fool," she said finally, feeling her limbs begin to tremble. He just kept looking at her, and *looking*.

"No," he murmured, "you're not a fool." His mouth slanted over hers and she watched it descend, closing her eyes the instant before it captured hers, quelling the fear of being intimately touched by someone like *him*.

Someone like him, whose lips were firm and soft against her own, gentle, probing, rimming her inflexible lips with delicate moist movements of his tongue.

"No!" She shook him away, mentally berating herself for not being able to just let him have his way. He would anyway; his hands held her just so, she couldn't get away, and his mouth claimed hers again, purposefully this time, as if he meant to make her understand that his demand must mean her compliance.

Or did it? She was swamped with feelings as he stormed her mouth, filling it, tasting her, urging her response with an emotion akin to voracious hunger. He delved deeply and fully into the honeyed softness of her with an almost repressed longing. She could feel it, and she could feel herself softening. She was so tempted to give in to his demand. Any kind of response would gain her time, would gain her his trust, she thought fleetingly; it was so easy to let him sweep her away. She wouldn't even count the cost; she would do anything to save herself. She *was* saving herself, she was.

In the end, she did not know what she was doing. He overwhelmed her totally until she could only try to seek her own gratification. She didn't know what she felt; everything within her was in brutal conflict—reality fought with sensuality for the upper hand. She could never have said she was a creature of the senses, and yet she had succumbed to the seduction of his mouth, and when, finally, he removed it from hers, she felt both bereft and overcome with shame.

His eyes flamed with triumph, a dark lord, embodiment of evil to her suddenly. "Well, well, well, Lizzie . . ."

"It doesn't mean a thing," she snapped, pulling at his hands.

His face hardened. "I expect it didn't," he agreed softly, dangerously. "A pleasant interlude . . ."

"Meant to reinforce exactly who is the boss," she interposed waspishly, to hide her roiling feelings. "As you said, now we know. You're bigger, stronger, more masterful, you've got the gun, you've got my clothes, you've got my body . . ."

"Would that I did," he murmured. "But be that as it may, it *is* a hard lesson to learn, Lizzie, so I won't take your body— yet."

Her hands shot out, aiming for his face, his eyes—anything. He had confirmed everything she was thinking—everything. She wanted to kill him. She felt dirty, filthy for having one kind of feeling about him, one impulse of being moved by his experienced play on her emotions. He knew exactly what he had been doing right off, and she—innocent that she was— knew nothing.

He grabbed her hands, deflecting them over her head. "Don't try it, Lizzie. I'm going to be *very* nice tonight; I'm going to let you sleep on everything that has happened."

"So kind," she spat at him, her eyes reflecting a moment's hesitation. Sleep—where? And how? She almost thought she hated not knowing anything more than she hated the situation he had brought her to.

"But I am," he agreed, shifting himself upward and pulling her with him. "I truly am . . ." He was on his feet, still holding her hands so that she came upright with him in one wrenching motion. "Now, come . . ." He pulled her toward the table, his pitch black gaze never leaving her rebellious face, his free hand feeling for the handcuffs on the table as she twisted away from the relentless grip of his left hand. She knew she was no match for his strength, and he yanked her right back to him again, forcing the metal cuffs over her wrists in front of her. So considerate of him, she thought scathingly, to give her some limited use of her hands.

"I *hate* you," she hissed as he inexorably snapped the cuffs shut. "I hate you! You're despicable, and strange, and everything I've ever heard about you. They were right. You're a bastard. You could have let me go. You *could* have!"

"Shut *up,* Lizzie." He was fast losing patience with her, and her sassy mouth and destructive words.

If she could only see herself, he thought, standing a pace or two back from her wild barely clothed body. If she could see the tumbling gold-glinting hair, and bandanna around her neck, and the cuffs that gave her the look of being someone's slave . . .

His slave. Her body was beautifully curvaceous; the long fiery fingers of the lampglow indented her waistline and heightened the tilt of her breasts above her threadbare chemise. One wrong move and her breasts might well push right out of her stays. One end of the bandanna grazed the tempting cleft between them.

Her vigorous motions made them bobble as she paced agitatedly up and down. "I will *not* shut up, damn you; *I* didn't ask to come here and you had a damned reasonable chance of escaping, without dragging me . . ."

She became aware suddenly that he was not listening, that his dark eyes were fixed on her moving body, on her breasts, on the fact that there was very little between her nakedness and the growing awareness she saw in his jetty gaze.

Her words grew frantic. "Don't look at me that way; don't you even think what you're thinking, damn you. I want to go back to the sheriff—*now!* Do you hear me? I will *not* go with you, not an inch farther, you hear? I won't . . . I . . ."

She was hysterical; she could hear herself getting worked up while the cool side of her brain that was still operating kept cautioning her to stop and stop quickly because *he* couldn't take much more.

And she couldn't stop, so he finally lifted her up and hoisted her over his shoulder, banked the flame in the kerosene lamp, and took her into the room beyond the living room.

It was cold and dank in there, damp and relentlessly dark. The prospect of it quelled the flow of her words and brought her to the realization she was slung over his shoulder.

Like an animal, for God's sake, she thought resentfully, damn him, and damn him . . . her manacled hands began pounding his broad back mercilessly.

Goddamn him, and he didn't flinch once as the heavy metal cuffs bit into his shoulder blades, and she just kept pounding and pounding until he swung down onto a surface—a bed, she thought she perceived it was a bed; her weight depressed it and it was covered with something coarse and abominably

30

unpleasant to the touch. "I can't see," she moaned, and suddenly a light appeared, with him behind it, his face predatory and devoid of any expression.

"We sleep here." Even his voice was blank. He set the lamp down on a crude washstand, and by its glow she could see that they were in another rudely furnished room that contained an iron bedstead on which she sat, a wardrobe, a smaller stove in one corner, and a crudely covered window.

"We?" she questioned, her voice rising. *"We?"*

"Yes, by hell, *we,*" he repeated harshly. "You won't spend a minute out of my sight, Lizzie, without I know exactly where I've shackled you." He crawled onto the bed and wrenched her hands out. He held the key, and he swiftly unlocked the cuffs, freed one of her hands, and snapped the open cuff onto his own wrist. "Pleasant dreams, Lizzie," he murmured mockingly. "Go on."

"I won't," she said adamantly, folding her legs under her.

"God, you waste a lot of energy on fights you can't win. We're going to sleep, woman; we've got a lot to do in the morning." He pulled her downward with hardly any force at all. It was almost as if she were glad to be lying prone. He turned down the light by stretching his arm as far as it would go, and even then, because she was no help, he almost knocked the damned thing over.

"What have we got to do in the morning?" she asked into the darkness.

"Things," he said, settling down next to her. "Just things." He eased his head onto the mattress. Damned uncomfortable. Lonita must have taken everything when she left, every goddamned thing, including her husband's life.

The mattress gave in the center as he tried to find a comfortable position, and rolled him gently hip to hip with Elizabeth, whose cuffed hand rested provokingly on her midriff. Which meant *his* hand nestled just beneath her breast. *She* seemed unaware of it—or perhaps she wanted it that way, he didn't know, but his intention of catching some sleep went out the window at the disturbing closeness of her body.

All he could think of was her beautiful breasts so clearly outlined by the thin material around them. Her breasts and the

31

reluctant, arousing heat of her unwilling mouth. God, she was a fighter. She would fight him every inch of the way. His back ached from her fighting spirit. His shoulder felt the pressure of her feminine curves still. She was so incredibly unexpected, he thought, trying desperately to turn his mind away from her alluring body and the memory of the one moment when her avid mouth capitulated to him. He would have to fight *her*, there was no other way; conquer her by any means at his disposal.

Yes, but he knew what he wanted to do, really wanted to do. And he *would* do it, and he would make her like it, and want him the same way he already wanted her. He wondered what she was thinking as she lay so tensely beside him, as wide awake as he, volatile and angry.

She couldn't bring herself to move, or even say anything. She was devastatingly aware of his heated presence beside her, and his large long-fingered hand so close to the underside of her breast. She refused to reposition her own hand. *He* had locked them together, so let *him* beware.

Besides, it wasn't as if she weren't used to being this close in bed with a male. In the halcyon years before her mother effectively separated from her boisterous brothers, she had shared all their adventures, climbing into one or another of their beds in the dead of night to plan this escapade or that, and falling asleep beside them, her limbs innocently entwined with theirs. But they were gone now, all of them, and this was explosively different.

All of her senses were fully alert. Every shift of his body seemed to bring him closer and closer still until the firm line of his hip and thigh almost joined with hers.

She could feel the heat, the magnetic contact of his body. She could feel the desire surging in him, and she wondered at his self-control. She felt as if the very air surrounding them vibrated with their heated awareness of each other.

She could barely breathe, suffocating with the need not to draw attention to herself and her thinly clad body. *His* breathing was deep and even, as if he didn't have a care in the world, damn him.

His mind wasn't roiling around agitatedly like hers; *his* body wasn't covertly straining to keep as far away from hers as possible. *He* wasn't worried about saving himself or whether she intended to harm *him*. She hated him for his impassivity, his pitilessness, his merciless strength.

She didn't know how she could hope to combat him. And she didn't know that he didn't intend to harm her, or that he was not a murderer.

She had no choices. She went over and over it in her mind. She could keep trying to escape, certainly, but that would surely bring down his wrath on her, and possible retaliation. She could pretend to cooperate and seek some other means whereby she could free herself, but she wasn't even sure that would work now that she had given him cause to distrust her.

Insane to think she had to earn her captor's trust! But that was the only conclusion she could reach: she would have to do what he wanted, and maybe, just maybe, he might relax enough to allow her some freedom.

But there were even dangers inherent in that decision. And finally her thoughts settled on the thing she had been refusing to think about: he could use his steely strength to overpower her sensually, just as he had done tonight.

And that was the crux of it, she decided, stiffening her body still more against the encroaching feeling of his nearness. She was appalled by her response to him, horrified that she had felt even a moment's flowering of some kind of feeling for a man who had threatened to maim and kill her.

He could still threaten to maim or kill her.

He could do any damned thing he liked with her.

She stifled the shudder that coursed through her at the implication of that thought. But the facts were there. He had told her the sheriff would not find them. He had stressed that wherever he was bound, she was bound to go with him. He had said he would never let her go.

There was not a particle of kindness in him, and she perceived that he meant what he said. His reputation in the tiny settlement town of Greenfields confirmed it: he was seen as an irascible loner who might even have killed his own wife.

And she had kissed him, she had felt herself being aroused by something about him. She had almost allowed herself to succumb to him.

My God, her inner self groaned. And she lay next to him, less than a breath away from being seduced by the warmth of his body! Her mind was going haywire, she thought. It wasn't possible to be sane, and to be so clearly assessing the situation and realizing that *this* could be happening: out of all rational thought and behavior, her unruly body and senses were fighting for the upper hand in response to a man who might still hurt her.

She felt as if she was slipping over some boundary, and she had to marshal every ounce of her own not inconsiderable strength to erect a barrier between her emotions and her intelligence.

She had to do what he said; very simply she recognized that was her key to survival. She would have to do whatever was in her power to comply with his wishes and hope for the best.

And she supposed that was what she was rebelling against: that she could only hope for the best. And then the possibility that at the end of it all, her willing cooperation still might earn her certain death.

She hated it; she hated feeling helpless and out of control, and not knowing what her fate was to be, and she felt a despair so endless and immutable that the only escape from it was to allow herself to tumble headlong into it, and give herself up to the welcoming void of sleep.

Three

She came awake suddenly to the certain awful perception that she was alone in the bed, alone in the room, alone in the cabin. And she was shackled to one of the iron posts of the bed frame.

He had left her!

She was going to starve and die on that dreadful rusty stinking foul-smelling excuse for a bed in a musty godforsaken cabin where no one would ever find her. The bastard! The lying stinking rotten bastard to do this to her! Damn him! Damn damn damn . . . ! Her panic was overwhelming and absolute. She could *not* die this way! That skunking fiend!

She shimmied her body upright, twisting herself so that she was on her stomach and in a position that would not pull her arm out of her socket.

Not a murderer! Not a killer! Oh, blast his rotten lying soul to hell, to leave her like this! She pulled frantically at the end that was snapped around the iron bar of the headboard. She would kill him with her own bare hands if she ever got free . . . and she would, even if she had to drag the bed single-handedly out of the cabin. If she had to break down walls, and carry it on her head straight back to Greenfields.

No matter how long it took, she would get out and she would retaliate. She swore it, in a fervent prayer. He would not get away with it.

But she was forced to admit, after a long time, that there was no way she was going to disengage the handcuff from the frame. She had to calm down. She had expended a great deal of her energy already in her furious pulling and pounding, and her steaming rage. She was panting with the effort, and not a minute closer to freeing herself.

She had, she realized with a touch of irony, all the time in the world. She sank back against the headboard to think. Crying and cursing would get her nowhere, even though it released a lot of her tension and her fear. Yes, her fear. It just was not possible that she was meant to die here.

She looked up at the adjoining wall where, slightly above her head, was a window whose rude curtains were drawn. She got to her feet and braced herself against the headboard, and with her free arm, and her leg, she tried to strain her body across the space between the bed and the wall to reach the curtains.

Damned cuff. Damned man. She couldn't reach it. She couldn't . . . she couldn't . . . she pulled and stretched her arm and her body to the utmost until her groping fingers could just reach the ragged hem of the curtain. Her thumb and forefinger pinched at it, caught hold of just the barest edge of it, and she snapped her arm back, almost dislodging herself in the process.

The curtain tore in a long skewed slit, and revealed the papered-over window. She could never reach it, never look out to see where she was, or call for help.

Devil the bastard, she thought, recklessly jumping back onto the mattress. She landed hard, feeling every coiled iron spring beneath the thin feather ticking, and wrenched her arm as well, which caused her considerable pain. She curled up in the most comfortable position and lay very still for a long time.

What time had it been when she'd awakened, she wondered fitfully. How long could a person live without sustenance? If the bed were so rickety to begin with, wasn't it possible that the frame was in as sad a shape? Could she push out the iron bars somehow? Or dismantle the frame itself? Should she do it soon before her exertions sapped away all her strength?

She turned onto her stomach and inserted a hand between the mattress and the headboard. The ravages of use were worse there, but no amount of strenuous pulling on her part yielded even the slightest movement of the bar. Her hands came away from the task orange with rust and black with dirt, and her anxiety grew with this clever and unsuccessful ploy to free herself.

She pulled up one corner of the coarse sheet and wiped her hands as thoroughly as she could. Her mind was a blank. She felt as if she could only concentrate on one small thing at a time.

Her terror totally overset her and she sank to her knees and began screaming, screaming for help, screaming imprecations, screaming Galt Saunders's name as though she were invoking the devil.

And then the door opened, slowly.

"Lizzie!" His voice cracked into the room.

She couldn't believe he was standing there so tall and lean and angry at *her*.

He had changed his shirt, he had obviously washed, for his jet black hair was still wet, and he held a coffeepot in his hand. Of course, she thought, with a bubble of hysterical amusement, just your average homey morning, where the man of the house is making the coffee while the woman of the house is handcuffed to the bed.

"What the hell is all the shouting about?" he demanded roughly, the tone of his voice not nearly reflecting how affected he was by the sight of her kneeling in the middle of the bed in chemise, stockings, and pantalettes, her hair in honeyed disarray, her eyes dew green and moist with rage, her manacled wrist raw with telltale violence, and her neckband skewed around so that her makeshift bandage had dislodged and now lay with its blotchy red side face upward on the floor.

"I thought you'd gone," she snapped. "I thought you'd left me to die." She was astounded at the thunderstruck expression on his face.

"I had things to do," he said shortly. "Things better done alone. I thought *you'd* sleep late."

She sent him a hostile look. "I didn't," she answered in kind, discomfited by the fierce expression in his intent gaze. And then the mask flipped back over his face. If he sympathized with her pain and distress, he was not going to show it.

37

He turned to the door and threw over his shoulder, "I would never have left you like that, Lizzie."

"So you say," she muttered, burying her face in her hands, not seeing him pivot back to her in time to see her curl into a protective posture of abject relief.

"I'll put up the coffee and then I'll come get you," he said.

"All right." Her tone was as bland as his. It wasn't all right, she wanted to scream. Nothing was all right, least of all his taking her prisoner. And leaving her. God, she would never forgive that. No matter what else happened, she would always consider that the worst.

She schooled her expression as the aroma of brewing coffee began to filter into the room. Her stomach growled, reminding her of her insane desperation of moments before.

When he entered the room once again, she was ready for him. Her obedient would-have-been-daughter-in-law expression was in place, the one she always showed to the Healeys, and she was ready to bargain with him, and to concede anything as long as she had a chance to stay alive. She just wouldn't forget anything. It all went into a little mental notebook in the forefront of her mind.

She watched with detached interest as he unlocked the one cuff and then snapped her other wrist into it.

She said nothing as he led her into the living room area, and motioned her into a chair, nothing as he poured her a cup of coffee, which, she found, she could awkwardly manage with the handcuffs on. Its warmth trickled right down through her body to her toes.

He had even found some nasty-looking slabs of bacon and some eggs which he was expertly frying up on the recalcitrant little cookstove.

She watched him for a while, trying to decide when to speak and what to say. Paramount, she determined, was his disclosing to her exactly what his plans were. Somehow she had to convince him of her sincerity to help him, and her realization that her struggling to escape would get her nowhere, and that her wisest course was to do what he wanted.

A sardonic little smile played across her mouth. Some assignment, convincing that big brute of anything. The evidence of her wrist had already given him a clue to her desperation this morning. He must have been aware that if she could have gotten away, she would have.

She sipped her coffee. He finished the sketchy meal and slid equal helpings onto two chipped ironstone plates and set one in front of her.

"Sorry you thought I'd abandoned you," he said laconically, folding himself into one of the chairs opposite her.

"I thought you'd left me to starve and die," she said with a hint of anger, staring at his strongly marked dark features that seemed only slightly more approachable in the light of day. The gray streaks in his pitch black hair were more obvious, more plentiful. It struck her that he seemed older than perhaps he was, because of the gray, and the hardness in him, the deeply cut lines that roweled his face between his perfectly shaped black brows, and down his cheeks from the straightness of his nose to his firmly molded mouth, which was fixed, as always, in that inflexible line beneath his gray shot mustache.

He looked as if he was capable of anything. The deep-seated emotion was there, kept rigidly in check, held close, not for observation by any casual observer.

His jetty eyes snapped and flared at her statement. "I reckon you could have had cause to believe that," he agreed finally. "But I would not have done that."

"Which is easy to admit after the fact, and which *I* have no cause to believe anyway," she retorted, frustratedly stabbing at a piece of bacon with a greasy fork. She speared it and lifted it to her mouth, turning the fork as she did to a better position for her to bite from it. The bacon fell off, disconcertingly, and landed back in her plate.

"An impasse, Lizzie," he said quietly, taking her fork and feeding her the bacon with the gentleness of a father with a baby, ignoring his reaction to the exposed swell of her breasts as she leaned forward to bite the bacon with a ferocity that said she would like to bite *him*.

"Don't call me Lizzie," she growled with her mouth full.

"You, however, may call me Galt," he said kindly, lifting another piece of bacon to her mouth. "Seeing as how we're going to be together for a while."

39

"Was that definite?" she mumbled, reaching eagerly for the food. God, she was hungry, hungry and worn, and if her heart ever stopped pounding, she might still be expected to live. She chewed furiously, extracting the last little bit of flavor from the obviously well-past-its-prime bacon. It was the most delicious thing she had ever tasted, that and the eggs. And the coffee. The warmth. The slight flash of amiability in the eyes of the alleged murderer. She might, just might, survive after all.

"I told you," he said, and the implacable note was back in his voice. She just wouldn't stop fighting, he thought, sipping his own coffee pensively. He hated shackling her hands, the hands he had observed so intently all those weeks in prison; he hated stilling them, and making them move awkwardly, making her appear clumsy, and afraid. Above all, he wanted to convince her not to be afraid.

"I believe that," she said finally. "And I believe that I can't keep defying you and trying to run away without some cost to me that might be more devastating than anything you could do."

"You're right," he agreed noncommittally. Anything he could do, for God's sake, like he was an ogre, a rapist, a murderer. Damn to hell.

"Which you proved with admirable demonstration yesterday," she went on, a faint flush tingeing her cheeks as she steered by any reference to his kissing her.

"So I did," he said equably, standing up to clear the table.

She gritted her teeth. He was still giving away nothing. "Devil you, you're so damned closed up! Say something! Say you're glad I came to my senses or something!"

"I knew you'd see it my way, Lizzie," he said gently.

"Don't call me Lizzie," she hissed, totally out of patience with him. "I can't stand this, I can't. How can you expect cooperation if I don't know from one minute to the next what's going on or if you're planning to dispose of me somehow when you're free of Greenfields territory?"

"I reckon you can't," he said, sliding his chair around so that the back splat faced her and he could rest his arms, when he finally sat down, across its back rail.

"Are you going to kill me?" she whispered.

"Hell, Lizzie." He couldn't bear that. He shot up impatiently and began pacing the room, a six-foot-plus tower of fury. "What else, woman?" His voice grated, as if his patience were going again.

She took a deep breath. "Where are we, that you were so sure the sheriff would never come looking?"

He considered her face for a long breathtaking moment. It really came down to whether he would trust her—with some of the essentials. It might make things easier. It might not. He had to decide whether to chance it. There was no reason for her to know. All she had to be sure of was that he did not mean to harm her. And yet . . .

"This is the McCreedy ranch," he said at length. "I would have thought you could have figured that out yourself."

She took a deep shaky breath. He could have come down hard on her for that one. He could have refused her anything. He could have tied her feet and gagged her and really left her alone in that room. All the things he could have done, the least of which was answering her questions. Yet, he had apologized for scaring her, and he had told her what she wanted to know. She felt a shot of hope.

"I never guessed," she admitted. "I assume you were counting on the sheriff going out to your place."

"As he did," he concurred. "And it's not too far away, so I plan to get out of here today. With you."

"I won't fight you," she assured him, and he sent her a skeptical black look. "Where are . . . we . . . going?"

"Do you really need to know that?" he asked edgily.

"I'm going crazy not knowing anything. Please tell me. I promise, I promise I will help you."

She looked so beautiful with her pleading green gaze. Her beautiful mouth formed the words readily enough. She seemed to have relaxed somewhat with his assurance he would not harm her, but even that could be a pose. He didn't know, he just didn't know. "I'll tell you everything when we're on the road," he said finally.

"And how soon will that be?"

"Within the hour, Lizzie. As fast as I can put a wagon together and you can scare up some clothes from what's left of

Lonita McCreedy's wardrobe."

He had already begun rigging up a makeshift Conestoga wagon, and where he had gone, he told her as he showed her what he had done, was back to his ranch in the early hours of the morning to appropriate certain supplies and stock that were not available at the McCreedys': two fast horses; a huge keg of water from his own cistern, which was lashed to the side of the crudely reconstructed wagon; and some dried stores, which were stuffed into a corner beside one of the two rickety dressers from the McCreedys' house that he had positioned at the back of the wagon, against the driver's perch.

He had fashioned and fastened a line of ridgepoles to the side of the wagon to support a huge drooping flat-topped canvas tarpaulin stretched over them. Inside, on top of the dresser he had put the kitchen table, upside down, and fitted two of the kitchen chairs, also upside down, into its base. Wedged into the space above that was a huge sack of flour. In the drawers of the dresser he had stored all of the pots and pans he could find that he thought were viable for cooking over an open fire, sacks of cornmeal, salt, flour, rice, beans, and tins of coffee, sugar, and baking soda. In the top drawer he'd placed tin plates and cups—so nicely unbreakable when the wagon was lurching over uncertain, rutted roads—forks, spoons, knives, including a long sharp one for gutting game, which elicited a quizzical glance from Elizabeth, who was kneeling beside him on the straw mattress he had shoved in front of the dresser.

"Oh, I figure by the time I get to use this, you'll be so dependent on me, you wouldn't dream of trying to use it." His tone was light, but there was a thread of seriousness beneath the words.

"Don't be too sure," Elizabeth murmured, staring down at her cuffed hands resentfully.

"Can you cook?" he asked abruptly.

"No, I never learned, and Martha never volunteered to teach me." Her eyes sparked jade as she met his.

"Thank God," he muttered, pulling out another drawer. "I will." He dug into its contents. "All right; there's matches, a couple of lanterns, kerosene here, soap, toweling in this drawer, a mirror . . ."

"You're vain too?" she quipped, ignoring the little dart of pleasure at this thoughtfulness which also included a comb for her. He'd also packed a sewing kit because she would certainly have to restructure some of Buck's clothes he had packed helter-skelter into a trunk, along with a vast number of odds and ends, including India rubber sheets to protect them in a rainstorm.

"You could cut down some of Buck's trousers, or make them into a skirt," he said helpfully as he worked the trunk into the space on the other side of the dresser.

"I can*not*," Elizabeth contradicted. "I can't sew."

"You can't sew? You *can't* sew! You can't cook. Damn to hell, Lizzie, why not?" He sank back on his heels in amazement, guarded, as if he thought her denial of these womanly arts was some trick.

"There was always someone else to do it," she murmured, not quite meeting his fathomless black eyes.

"A houseful of servants, I expect," he muttered ironically.

"Well, yes," she whispered, and was not surprised when his head jolted up, and that smug knowing expression flashed in his eyes.

"I should have guessed," he said mockingly, "but it's to no point, woman. You'll learn, and I'll teach you and that's that." His eyes skimmed her face. There was no vacuousness there, only a sure throbbing intelligence. She was *not* a pampered belle; he would have bet on it. And yet . . . a houseful of servants to do those things . . .

Her eyes flashed as though she were reading his thoughts. "Yes, you'll make *sure* I learn *everything* I need to stand me in good stead—with a *man*," she sniped nastily, and she felt her whole body twang as the sardonic light in his eyes deepened into something quite different. She was again terrifyingly aware of how little she had on, and how wrinkled and revealing the thin cotton underclothing was to his knowing penetrating gaze. And how, when she was forced to stand on her knees, as she was now, her breasts thrust forward in a most undeniably feminine way.

And how his pitch dark gaze rested on them, and his voice deepened a shade as he agreed, "Everything, Lizzie."

Her face set for an indefinable moment as she sifted the feelings that churned inside her. He wanted her. Those outlaw eyes flamed with the very hunger she had felt in his ravenous kiss. She felt the same detached schism of her senses, all at once aware of his masculinity, and his threat, and the two halves were part and parcel of the whole.

Her voice caught as she thought how she could use this to her advantage.

"Won't you please tell me what you're planning to do?"

Her halting question hung in the pulsing air between them.

"No," he said abruptly, and the simmering heat cooled as quickly as if it were a flame doused with water. "C'mon, Lizzie." He crawled forward on the mattress until he reached flooring, and the wagon gate, and slid onto firm ground. His hands reached for her, caught one leg, and pulled her down onto her back and forward out of the wagon.

"Here." He had found an array of hats, for himself, for her, including a bonnet. His wife's, he said. He popped it on her head, ignoring her blazing jade eyes, and she immediately shook it off. His wife. His mouth tightened as he picked it up, turned away, and shoved it into a corner of the wagon.

"Into Lonita's bedroom now, please," he said inflexibly.

"*Really?* Lonita's bedroom?" she asked quizzically, unaccountably annoyed that *he* knew about Lonita's sleeping arrangements.

"Certainly. You can't travel like that." His hard gaze swept her slender full-bosomed body appreciatively. "Though *I* might not mind if you'd agree to stay in the wagon."

Elizabeth looked down at her wrinkled pantalettes and ruined chemise. Her breasts were almost ready to fall out of their confinement. And her boots looked utterly ridiculous with such deliciously feminine garb. "Oh, I don't know. I rather like the costume. It's cool, and it's rather refreshing not being impeded by a skirt," she answered mockingly, slanting an impudent glance at him.

He wasn't smiling. He grasped her arm and pulled her into the house, past the bedroom they had shared, into another,

44

smaller room.

No wonder Lonita McCreedy had left town, Elizabeth thought viciously, looking around the mean little room. Its bedstead was made of only a slightly better quality iron than the one she had slept in. The washstand was plain pine, the ewer and basin on it undecorated white ironstone. There was another of those rag rugs on the floor, and an even smaller stove in one corner. A curvy cane-backed plank-seated rocker was by the window, which overlooked the barn area.

And the wardrobe that Galt was rummaging through looked like something Buck McCreedy had nailed together out of four flat pine boards, haphazard and uncaring.

The closet was appallingly empty except for two plain skirts, and one unadorned inelegant gray-tinged white shirtwaist.

"Damn it to hell," he muttered, tossing the clothes into her arms. He seemed distressingly disappointed, as if he were intimately familiar with Lonita's room and what her clothes closet contained.

"These are ugly," she snapped, letting them fall on the floor.

"You don't have to be pretty on the trail," he said sarcastically, picking the skirts up and examining them. One was a colorless dun shade, the other black. "Wear the black. We'll figure something else out later. Go on, get dressed."

"I can't," she gritted, lifting her arms, fully expecting again he would unlock the damned pestilent cuffs and let her get *on* with things. And then what? She couldn't race out of there totally undressed. Damn him. "I won't wear Lonita Mc-Creedy's castaway clothes," she added with a touch of peevishness.

He looked down at her, considering her mutinous expression for a moment longer. He had never quite perceived how tall she was. She didn't have to lift her head very far to burn him with that heated green gaze of hers. He wouldn't have to bend very far to taste . . .

He shoved the thought away, and shrugged. "Fine with me," he said noncommittally, giving one last lightning look around the room. He never had liked it that Lonita did not share Buck's room. But she never did like Buck. And that was something else again.

He edged his way out the door, leaving Elizabeth standing, fuming, in the middle of the roughly furnished room.

Stupid men, she thought maliciously. Dumb stupid men, all of them. She stooped and picked up the black skirt. And how the devil did that miscreant think she was supposed to dress herself? Devil him and damn it all. Stupid of him not to think of that! She stamped her foot in frustration.

And then the thought occurred to her that every minute she delayed might be time gained for the sheriff and his men to find her.

"Lizzie!" He appeared in the doorway almost as if he had divined her thoughts. "Hell, woman, you are either screaming, or cursing at me, or planning to run away, and I don't know what I'm going to do with you."

"Let me go back to Greenfields," she suggested tightly, whipping the black skirt into his large hands. She watched curiously as he threw the garment over his shoulder and stooped to pick up the dun-colored skirt, then carefully began folding it up instead of rising to her obviously impossible suggestion.

Then he looked at her, his black eyes inscrutable, his voice hard as he emphasized, "You are coming with me, Lizzie. Dressed. Or not dressed. But soon. So don't tell me what you'd *like* to do; that's what you're *going* to do, one way or another, if I have to dress you myself."

"I can't wear Lonita's skirt," she said stubbornly. "She's a lot smaller than me . . ." She trailed off as she saw his glinting eyes rake over her body in that all-encompassing way of his.

"She quite obviously is," he agreed, with that faint edge of humor in his rich voice. "But I expect you might—just might—be able to squeeze into that black skirt."

He obligingly unfolded the black skirt from his shoulder and held it out toward her to step into.

"I expect I might," she said frostily as she unwillingly moved toward him. Her eyes crackled with green fire as she bent forward slightly to balance herself to lift one booted foot into the circle of the skirt. Her manacled arms pressed against the sides of her breasts at that instant and squeezed them forward so that as she straightened up, they fell out of the

46

beribboned vee of her neckline.

A hot wave of embarrassment suffused her whole body as her cuffed hands vainly tried to tuck her breasts back into the chemise. The compressing motion of her arms only made things worse, pushing the creamy pink-tipped mounds even farther from their confinement.

Finally she straightened up and stared at him, daring him to say a word, or to look at her, or touch her.

Oh, but he *would* look. His dark devil gaze kindled with a blazing jetty light that devoured each upthrust breast with his hungry sensual gaze.

She felt like beating him with her hands again, like screaming as his eyes slid all over her nakedness and back to her stone-hard unforgiving face.

He dropped the skirt and lifted his hands to her breasts. His hands were so large, she thought abstractedly, holding her breath, ready to spit in his face if he did the merest wrong thing; his hands were so large, she thought, holding her body tautly, which only pushed her breasts forward wantonly, so large he could hold each of her breasts and cover them completely.

The thought shocked her, and in the next moment, the feeling of his fingers brushing against each taut nipple utterly shattered her composure as he gently lifted the material of her chemise and slid it as carefully as he could over her exposed breasts.

Her whole body tingled at the sensation of his hands touching her, and at the cast of her thoughts, and his heated closeness as he efficiently tied the frayed ribbons, and his impenetrable gaze rested on her covered breasts. Only the thin cotton hid nothing; every contour was fully revealed to his knowledgeable black outlaw eyes.

Without a word, he stooped and held out the skirt for her to step into. Without a word, she lifted her leg and let him pull it up around her waist, let his deft hands pull and tug the damned waistband together in a way Lonita never would have had to do, while his eyes never left the profile of her breasts and her taut nipples.

He was so adept, she thought, shaking with a consuming

anger. A murderer at home with women's clothes and pots and sewing equipment, who knew with a surety just how to touch and excite. Who knew just how to play with her emotions and her life.

"You're sure to lose some weight on the trail," he murmured confortingly as he finally managed to secure the waistband. She almost thought there was a humorous gleam in his eyes, that his expression had lost that ravening hunger that was so appalling to her. He was looking at *her* now, and not her treacherous body, and his mocking suggestion that she was, perhaps, heavier than she should be passed by her like lightning.

All the hot coursing sensations ceased as the tenor of the atmosphere between them changed. "You'll have to wear one of Buck's old shirts," he added as she trailed him into the bedroom they had occupied.

Buck's shirts, she discovered, were miles too big. Galt unlocked one cuff so she could slide her hands into the sleeves of the cleanest one, and button it, and then wrenched them together again. He rolled up the sleeves, kindly removed the bandanna that had been chafing her neck wound, and found a ratty-looking leather belt that he cut down and notched for her so that she could cinch the shirt around her waist.

"I hate this," she growled fervently.

"I hope we're finished, Lizzie."

"I need a moment of privacy," she countered suddenly.

"There's an outhouse."

"My hands?"

"You'll manage," he said confidently. "Let's go; we've got to get out of here. Look around. Anything else you can think of to take?"

"No," she snapped, heading for the doorway adamantly. "You've taken everything—including my freedom."

Four

His plan was ingenious, she thought scathingly hours later as a pair of plodding oxen, liberated from the McCreedys' barn, finally pulled their overloaded wagon, with the rocking chair rungs sticking incongruously out the back flap, across the county line, up toward the Kansas border.

"*That* far?" she demanded in consternation.

"That far," he said grimly, and she couldn't fight the determination she read in every line of his set expression.

"You bastard," she hissed, fraught with impotent anger once more. She felt like swinging at him across the high-perched wooden wagon seat with the rusty iron arm rests. The son of a bitch really thought he was going to find Lonita McCreedy and drag her back to Greenfields—by the roots of her hair if necessary—to clear his good name.

That was what he had said: he was going to find Lonita. And he was sure he might have to go as far as Rim City to trace her.

"Sure, and the sheriff won't be chasing after you, or anyone else for that matter," she had flung at him sarcastically. She, in fact, was as sure that Edgar would trace him sooner than ever he thought possible.

"My dear Lizzie," he drawled, turning his hard-lined face and his snapping black eyes full force on her resentful countenance. "Who is going to look twice at a newlywed couple on their way west, toward the Missouri River, who are hoping to join up with a wagon train in either Independence or Rim City?"

She was struck dumb by the simplicity of it. All the little details he had taken care of in the dark of the night, the way he had outfitted the wagon, down to the kitchen table and the rocking chair, were smokescreens designed to fool the casual observer into thinking they really were what and who they were pretending to be.

He had a dramatic eye, she thought with consuming rage, and she held up her hands. "Do you truly think that anyone will regard my handcuffs as some innovative new kind of jewelry?"

"I think no one's going to care for the first hundred miles," he retorted calmly, and that sent her into a fuming silence again. He had an answer for everything, except what he was going to do if Lonita McCreedy was not to be found anywhere between Greenfields and Rim City.

That was his problem, she thought bitterly; hers was to survive the trip. A trip he had planned, spur of the moment, while thinking about escaping jail, to follow someone on a hunch, based on a conversation, or perhaps several—he hadn't elaborated on that except to say he had reason to believe Lonita might be headed that way; but still—a wild-goose chase, even if Lonita had been serious about her daydreaming about a livelier existence in one of the provisioning towns on the Kansas frontier.

And why hadn't she talked to Buck about it? Oh, she had talked to Buck about it, and Buck was all full of ranching and building a herd, expanding a cattle operation, raising horses. Buck hadn't listened.

And Lonita had never known a life like that, Galt said, as if that excused it. Lonita was like his wife, he said, which made Elizabeth's ears prick up, and her unruly mouth immediately mutter in an undertone, "Of course," as if that explained everything for *her*.

It explained nothing, and she knew she could not ask him about his wife—not yet. He was barely being civil answering questions about Lonita.

And she still didn't understand, except she now saw quite clearly why he "needed" her. She was his cover, his blind, the thing that would make him unremarkable in the public eye, that would color him different than he was.

It was so clever. No wonder he had watched her so intensely. He probably knew all about her. Her rage boiled up again, at the thought of how many ways he was using her, how many ways he could . . . and then what might happen if and when they actually stopped in at a settlement? What would he expect of her once he had announced to one and all who they were and where they were going?

The ramifications were staggering; they would always, of course, be put in the same room. And she hadn't even thought to demand separate sleeping arrangements on the trail—she had assumed, since he had packed two bedrolls besides a wad of bedding for the straw mattress, that *he* would be sleeping outside the wagon.

But what if—the what-if questions were mounting unceasingly; her spuming fury gave way to a ragged pounding headache. None of these questions and answers mattered; she was trapped with a murderer—a man who could and would do what he wanted.

She felt a glimmer of relief as he pulled the wagon off the road finally, and wordlessly jumped down to unhitch the oxen.

"Let's go, Lizzie; no rest for the weary here."

She watched without comment as he rooted out three stout branches and planted two in the ground to support one crosspiece from which he suspended a bail-handled cast iron oven from a hook. "C'mon, Lizzie, fill this damned thing with water and start the fire."

She looked at him blankly. "Galt, I am not playing games with you. I don't know how to do those things"—she almost bit her tongue saying it—"and I couldn't do them, even if I did, without the use of my hands."

"Another useless woman," he muttered exasperatedly, throwing aside his hat then coming around to her side of the wagon and extending his arms to her.

"And *what* do you mean by that?" she demanded, not moving.

"I mean I've yet to encounter a woman who could take care

51

of herself in the damned wilderness, is what I mean. Hop to it, Lizzie, because you're going to learn." He reached for her then, and there was no way to avoid his large encompassing hands that lifted her down as easily as if she were a sack of foodstuffs.

Wordlessly, he unlocked the right cuff, so that the whole thing dangled from her left wrist like some kind of bizarre bracelet.

She didn't bend a bit under his formidable jet gaze. "So," she said with just a hint of forced cheeriness. She knew he would hate it. He handed her a small tin bucket. "About three of these in the cauldron. Then pick through about two handfuls of beans you'll find in the back."

"Pick through?" She made the words sound as though it were the most distasteful chore, and counted herself lucky that the sky was darkening and he couldn't quite see her dismayed expression. Never had she done anything like this. One had "other" people to do things like this.

"Go through them for rocks and dirt, Lizzie. We can't waste water draining them." His tone was guarded, as if he had not fully expected this kind of ignorance.

"For dinner tonight?" she asked hopefully as she began siphoning water from the cask.

"Tomorrow night; tonight we make do with bacon and some dried fruit I found in the McCreedys' winter cellar."

She wrinkled her nose. What an abomination of a make-do dinner! And she was starving. She dumped in the water, three buckets of it, then crawled back to the dresser to search around for the beans, which she found in a large flat tin. She added two handfuls to the water as directed, after dumping them in her skirt and running her fingers through them, thinking she wouldn't know a rock from a bean if she saw one, and she hoped he would choke on one if she *had* overlooked it.

He meantime had gathered an armful of brush for tinder, and several long crackly-looking pieces of wood, and arranged this under the iron kettle. "Matches, Lizzie," he snapped out, almost as if she were his servant and should have anticipated his request.

She had, of course, and watched impassively as he fired the wood, then arranged a little circle of rocks around the campfire.

52

"A precaution," he explained, as the fire flared up as it caught, and then died down. The sky darkened ominously as he sliced several huge slabs of bacon from a thick cut that he had strapped to the other side of the wagon. He diced one of these and tossed the pieces into the bean pot. The other strips he cut went into a large cast iron frying pan, which he drew out from a little platform under the back of the wagon, along with the coffeepot. "Most used items," he elaborated, after she had crawled back into the wagon to return the beans to their drawer and bring him back the coffee.

She didn't say a word, just gave all pretense of watching and absorbing, ignoring the piercing glances he sent her from time to time across the fire, and admitting finally that even bacon, dried fruit, and coffee were a more than adequate meal if one were hungry enough.

He fed the oxen and the horses, which were also unhitched from the back of the wagon, and watered them, then buried the covered kettle with the smoldering embers of the dying fire. "Tomorrow—beans. And breakfast. Tonight—I trust you can lay out the bedding properly."

"I believe I can figure that out," she agreed amicably.

She climbed into the wagon still again, and tossed the bedrolls to one side. The rectangularly folded sheets and coverlet unrolled easily over the mattress. They'd come from Lonita's room, she thought suddenly. The sheets were smooth and silky, and the coverlet was thick and soft to the touch.

She couldn't wait to lie down, to be alone and unencumbered.

Galt's voice, Galt's hand lifting the flap which had given her that precious moment of privacy, sliced through her pleasure. "You're taking up all the room, Lizzie; where do you expect *me* to lie down?"

She bolted to her knees; as he hung the lantern he was carrying from a hook on the nearest ridgepole, she reached for one of the bedrolls. "On the ground," she retorted, heaving the thick roll at him furiously, "like the gentleman I had supposed you were, in one of these which I stupidly thought you had provided for that purpose."

"I suppose I might say I provided them for your accommodations," he rejoined, climbing into the wagon bed

53

with one lithe movement, "but I wouldn't be that 'ungentle-manly.' We share the bedroom, Lizzie. I hadn't intended anything else, and you were naive if you thought so."

She sent him a fulminating look as he extinguished the light. A moment later she felt him reach for her left hand.

"Don't do that," she said quietly.

"I have to, Lizzie." His voice was equally dispassionate.

"And don't call me Lizzie," she added uselessly, as she felt him ring the empty cuff around his wrist, and heard the ominous click as he snapped it shut. "I'm really a very restless sleeper."

"Not last night," he contradicted gently, pushing her down on her back, easing his body into a turn so that he could lie on his back and not wrench her arm.

"I didn't sleep," she said flatly.

"Neither did I," he countered, positioning himself carefully beside her. He heard her heave a deep inward breath as he settled his head back against the soft coverlet. He heard her mutter under her breath, "Oh Lord . . ."

"Lizzie . . ." He propped himself up on his left arm and reached across to touch her.

She beat away his extended hand. "Leave me! Devil it, you took me prisoner, you shot at Edgar and his deputy, and I'm sure as I'm sitting here you meant to hit them, you locked me up, and forced me to go with you, you're keeping me in handcuffs, and you expect you can *say* something to comfort me? Are you crazy?"

"Are *you?* Damn to hell, woman. I did not kill that son-of-a-bitch Buck, and I don't expect to go to my grave paying for it. And if what happened is what it takes to clear my name, damn it, that's what it takes."

"Sure, and the devil with everything else," she spat at him in the dark, pulling frantically at her manacled hand.

"That's right, Lizzie." His tone had gone softer. "The devil with everything else." He eased himself back down onto the mattress.

"Let me go." Her own voice lowered. She knew there was the faintest hint of pleading in her request, and she knew he was not a man who would be moved by such a plea. Yet if he were as honorable as he claimed, surely he could continue his pursuit without her; he could find Lonita without her and he could demand restitution, all without *her*.

"You're so clever, Lizzie. You're asking me to let you go to prove I'm telling the truth."

"How clever of you to see that."

"I won't let you go," he said flatly.

"And I'll keep trying to get away," she promised with equal determination in her voice.

"May the best man win," he concluded with a touch of irony in his tone. "Rest easy, Lizzie. I'd never hurt you."

"Yes, you've said that, but I'm still in handcuffs."

"And you said you'd help me, and you're still issuing threats," he countered. "So you don't believe me, and I don't believe you, and we still know who is in charge."

"True—the man with the gun."

"Really? *Have* I threatened you with a gun recently? It seems to me," he added thoughtfully, "there are other more potent persuasions I can use. Think about it, Lizzie. You haven't seen that gun since you entered the McCreedy cabin."

"That doesn't mean you aren't carrying it, or you wouldn't use it."

"Or that you wouldn't, *if* you could get hold of it."

"That's right," she agreed, feeling as if she were on a speeding train and running out of control.

"Anything else you'd like to add?" he asked kindly.

"Oh, I've got *miles* of things to say to *you*," she growled, shifting restlessly now, knowing her reckless words weren't doing a thing to anger him, and wondering *why* she wanted to anger him at all. She was on such shaky ground. Her only weapons now were words. Words that could get her in deeper and deeper trouble. Words that could provoke him into doing . . . what?

"And you'll have miles and *miles* to say them," he said, still in that smug indulgent tone, as if she were some kind of child to be humored. "Go to sleep, Lizzie. There's nowhere you can go, tonight."

She stiffened at the words; nowhere she could go, physically or verbally. He had her both ways. His strength would defeat her every time.

She moved restively against this conclusion, and her body slithered against his, and just as quickly shimmied away.

"We're bound to bump into each other, Lizzie." His voice had just the faintest trace of amusement in it.

"Indeed," she agreed sarcastically, "we *are* bound."

"And you're going to be *bound* by the next word that comes out of your sassy mouth, Lizzie." There was an undercurrent beneath his dark-toned voice and she sensed he meant the threat, and that the threat was sensual.

She shivered at the implication of it. There was something about being alone with him, and close to him in the thick enfolding darkness. She was so very aware of him next to her. He had a long, lean presence that seemed imprinted on her consciousness. She could not turn to get away from him; always she was aware of his huge hand clasped to hers, and the sinewy muscle of his arm side by side her own.

It seemed to her that he meant for her to feel the all-enveloping sense of him, and his heat, the long line of his body, and his tautly controlled desire. That he wanted her to know that he could have demanded anything of her that he wanted, that all that leashed power could have taken anything.

Oh, but she knew it.

As the darkness wove tightly around her, and made her resist more violently his sensual lure, she knew he could have stormed her senses in the very way he had done before, and she knew her divided emotions would wage a terrible battle against her.

For now, he was satisfied she wouldn't challenge him again this night. Even she did not know whether she would. Some part of her wanted to, and it terrified her. There was some depth in her that wanted something, something she couldn't define.

Of the two of them, she thought, she was the one who would lose to any challenge that was issued, either hers, or his.

Her body tensed at the thought of the implications. She was shocked, as she shifted her body once again to avoid touching his, that she felt just the tiniest tremor of anticipation.

56

Five

Galt was hunkered over the morning fire cradling a cup of coffee when he heard the movements within the wagon that indicated Elizabeth was awake.

He set down his tin cup and put aside the plate of beans he had been pushing around with his fork. When he lifted the canvas flap over the wagon gate, he saw Elizabeth sitting at the edge of the mattress with the mirror propped up in an open drawer, trying vainly to comb and braid her tangled tawny curls.

"Sorry I didn't have time to sew a couple of pockets onto the tarp for your personals," he said acerbically, climbing into the wagon and settling on his knees behind her. "Give me the comb."

"Don't be silly," she snapped, pulling through another handful of strands so violently that the loose cuff hit her in the forehead. This was insane! Her nerveless fingers gave up the comb as he reached for it, and she watched with a kind of fearful curiosity as he calmly began combing through the knots and tangles gently and thoroughly. He knew just how to do it, too, she thought, her tension mounting as he lifted the heavy fall of her hair and stroked the short hairs underneath. His hands were so large, they could hold the whole mass of her hair in his palms.

Patiently, he worked out each tangle, unsnarling each knot efficiently and painlessly, and then combing through the bulk with long soothing strokes that she felt deep within her body.

And when the tangles were smoothed out, he didn't stop. He just kept combing and lifting her hair, spreading it over her shoulders, parting it to check the puncture wound which still was a dot of angry red, handling it, speaking finally in an undertone as he kept working the comb through, the timbre of his voice rich and low.

"You slept last night," he said, very well aware she was watching him very carefully in the mirror, as he was watching her, when her head tilted back, and her eyes closed as he stroked her glossy hair.

"Did I?" she murmured. It didn't seem as if she had, yet she knew she closed her eyes at one point when the unbearable strain of lying next to his hard heated body had gotten to her. Every muscle felt tight this morning from the effort of keeping her arm away from his, her body rigid and as removed from his as such a narrow space would permit. Every time she had moved, he had moved correspondingly.

She met his glimmering eyes in the mirror. She had an uncomfortable hot sense that sometime in the night she had been close to him, too close, too warm, liking it too much, relaxing enough to close her eyes. Had he held her? She would never know. But as her suspicious eyes narrowed as she looked at his reflection, his firm chiseled lips grimaced wryly under the concealing brush of a mustache and he lifted one thick black brow quizzically.

"You slept," he said slowly, and there was a wealth of unspoken meaning behind the words. The very way he said them told her that her innermost feelings had been correct, that she *had* been cupped against him, and that the hard heat she thought she had imagined had emanated solely from him, and that perhaps in the depths of the night, and in her dreams, he had held her in ways she would never know.

Another shocking thought assaulted her: she *wanted* to know. Her kindling eyes slashed back to meet his in the mirror. He shrugged, and began carefully combing through the ends of her unsnarled gold-brown curls once more.

She closed her eyes as the comb swooped from the crown of her head down through the lengths of glossy hair that he held in thick sections in his hand. First one side, then the back, then the other side, then his long firm fingers sliding through the tawny mass feeling its texture and its weight, lifting it and letting it cascade in a thick molten curtain all over his hands.

He watched her face in the mirror as he played with her abundant lustrous hair. Her head was thrown back, her eyes closed, and her firm lips parted just that little bit, as if she had surrendered her whole body to the ministrations of his hands. She was totally his at that moment, the way he wanted to see her surrender wholly and completely to him.

But not that way, and not just yet. It wouldn't happen soon. He pulled the comb once more through her heavy silky mane, and then lightly began separating out three sections of her hair. With quick adept movements, he began plaiting the strands; her eyes shot open wonderingly at the firm yet sensuous touch of his hands. Their eyes locked in the mirror.

"You know too much," she muttered, loving the gentility with which he twisted and turned her hair. She could have sat like that forever, but that was something she would never admit to him. She handed him a piece of elastic to fasten the ends with a brusqueness that belied her real feelings.

"I was married," he reminded her, handing her the comb.

She felt an interesting stab of feeling she could not identify. She knew she couldn't care less that he had had a wife. Everyone knew what had happened to *her*. "Well, that explains it," she said briskly, tucking the comb and mirror into the drawer, and twisting around to face him.

His eyes stopped her; they were alive with feeling. "Really, Miss Lizzie? What *does* that explain?"

His cold question stopped her. He loomed up over her suddenly, threatening, frightening. "Why, it explains how come you're so good at fixing a woman's hair," she said with some asperity, pushing herself as upright as she could on her knees. He was not going to cow her with that godawful formidable expression of his that seemed to carve the lines deeper into his face. She had struck some kind of nerve with her artless comeback. So be it. Words were her weapons, and she could see that some of them had homed in straight and true. There was something about his wife he did not want to talk about.

He was so immobile for so long she began to feel a shimmer of fear. And then he finally growled, "Maybe I've never combed a woman's hair in my life."

She made a negating motion with her hand, and he grabbed it. "Maybe," he added, "I've never kissed a woman before either."

"Galt . . ." Her fear returned tenfold. She didn't want him to touch her. She was still feeling the softness of his hands on her hair, and the chill of the mystery about his wife, the uncertainty of his part in Buck McCreedy's death.

"Shut *up*, Lizzie. I am going to kiss you." His pull on her resisting hand was inexorable as he reached for her, his dark outlaw eyes blazing, his impenetrable expression revealing nothing as his mouth descended and captured hers with that devastating invasiveness that almost sapped all of her will. Her cuffed hand beat at the unyielding stone-hard flex of his arm muscles, the empty cuff slashing at his shoulder blade hurtfully.

Yes it hurt, she could tell it hurt because he removed his mouth from hers long enough to rasp, "Don't keep it up, Lizzie. Just don't," and his tone was enough to stop her cold, just as the heat of his mouth crashing back down on hers was enough to kindle her senses to a blazing awareness.

Not this, not . . . she could even hear her mental voice reciting a litany to prevent her reeling senses from responding. She didn't want to have feelings for him. She wanted nothing except that he let her go back to Greenfields. Nothing. Surely not this . . . this closeness as her body molded tightly against his, immovable, inescapable, so that she felt that there were only the two of them in an increasingly tightening little world that consisted solely of heat and sensation. Certainly not this, this uncoiling of pleasure from the knot in her stomach that slowly curlicued its honey-thick way through her veins down to her toes.

Never ever this invasive *male* exploration of the taste and texture of her mouth, demanding, inviting, dominating all at once. Her body curved and melted against him, and she felt his hand cradling her head, and then a sense of being gently laid down, still enfolded in his heat and in the tremulous world of sensuality.

She was surrounded by an all-pervasive awareness of him, his scent, his strength, his hardness, his taste. Nothing seemed to exist outside of the circle of his arms which still enveloped her. His body, pressed snugly and familiarly against hers, became an extension of her own. Waves of sensual heat engulfed her.

From a mere kiss. And a man who might be a murderer.

Had he kissed his wife like this?

Whatever it was in her that wanted to oppose him doused her rising excitement with the thoughts, with the questions. How easily he overcame her resistance! She mentally shook herself out of her carnal fog. He had other means of persuasion, he had said, she thought wrathfully, and he had just shown her how easily she could succumb. She couldn't believe it. She couldn't understand herself. She felt cold, lusterless, and he felt her withdrawal palpably.

"Lizzie . . ." His voice was hoarse with some kind of emotion, probably, she thought, the ignominy of being thwarted. He couldn't move her with his emotion now, she was beyond him, back to herself, feisty and fighting mad that she had even allowed him to touch her, let alone kiss her like that.

Her own response shamed her; but she wasn't going to think about that. "I'm hungry," she said flatly, pushing herself up onto her elbows.

His face was shadowed as he propped himself up beside her. She couldn't tell what he was thinking. She didn't care. But she was aware of a retaliatory anger in him that focused itself on her with an almost living vibrancy. He knew what she was thinking, as he seemed to know everything. She felt his eyes rest on her lips. "Maybe," he said mildly, the slight hoarseness in his voice disguising his peculiarly male vexation, "you've never kissed a man before, Lizzie."

She slapped him. She put every ounce of strength into that swing, and she felt the reverberations from it all the way up her left arm. She felt the metal cuff catch him behind the ear, and the rasp and scrape of his skin, bristly from two days of not shaving. All of that she felt, and above it, his towering rage at her sheer gall. Already, the yellowish marks of her fingers stood out against the bruising red of the blow.

"You only get one of those, Lizzie. I'll tell you right now, you hit me like that again, you take the consequences. Fair warning." He was up on his haunches staring blackly down at her, menacingly angry. His body seemed to fill the wagon, almost as if his fury expanded his size. She felt the urgent need to get upright herself, because she felt so vulnerable lying prone, supported by her elbows, and her still tingling hand.

"Let me go then," she countered. "Just—"

"You don't hear good, woman," he interrupted harshly, bending over her now, supporting himself on his arms, which he planted on either side of her reclining body. "You are going nowhere except with me."

"For the time being," she muttered, her stormy jade eyes meeting his equally fierce jetty gaze.

"You can be sure I've taken that to heart, Lizzie," he said sourly, lifting one hand to cup and touch her smooth cheek. She felt his long fingers move provocatively against her skin. She shuddered in spite of herself, angry that she could respond to something in his touch that she could not even define.

He's going to have some interesting trip if he persists in keeping me with him, she thought, vengefully holding his eyes and stiffening her body against the sensual stroking of his fingers. She was not going to knuckle under to anyone. Whatever he thought of her from observing her from the jail cell window, he was going to find out his perceptions were inaccurate. Totally. She was not someone he could beat down or subdue with pretty words and a casual caress now and again.

Nor was she going to go with him any farther than she could help; she was going to take every opportunity she could to try to get away.

He read her decision in her defiant verdant gaze and his mouth twisted into that hateful sardonic smirk. He pulled himself back onto his haunches again and held out his hand. "Nonetheless, Lizzie," he said mildly as if he were continuing a conversation with her, "you've got to pull your share of the weight until—and if—you do manage to escape me."

She stared at him wordlessly, not moving a muscle, and he lifted his shoulders once again.

"Up to you, woman; just get the hell up and get out. Now." The last word cracked into the silence, betraying his building frustration. He edged his way slowly backward until he could swing himself out of the wagon gate into fresh air, and sanity. He wasn't sure there was any sanity where dealing with her was concerned. He shook his head disgustedly, annoyed at himself for letting her get to him. Yes, she got to him. Even as he stood waiting for her, he was beguiled by the sight of her crawling forward toward the back of the wagon, her braid swinging over her shoulder like some living thing, her handcuff thunking against the mattress.

"Cheer up, Lizzie," he said as he helped her out. "I'll get you up early enough tomorrow so *you* can do the cooking."

She shot him a baleful green look and wrenched her arm away from his hand. She *would* get up early enough to do the cooking, damn him; she would—and until she could get away from him, she swore, as she allowed him to pour muddy-looking coffee into one of the dented tin cups, she would pull her own weight.

Silence. The wagon creaked forward slowly, tailing from side to side, as the stolid team of oxen resignedly pulled them down the well-worn dirt track.

She had a bad taste in her mouth from the coffee, which he had brewed strong and thick as mud. The beans, of which there had been a fair amount remaining in the kettle, had settled into a huge bacon-scented knot in her stomach. She raged over his treatment of her, particularly because her manacled right hand was now shackled to the rusty iron armrest of the driver's perch.

On her head was the shovel-brimmed bonnet she had never wanted to see again, and she wasn't even remotely grateful for the way it shielded her face from the sun. All his considerations went for nothing. She wanted to escape his thoughtful ministrations so badly she could taste it. It and the beans and coffee.

He shrugged when she commented on it. "You made the beans, Lizzie."

"You taught me how," she retorted, and turned away, letting the heavy sultry stillness fall between them. She had nothing to say to him. He had made it crystal clear he didn't trust her, and was infuriated because her unruly thoughts prevented him from having his way with her.

Fine. The silence stretched into miles. And more miles of dust and dirt, and rolling fields that were now coming out of years of lying fallow because there was no one to work them, or they had been abandoned altogether during the war.

Elizabeth bit back a strangled sound as the familiarity of the unfolding scenery spoke to her.

"I feel that way too," he said, shattering the silence with the depth of emotion in his voice.

"How could you," she responded without even thinking, and a nervous quietude followed her words that made them stand out in the hush as if she had shouted them.

She heard them resonating the way he had heard them; she didn't regret saying them, but she knew they sounded vindictive, and she waited for the explosion she knew would come.

It did. "How could I damn *what*, Lizzie? Feel? Respond to things that move me? What am I, a stone statue or something? What the hell are you talking about?" He pulled the wagon to a jarring halt so that he could turn to her and have his hands free to shake her, as he almost knew he would if she kept up this way. And he waited with a tense exaggerated courtesy for her answer.

She wouldn't apologize; even he knew that. "Who can know anything about you," she threw back. "I'm not exactly in the kind of circumstances to make a judgment, am I? Let alone a fair one."

"Oh, you've made judgments already, Lizzie, and you're right, none of them are fair. Don't think I haven't heard those jibes about my 'strangeness' and my 'reputation.' Don't think I don't know what they say about me."

"Yes, and now they say you're a murderer and kidnapper; and you want me to sympathize with misplaced emotion about the scenery rolling by?"

"'They,' and *you*, know nothing about me," he grated, picking up the reins again.

"'They' and I know you killed Buck McCreedy," she retorted, her body shunting forward unexpectedly as the wagon began moving again.

"I didn't kill Buck."

"Sure, and I'm not handcuffed to the armrest of this damned wagon," she agreed sarcastically. "'They' say," she added venomously, "you killed your wife."

"Well, now you know everything," he snapped. "There's nothing more *I* can tell you."

"I was at your hearing," she said suddenly. "Even Edgar bore witness against you."

"He *was* rather conveniently on the scene," he agreed dryly. "He was sure positive about what he saw, wasn't he?"

"You didn't defend yourself too heatedly either."

"Edgar was positive; so was Lonita. She was hysterical, screaming at the top of her lungs that I had killed Buck. No one else was there; no one came when she started screaming . . ."

"None of their hands?" she questioned.

"You heard them testify: it was payday; they had all gone to town." He slanted a cold black look at her. "Draw your own conclusions."

"The jury did."

"They did."

"You could have killed him."

"I could have."

"*If* Lonita were telling the truth," she added a little daringly. One to one, *he* sounded convincing enough. The story could have had two endings, as he had claimed. He could have been set up. Lonita could have been lying. But it sounded so plausible, the way she told it; so reasonable. She was a ranch widow; he was a lonely unambitious man who was her husband's partner, who ran his cattle. Who made love to the boss's wife, and made promises he fully intended to keep if he could get Buck out of the way. He had wanted Buck's land, stock, cattle. And Buck's wife, completely and desperately.

That night, Lonita testified, when she told him it was impossible, he had gone a little mad.

Galt Saunders, a little mad? Elizabeth thought wonderingly. She had seen him desperate, she had seen him formidably angry in these past two or three days, but she had not seen him so far gone in his emotions as to be "a little mad." It seemed impossible that someone so self-contained as Galt Saunders could lose all control. She sent him a quizzical little verdant look. He was facing straight ahead, his dark eyes on the road as if he were picking out each and every rut so he could be careful to avoid them. His set expression told her nothing. His profile was hard, blunt, shadowed by the deep brim of his hat. His mouth was a taut line under the black streak of his mustache.

Draw your own conclusions, he said. She didn't know what to believe. *He* could also be an expert liar.

He had a gun, Lonita had said. He had come that night with a gun. He had planned to propose, planned to take her away that night because he knew everyone would be in town. It would just be the three of them: him, Buck, and Lonita. He wanted her so badly. And no, she had never given him cause, ever, to *think* she would ever leave Buck because of *him*. Why, she was even a little afraid of him; he was so dark and forbidding, full of undercurrents she never understood. And he wouldn't talk about his wife, she said.

She might have flirted with him—a little, she admitted when pressed. What woman wouldn't? He was willing, and Buck was hardly ever around. She felt lonely, and she *never* thought he would take it as seriously as he had.

She was every inch the grieving widow, Elizabeth remembered, and every man jack of the jury went overboard in sympathy. No doubt every one of them to a man had heard often about the overwhelming loneliness of being a farm wife in a frontier border town. Every man of them had heard the same protestations from his own wife: she had loved her man. Hadn't she come west with *him?* She hadn't elected to stay put with friends and family in, in Lonita's case, Texas. She had stood by Buck and his decision to make a new life in the West, purely that.

It was just that sometimes he was so *busy*. And Galt was always there. Often. She realized it very suddenly when he began to take her little kindnesses seriously.

Had Galt been so isolated and so lonely? Elizabeth wondered as the oxen plodded on, and the scenery disappeared behind her. She envisioned a playful Lonita McCreedy with her glossy black hair and moist blue eyes flirting with Galt and his disapproving outlaw face. Envisioned him touching her with those long sensitive fingers, touching her hair, running his hands through it, kissing her . . . no! Yes! Like he had kissed *her*, yes! Envisioning a hungry, empty, desperate man who had, deliberately or not, immured himself in the Missouri wilderness to raise horses and run cattle first with a wife who had mysteriously died, and then in partnership with a man who, willfully or not, neglected his wife, and precipitated a situation ripe for a crime of passion.

Yes, she could picture it, Elizabeth thought with a frisson of dismay at her strong reaction, and that it had happened exactly the way Lonita had described it.

She slanted a long thoughtful glance at Galt's bluntly shadowed profile, and his large capable hands that flicked the reins so competently. Yes, she could imagine Galt making love to the delectable Lonita McCreedy. She could imagine a lot more than that, and her face, shielded by the sides of the pasteboard-stiffened bonnet, burned with pictures of everything her overactive brain could conjure up that he and Lonita McCreedy might have done together. And where they might have done it.

While Buck was in the fields and chasing cattle to pasture.

Oh no, it seemed a lot less possible that Lonita had engineered coincidences and provided somehow the sheriff on the scene to witness an unfortunate "accident."

It didn't seem remotely plausible to her. Lonita had not seemed to have that kind of guile. Lonita's story made the most sense, and she didn't like that conclusion. She wanted to have some hook to believe that Galt was not a murderer. It meant her own life would not be so completely at stake.

But she couldn't see it any other way but Lonita's. And she knew he was waiting for her reassessment of her judgment.

"How could Lonita not have been telling the truth?" she demanded, in answer to the unspoken question in the air. "How could it have happened any other way?"

"Amen," he agreed harshly, not looking at her. "I suppose it *was* rather too much for me to expect a fair flower of the South to use her obvious intelligence. It's just easier not to contemplate the truth. Gives you lots of room to fight, doesn't it? Fine."

The dead finality in his tone made her want to scream. "You tell it then, you tell me just how it happened, and see whether I believe it or not," she challenged him angrily.

"It doesn't matter, Lizzie; it won't change anything," he told her flatly.

"No. No—because nothing can justify what you're doing to me, Galt Saunders, nothing; I deserve to know *your* truth. I do." She struck back at his impassivity, his certainty. She saw him chew his lip under his mustache in response to her words and then shake his head.

"No, Lizzie. Tell you what though, *you* try to think of a good alternate story that fits the facts. You might," he added, his rich voice terse and unrevealing, "surprise yourself."

She drew in her breath sharply at the insulting tone. "Why," she asked, just as brusquely, "should I bother?"

She could have killed him for his impassive shrug and response. "It passes the time," he said, with just the faintest hint of patronizing behind the flatness. "It's just an exercise to fill the time, Lizzie."

They nooned on the edge of what looked like a turned field. They drank cold coffee and ate the last of the beans. Elizabeth whisked out the pot grudgingly, feeling as if Galt had deliberately caused the stubborn residue to burn onto the bottom.

"It'll cook into the next batch of beans," he told her with that same hatefully indifferent tone with which he had spoken to her earlier, and she felt like throwing the pot at him.

She *could* have thrown the pot at him . . . she realized suddenly, hefting it in her still-free hands. She could have whanged him right over the head with it . . . right now—his back was to her. . . .

She lifted it. . . .

He whirled. "Hell, Lizzie. Don't even try that."

"It was a thought," she said stonily, setting the iron pot down again.

"Well, I'll tell you, woman, I'm not doing all the cooking

68

myself, and I expect you to do what you can. If I can't trust you, you'll be confined, and that's the end of it. It's okay with me. We've got another two or three days till we reach the border." He stood, arms akimbo, staring at her, daring her to confront his coal dark eyes, and ask the questions that he saw springing to her lips in response to his statement. "You decide," he added, and turned his back on her to finish stowing away the coffeepot and draw the water for the horses and oxen.

She lifted the pot once again. God, but it was tempting. It *was* tempting. And she would have the wagon and the stores, and all the time in the world to . . . *go back.*

She hoisted the pot once again by the bail handle. It swung nicely and with elegant solidity against her arms.

But she would be alone without protection, the little voice of reason inside her protested. She'd have the gun, her desperate side countered triumphantly. Surely she could make it to the next settlement town with the wagon and the gun.

Her eyes streaked across the small space between them as he knelt down to shove the coffeepot in its storage space under the wagon gate. No gun, on either hip.

She licked her lips, and she knew suddenly that he was very aware of what she was contemplating doing, waiting for her to do it—no, to try to do it, before he leapt up and slammed her down. She could feel it palpitating in the air between them, even though *he* was at the disadvantage and *she* had the weapon.

Fool, she thought, and reared back with the pot in her hand, and with all her strength she pitched her body forward and swung her arms downward.

Instantaneously, he rolled onto his back and caught her legs, deflecting her aim. She went down on top of him, hard, with the iron pot slamming into his muscular thigh.

"Damn to hell, Lizzie!" he growled, his mounting anger almost murderous. His body heaved upward and she toppled off him and hit her head against the axle of the rear wagon wheel.

She lay very still. Behind her closed eyes, she could just see him thrusting the infernal oven away from his body, she could hear the scraping sounds of him slithering across the dirt track toward her.

She felt him touch her, shake her, gently at first, and then with increasing impatience, as his large hands cupped her shoulders, and then her face, and then lifted her upper torso against his hard warm body. "Open your eyes, woman."

She kept them resolutely shut. She felt him drop her right onto the ground, with no care, no mercy, and her eyes shot open at his callousness.

"You're a fool, Lizzie," he said without rancor, and there was a note in his voice this time that she couldn't define.

She struggled to sit upright, and gingerly felt the back of her head. He pulled her forward roughly, and pushed her hand out of the way. In an instant, he found the right spot, and intentionally or not, he pushed his long fingers against it, hard.

"Ouch!" she gritted, trying not to verbalize her pain, but those long fingers were not sympathetic; they prodded what felt like a hard lump with his usual brisk efficiency. It ached.

"You'll live," he said dryly, and she reacted to the caustic tone; her hand shot out and she pushed his crouching body. He went down on his backside, startled. "And you never learn," he added acidly. "But you will."

"Or you will," she retorted with equal acerbity.

The sardonic twist of his lips appeared beneath his mustache, and he levered himself to his feet. "There's a farm yonder. Just maybe we can get some fruit and vegetables. Just maybe I'll share them with you. Just you don't forget who's paying the fare here, Lizzie. Don't show your gratitude too openly, you might spoil me."

"Not a chance," she muttered as he sent her a satirical black look, and reached for her hands. "I didn't know you had money," she added as he pulled her to her feet.

"There's a lot you don't know, so don't get any ideas," he retorted, pulling her wrists together ruthlessly. "Lock up your emotions now, Lizzie. I can't risk another whack on the head."

She pulled away from him hard. "You're not the one with the risk," she snapped as he wrenched her hands back again. Useless, she thought, to resist, but why let him feel she was acquiescing so easily? Her body pulled against his grasp of her hands. He yanked her right back again. The hated cuff snapped

70

back around her left wrist with an ominous click.

Nor did she like the necessity of his picking her up like a sack of flour and depositing her on the wagon seat, or his arranging the hateful bonnet just so on her head, or his last-minute added touch of tying a coarse canvas apron around her reluctant waist.

"Where did you get *that?*" she demanded cuttingly. "I suppose you whipped it up with your handy needle and thread while I was asleep?"

"My wife's," he said shortly, pulling her hands underneath the scratchy material and fastening her cuffed wrists to the armrest.

Oh yes, his wife's; conversation stopped abruptly at the mention of his wife—always, she thought mordantly, tugging at her bounds. Damned wagon seat was hardly rusted enough to give with her pulling, but she had to try, even with his pointedly trenchant jet gaze watching her every move. She didn't want to hear about his wife.

His eyes never left hers as he walked back to the opposite side of the wagon, and he climbed onto the perch and picked up the reins.

In her mind's eye, she pictured the perfection of the disguise.

They surely looked every inch the overland couple. This first stop was to be a test, and he was going to play it to the hilt, she surmised as he jammed his punched-down hat onto his head impatiently.

There was an unspoken dare between them: if she started anything untoward, she would pay the consequences, and they would be dire. If she even said yes or no, that would be too much. Her mouth thinned defiantly as she considered what her chances might be of trying to appeal to strangers for help.

He watched her profile, barely visible against the stiffened rim of the bonnet. He knew she understood. He nodded to himself, snapped the reins, and started the wagon down a well-worn dirt track.

Six

"But wouldn't you and the missus like to stay overnight?"

"No, ma'am, but I thank you kindly for the offer. I plan to push on another four or five miles by nightfall," Galt said respectfully, holding his hat in his hand and deferring to the tiny calico-garbed woman who stood in the doorway of the rude cabin that was the big house of the farm.

"But surely your wife—she looks plumb worn out. We've got the barn, you know; and it does look like rain. I feel I'm not helping a bit just sending you on your way with a basket of dried apples and a bucket of milk. Truly . . ."

"I couldn't impose," Galt said firmly, casting a speaking look up at Elizabeth. "And besides, we're on a schedule," he added smoothly. "We've signed on to join a wagon train in Kansas."

The woman made a disclaiming motion with her hand. "But there's always a train—"

"But we've *paid*," Galt interrupted, "so we have to push on. We're grateful for your kindness, aren't we, Lizzie?"

"Very," she agreed fervently, clenching her fists under the apron as he heaved the milk bucket into the perch beside her and climbed up again next to her.

"It's little enough to do," the woman said. "It's too little. It's not easy out there." She waved at the horizon. "How many turnarounders we've sheltered, I couldn't begin to tell you, with their horror stories of Indian attacks and plain highway robbers who've stolen gold, or every other personal possession you can imagine. They can't take it, I couldn't make it much farther myself. But the land was here, so my husband was satisfied to settle. I hope you have better luck."

"If everyone is as kind as you," Elizabeth started to say, and was emphatically hushed by a compelling hand on her thigh, grasping it hard.

"We plan to," Galt said confidently. "You sure that's all the payment you want for the milk?"

"More than enough," the woman said as he clamped his hat onto his head and picked up the reins again. "Good-bye, I'm sorry my husband wasn't here to meet you; good luck—I hope I don't see you back this way . . ."

Her voice was lost as he maneuvered the wagon around and back down the track from the house. Elizabeth fumed that she couldn't even wave to the woman, couldn't express her own gratitude.

"You beast," she hissed at him when the woman was finally out of view. "She was dying to talk to another woman; I bet she hadn't seen another woman for months. How could you do that?"

"I know about all that," he grunted. "It couldn't be helped, and I have no way of knowing anymore what you'll take it into your head to do, woman. It's too bad, and I've heard the whole story before. We used to put up turnarounders ourselves, and you can bet every damned story scared the loving wits out of my wife, and she wasn't too happy about settling in Greenfields. I feel sorry for that woman, but she looks like she *might* have the stamina to see it through. If there are no Indian raids. And *if* they get a crop together, and *if* they survive the winter, and she doesn't have trouble . . . giving birth . . ."

His voice trailed off, and she looked at him quizzically, her leaf green eyes soft. He was telling her about himself. About his wife, his mysterious wife who had died soon after they had settled in Greenfields.

"She died giving birth?" she whispered, but she knew; the raw, real emotion in his voice told her, and he hadn't even heard the question, so lost was he in his own dark memories that the farm woman evoked.

"She died," he said suddenly, his voice hoarse and ravaged

73

with feeling, "because she needed too much, and I gave her too little."

It rained.

Sometime during the night, the storm began pelting the ground; she awoke to the thrum of it over her head, aware that Galt lay sprawled beside her wet and wide awake himself.

"I laid out the rubber sheets," he said quietly, "on the tarp and the animals. I don't think we're going anywhere soon tomorrow."

"All right." The ramifications were endless. They wouldn't be able to cook, and they might not be able to move. They had feasted on the milk and berries he had found two miles beyond the farm. They had traveled well past twilight, saying little. There was nothing to say. He was wrapped up in some dark place she could not go. And he didn't want her there. She had gone to sleep finally, tossing, restlessly thinking over this new tidbit of information that put the gossip about him in a new light.

She wanted too much . . . the words echoed in her mind as she lay stiffly beside him on her back, her hands still manacled in front of her. Or he had wanted too much, she thought. He had wanted Lonita. What if his wife had still been alive? Her body tensed up. Was Lonita the kind of woman who could lure a man in spite of everything? Would she have been so "nice" to Galt if his wife had still been alive?

It was impossible to picture that sultry quartet. Think up another story, Galt had said. Her brain was reeling with thinking. All she had had to do for all those past miles was think. She had thought about Galt's poor wife, the baby, about the woman they had left who might or might not be there on their return trip, about Galt's pain. About her own impossible situation. About the inflexibility of the man whose body almost hummed with perceptive pulsation as he lay silently beside her, absorbed in some internal world she could not penetrate.

"Give it up, Lizzie," he said suddenly, with the faintest glimmer of amusement coloring his rich voice. "You'll think

74

your poor brain out."

"Then tell me," she challenged him boldly, wondering as the words spewed out of her unruly mouth *why* she wanted to know about Galt's wife. Ridiculous; mere curiosity to pass the time, she told herself, waiting, and roundly cursing him when he did not speak.

"There's nothing to tell," he said after a long long silence as he seemed to be considering whether he should.

She waited, gritting her teeth, feeling as if she wanted to bite him because he was so closed in and reluctant to talk. He didn't want to make her understand, and she couldn't comprehend it when he also wanted her to believe in his innocence.

"Make up your own story," he said after a while.

"Such an easy answer," she sniped at him, out of patience. "All right. Here it comes. You fell in love with Lonita and you got rid of your wife. You spread the word that she had died giving birth so that everyone would sympathize with you instead of being suspicious and investigating. And you planned to kill Buck. How's that?"

"Unassailable, and essentially what was hinted at the trial." His flat tone did not change. No hint of expression revealed what he felt about what she was implying. No one had ever accused him of making up the story of his wife's childbed death. He felt a slow burning sensation coursing through his body at her acumen for providing the reason why. It probably was no more than gossips were saying, he thought, staring at the side wall of the tarp which was slowly soaking through with the intensity of the rainfall. "That hardly took any thinking at all, Lizzie. We could make better use of the time by getting together something to eat." He hoisted himself onto his knees, crawled over to where the lantern was hanging, and lit it, out of patience with her and himself for catering to her.

An eerie glow suffused the interior of the wagon. Elizabeth watched as he rummaged around for the tin cups and what remained of the berries and milk. He poured a handful of the berries into a cup and milk over them. "Sit up, Lizzie; today you don't have to get breakfast."

She shimmied her body into a sitting position and held out her cupped hands to take the drink. Her fingers closed around the handle, as one palm balanced the bottom of the cup; she lifted it to her lips, watching him narrowly over the rim. She sipped and found the milk was warm, just bordering on spoiling, and the berries were soggy already from having been squished together in a pail.

He made a face himself after tasting the concoction, and said, "The apples are for later."

She nodded, and continued sipping very slowly, which made the pungent taste of the milk bearable at least. He set his aside and crawled out from the wagon into the storm, wrapping himself in a long rubber coat before he swung outside. He returned moments later. "It's coming down in sheets out there," he reported, divesting himself of the slick wet coat and his drenched hat. "So we're stuck, Lizzie. What would you like to do? Sewing lessons? Cooking hints? Desultory conversation?"

"Not possible," she said, putting aside her cup. Her eyes flicked up at him. He was staring at her as he knelt, still, by the wagon gate, his eyes opaque and unreadable.

She looked like a child, he thought, in the wrinkled oversized shirt, and her black skirt hiked up around her knees as she sat tailor-fashioned, leaning against the rickety bureau. Her hair curled wildly around her beautiful face, with tendrils escaping the long braid. She seemed unaware of it, and how her eyes darkened to jade as the tense air between them thickened. Alone together, in the depths of a storm, he could almost hear her thinking. And what he could do, with her helpless—hardly helpless, he thought mirthlessly when he remembered what those cuffed hands could do to his back. No, not helpless. Without a doubt she was desirable. Her oversized shirt hardly hid her feminine charms: the contrast only made the thrust of her breasts against the coarse material that much more obvious. The rest he could imagine very well. Too well. And her hands, now that she had learned to manage with them shackled together, had lost the abrupt spastic movements that had made them seem so awkward.

She was quite amazing, he thought as he sent his lambent gaze skimming upward to rest on her uncompromising lips. She expected him to try to take her now, in the close isolated

76

confines of this musty wagon, with the rain pounding an accompaniment to the deed, and she fully expected to battle him every inch of the way.

A faint smile of real amusement played over his chiseled lips. "It's okay, Lizzie; I'm not going to ravish you—today."

"I'm relieved." Her voice was equally tart. "For now."

"Good then. I'll teach you to play poker instead," he said in almost an offhand tone, and she reared back, startled. "Isn't that what we've *been* playing, Lizzie?" he added softly, enjoying the astonishment reflected on her face and in her eyes. Truth to tell, he hadn't quite expected to say that himself, except he knew he had to divert the direction of his unruly thoughts, and quickly. And it was the same: they each had to determine who was bluffing and who was not.

So far, he thought wryly, he had held the winning hand.

She watched him warily as he reached across the space of the mattress to where she was sitting, and motioned her out of the way so he could open the bottom drawer, out of which he produced a worn pack of cards.

"Aren't you a man of many talents?" Elizabeth murmured appreciatively as she leaned back against the dresser and watched him expertly shuffle the deck. "You can cook and sew, and break out of jail, kill—gamble—"

His steaming black eyes stopped her before she could go another word further. "Choose the stakes."

"My freedom," she snapped.

"Your kisses," he countered grimly.

"Beans," she flung back.

"Hell, Lizzie—"

"You are *not* going to touch me," she stated unequivocally, scared now because he could insist; he could demand a lot of things, and he could take everything he wanted, and her puny attempts to dissuade him would be ineffective as usual. Only her defiant spirit stood between her and his now quiescent desire, but anything, she thought, could set him off. She had learned enough about men to know that. Her jade gaze held his glowering eyes unwaveringly.

"Beans, then," he gave in finally, and reached behind her again for the tin. "A dollar a bean."

"A gambler," she reiterated in some satisfaction.

"And how would a nicely reared young woman know about such things?" he wondered as he poured out a handful of beans and laid half of them on her lap.

"I know some things, Galt Saunders," she said testily, counting the beans painstakingly.

"*Some* things," he agreed in a suggestive drawl, and bowed to the flashing green eyes that skewered him the moment the words issued from his mouth. "Well then, Miss Lizzie—they did call you *Miss* Lizzie, did they, your servants?" he asked casually, slanting a curious look her way.

So he remembered *that,* she thought wrathfully. "Miss Elizabeth," she corrected haughtily, "but *you* can call me Miss *Barnett.*"

"And didn't you say that in just the right tone of voice," he marveled, expertly flipping the cards together one more time before he held them out to her. "Your choice, Lizzie—excuse me, Miss Lizzie."

"The devil with you," she said coolly. "You choose. What do I know about . . . cards?"

"What indeed," he murmured. "All right, five card stud. It's fastest. Ante up now, woman."

"Meaning?" Her narrowed verdant gaze swept over his face with, she hoped, the right balance of suspicious curiosity.

"Beans. In the pot."

"Oh. All right, I bet one dollar," she decided, her voice searching for the right note of guilelessness as she tossed one bean into the space between them.

He matched her bean, shaking his head. A way to pass the time, he thought, bending his dark head to deal two cards, each facedown. "You can look at it," he said helpfully, "just don't show it to me." He lifted his, and then passed out two more, face up. "So. Lizzie queens it over us all. Your bet, milady."

She sent him a virulent gaze and tossed two more beans between them.

"Ah, the ante is up. Most interesting. And here I sit with a lowly knave." He tossed in his beans and dealt two more cards to each of them, face up.

Elizabeth sat looking at a queen and a king; his second card

78

was a queen. She reached down and tossed two more beans into the pot, and sent him a speaking glance as he looked at her.

"You're either a fool, or you know what you're doing," he said finally.

"I know which cards are high," she evaded, and he silently dealt the third card to her, a three; his, a ten.

"We're working on a pair of queens, pair of kings. Eight for you, no help there, Lizzie. Your pair possibility is a little scary, always assuming *I* don't have that second queen"—he dealt himself the next card—"a six—nothing there. High card bets, Lizzie. Or folds."

"I'll never fold," she said coolly, and tossed two more beans into the pot.

"I like your spirit," he said, matching that. "Turn 'em over."

She flipped over the card to reveal a queen; he swept his cards together disgustedly.

"What did *you* have?" she asked kindly, pulling the beans over to her side of the mattress. "A jack. So two queens beats two jacks. What else beats what?" Her voice was just the slightest shade patronizing, but she couldn't help it, she *couldn't*.

And still he wasn't warned; he explained briefly and she shook her head. "Oh, I'll never get all that flush and pair stuff straight. I'll trust you—but only on *this*."

"You drive a hard bargain," he muttered scathingly as she tossed two beans onto the mattress. "You're positively heady with success." He matched her and dealt the cards.

She lifted hers, and threw two more beans between them. He added his, and dealt again. "Two, Lizzie; pride goeth before a fall. And—nine. All right." Two more beans, matched by her two. And the next card—"six on Lizzie; can't be helped. Ten, possible straight." They bet, and he slapped the next two cards down. "Pair of sixes on Lizzie, nine, ten, queen, possible straight working, and next—last card now, Lizzie. I wouldn't bet on either of us who could win this one."

"But a pair of sixes *could*," she countered, hesitating to throw her beans into the growing pot.

"Could," he agreed, watching her manacled hands deftly

79

scoop them up and add them to the others. He put in his two, and laid a ten down on her cards. "All right then, pair of sixes, possibly three of a kind, two pair if you're lucky, but I don't think you are. A five on me, no help there. So what do you think, Lizzie?"

"I've got the sixes," she shrugged, and tossed three beans onto the others.

"Holy hell," he muttered. "I could have a pair of nines or tens or even queens for all you know."

"I'll gamble," she said brightly. "Let's see if you do." She reached across and turned his down-faced card—a four. She turned hers. "Another six. Three of one kind, right?" She swept in all the beans. "You know, I might be able to ransom myself at the rate this is going."

His exasperated look told her he didn't like the "way this was going," and his impatience was evident in the way he shoved his beans onto the mattress and dealt the first card of the third hand.

She peeked at it and smiled. Two beans went in the pot. And two more. He dealt: a jack to her and a four. Two more beans, matched by his two. A ten to her—possible straight; a king to him, no help. She bet again, wildly this time, four beans, and he added his, grimacing.

"Nine to you, Lizzie, working on a straight; ace to me, no help." Another four beans—he didn't like it, but he matched it, and dealt the final cards: an eight to her, and an eight to himself.

"Lizzie?" His black gaze caught her looking pensively at her hand.

She smiled enigmatically, and threw in four more beans.

He narrowed his eyes. He had a pair of fours. He reached over this time and turned her down-faced card. A ten. She took him again with a damned pair of tens. And throwing around money—beans—as if it were a straight.

"You bluffed that through neatly," he said calmly, shuffling again.

"Beginner's luck," she said deprecatingly, placing her bet and lifting her card. Two beans on that one, and king high to her, possible pair. "I'd fold now," he muttered, scowling at his

80

face up three and throwing in his two. "Pair of kings. Lizzie holds the luck; nine on me, no help." Four more beans hit the pot. "Queen on Lizzie, jack on me—nothing." Four more beans; final cards: a nine to her and an ace to him—his luck holding. He added his beans, and turned his card: an ace.

She grinned at him, her jade eyes sparkling, and flipped over her card: another king.

"Lizzie . . ."

"Let's keep playing, this is fun." She purposefully ignored the storm warning in his voice.

"Lizzie . . ." His tone was ominous now.

"Yes, Galt?" She tilted her head, looking like a curious little bird. "*Can* I buy my freedom? I've got—oh, it must be fifty— beans here."

"Who taught you?"

"You did," she said lightly, running her hands through the beans. "You're a good teacher," she added, loving the fact she could tweak him about this; she didn't have to tell him anything. Not anything. But one telling look at his blazing eyes said she had better, that he was serious about his cards, and about being taken for a fool. "All right," she said grudgingly, picking up a handful of beans and tossing them at him, "my brothers."

His eyebrows shot up. "Your brothers? *Brothers?* How many—brothers?" He was totally nonplussed; he had never thought about her having a family before. It was almost as if she had sprung up fully grown on the sheriff's doorstep, a goddess created solely to marry his son. But of course she had family. And brothers . . .

"Three. There were three," she said slowly. "All older. All," she added, with a break in her voice, "gone now."

"How?" he asked roughly as he gathered up the cards first and then the beans.

"The war," she said stonily.

He put the deck away. The war; he should have known—the war. The war killed, it maimed, it destroyed, it made people run from its hard memory. He knew all about the war.

They sat in silence for a long time. He didn't ask any more questions, and she would have refused to answer them. The war had taken everything: her father, her brothers, her mother, who had died of despair and a broken heart, and ultimately, the thing that had brought her to Greenfields, her home. Two loyal servants, who had stayed with her till the end, gone as well, to work for wealthy speculators for a salary, and only after Martin's letter, begging her to marry him, to come to Greenfields to his family, to make a new life, had precipitated that decision. Her home, Longview, had been bought for back taxes that she could not have paid, and she had no other choice.

She hadn't even known, as she rushed forward making preparations to join Martin Healey, whether she loved him or not. She had felt deep feelings for him, when he and his fellow officers had commandeered Longview for their headquarters late in the war. And she knew he had instantly been smitten with her.

No, she couldn't think about that; Martin had betrayed her, and there was no point to any regrets. Nothing would bring back her home or her parents. Never again would she have the companionship of her rowdy boisterous brothers. There was nothing. There was only the disapproving coal hard stare of Galt Saunders, her captor.

Her stony jade glance bounced off his. Her captor. She couldn't understand him. He kept her in handcuffs and taught her card games. He threatened her but he didn't carry his gun. He was using her, but he wouldn't let her go. He had the strength to overcome her resistance, and he hadn't tried to force her to do anything. Not really. He swore he was innocent, and all the facts said he was guilty.

She felt no threat from him now, only an iron determination. He was watching her as closely as she watched him. They didn't trust each other, he had said it, and they exacerbated each other with words and, in her case, easily thwarted attempts to escape.

He just didn't need her anymore, she thought. He was far enough away from Greenfields to be sure he would not be caught, and to lose himself in the anonymity of the vast Western spaces. Even if he could find Lonita, even if he brought her back, he wouldn't be gaining that much: how much could a struggling horse ranch be worth to him? She didn't understand it. She just didn't.

He watched her struggling with her thoughts, much as he was wrestling with his own, his memories, and the new sparse information about her. He shook his head wonderingly. Brothers, and servants, and who knew what all? What had possessed someone like her to come to a settlement town like Greenfields to marry someone like Martin Healey? He wanted to know that more than he wanted to know anything else at the moment. She played poker. She was game to tackle anything. She had a fierce, now understandable, competitive spirit. She was beautiful.

He would have given his life to be able to touch her just then, to hold her, soothe away her troubling questions, assure her with some kind of real proof that he was what he said he was.

But he knew what she saw: a ruthless man with a stone-hard disposition, and a rock-hard tenacity that would not be swayed by anything outside its purpose. He was absolutely like that, and he couldn't change. No more could she.

Only that kind of man would have slept with her side by side these several nights and not touched her. Only that kind of man would have clamped down on his unholy desire and left her alone.

Only that kind of man would have yearned to have her with an unending hunger in his soul that could never be sated. Only that kind of man would have watched her, with impassive eyes, as she lay down on the mattress to listen, as he was, to the drumming of the rain on the rubber-shrouded roof, and to watch it soak through the tarpaulin curtain on the opposite wall.

Seven

Mud. Everything was awash in sludge and sun-drenched dew-kissed light. "Let's go, Lizzie." Galt shook her impatiently. "You get up the fire and the coffee this morning: four palmfuls in the pot, please. I like it strong if you don't."

She shook her head to clear it, but he had leapt out of the wagon before her sleep-clogged eyes could grow accustomed to the light. She groped her way to the front of the wagon, aware suddenly that her hands were not trussed together. Well, of course: she was making breakfast.

She slid down from the wagon gate into a morass of mud. "Devil it," she muttered, reaching back and grabbing for the bonnet, which she shoved onto her head. Only today would she allow herself to be grateful for its broad shading brim; she had meant to throw it into the nearest body of water they came to. For now, however, its cradling shadow blocked the intense morning sun very effectively, and she saw that she was standing in a slimy pool of wet mud that was fast being soaked up by her boots and hemline. She stepped out of it gingerly onto a little grassy hillock nearby which looked like a good spot to lay the fire.

She didn't know where Galt was, but as she gathered twigs and got the matchbox, she saw him under the wagon, assessing the difficulty of moving it. His temper didn't improve with coffee, dried apples, and a rasher of bacon. "The road's awash in mud. We'll just have to plow on. The team is ragged out from the rain anyway. We're not going to make ten miles today."

84

"What difference does it make?" she asked into her coffee cup.

He scowled. "It makes a difference."

She hated his assurance. He was not to be dissuaded from this fool's chase; he meant to find Lonita somehow. She cleaned the cups and plates and stamped out the campfire resentfully. When she had done, and packed everything away, he helped her onto the wagon seat and locked her handcuff onto the armrest.

"I didn't try to get away *this* time," she pointed out.

"And next?" he retorted, climbing up next to her. He cracked the reins and the oxen began pacing forward sluggishly.

It was slow going all the way, until the wagon rounded a bend in the road and the wagon wheel slipped off the track and into a mudhole. The wagon immediately tilted sideways as Galt pulled on the reins to halt the oxen, then he jumped off the seat, which dipped alarmingly downward. Behind them, they could hear everything in the wagon shift toward the slant. Galt's fuming curses rang in the clear air. "Grab the reins, damn it, Lizzie!"

"I can't; you locked me up like—"

"Oh, hell . . ." He jumped up onto the perch and unlocked the right cuff. They both felt the wagon lurch forward as the oxen moved toward the slime. "Get the reins, now—shorten them, try to pull them to the right—*now!* He jumped off again, and around to the rear of the wagon.

She felt a mighty push at the left rear wheel and nothing, as she grabbed up the leather straps and pulled with all her strength to foreshorten the lead and pull the team's heads to the right.

The wheel slipped backward. Galt shouted: "*Again!*" And she hauled in the reins and jerked her body across the slanting seat to force the animals' heads—and nothing. And then they moved—to the left—and she felt the right wheel sink into the morass, and the wagon slide sideways, and tilt, and the right wheel sink still farther . . .

And then she felt her body slide down the seat as she vainly grasped the reins, and fall off the wagon into the mud pit.

"Lizzie!"

Galt's voice, panicked, was somewhere above her. The hole wasn't deep—it was a little incline, a little gully off the side of the road, and it was filled with a wash of dirt and grit, and she felt buried in it by the time his frantic hand reached her. She was covered with it, so angry, feeling such futility, that when he grabbed for her, she yanked his arm hard and he wound up in the mud beside her, stunned by her strength and the depth of her vexation.

"Run, Lizzie," he urged her, but his tone was mild, and he was vaguely reassured that she wasn't going to attack him.

"I'd get far," she said disgustedly, standing up and swatting at the mud with both dirt-encrusted hands. "What *do* we do?"

"We push, my dear Miss Lizzie. And then somewhere, somehow, we take a bath."

So they pushed, and their combined strength, and his muscles with her pulling at the oxen to veer them away from the hole, eventually got the wagon onto the track again. But it took hours. And then he decreed they had to continue traveling—by foot until they could clean themselves off.

"That's crazy," she shrieked.

"You haven't looked at yourself." Again his tone was reproving but not angry. "And don't go after the mirror; no one's going inside the wagon until we get this muck off us."

"Easy for you to say," she muttered as he got on one side of the team and motioned her to the other.

"Just do it, Lizzie. I promise this will seem funny in a few days."

It didn't seem funny at all as they trudged into the depth of the midday heat by the side of the wagon, impeded by the slow pacing of the team and the drag of the drying mud on their clothes. Nothing seemed funny, and he refused to waste drinking water on washing, and as the mud caked into her hair and on her skirt, she felt he was doing it deliberately.

Hours later, when conversation between them had come to a pitched battle as to who could complain the least, he suddenly pulled the team to a stop. "I'm going to climb a tree," he announced, and sent her a sour smile when she reacted just the way he could have predicted.

"I suppose then you'll slide down and all that dried mud will just flake off your clothes," she said meanly as he grasped her left hand and fastened its cuff to the front wheel. "The devil with you," she groaned. "*Why?*"

"I believe you can answer that," he answered tartly. "*That* tree, Lizzie, to see if I can spot a water hole anywhere around here." He pointed, and her fulminating gaze followed his finger—longingly, he thought curiously, contemplating her expression. "You used to climb trees," he said resignedly, understanding her pining look very well. "Your brothers . . ." She nodded, and he wheeled away from her shaking his head.

Yes, she had loved to do the things her brothers had done, and she had been good at them too. She watched as he catapulted his mud-slathered body up onto a thick branch of a solid-looking tree a few hundred feet ahead of them. And up, climbing slowly, pausing to look at the surrounding area as he proceeded higher and still higher. Misplacing his foot once, almost slipping another time. She was amazed she felt fear for him, and relief, finally, when he made his way downward again.

"Over that rise," he said when he came close enough, turning around and pointing, "off the road, though, and through a small thicket of trees. But there *is* water, and we can make it."

Making it meant walking, and they walked, after he had released her cuff and fastened it again in front of her. And when she got tired, he hoisted her onto the wagon seat, and *he* walked some more. Shadows were lengthening onto the road when they finally cut off the track and into the little forest.

Just beyond it, the sparkle of water, as the sun danced on its lapping waves.

She eagerly jumped from the wagon of her own accord. "It looks lovely. Where is the soap? What will you do while I bathe?"

He stared at her, bemused, and then one thick black brow arched upward in amusement, and his firm lips under his bristly mustache curved into a cynically amused smile. "Oh no, Lizzie; I'm not going to allow you any false modesty. I've

87

had e-damned-nough of holding that benighted skirt up in front of you to give you privacy while we travel. You take off your clothes here and now. We bathe together."

"I will *not*," she contradicted indignantly.

"But you will," he disagreed coolly, and swooped his arm around her midriff and lifted her up as easily as if she were a child and strode determinedly toward the edge of the water with her cuffed hands beating at his muscle-corded arm and her feet kicking wildly at his legs.

He plunked her down unceremoniously and briskly unlocked the one cuff so her hands were free to remove her shirt. He looked down at her with that uncompromising expression, his black eyes fathomless and unreadable. "Do it, Lizzie."

She met the look with a stubborn set of her lips and her eyes darkening in anger to that deep jade that he knew already was a barometer of her emotions. "It's time you trusted me."

He laughed. She couldn't believe it; he stood there and laughed at her with a kind of deep chortle that rose up from deep inside him. And then he stopped abruptly. "Just take off your clothes, woman."

"I won't," she reiterated stubbornly even though she was longing to get into the water and to feel clean again. She just didn't want him to have it all his own way, but she saw, as his face darkened with exasperation, that he was going to have everything his own way whether she liked it or not.

"It will be my pleasure then," he said in a deceptively ingratiating tone as he grasped her mud-caked braid and pulled her toward him.

"I suppose," she said nastily, resisting the pull which hurt her and did not in the least stop him, "you have to take your pleasure where you can find it. Isn't that how this whole thing started in the first place?" she added for good measure as she found herself hard up against his broad chest with his scowling face above her.

"You've got a sassy mouth, Lizzie; you talk too much," he muttered, tilting her face up to him. "I know just how to shut you up."

There was no protest. Her lips parted and he claimed them before she could utter a word. She felt herself being drawn up against him, tighter, and still tighter, and her cuffed hand and arm being forcefully wound around his neck. His tongue demanded hers insistently, seeking her, tasting her, gentle with her, but still with some underlying feeling she didn't understand. She felt overwhelmed by him, his height, his passion against her own vulnerability.

She couldn't succumb, she thought even as her senses were dazzled by his hot seeking mouth. She beat at his shoulder with her cuffed hand ineffectually, her body struggled against him, which only molded her tighter to him as his arm constricted and tightened. Her body responded to the intimate pressure of his, and the strangely familiar sense of his elongated manhood that pressed against her now not-so-unwilling thighs.

She felt herself melting against him, her own body seeking that closeness, her lips responding to the continual gentle assault of his. And she continued to pound on his shoulder with her hand, a protest that turned into a kind of caress as her shimmering body reluctantly responded.

He lifted his head once to murmur, "I swear, Lizzie, I've got more scars from that damned cuff than I ever got fighting that damned war."

She felt his hand slide behind her head and guide her lips back to his, and slowly and deliberately, he fit his mouth against hers with such voluptuous intent that a curlicue of pure pleasure spiraled from the cold knot in her stomach right down between her legs, and her hips writhed against his in reaction to the feeling.

It was crazy, she knew it was crazy, her uninhibited and restrained response to the compulsive urgency of his mouth. It had to be something in her, something about herself that she had never known that allowed her to let this stranger kiss her this way—touch her this way—as his hand slid to her throat and then downward to the buttons of her skirt—make her feel this strange way.

She wrenched away as she realized his fingers were deftly undoing the buttons down the front of the shirt. "So—a ruse," she accused him. "You can't get her to do what you want, you seduce her into it."

He shook his head wonderingly, unable to take the leap she

had taken as to his motives. "I said I'd undress you, Lizzie, if you wouldn't do it yourself." He reached out and continued unfastening the shirt until it hung open to reveal her mud-caked chemise. "Not too seductive, all that muck," he added pointedly, and moved closer to slide the sleeves off her shoulders.

She flinched at his touch. His hands were so warm, so caressing, as he pulled each sleeve down her arm and over the tormenting cuffs. And she watched, almost as if she stood beside herself and were a spectator, as he unfastened her skirt, not without a little trouble, and let it slide down her legs to pool around her mud-soaked boots.

"Move, Lizzie; take off those boots, and get out of your underclothes." His voice was sharp, almost angry, as she crossed her arms over her breasts and stood glaring at him like some avenging angel. Rather than throttle her, he began unbuttoning his own shirt irritatedly, holding her verdant gaze with his own exasperated coal dark scrutiny.

Finally, impatiently, he wrenched the sleeves off his arms, tearing the button and gauntlet of one in the process. He threw it down disgustedly and began unbuckling his belt, aware that she was becoming less defiant and more vexed with him. "I'm going down to the skin, Lizzie, I expect you to do the same," he said, amused as her eyes narrowed with each ensuing garment *he* removed.

She didn't register shock at the sight of his bare chest or his removing his denims, and he laid that familiarity at the door of her phantom, now gone, brothers, who seemed to have educated her in ways her mother probably never dreamed of. It was an amusing thought, that this sassy-mouthed urchin of a woman who stared at him so stormily had had as proper an upbringing as any wealthy landowner's daughter would have, and she knew things that would have sent her mother into a dead faint if she had even so much as hinted at them.

"I'm glad *you* think this is so funny," she said tartly as he pulled off his boots and his undergarments and pants in one efficient movement. She was stunned by his naked body and his rampant manhood so fully and insouciantly exposed to her avid gaze.

He was beautiful.

The unguarded thought shocked her. Her brothers, whose handsome well-made bodies she had seen undressed many times, had never elicited that kind of response from her. But this was different. This was so different. There was such a latent power in this long lean muscular frame. His shoulders were so wide in comparison to the rest of him, his chest broad, matted with springy hair. His upper torso was darker than his muscular flanks, and every last inch of him, she thought, was as abundantly male as could be.

Wordlessly, she watched as he picked up his clothes and threw them into the water, and then he came at her with an incisive determination that made her hold her ground rather than—as anyone else would have done, she thought maliciously—back away in fear.

"The time is now, Lizzie; I'm not sleeping with a mud hen tonight," he growled, and reached out one long arm. His fingers grasped the frayed end of the ribbon that secured her chemise. He pulled, mercilessly, and the bow untied itself compliantly and dangled down onto her adamantly crossed arms.

She took a deep stringent breath, prepared to do battle, but there was no battle. The latent power of his nakedness unnerved her. When he reached for her arms to pull them away from her breasts, she let them fall without a fight.

He began unlacing the ribbon, his hot gaze intent on what his long fingers were doing and not her cutting look, or her tremulous shudder when the laces were undone and his hands began sliding the chemise from her shoulders.

She watched his face as his unreadable dark eyes settled on the swell of her breasts. It was easier to watch his expression than to see herself naked and sense his gaze caressing her, but she knew that was just what he was doing, and her treacherous body responded accordingly, arching itself slightly, her nipples tightening into tempting rosy peaks.

His jetty gaze burned into hers as he removed the rest of her undergarments, and forced her feet out of her boots, before he grasped her naked body and lifted her away from the pool of mud-caked clothing and crushed her against his body.

91

Slowly he slid her body downward so that he felt every nuance of her silky nakedness against himself; slowly he encircled her into the unremitting wall of his strength and his tumescent heat. Her thighs straddled him, feeling every long pulsating inch as his mouth found hers again and he forced her lips to his, and whispered against them, "Hold me, Lizzie."

"No!" No! she protested deep within herself. And no, because if she held him the way he wanted her to, it meant her surrender to him. And even now, the temptation was so great, he held her so close she felt bonded to him, with his one strong corded arm supporting her buttocks just above his hard male length, and the other firmly around her waist, just below her breasts, which were compressed against his hard matted chest.

"No!" she breathed again, but she knew the objection was useless.

The force of his kiss crushed it down, and he took her lips and tongue then with all the latent feeling she had sensed in him before. His mouth was a storm, overcoming everything in its path, boldly exploring every crevice and surface, discovering her, exciting her in unimaginable ways, forcing her response, claiming it for his own.

She moved against him sinuously, winding herself around him in an almost involuntary feminine invitation. She wanted to stretch her whole body against his, to open herself to him utterly and feel the heat of his hands exploring her as thoroughly as his mouth, to . . .

But that was insane, she didn't want that; she *didn't*—her unawakened yearning body wanted that, not her *self*. Not . . . his mesmerizing mouth plundering hers and sending every coherent thought from her head.

She felt suddenly the release of the pressure against her mouth, and she knew what he intended to do as he began lowering her body downward. She reacted instantly, beating him with the cuffed hand and pushing at him with her other arm and her legs.

"Damn you, Lizzie," he grated, dropping her rudely onto her feet.

"Damn you, Galt Saunders," she hissed, watching with not a whit of sympathy as he rubbed his right shoulder where she

92

had struck him.

"A pretty impasse," he retorted, placing his large hands on his lean hips. "What are you going to do?"

"What are you?" she countered, quickly crossing her hands over her breasts as she became aware of the intensity of his gaze. His erection, which had diminished, was showing life, and she wanted to squelch that and bathe and dress as quickly as possible.

She didn't expect him to step forward in his catlike way, and grasp her hands together and snap the cuff back onto her right hand.

"You didn't think I would give you free rein with my privates as well, now did you, Lizzie? Those damned things are lethal."

His caustic tone set her hackles up. "And I know very well how to use them," she said sweetly, envisioning him, for one delightful moment, totally at her mercy, naked before her and her free cuffed arm swinging at him. Yes, she would have thought of that—eventually—if her hands had remained free, and she would have done it too.

"So do I," he answered in kind, and her triumphal vision faded. She might have disabled him for several moments, she realized, but no more. He had everything else on his side, and the means to make her pay for such purposeful defiance.

Besides, she thought, she didn't want to hurt him there, she didn't. "So now . . . ?" she said tentatively.

He smiled unpleasantly. "We do the laundry."

She couldn't believe it; the sensual moment evaporated as if it had never existed. She watched, bemused, as he picked up her clothes and threw them into the water, and then waded out after them.

"You too, Lizzie. You're going to have to work those lily white hands of yours," he called back to her.

She stood at the edge of the water, loath to follow him. He had turned his back on her. She could even turn tail and run, much good it would do her, naked and cuffed as she was.

"*Lizzie!*" His voice cracked into the scorching silence

almost as if he had read her thoughts. She girded herself and put a tentative foot into the water, and looked up to where Galt was standing, waist-deep now, with his clothes and a bar of soap in one hand.

He was watching her with that arrogant lift of his brow that made her want to smack his face, and that incentive goaded her into the water. It was warm, silky smooth, and inviting. If only her arms were free, she could have dived right into it, and disappeared, she was sure, forever. How smart of him to truss her up again. She would never stop trying to escape him, she thought, no matter what sensual blandishments he employed.

She wondered if he had deduced, from what little she had said about her brothers, that they had taught her to swim as well. The mocking look on his face said he had, and he was waiting for her to try something.

It was easier just to immerse herself and let the soothing warm water cool off her heated body and her rising temper.

She felt his arms grasp her legs under the water, and they rose together from the depths with her flailing legs almost pulling them back under again.

His iron arms held her tightly from behind. "I'm so happy you proved my precautions were necessary," he murmured into her ear. She jerked her head away from him and he twisted her body closer. She was aware of every inch of him behind her, and the growing evidence of his barely contained desire. She could not let happen what had happened before. She was in too much danger from it, and from the enticing heat of his mouth that even now brushed her earlobe with disconcerting directness.

"Don't do that," she said, pronouncing each word with hard distinctness. "Give me the soap; I'll do my clothes and then I'll wash myself." Futile words, she realized as she said them just to fill the simmering silence.

He radiated sensual heat. He wanted her and he was intent, for the first time since he had abducted her, on having his way. It was like trying to contain a runaway steam engine, her useless words, her meager defense of her nakedness.

"I'll wash you," he said suddenly, his voice muted as he felt her fear.

"No, I—" she started and stopped, unable to see how she could wash herself with her hands bound together.

"*I'll* do it," he said again mildly, but she still felt some explosive emotion under the cool surface. How well he contained himself, she thought, her skin tightening with apprehension, as he released her and set her a foot away from him so he could lather up the crude bar of soap he still held in his hand.

His eyes were dark and mocking as they met hers, his large hands slick with soap.

She waited, her face stony, her eyes darkened to jade chips. He moved closer, slowly, and reached out for her shoulders, to turn her around.

And then she felt the shattering movement of his hands down her bare back. She had nothing within her to protect herself from the sensation of his long fingers massaging her back, sliding from her shoulders down her spine in one slithering shimmery motion, feeling every bone and hollow of her backbone, and resting finally on the curve of her hips.

Then the flat of his palms pushed gently back upward to brush against her neck and the healing mark of the puncture wound, and then slowly descended to her shoulders and slid over her collarbone to her chest.

Her whole body quivered against him and she watched with an almost abstract intensity as his hands moved downward still to rest against, and then fully cover, her taut-tipped breasts.

She thought she felt every pore of her skin being touched by him and the slick wetness all over his hands. They moved, she had expected them to move, but she did not expect the exquisite sensation from her nipples as he stroked them. She didn't expect her whole body to be suffused with a desire to have him continue to stroke that way, or cup her breasts and run his soap-slicked fingers lightly, just very lightly, over her sensitized nipples. She couldn't believe the flood of yearning just that one motion evoked.

She leaned against him in unconscious invitation; she gave her body into his hands as long as he kept on doing exactly what he was doing.

But his hands moved downward, toward her most private

95

place, grazing the golden brown thatch that shielded her secrets. "Let me in, Lizzie." His whispered request was a bare breath in her ear.

She shook her head urgently. Not there; she couldn't vocalize it, not yet. He sensed her perturbation. His hands glided away, and downward to her thighs, kneading them lightly, sensually.

His one arm slipped around her hips as he lifted one leg to run his soapy hand down its curving length and then back upward again, against her inner thigh, flexing his long fingers there as well, lightly, commandingly, circling it with his whole large hand. And she felt every movement, every possessive point of contact through to her bones.

And he was aware of it. He shifted her against him, nudging her with his tempting hardness as he prepared to soap down the other leg, and back up its length again to cup her thigh, and slide his hand around and under it to grasp her buttocks.

He repositioned her once again so he could wash down her buttocks with firm light strokes, insinuating his soapy hand between them, and all over them until her knees felt weak. His arm pulled her close before she sagged into the water, and began its torturously sensuous course back to her breasts. She knew he was going to hold her there, that he wanted to hold them again, and feel them. She pressed her body against his as new sensations assaulted her and his hands slicked up her body to cover her breasts again.

His hands were so big, so all-encompassing. Every ounce of the female in her responded to the way he touched her there. Her whole body thrust itself outward to be sure that he held her as fully as possible.

"Lizzie . . ." His breath of a voice in her ear thrilled her, and she twisted her head back to meet his lips. His mouth covered hers as completely as his hands covered her breasts.

Had she demanded his kiss? She didn't know; but she was aching for his caress, moving her body voluptuously against him to force him to feel her breasts, to cup them to feel their heft, to stroke the taut nipples so she could feel those molten sensations once again.

She was totally in his hands, hardly even aware he was

maneuvering her body against his, that one hand now guided her head and mouth in perfect alignment with his, while the other slid moistly down her slick curves, feeling every inch of her body from her shoulder bones to the curve of her upper arm, and the luscious weight of her breast, down to the indentation of her waist, and further, to the slope of her buttocks and the round fullness of her thigh, past her flexing, manacled hands, and straight to the core of her femininity.

Her entire body jolted against him as he inserted his long fingers into that moist haven, and she writhed in panic, trying to get away from the enveloping invasive sensation.

"Lizzie . . ." He removed his mouth from hers; his voice in her ear calmed her, his fingers lay quiescent within her. The silence between them was charged with his fiercely rising desire and her body's torrid acceptance of him there against her mind's will.

And yet, even as her consciousness rebelled, his firm hard touch began to feel ravishingly familiar. She sensed him watching her through hooded eyes; she felt the scrape of his unshaven cheek against hers as he waited for her to raise a hand against him to deny him.

She wanted to, how she wanted to. But she wanted something else as well. She was filled with the sense of him within her, and her body moved involuntarily against the penetrating solidity of his fingers.

"Let go, Lizzie."

She heard his rich whisper in her ear through a multitude of conflicting emotions. He had not moved either his mouth or his hand and she felt as though his command and his deep caress were seducing her beyond her own control of her senses.

"Never," she hissed, and wrenched her hips forward. A mistake. A huge mistake; she wasn't prepared for the fluming feeling of pleasure that coursed through her vitals. Everything in her pushed it away—her hands made a futile shoveling motion at his wrist even as her torso caved into the iron rod of his manhood.

Her protestation became an invitation as her body demanded more, and still more of the sensation, the feeling. What *was* the feeling? It was almost as if she had known it some

97

other time before, it was so dazzlingly familiar. Her body, her very own body, knew just what to do somehow; it moved with a feminine surety against his inexorable touch and everything in her, unmindful of her warring emotions, reached out to the thickening sensations he evoked.

They expanded as he caressed her, hot and shimmering at first, nebulous with promise. His free hand slid upward to force her reluctant mouth to his and he covered it ruthlessly. She met his kiss eagerly as she strained against his touch, and the luxuriant sensations, all satin, all silver, incandescent and glowing. Reaching, as his fingers pulsated deep within her, for the culmination of all the opulent feelings that rippled within her.

Pinpoints of light danced on her skin, rushing downward with a glittery heat, at one with the sun, glowing and centering suddenly at her core. And then all at once, spasms shook her, exploding and crackling through her body, cascading through her blood, as the fingers of her right hand constricted against his wrist in rhythm with each convulsive moan from deep in her throat. The voluptuous excitement of her culmination eddied slowly away and her body sagged against his. His chest was like an unyielding wall, there solely to support her. He was totally impassive as he took her weight against his nakedness, holding her just as he had been, unmoving, rigid, the ecstasy of her response settling in his gut, in his heart.

She ripped her mouth from his with a violent sound. "My God, my God, my God . . ." Her voice sounded muffled, disembodied—awed. "What did you do? What did you do? What *was* that?"

"The beginning," he whispered, his voice hoarse. His hand moved then, withdrawing gently from her velvet fold, to slide softly down her torso to grasp her long legs and lift her with tautly controlled ease into his arms.

"No!" Her enchanted surrender toppled headlong into defiance. Her legs flailed out, her body thrust against his frenetically, her cuffed hands lifted threateningly. "You bastard! Put me down, damn it . . ."

He ignored it all, striding steadily out of the water onto land before he said calmly, "You keep it up, Lizzie, and I'll drop you right here and now. I don't guarantee you won't break your neck either, now you can't float away from me."

"All right, all right," she gave in grudgingly. "What are you *doing?*" she shrieked suddenly as he swooped her down onto a grassy bank and dropped down prone beside her. His muscular right arm immediately clamped over her hips as she struggled to sit upright; his long muscular hair-roughened right leg wound meaningfully around her thighs. She looked into his snappy black eyes warily: they were coal hard, glittery with purpose. She fell back resignedly.

A brief cynical smile touched his lips. "You're learning, Lizzie."

"Yes, aren't I?" she snapped caustically, her eyes darkening to jade as they clashed with his. "You're not done yet, are you?" she added with just a touch of snide mockery in her voice. She knew she didn't have to ask that; his body was tight with suppressed desire, and a little muscle twitched along his jawline. There was tension in the arm that held her locked to the soft grassy tuft of ground, and his jutting manhood prodded her thigh urgently. He was all strength and aroused male hunger, and she knew very well what happened between two naked people in private. There was no question he could force her compliance now.

The way his piercing black gaze swept over her left her in no doubt that he wanted her. Want! What was want? What had she to do with his want except that she was at the mercy of it? It didn't hurt except once—or so her older brother had told her. The danger was that it led to childbearing.

The danger was a man did something unexpected to you that you had no knowledge of, no awareness of. Something that made you both wary and yearning for more. Something that prevailed over all reason and intelligence, over your own will, and wracked your body with an unimaginable all-enveloping feeling of pleasure. She had no weapons against that. It simply must never happen again. Never. "What *did* you do to me?" she demanded suddenly.

The air between them thickened as his jetty gaze considered her mutinous expression. "What do you think I did, Lizzie?"

"I think you robbed me of my sanity," she retorted, "and I

99

didn't like it."

"Didn't you?" he murmured chidingly. "Don't lie to me, Lizzie—and don't lie to yourself."

Her manacled hands lifted in a sudden sharp movement of frustration. The hand that confined her body instantly clamped over them. Their heated gazes collided as he slowly lifted her resistant arms and pinned them over her head with his left hand.

Her heart lurched violently as he grasped her wrists, and her body thrust forward, curving sensually toward the hard angles of his, and no amount of subtle movement on her part could prevent it. She knew he was aware of it; the light in his eyes deepened, his encompassing black gaze missed nothing.

"I suppose," she bit out to distract him just a little, "I suppose now you'll take your pleasure." She knew he would; it was in his eyes and the heat of his body. He was still, so still, and his desire was a tangible thing, the only movement his inexorable manhood that nudged her thigh, so absolute, so hard, so huge, so *there*.

"Oh yes indeed, Miss Lizzie," he agreed softly, the amusement patent in his voice, a smile crinkling his eyes, wafting across his lips, "now I will indeed take my pleasure."

She didn't know what to make of his tone of voice. Her body thrashed in protest at his words. His leg flexed against hers, a threatening, containing movement. She turned her head away from the mocking expression in his face.

"You can't escape," he murmured, and her body stiffened.

"How true," she muttered, snapping her eyes closed against his burning eyes and her burning fear. It only hurt once, just a little; the thought repeated itself like a litany—her brother would not have lied; he considered it essential she knew these things as he headed off to war. Her indomitable strength was not proof against things like these happening. He could never have foreseen this predicament, this abductor, this latent erotic feeling that a stranger could evoke in her so that her fear was tinged with an aching curiosity to experience more. Oh, no one had prepared her for this, this situation and this man . . . and the thought that had it not been this man, perhaps her captor might be dead.

Or she.

The morbid thought catapulted out of her mind as she became aware of his right hand skimming down her upraised arms and her uptilted left breast. She caught her breath as he molded his long fingers around its lush shape and held it. Just held it. She felt her nipple tighten at his subtle touch and she couldn't bear to open her eyes to see what he intended to do next.

She knew.

She thought she knew. He didn't move for the longest time, and the tension in her body held her just where she was. She could pinpoint separate distinct impressions: the unyielding strength of the hand holding her wrists; her body's torrid awareness of his nakedness so intimate with her own; the heated tautness of the fingers that surrounded her breast. The evenness of his breathing. The burning sense of something about to happen that stretched her nerves to the breaking point because nothing she *expected* to happen was happening.

And then she thought he wanted her to open her eyes, to see, or to lash out, perhaps to try to escape him—as if that were possible with his height and muscularity, and her useless hands.

She drew in a deep breath, cursing the lack of foresight that had prompted her to close her eyes rather than watch every last horrifying detail of his seduction of her. The waiting was harder; if she had challenged him, it would have been over by now.

And what was he thinking? More, what was he seeing with the total freedom of his eyes to rove where they would? Everything was bared to him except what she was thinking. He knew everything now, even her potential to respond to his hands. She stifled a groan. She had no defenses against him, and closing her eyes wasn't going to help her if he moved his hand one inch from where it rested this minute.

His fingers flexed against her skin, and his hand moved, sliding gently up and over the tip of her breast to contain the whole of it in his grasp.

Her eyes shot open as her taut nipple grazed the hard hot flat of his palm.

"So, Lizzie," he murmured encouragingly to her mutinous gaze as she caught her lower lip between her teeth.

"Devil you," she spat at him, wrenching her upper torso unsuccessfully against the feeling of his hand possessing her breast like some kind of undergarment. "Damn you, get this over with, for God's sake."

He shook his head sympathetically. "Lizzie, Lizzie, Lizzie . . . impatient Lizzie." He examined the antagonistic expression on her face with the benevolence of a tyrant who knows he has the upper hand.

Oh, she was a true martyr, he thought with that same beguiled amusement, full of gut and spit, and still an unawakened sensual animal. Her green eyes blazed out at him and every futile thrust of her body only brought her sleek body in closer contact with his pulsating desire. Her wet wildly tangled hair and finely molded lips ever open to spew imprecations at him gave her face a look of alluring invitation that was almost too hard to resist.

But he did, he waited; she had no idea what he intended to do, she could only credit him with wanting to do the obvious when in fact he had not intended to do anything at all. Her voluptuous response had caught him completely off-guard, and now—yes, he wanted her, and yes, she *was* his for the taking, but he knew right then as he inexorably held on to her writhing nakedness, that he wanted more than that.

He watched with a great deal of interest as she waited for what he would do next. He didn't know himself. He loved the feeling of holding the soft sensual mound of her breast with its taut protruding center grazing his palm and he loved looking at her straining nakedness.

And she didn't love it at all. She couldn't stand her helplessness and she was ready to kill him for that look of benign pleasure that lurked just behind his glowing jet eyes. She had no choice but to goad him. Her eyes narrowed and she focused on the hateful little smile that just curved his lips. Her mouth opened—and he forestalled her words.

"Don't say it, Lizzie."

"Oh, please," she groaned, "don't say what? Get on with it? Could we finish washing out clothes? Could I have something to eat?''

"But I'm the one who's ravenous,'' he countered harshly, and she saw with some satisfaction that her words had ripped right into his humor. His expression turned stony, his body tightened and lengthened against hers as the hand that grasped her wrists constricted with emotion, and the one that held her breast moved from its voluptuous contour slowly upward and upward still across the flat of her chest, and the delicate line of her collarbone to the base of her throat. His long fingers began stroking the indentation there, and his coal hard gaze took on a hungry, predatory look that was frightening because of its intensity.

She shivered; for one decimating instant she felt real fear that totally wiped out her defiance. Her lips parted once again to lash out with the only defense she had, and his mouth swooped down on hers with unerring precision to quell the spate of words.

He swallowed her words, her fear, her anger; he stormed her mouth with all the fierce desire with which he would have stormed her femininity. His body surged over hers, all heat and angles, and his hand began a torturous path downward, from the fragile hollow of her throat, to the lush curve of her breast, down still farther to the slope of her hip, and the long angular slide of her flat stomach to the seductive thatch at the vee between her thighs.

And she hadn't expected that. She had thought it would be quick, a brief stab, a pulsation and the finish of it. She hadn't armed herself against this bone-melting exploration of her body that went right back to her provocative center, to seek and tantalize, to feel the honey of the response she could not have withheld even if she'd wanted to.

What *was* this, that his hands could incite her to lose control, that his mouth and questing tongue could reduce her to yearning for something she had no knowledge of whatsoever, that her body, over which she thought she had mastery, only ached to be mastered by his.

His hand moved, engulfed by her essence, satiated; he was leaving her, and she wanted to cry out against his rapacious mouth in protest as the heightening feelings within her slithered away, and were replaced with a keen urgency that had nothing to do with her thoughts or will.

But she must have made some sort of sound deep in her throat. He tore his mouth away to breathe against her lips: "Yes, Miss Lizzie of the sassy mouth; tell me with your words now, my Lizzie. Tell me what you want."

"Nothing," she whispered, unable to curb her defiance, and unable to restrain the traitorous movement of her heated body.

"Everything," he contradicted with a growl, crushing her mouth again, never letting her get away with denying what she was feeling. His mustache scraped the delicate skin above her lips as he voraciously plunged into her mouth, seeking the affirmation her words refuted.

It was there; she moved toward him, her lips and tongue eagerly reaching for his. Her body shifted just the faintest bit upward, closer, and with a groan he released her imprisoned hands to settle them down around his neck, to free his arm to slide around her and cup her closer still. His long strong leg that held her around her knees slid roughly downward, and gathered her legs in the circle of its muscularity. His right hand claimed her body, caressing its line from the horizontal stretch of her arm, down her back, under her breast and around it, down the alluring curve of her hips and thighs, to the lush cushion of her buttocks where he held her tightly against his hips. His body worked against hers, attenuated little thrusts, barely there, the long hard length of him throbbing against the enticing roundness of her hip and belly. His hand played a frenzied tattoo up and down the small of her back, feeling and rubbing alternately as if he could imprint the texture of her skin on his.

She felt possessed by him, his hands, his voluptuous mouth, his encircling body that, in his fevered movements, had mounted hers so that she took his weight again with a firm sense of knowing it, and more—shockingly—of wanting it. He was all over her, body, hands, mouth, tongue, thrusts pressing, compelling, forceful, and then a prolonged lunge and his body tightened like a bowstring; she felt the wet, and the heaving sweatiness of their bodies locked together, and the long low groan deep from within him as he ripped his mouth from hers.

104

He didn't move, didn't want to move; hadn't planned for that to happen, and yet—she *had* been with him, and knowing that, and in spite of her resistance, he wanted desperately to hold her more tightly to him.

His arms tensed around her to draw her closer, to quell the restive motion of her hips. She pulsated with a deep yearning heat compounded of both need and a sense of wonder. It was as if her mind were dissociated from her body, the one absorbing the fact that, in spite of the odds and his ferocious masculinity, she was still whole; and the other, almost against her will, demanding the exquisite release that saturated her memory to the exclusion of almost everything else.

Her clamoring body told her—told him—it was still possible. Her arms around his neck began a rhythmic pummeling across his shoulders, and at that, finally, he lifted his head and looked at her.

A mistake. There was no triumph glowing in his eyes; they were shuttered, curious, and the lines in his face seemed to have carved themselves deeper, and wiped out whatever joy he had allowed into his expression. And she had not seen it, and she hated him for making her want to have seen it, and for craving a repetition of the explosive sensation he had evoked before.

"No!" She heard herself actually saying it out loud as she consciously clamped down on her quivering body.

He stared at her furious expression for a long moment. Her lids had come down so that her long dark lashes shadowed the true feelings reflected in her heated verdant gaze.

"Surely, Miss Lizzie . . ." he began.

"I won't. I won't let you do this, Galt. You've done enough. You have. You've just . . . done . . . quite enough . . ."

His snappy black eyes narrowed as he listened impassively to this distraught little speech, and a slow disbelieving smile skimmed his lips. "Beg your pardon, Miss Elizabeth, but I assure you, I haven't done nearly enough."

She bridled at the amused note in his deep rich voice. "But what more could you do?" she asked with a deceptive tone of innocence. "I thought that was all there is."

His smile reached his eyes this time, crinkling the lines

around them with a thought she never would know. His two large hands moved to cup her head and tilt it upward to force her to look at his face. She hated the knowledge she saw there, and he could see it reflected very well in her jade-darkening gaze. "I truly appreciate your solicitousness, Miss Lizzie," he said softly, and slanted his mouth over hers. "Are you sure you don't want to change that story?"

"Seems to me," she managed to whisper as she watched the inexorable descent of his firm lips toward hers, "the only story we've been discussing around is—yo—urs . . ." His mouth covered hers as she breathed the last word, his teeth nipping at her lips with no intent to part them.

"Oh, I think there are more stories here," he murmured against her rebellious lips. "I think there are lots of stories about Miss Lizzie and her servants, and her brothers, and how in hell she wound up in Greenfields with the sheriff's son, and how she finally came to be the compliant Lizzie I have in my arms this very minute." His lips grazed hers again, meaningfully, and he ignored the pounding of her fists against his neck.

She tore her mouth away. "Compliant! Compliant! My good God, Galt, you . . ." Her body twisted furiously under his futilely, knowing she could not escape him. "Compliant! You'll never have compliance from me, Galt Saunders—never!"

His jetty eyes roamed over her enraged expression, and the small knowing smile danced on his lips and in his eyes. "That's what makes it all the more interesting, my dear Miss Lizzie. I do caution you, however, not to make such rash pronouncements. Who knows but it may be you might have to take them back."

"Devil you," she muttered, "I will *not*; one of us hasn't forgotten who abducted who and who has who in handcuffs."

"You're right; such an easy thing to forget," he agreed lightly as she shot a baleful glance at him. Oh, definitely he had the upper hand now, she thought wrathfully, quelling all her misspent urges. But he wouldn't be lying on top of her forever. He wouldn't have her at his mercy so easily again. Never would she let him have a chance to evoke these disastrous feelings again if she could help it.

106

But how would she help it if he touched her the same way again? she wondered with a sinking feeling of hopelessness as she watched his expression harden purposefully. "It went right out of my head," he added, his rich voice deceptively gentle. "I promise I will keep it in mind next time."

He watched her face, which changed predictably with each encroaching word. Not helpless, he thought, his neck and shoulders starting to ache from the throttling of her cuffed wrists. He shoved it out of his mind. But it was too late for her now; he could never pull her back enough from this mood to generate that volcanic response again. His right hand, almost of its own volition, began tracing a light sensual line down her nakedness again, almost as if it didn't believe his conclusion. But it was true; her face schooled itself into a blank expression as she felt his fingers trailing across her midriff and slowly downward to her thighs.

And she felt it; the danger was, she thought, no matter what her resolve, he had this unrelenting power over her. Her body tautened perceptibly and she followed, with careful attention, the sense of his hand touching her, and he watched her and every nuance in her face.

She would not let him, he thought. It would be a clash of wills, his to give and hers to resist. But he couldn't desist. He wanted to feel again her provocative femininity. His hand closed over her seductive mound.

A hot velvet stillness rose between them. She dared him to proceed further, her every pore aware of his long tensing fingers just at the entrance of her feminine fold. He dared her to invite—one move, one shift of her hips, one moan, and she knew it, and she knew what culmination would follow. He dared her to repress her need, which he could arouse again so easily.

Too easily, she thought again, tense with the strain of hiding her feelings.

"Lizzie!" He was not amused now; his voice cracked with hoarseness.

"I thought it was done," she said, her voice on the edge of poutiness purposely to push him away.

"We're not done," he contradicted. "But you know that."

He shifted his body slightly so that he was braced on his arms as far upward as he could move with her arms still around him. Even so, her body arched up with his, as he looked down on her, and her golden brown hair, now dry, hanging down her back, and her darkened jade eyes impaled him as he lifted her still farther up and against his steely nakedness as he got to his knees and then to his feet.

He lifted her arms from his neck gently, a crooked little smile playing across his firm lips which was almost obscured by his mustache.

She stalked away from him, and then turned to look at him as he stood, arms akimbo, her own stance defiant. And *looked* at him, her resistance wavering, as her glittery eyes feasted on the long sleek line of his body, and the matted hair that covered his chest and crept beguilingly downward toward the dark center of him that was enshrouded in the same springy thatch.

He was amused by her scrutiny. Her anger had seeped away and he could not tell what had replaced it: curiosity, perhaps, or even desire if that explained the lambent light in her eyes which flickered as her derisive green gaze swept up to meet his.

She was a fighter all right, he thought, as a dart of pure male desire pierced him; and yet, underneath all the bravado and the words, she was still consumed by fear. And he couldn't change that, either by will or by deed. He couldn't take the chance that she might run away. He had to keep her with him with threats or by force. He even had a fleeting regret he had not seized the moment and taken her as she had so obviously expected him to do.

He watched her as warily as she watched him, and wondered what she was planning to do.

Eight

She moved first, not even thinking, just assessing the distance between them and whether she could get some kind of start on him, and reach a copse of bushes, perhaps, where she could find refuge.

Futile. His voice bellowed after her and echoed through the tall trees: *"Lizzie!"* And a taut obedience stopped her in her tracks. She sensed him behind her almost instantly, his large hands grasping her hips from behind and lifting her with shocking ease. "You witch," he hissed in her ear as her legs dangled against his purposeful strides, "don't you understand I won't let you go?"

"I have to try," she retorted grittily, pounding her manacled wrists against his iron bar of a forearm that held her like a vise.

"Yes, you do," he muttered, plunking her down suddenly in three feet of water, and turning her around to face him. "And I have to keep you with me."

"You're crazy," she said acidly, edgy at his closeness, his determination. Nothing she could say would sway him, and she knew it.

He pulled her head down suddenly, roughly. "Stand still, Lizzie." She felt him pulling at her hair, and reared back at the lancing little pain. "I have my reasons," he added abruptly, drawing her back to him.

"What are you doing?" she demanded, wrenching her head around to look up at him. "And when may I know these so-called reasons?"

109

"You've got straw and burrs tangled in your hair. I'm removing them, Miss Lizzie, and I'm pleased of the opportunity to be of service to you. Did I"—he yanked several strands particularly hard for emphasis—"get that part right? Is that how your servants phrased it?"

"Devil you," she retorted under her breath, as he jerked her around to avoid her hands again.

"Idle hands," he murmured as he kept pulling and picking God-knew-what from the tangled curls of her hair. "You'll have to wash it now, Miss Lizzie."

"I would love to. Just uncuff me."

"No, I think not. I think I'll play your maid some more. It's rather enjoyable. And then, if you try to swim away, I can drown you."

"So you have it, as usual, all ways."

"Always," he agreed silkily, wading toward the shore to root out the precious piece of soap he had brought.

She watched passively as he appropriated it and turned back to her. The sun was behind him now so that all she saw was the line of his body angling toward her limned against the light. He was like a creature risen from the sea, and in that moment, as her imagination ran riot, she was entranced by a magical moment out of time that had nothing to do with her predicament. She was Circe, and he was seeking her—only her.

And he came to her steadily, resolutely, came *for* her, the water barely rippling under the force of his firm stride. Beside her now, a steely dark god, lifting her into his strong arms, lifting her to heights never dreamed of, his eyes caressing her face, her mouth. Just for a moment, with the sun glistening over him like a halo, she thought—or hoped?—he might kiss her. She felt as if she were being transported on a cloud. Her eyes, softened to the color of spring green leaves, never left his face.

And then, on the whim of a god, he dumped her unceremoniously into the water.

She sat huddled in a corner of the wagon, her arms wrapped around her still bare legs, her mutinous face buried in the rough cotton collar of the second of Buck McCreedy's shirts that comprised her wardrobe. Everything else was spread on bushes, on the tarpaulin roof of the wagon, and across the backs of the animals to dry. The second skirt, she had discovered to her chagrin, did not fit, and Galt had been entirely unsympathetic. "Alter it," he had shrugged, and tossed it onto the bedding where she had crawled to warm up from the vigorous dunking and washing he had given her.

"Alter it," she had repeated faintly. Of course. Just cut it open—how? Expand the waistline—how? And with what? And there you were. Simple. As if he would let her have a cutting instrument—or a needle, even *if* she had known how to use it. She would jab it right into his posterior, she thought venomously, tossing her still stringy wet hair away from her eyes.

She couldn't even think of the ignominy of having him wash her hair like a child, and then her clothes, like her laundress, or of being forced to parade around buck naked until he could return with her to the wagon. She had been astounded—once the fierce desire within ebbed—at how embarrassed she felt, how uncomfortable in her unclothed state, and how it hadn't seemed to bother *him* one bit. She had found she could not look at him, not when her skin was cold and bumpy and wet, and her improper yearnings had turned to something akin to shame.

She had spent at least the last hour like a chastised child in its room, scared to come out, fuming at the circumstances, and too aware of her state of deshabille.

She stretched her long bare legs out in front of her, and wriggled a little to free up the long shirttails of Buck's too large shirt to smooth them down over her thighs. They hardly came to her knees. She nudged the misbegotten skirt that was draped over the edge of the bedding disgustedly with her foot, and then slid it upward toward her with her heel. Crossing her legs under her, tailor fashion, she leaned forward to pick it up.

Alter it. The waistband was attached to it in one piece, neatly stitched over the two seams that ran up either side. Really, alter it. Ruin a perfectly good skirt.

She grimaced, opened the circle of the waistband, and slid her legs into it. Very carefully she got to her knees, pulled the

111

waistband under her shirt and took a deep heaving breath. And—damned Lonita must have had a good corset, she thought angrily. And the leather belt she had worn to cinch the shirt around her waist was water sodden too.

There had to be something; she wasn't about to climb out of the wagon skirtless to satisfy her curiosity as to what Galt was doing. There was a suspicious lack of any kind of noise from beyond the wagon gate. She hadn't seen him since he had tossed her the skirt. And good she hadn't. She never wanted to see him again. She didn't want to feel grateful that he had freed her one hand so she could dress herself. And she had to be very careful not to let the damned cuff thump on the wagon floor as she explored his belongings to find a belt. She did not want him coming to see what she was doing.

She had a moment's feeling that she was thinking incoherently, that nothing could make any difference. She was in the wilderness now, and until they came to a provisioning town or ferrying place, she was his companion, like it or not. She wasn't stupid enough to try to get away. Or desperate enough. Or was she?

He had, she discovered, less than she in terms of clothing. Another set of undergarments and socks. Another pair of denims, which he had appropriated, and his one shirt and hat were out to dry.

So he didn't need a variety of belts. So his very lean hips supported his ... her whirligig thoughts veered around following that notion to its conclusion.

Perhaps, she reasoned, a piece of rope. Rope. Rope: he had used a length of it to secure the table to the chest. God, and he knew how to tie a puzzler of a knot, she discovered as she examined the table base. Devil it, and devil damn, she thought viciously, sinking back onto the bedding. She was becoming a savage over a piece of fastener for a skirt that belonged to a woman she despised to shield herself from the man who had abducted her and almost seduced her.

Perfect.

And why hadn't he?

No! There was no time to ruminate on him and his whims and reasons. She eyed the bedding consideringly, and then

112

twisted her body to reach for the far corner to pull out the edge of the coarse sheet. With a grimace, she tore a long strip from the length, feeling that she would have liked to tear a strip out of Galt Saunders in just the same way.

She was very satisfied that she had to wind the length of sheeting around her waist twice before she could tie it, and even then the ends dangled well down toward her knees. The shirt hung over her makeshift belt, covering it, covering her in a way that could not possibly compel any kind of untoward thoughts.

Pleased, she tucked what was left of the sheet under the corner and began crawling toward the wagon gate, unaware of the faint movement beyond the tarp and soft rustling sound of a footstep, just beyond, that signified the retreat of an interested onlooker.

He was barechested and barefooted, and seated hunched over by a newly made fire where the coffeepot bubbled, its aroma just beginning to permeate the sweet early evening air. On his lap, he held his shirt, and he was bent over its cuff, laboriously pushing a needle in and out of the rough material.

He slanted an amused look up at her as he sensed her presence. "I hope you've used this time to good advantage, Miss Lizzie."

"Certainly," she said primly, thrusting her legs off the end of the wagon gate and sliding onto the ground. The skirt fell around her legs like a curtain on the last act of a play.

A twisting little smile flashed across his mouth. "So you have. I'm impressed. You need no instruction at all on the housekeeping arts. I appreciate the joke, Lizzie, truly I do."

She felt like stamping her foot. She felt frustrated, hungry, and just like she was battering her head against a great stone wall. He was imperturbably—and disturbing—her enemy and perhaps her savior, if she was to come away in one piece from this adventure of an abduction. And she had to trust him; with all her wits she had to trust him, and the heavy silvery cuff that weighted down her wrist reminded her she couldn't trust him at all.

113

She edged her way over toward the fire, all the while watching his hands covertly as he worked the bedeviled needle through what now she could see was a horn button, in and out with quick, sharp little stabs, and that faint knowing smile playing across his firm lips because he knew she was watching, and he was so competent doing it.

Finally he thrust it aside. "Tore the button, Miss Lizzie, and I had to find it first, of course. Small things like that, a man has to learn to do if there's no woman to do for him."

She made no response to that; it was easier just to ignore him and sink down opposite him, and tuck her telling bare feet under her before she looked up at him. He could even read her thoughts: he had had a woman to "do" for him, and look what became of her.

"Some coffee, Lizzie?" he offered, still in that benign tone of voice. "It might take the edge off your temper." He leaned forward to lift the pot, while his other hand grasped the two cups nearby. He didn't wait for her answer. He poured and handed her a cup, then poured his own, sipped, and looked at her quizzically over the rim. "So say your piece, Lizzie. God knows you look like you're going to explode."

She opened her mouth and then shut it again. What good was making demands or yelling, or threatening? She looked at the dangling cuff. "Can't you just take this off?"

His smile reached his eyes this time. "Wish I could, Lizzie, but we have a long way to go yet."

"And don't you sound regretful. Tell me where I'm going to get to in this wilderness?"

He shook his head. "We're heading out of wilderness, and well you know it. The question is, what will you do when we reach the next town?" He rose up suddenly, looking impossibly tall against the lowering sun behind him. Slowly he moved around to where she sat and hunkered down next to her. "I think," he said gently, "we both know the answer to that."

She didn't look at him as he drank deeply from his cup. "Where *are* we going, Galt?"

"I thought you were perfectly clear on that. We're going to find Lonita McCreedy."

114

He said it without rancor, as if it were a fact, logical and well thought out. A fool's errand, she thought contemptuously, unsettled by his nearness, his naked warmth emanating from his golden skin. Oh, there was something about him. He was so sure what he planned to do was valid and accomplishable, up to and including taking her with him. And it was just as totally incomprehensible to her. But how could she make him understand that? His only choice was to leave her at the first habitable place he could. She would find work; there was always work in a frontier town. She could take in laundry, or sell at the mercantile store. Or teach children. Or something. Until someone was returning Greenfields way.

"I don't understand," she burst out finally. "I just don't understand why you want to find Lonita. How on earth will that do anything for you? You think Lonita will come willingly back to Greenfields and recant her testimony? You're crazy. She would run as fast as she could the other way. She wouldn't let you find her if she even knew you were trailing her. Why should she? Why, tell me, *why*?"

She felt as if she was on the edge of hysteria. And he didn't move, didn't say a word. There would be no explanations. Only her handcuffs and an endless mindless trip to nowhere.

"You could just go on from here," she went on. She was wound up, her words spewing out like an uncontrollable flume of water. "You could *lose* yourself in the wilderness. You think Edgar could find you if you headed out to Dodge? Or if you took the wagon across the Santa Fe? You could make a whole new life for yourself, and Edgar would never ever find you."

His body tensed almost palpably, as if she had struck him. He turned to look at her, and she could almost feel the ruthless purpose hardening in his face. His rich voice, when he spoke, sent a chill through her; each word cracked with intent and emotion she could not identify.

"But I'd still have to live with myself, Lizzie. *I'd* still know my name was good for nothing in Missouri, wouldn't I? You above anyone should know what a man's honor means to him. Three years ago, I didn't have much left to fight for, but I loved my life, Lizzie. My daddy taught me to love my life, and then suddenly I had a family, and not long after that, I got my own

115

land, something my daddy never would have thought to see; he wouldn't have left Primrose Plantation if the war hadn't come. He would have stayed there forever, loyal, honor bound, Lizzie, to my wife's family—and less so to his own. But there was only me by then. So when war came, and Lydia's family went, we stayed—for honor, for the land, to preserve the land for them. Land was the most important thing, my daddy said, land and family. The land survived; and he, who didn't survive, expected that I would go on in his stead, on the land— someone else's land. He didn't reckon on dying, and he didn't reckon the war would eat up the land and destroy the family." He broke off suddenly and stared past her across the flames which lit the ever darkening circle of their camp.

"Galt—" She felt so cold; she knew nothing of this . . . honor. She only knew finally what it had been like to be without what she was most accustomed, what he had never had. And she didn't want to hear more. His reasons didn't matter. She had never understood the concept of honor. Her brothers had understood. Their debts, their peccadillos, how their community perceived them had mattered deeply to *them*, never to her. Honor. It still made no sense that a man with a sense of honor would almost kill to escape a false murder charge and abduct an innocent bystander in the bargain. What had his honor to do with that?

"He didn't reckon that honor would compel the marriage of the overseer's son to the impoverished daughter of the house. He never would have understood that. Never. Or that honor compelled him to leave, to make his own place, to find his own land, to have it all in *his* name, Lizzie. And no one has the right to take it away from me, *no one*. And I will find her, and I will clear my name, and then I'll go on. Maybe I'll go on. But the name *Saunders* will never be branded a murderer—anywhere. *Any* damned where, Lizzie. And that's final."

His words chilled her. He sounded as cold-blooded as a killer. "Fine," she said finally, her voice husky. "But what about me?"

"What about you?" he asked after a long moment, a contradictory note of amusement creeping into his voice that almost made it seem as if she had imagined the emotion behind his previous words. "You were there, now you're here."

116

"Yes, and then what?"

"We're traveling together, Lizzie—not to dodge Sheriff Edgar now so much as to allay suspicion when we finally catch up to Lonita."

"Oh? And you're so sure we're going to catch up to Lonita?"

"Lonita went to Rim City."

"You know this?"

"I know what she intended."

"Because what she said on the stand was true," Elizabeth hazarded with a great feeling of setting off an explosive, and knowing she wasn't going to like the answer.

"Because she talked so much," he rejoined grimly. "To anyone and everyone who would listen."

"Oh, really . . ." she scoffed, burying her nose in her cup again.

"Let me remind you, Miss Lizzie, that what *you* think doesn't much matter."

"I guess it doesn't," she agreed caustically. "Of course, if I weren't here, it wouldn't much matter either."

"I beg to contradict you, Miss Lizzie. It matters to me."

Her comeback died on her lips. What the devil did he mean by *that?* She let a little beat of silence go by and then she asked, "*Why* does it matter to you?"

She sensed his smile, the real smile, the one that crinkled his eyes and creased his lean cheeks. "Now, do you really think I'm going to tell you that, Lizzie?"

"One can always hope," she muttered darkly, and took a quick sip of what was left of her excruciatingly cold coffee.

Silence fell between them once again as he fried up several rashers of bacon and she threw a few handfuls of dried apples into two plates.

"Not much of a dinner," she muttered, eyeing the crackles of bacon disparagingly.

"I'll be happy to let you take over the cooking, Miss Lizzie. Sometimes a meager meal like this can taste like a real banquet—the kind," he added with a spiky little look at her, "I'm sure you all were used to."

Elizabeth returned the look balefully, and dug a fork into the

117

bacon strip. "Yes indeed. We had regular five-course meals every night. Longview was known for its hospitality; we never had fewer than five guests to table at any dinner before the war. We had a cook, Rilla—she stayed on after—and Herod, our butler, such a stately man, he would usher all the guests in, to where Verdine would have laid such a table . . . Mama's silver, that went back two generations, her family brought it over from England, was always laid out, and the china that Father gifted her with when they were married." She shot Galt a covert glance from under her lashes as she spewed out the details in her best debutante drawl, and she could see he didn't like hearing any of it one bit. "Why, there must have been a hundred pieces or more to that set. I don't know but what Rilla or Verdine buried what was left after the Yankees came through; it could be there still.

"Anyway, Rilla was such a cook. Her pastries, especially. And she'd wrap that flaky dough around ham and bake it . . . I can't tell you, Galt. And after, when we had nothing, she made do with nothing and she still fed us royally until Mama died. I don't know how. I don't know why she stayed either, except for loyalty to Mama, because she had been with Mama's family for years. She used to call me Little Missus when I took over running the place. My brothers were in the army, and Father was an adjutant to General Johnston. He died in the Peninsular Campaign . . ."

Her voice trailed off. She was talking too much, about things that still had the power to pain her deeply. After they had heard about her father, she had watched her mother's health go into a deep decline. Her world was falling apart, and her only daughter, her husband, and her sons could not save it for her. She still felt her mother's lament in her bones; *her* world had fallen apart too with the unexpected death of her father. He had never considered, in his ardor, that his life was on the line; they had all thought her father would go on forever.

She, Elizabeth, had not broken under the grief. She could not let herself. She mourned at night, late at night, when she was alone and everyone was asleep, and her mother dosed with the little laudanum that was left in the stores to ease her nightmares. Her mother was dying then, and only later did she realize it. Only later did she understand she could have saved

118

the medicament for other purposes, a harsh judgment she had come to as she watched her mother waste away, and she had no regrets for making it. Everything was on her shoulders by then, all the field hands but the two or three eldest, who could not have made their way anywhere else, were gone. Rilla left for a paying job cooking for a town family. Verdine was considering one. Her brothers she never thought about at all lest she give in totally to the pain of their loss and she knew that would have rendered her totally inactive, powerless to direct any of her future.

And that had been when Martin Healey walked back into her life.

"Tell me," Galt said into the heavy silence that stretched between them again, "about your brothers." His voice had just the right neutrality in it, as if he had guessed where her thoughts were going, and he meant to distract her by conjuring up joyful memories rather than sad ones.

But I don't want to talk about them, she thought disconsolately. Just the thought of them shot pictures through her mind of events, incidents, playful moments, serious times; her father chastising them—and her—for some irreverant prank; herself as a child tumbling out of the hayloft into a mountain of new-mown sweet-smelling hay after her brothers, determined to do everything that they did. When had her mother stopped allowing that? She shook her head vigorously to clear the haze of the past. It didn't matter; all of it sat in a comfortable little rocking chair of memory in the back of her mind, in a place where she could retreat, where she used to retreat when times got too hard.

Times were not hard now. Her reality now was to be home until she could change it, just like she lived with Martin's jilting her, and the sheriff's using her under the guise of protecting her. Galt would use her too. And even though she was on the verge of believing he might not harm her physically, she knew just as surely that he could now hurt her another way. A way she did not want to think about either because it opened doors to avenues she did not want to explore. Nor did she want him to explore them either, and in the lowering night, with them sitting so closely together and his naked torso vibrating next to her, she felt a connection to him that was both all enveloping and comfortable, and disquieting to the point of panic.

She allowed him to refill her coffee, avoiding the quizzical look in his sharp eyes, avoiding looking at his body and the way the firelight played in the hollows and bulges of his arms and chest.

"You don't want to talk about your brothers," he mused slowly, settling down next to her again, folding his long legs under him this time, and cradling his own refilled cup in his hands to warm them. "But you see, Miss Lizzie, I really have to know what I'm up against. For example, I have a real strong feeling that if I were to uncuff you, I'd find that, sometime, in the dead of night, you'd have stolen the horses and gone off bareback, now wouldn't you? I just know you can ride without a saddle." He paused expectantly and a reluctant little smile tugged at the corners of her mouth that was easily perceivable even in the dim firelight. He nodded in satisfaction. "So?"

She answered without thinking, "If you really think that, why would you suppose I'd willingly give you *any* information about my more unusual accomplishments?"

He smiled then, a slow real right to the eyes smile, and began lifting himself upward in a lazily lithe movement that arrested her attention. "You're right of course. I can see already you know the things that count." He held out his large hand to her, and after a moment's hesitation, she grasped it and allowed him to pull her to her feet. "And tell me how you secured the skirt?" he asked, surveying her enveloped body with interest.

"I tore off a strip of sheet," she said blandly, not meeting his eyes.

"I knew you'd figure something out," he answered in kind, motioning her toward the wagon, and then bending to take a handful of dirt to throw on the fire.

She watched him damp out the flames impassively, with only her hands restive, because of what was to come. He would lock them together yet again, and she would sleep once more on the edge of apprehension as to his intentions. A semblance of camaraderie before the fire was one thing; sleeping next to the man was another.

And the thing that threw her the most was his warmth. His

120

whole body pulsated with it, and it was a reaching and enfolding warmth, a dangerous warmth that she could very easily allow herself to get caught up in. Too easily. His hands and his body, were warm. So were his words sometimes, and the way he looked at her.

And still she wore manacles; he knew he could have her, and he hadn't taken her, and he kept her in handcuffs. It made no sense, none of it: his reasons, his throbbing swirling warmth . . . his patience, she thought unexpectedly, as she watched him withdraw the handcuff key from his still-drying pants and slide it into his right back pocket. His need for vindication. Maybe she could understand that. But just maybe. That had to do with the male things she could not be a part of with her brothers. Things they knew and she didn't, couldn't. Rights and privileges they had that she could never have. Amorphous things, like honor.

She shook her head impatiently and thrust the fruitless thoughts and mental arguments out of her head. The fact still remained that Galt was stronger and she was in handcuffs, and for the time being, she was going to have to do what he wanted.

And what he wanted now was for her to climb into the wagon. She was so tempted to be testy; she wasn't one bit tired, and her overactive brain was still circling around the puzzle of Galt Saunders and his abduction of her and pursuit of Lonita McCreedy. Even when she resolutely told herself she wouldn't think about it, it still floated around the periphery of her consciousness. And took just that bit of precedence over her even ruminating about her response to Galt this afternoon. Oh no, that was not for examination at all, that was to be shoved well to the back of all her problems, she had thought, but she had not counted on the difference it would ultimately make this night when he was finally bedded down beside her, dressed only in his tight denims and reaching with his large warm hand to take the unused cuff and secure it to his own wrist.

"Must you?" she demanded ungraciously.

"I think I must, Lizzie." The snap of it catching around his wrist sounded like the crack of a gun in the small confined space. It startled her in the heavy darkness between them. She couldn't see him, he had not lit one of the lanterns that hung suspended from the frame. She couldn't see his face, she

121

couldn't tell what he was thinking. She almost felt as if she had to rush into words to distract him from anything he might be thinking.

What could he be thinking? That she was naked under her clothes. That despite all her protestations this afternoon, she had let him touch her in that unfamiliar sensual way that was now too familiar, and too well desired now she knew she could not allow it to happen again.

And what was happening to her?

"It would serve you right," she told him roundly, "if I just stole the damn key out of your pocket and snuck away from here on one of your horses."

What was it about him, she wondered the second after she uttered the words, that made her totally able to perceive when his humor was piqued. She could swear, in the deep, deafening silent dark, that he was smiling again, the crinkle-eyes smile, the one, she admitted reluctantly to herself, that she liked and liked too much.

"I'd love to see that, Lizzie," he said after spending a tantalizing moment or two wriggling around the mattress to get comfortable. "The thought of feeling your hand groping around my pockets leaves me breathless with anticipation. I encourage you to try."

Damn the man, she thought, pounding her cuffed hand to the mattress with frustration, weighting his hand with it. "I leave you to your anticipations. You can't think I would advertise the day and time the event is to take place, do you?"

"I won't sleep a wink from now on," he promised, and again, she swore he was smiling. God, he was so very different from the man who had taken her by threats and gunpoint, and too different from the man the townspeople of Greenfields gossiped about.

Who was he, really?

The thought caught her fancy; it was something to tease her mind for the rest of the night, for she was absolutely sure that, in spite of his bantering promise, Galt Saunders would sleep very well tonight. And she knew the same could not be said of her.

122

Nine

"Biscuits? *Biscuits?* I never made biscuits in my life," Elizabeth complained, squinting her eyes to look up at Galt, who was on his knees above her, his dented coffee cup in his hand and his fingers poised to dip into its contents again, and lop cold drops of water on her face.

"Time you learned, Miss Lizzie. You have to pull your weight around here; you can't always find a solution in the bedclothes. Let's go."

God, he was unmercifully cheerful this morning, she thought irritably. "Have pity; I didn't sleep at all last night."

Her grumpy words arrested his progress toward the back of the wagon. "Is that so? I'm truly sorry about that. Did you get a chance to search me? I'm sorry I missed it."

His dismissal of what he implied was her lightweight effort to locate the handcuff key jolted her upright. "If I had touched you, *anytime,* you would have known it," she retorted grittily.

"I'm pleased to hear it," he rejoined blandly, and then his voice sharpened. "Get moving, woman."

He vaulted out of the wagon, leaving Elizabeth staring after him in a state bordering on bewildered exasperation.

The thought of that key nestled so provokingly close to her, in his back pocket, the one she could easily reach if he were as soundly asleep as he had been last night, had tempted her the whole night. Planning just how to do it had driven every other thought out of her mind. It was within her grasp, the key to her freedom, and accomplishable with a moment's daring.

123

Any time, in the deep of the night, she could have propped herself up as best she could on her cuffed hand's elbow, and slowly reached across his recumbent body, which more often than not inclined slightly toward hers, and as gently as was humanly possible, worked her hand into that back pocket and slid the key out. Any time, as he slept soundly; she had gone through it in her mind step by step as she listened to his deep heavy breathing.

"*Lizzie!*"

His vexed shout jolted her out of her reverie.

"All *right!*" she shouted back, and began crawling to the wagon gate. "Throw in my boots and socks, will you?"

"You don't need 'em. Come *on*, Lizzie. I would think you couldn't wait to learn something of *real* practical use," he added with a glint in his eye as he watched her slowly maneuver out of the wagon with an eye to preserving what modesty she could in the face of his crackling all-aware gaze. "Don't you look all fresh and raring to go—in spite of your lack of shuteye."

"Galt—"

"Never you mind, Lizzie; the biscuits are more important than your temper this morning. I'm damned hungry. And I'm waiting on the coffee too."

"And you're determined take it all out on me," she muttered nastily as she caught up the pot and headed in the direction of the water. She was disconcerted to see Galt right beside her. "Good lord, Galt, you want your coffee and you're tailing me like a bodyguard."

"Damned right, Miss Lizzie," he agreed amiably, matching his stride to hers as he slid his long arms into his now dry shirt, which he had caught up from a nearby branch on the way. "You never know what's lurking in the bushes when you're in this kind of desolate wilderness. You never know," he added obliquely, "what a person might take it into his head to do."

"You never do," she concurred, smiling tightly as she knelt near the water and began washing out the pot. He stood watching her, his head cocked, his hands on his hips, as if he knew what she was thinking. Not hardly, she thought viciously, toying with the idea of flinging a full coffeepot of

124

water at him.

"Miss Lizzie . . . ?" His rich voice was ever so gentle, but the steely thread underlying it could not be missed.

"Yes, Galt," she answered ever so sweetly, gritting her teeth as she stood up. She wondered if it were a test, if he expected her to do something. If he was giving her enough rope to prove he still couldn't trust her. What freedom might he allow her if he thought he *could* trust her? she mused, not looking at his tall lithe body as he walked her back to their little camp. What would he do if he thought he couldn't?

She didn't care to speculate. Automatically, she reached into the wagon for the coffee tin, which was now kept near the wagon gate, and she opened it and began adding the requisite amount of coffee to the pot. Then, deftly she uncorked the water barrel and measured in the liquid by the feel and heft of the pot. She marveled at the aplomb with which she capped the barrel and popped the pot onto the fire to boil, all under his lively interested black scrutiny.

"I'm a good teacher," he said as she looked at him expectantly.

She sent him a scornful look.

"Biscuits now, by God."

"I still don't understand why I'm to make them. *I'm* the captive here."

"Now Lizzie, you've got to learn a little bit about how to care for yourself on the run. What if something happens to me? What if—unlikely thought—you managed to get away?" He regarded her with that same light in his snappy jet eyes, that amused what-might-she-say-next light, the one that blotted out the outlaw aspect that she had not seen, she thought interestedly since they had made camp, and he had . . . Oh no, she still felt like growling at him and biting him right at that very moment. *If* she should manage to get away indeed! A challenge to be met, she decided, no more no less.

"Aren't you the least bit interested?" he prodded gently.

"Not in the least," she answered testily, crossing her arms; the loose cuff smacked into her elbow. He ignored her response.

"I'll get out the flour. We also need the salt and some

powder. I think I put a little package of it in the bottom drawer of the dresser. If you don't mind, *Miss* Lizzie . . . ?" His thick eyebrows quirked and he stood staring at her, a hard determined look now that said very definitely she would do what *he* wanted and not vice versa.

She glared at him and climbed into the wagon, all under his very fascinated observation. Then he went to unlash the half-used twenty-five-pound bag of flour from the side frame, lifted it, and set it down nearby the fire as he waited for Elizabeth to climb back out of the wagon. She could do nothing demurely, he thought with exasperation as, without warning, she tossed the tin of salt and the package of baking powder at him one after the other. He caught them deftly; he was not a man to be surprised easily off-guard. As she approached him, he handed her the cast iron oven and told her to fill it with water.

She did not like taking orders either, but he had known that. The set of her shoulders was grudging, resentful; the pot was heavy, he was stronger—he could almost recite what she was thinking. Nonetheless, she went to the water keg and got the water.

When she returned she saw that he had in his hand his tin coffee cup, and he was digging into it with a spoon. "What's that?"

"Drippings. I saved them from last night. There. Now, here's what you do, Miss Lizzie—"

"What *I* do?" she echoed faintly. "*I* don't want to *do* anything. *You* want biscuits, you make your own biscuits."

His dark head lifted, and he met her green gaze head-on; the lines in his face deepened as he considered this rebellion. The outlaw look, ruthless and inflexible, hardened the amused light in his eyes in an instant. "Surely you will, woman. You're going to get mighty hungry if only *I* do the cooking. I don't tend to share with people who don't share with me."

And that, she thought ruefully, staring him down with her haughtiest look, was about as far as she might be able to push him.

"I didn't ask to come on this jaunt," she reminded him tightly.

"This is true," he agreed, his tone softening a little. "You ought to be thankful I didn't make you do all the work." His lips curved slightly as the militant look turned her eyes a trenchant jade. "But at that, I expect we would have starved to death by now. Come on, Lizzie. I have a feeling you'll be forever grateful to me for teaching you how to do this."

"Not likely," she retorted ungraciously.

"I promise *you* are the one who is going to make the biscuits. Now, I reckon we could pull and tug over this all day if that's what you want, and that's fine with me. I would have liked to have made the ten miles today, but damn to hell, if you want to fight about biscuits, Lizzie, well, you just go right ahead. Maybe when you get hungry enough, you'll see it my way."

He bent his head over the cup again and began spooning out bacon grease onto a plate, all the while aware of her ambivalence. This was a small matter, her giving in on this point, but he knew it was part of the larger issue of her powerlessness against him. She hated it, and he hated it too, if the truth were told. Elizabeth Barnett was not a woman to be broken; she was a woman to be savored, a woman of so many facets it would be a pleasure to explore. Not the least of them was her curiosity. He was counting on her curiosity to make her bend. He knew she wouldn't give in without a fight, and he watched, with increasing appreciation, as her inquisitiveness outweighed her defiance, and she approached him.

"What in God's name is that for?" She waved her hand at the melting glob of bacon drippings.

"Oh, that's for flavoring the flour, and for greasing the pot, which I can't do till you add the water to the flour, Miss Lizzie. I don't suppose you'd care to . . ."

"You're so almighty reasonable, aren't you?" she said nastily.

"I am indeed, and don't you dare toss that oven and that water all over me." His flaring eyes told her she would pay a price for *that* attempted audacity.

"Well, let me tell you, Galt Saunders, nothing can reasonably explain what I'm doing here right now with you in this devil-damned wilderness thinking about actually mixing up a batch of biscuits with a damned handcuff hanging from

127

one wrist. You explain *that* reasonably, and I'll do whatever you want." Rash promise, she thought wildly as she uttered the words. It was like a duel between them; no matter what justification he thought of, he would call it reasonable, and she would, no matter what he said, deny it was. What could possibly vindicate his actions?

He didn't even try to explain. He shrugged his shoulders and murmured, "Fate."

"Devil you! *Fate?*"

"You got in the way, Lizzie."

"You could have let me go," she argued. "You could have left me at the McCreedys' ranch; someone would have come. I would have gotten away. I promise you, I wouldn't have died there."

"You almost died of frustration when you thought I had abandoned you," he pointed out sharply. "And by that time, woman, I made up my mind you were coming with me. Let's just say I thought you might—but only might—be good company."

Her indignation almost choked her. "Good—*company?*"

He sighed. "I was damned wrong about that; you can't cook, you don't want to learn. You want me to abandon you now in the middle of the woods instead, and leave you to fend for yourself . . ."

"Which I can do *very* well, thank you," she interpolated angrily.

"Yes, I see," he appended, motioning with one large hand to the flour bag. "And for some *reason* I can't make sense of, you want to get yourself back to Greenfields. Now what in damned hell do you think is back there for you?"

His words hit her like little electrical jolts. She hadn't forgotten she had been aching to get away from Greenfields; it was just one of the many things relegated to "back there" in her mind, things she wasn't going to think about, not yet. Not while she was trying to cope with what she had thought was a life-threatening situation. She had never in her life thought her captor would be questioning her motives for wanting to return as closely as she had questioned his.

"I have a life there," she said stiffly after a while.

"So did I," he reminded her. "Maybe, Miss Lizzie, we have something in common."

"Maybe I thought you might kill me."

He shook his head. "No, you couldn't think that now."

"Then take off this pestilential handcuff."

A small sour smile wrenched his lips. "Not yet, Lizzie. I don't think I'll feel right about it until we make Kansas."

"I'm a good swimmer," she said darkly, divining his thoughts.

"I don't think you'd care to try the Missouri in the spring, Miss Lizzie."

"I know other ways," she interrupted.

"I'm damned sure you do," he agreed easily, "and that's why you stay in handcuffs, and you stay with me, and you share the work *and* that's all there is to it, woman."

He tilted his head back to look at her more closely. She stood several feet away, looking impossibly desirable even in her raggedy overlarge shirt and dust-hemmed skirt. Her tawny hair was tangled from her night's unrest, and the sun, moving inexorably overhead, glinted off its golden strands. She looked rumpled and tired, and he was sure if he could see her face, she would look totally out of patience with *him*. The thought made him smile. "Sit down, Lizzie. Let me tell you just how to do this."

"I'll agree to your *showing* me," she temporized.

"You're not going to win this one, Lizzie. I guess it *will* depend on how hungry you get."

"Or you." She had to have the last word; he irritated her beyond measure with his smugness, his surety. Over and above that, she was keenly aware of the way he was looking at her, with a knowledgeable warmth, that same enfolding warmth that she knew could be so dangerous to her. It was almost as if she *wanted* to touch off the explosive desire she was sure lay just beneath this surface.

But *why?*

She knew why. In one telling instant, she understood exactly why she felt such contradictory things about him: he was becoming too likable. She shoved the thought away. It didn't bear examining, not now. It was dangerous to like him.

129

She still had no conception of the lengths to which he might go to clear himself. No feeling at all as to what he might do with her. No, she couldn't relax her guard, she couldn't afford to like him. She couldn't afford to cross him either.

"I'm not sure I could survive the pathetic picture of you watching me down a dozen nice hot biscuits by myself, Lizzie. The guilt would unman man. So I think, because in spite of everything I *was* raised to be gentlemanly, I will *act* like a gentleman and go hungry with you."

Her hands balled into fists at her sides. Impervious rock, she thought viciously. He had an answer for everything. He was immovable. *Unlikable*, to amuse himself at *her* expense. And he *was* amused.

He turned away from her, and picking up the tin plate, he slanted her an acerbic black look and began scraping the drippings back into his cup. "Coffee's ready," he added helpfully. "You're entitled to have some of *that*. Then we'll get moving. I believe we can make ten miles today, don't you?"

He leaned forward to take another cup and reached out his hand for the pot. Without thinking, Elizabeth reacted and slapped the cup out of his hand. "*My* coffee," she said derisively.

His face changed abruptly from affability to cold hard purpose and his hand shot out quick as lightning to grasp her arm like a vise. He pulled her down next to him, close, so close to his ominous threatening outlaw face that she finally felt scared; scared and threatened. "*My* coffee," he rasped, his mouth nearly touching hers. "My stores."

"Yours," she whispered, her body quivering with fear.

He released her arm. "Good you understand that much at least. Take your coffee, Lizzie." He poured it into her cup and held it out to her.

She sank down next to him, her legs rubbery, and reached her shaking hands out for the cup he offered. The warmth of it calmed her trembling somewhat, but not her sinking feeling that she had just seen the real Galt Saunders, the one the town of Greenfields had gossiped about; the one who had had the steely nerve to break jail and take her with him.

"I'll make the damned biscuits," she said suddenly.

"Why would you ever want to do that?" Galt asked, his rich voice perceptibly softer.

She slanted a considering look at him as he sipped from his own cup. The implacable note was gone from his voice now, the unyielding harshness from his face. Why indeed, she wondered caustically, if he could scare the wits out of her with just a few hard words and that look. She had best be wary with him, she decided; she would do whatever he wanted, and she would keep trying to escape him. Tonight if possible, she would attempt to steal the key. And this morning, she would make the damned biscuits and lull him into thinking he hadn't frightened her with his outlaw face and uncompromising words.

"I'm hungry," she said finally.

"And I wonder why I don't believe that," he countered. "But for God's sake, don't look like I'm going to murder you over a pan of biscuits."

"Nonsense," she snapped, turning her verdant gaze away hastily lest he read the truth of that surmise in her eyes. He *was* capable of murder, she thought, and now she knew. There was something hard in him, arrogant and unbending. If something got in his path, he was capable of eliminating it. How easily he could eliminate her!

"I would never hurt you, Lizzie."

Her eyes shot back to his at the muted note in his voice.

"I believe you don't intend to hurt me," she said after a little pause. "Now tell me how to make those pestilential biscuits."

He shook his head and set aside his cup. "No. I'll do it."

"Don't be absurd. You are absolutely right. I should know how to do these things. Especially if I should happen to get away from you." She sent him a guileless look that didn't fool him one bit.

"Lizzie, if you rile *me* to the point where *you* feel threatened, then I want to show you it doesn't matter a damn to me whether I do them or not."

"Well, that's fine, but I'd really like to make them."

"I don't believe you, and I'll do them. I'll do them better anyway, and I *am* hungry."

"I insist that I do my share."

131

"You were right, Lizzie; you have no share since you're here by force."

"Nonetheless, I don't want you *doing* for me," she maintained resolutely, wondering why she had the feeling he was laughing at her. The expression in his eyes was perfectly neutral, and there wasn't even the faintest curve of a smile on his lips. But he didn't look at her. His long fingers absently stroked the warmth of his coffee cup as if his thoughts were elsewhere, but she sensed that all his attention was centered on her. And that unholy amusement that he contained so well.

He shrugged in answer to her declaration. "It's just as easy to *do* for two when I'm doing for one."

"But why settle for that when you can have a *woman* to do for you?" she asked with a silkily spiteful little note in her voice that she tried hard to suppress. He was so adamant she felt like swinging at him; her fear pitched headlong into pure frustration.

He turned his head slowly and leveled a long thoughtful look at her. "That's a mighty convincing argument, Miss Lizzie," he drawled at last. "I'd be delighted to have you prepare our breakfast."

She started. She hadn't expected such a quick capitulation. His slow smug smile fanned her burgeoning rage as she became more and more certain he had meant for her to do this morning's cooking all along.

"I'll just go and wash my hands," she said, hoisting herself upright so that she could look down on him. Her hands were just even with his chin as he looked up at her, and she was so tempted to swing them forward. So tempted.

"Use the drinking water," he said, just as if he didn't have any idea what she had in mind. "Think about how it would be in the wilderness alone, Lizzie, without food or water, no idea what direction you're heading, with the sun overhead endlessly, and who knows what scum marauding through the woods. Sure, you'd have a horse, and maybe a knife, but how far—really—do you think you'd get alone?"

His eyes held hers, dark, jet dark, disquieting, knowledgable. She turned away abruptly. She couldn't fight his words here, now, this morning.

132

Her mind worked furiously as she rinsed her hands. No matter what he said, she *had* to try to get away. He was a threat to her, and she recognized it, the double-edged sword of his ruthlessness and his attraction. Her fear had dissolved; her eyes riveted on his hands as she turned back to the campfire, aware fully that this was the danger, and the heart of her feelings about him. She couldn't mesh in her mind the sensuous things those hands could do to her with their ability to calmly dispatch an enemy.

She studied him for a brief moment before she began walking back to the fire. What was it about him? He sat tailor fashion before the fire, cupping his coffee in his hands. His profile was to her, blunt, strong featured, the blazing sun detailing every line in his face, every gray hair in his dark head, the grizzled two days' growth of beard on his cheeks. Something in her stirred at the sight of his strong long lean body compressed that way, and it wasn't sympathy, fear, or desire. It was some combination of all those feelings coupled with the knowledge he had given her of her own rampant desires.

But she didn't feel desire now. She felt exasperated, and it seemed to her that defined very clearly the sense of her emotion about him.

He didn't move as she came up behind him, but she knew he was aware she was there. She felt a curious excitement as she hovered a moment longer than was necessary. She wanted to touch him, and she didn't want him to see it in her eyes.

"No games, Lizzie." His voice held the slightest gentling warning. He didn't turn to look at her, but she sensed the steeliness in him, the determination once again. He was ready for her should she try anything; his body tensed, shifted slightly, and if she had not been looking at him as minutely as she was, she would have missed it.

She marveled at how finely she was coming to know the telltale movements of his body, the registers of his rich tone of voice. And she wondered why she should want to know him so well. All she wanted at that moment was to get the bedeviled biscuits out of the way.

To prove you can do it, a little voice within her amended. To keep him from getting so angry again, she contradicted it in her thoughts.

"No games," she echoed, moving slowly into his vision. "Biscuits."

He smiled ruefully. "Open the flour sack now, Lizzie, and here's what you do: a big pinch of that salt in your palm, an equal amount of the baking powder, then shake that on top of the flour."

"In the bag?"

"In. Here—scoop out the drippings over that, and then you'll measure out about three cups of water and pour it into the flour."

"In the bag," she muttered to herself as she followed his instructions.

"Truly, in the bag. Water too, really."

She sent him a sullen green look. "Then what?" she demanded, suspicious of the bland expression on his face.

He picked up the emptied iron pot and began smearing its interior with what was left of the bacon drippings. "You put your hand in the bag and work it around till the water stops taking up the flour," he answered with his head down.

"In the bag?" she repeated in disbelief. "I'm to put my *hand* in that mess and mush it around?"

"That's about it, Miss Lizzie. That's what you do."

"I *won't.*"

"But you're hungry," he reminded her gently, his firm lips twitching as he lifted his head so he could look at her indignant expression.

"Doing *that* will make me lose my appetite."

He shrugged. "I said I'd do it."

"I will. I *will,*" she ground out, and gingerly put her uncuffed hand into the burlap bag and slowly lowered it into the flour and water mixture. "Ugh—it's cold—and slimy."

"Just work it around with your fingers. It'll start to ball up very soon."

"Not soon enough for me," she grumbled. "Oh Lord, this is awful. It's sticky! You mean Verdine used to do this *every* day, two and three times a day? I can't believe this. It's still wet, Galt."

134

"Keep going. Use your other hand if you have to."

"If I use it with the damned cuff on, you'll have *beaten* biscuits—to a pulp."

"My favorite kind," he said with equanimity, enjoying her struggle as she screwed up her face and squared her chin with distasteful determination.

"It feels like my hand is in a swamp, in mud," she complained. "I can't believe this is how you habitually make biscuit dough."

"Oh no," he agreed smoothly, "not habitually; just when you're on the trail and you have limited resources." He smiled at her benignly. "It should feel drier now, and like you can't mix it anymore."

"It's damned hard."

"Lift it out then, and you'll work it a little with your hands."

"With my hands?" she echoed faintly.

"I forgot to take a breadboard," he said apologetically, hiding another smile. "The oven's ready. I'll make a fresh pot of coffee. Just—take it out—"

She pulled her arm out and lifted a thick ball of flour into the air. "There it is." She regarded the flaking pieces of dry flour with a disparaging look. "Isn't it supposed to be smoother?"

"After you knead it a little with your hands it will be."

"Knead it? I have to—knead it now? Can't I just pop it into the pan like this?"

"Nope. You have to kind of squeeze it and fold it and roll it a little, not much, just enough to finish working in the ingredients."

He smiled at the doubtful look on her face. "I promise, Lizzie. It works."

"It's stiff, I can hardly squish it."

"You *are* the complainingest woman, Lizzie. You should be thanking me. You can use your skirt if you need a surface."

"My skirt! It's all covered with flour dust anyway. I can't put this on my skirt, are you crazy? I ought to throw this right at your unsympathetic heart, Galt Saunders. You can't tell me my Verdine used to do this."

"She really did," he affirmed as he watched her fingers dig into the stiff ball of dough. "She had a table, of course, and an

135

oven in a fireplace, time to let it rise and all, but—you're doing fine. Now all you have to do is roll it lengthwise a little and then you'll pinch off the biscuits."

"Does this floury stuff come off?" she demanded as she worked the ball into a snakelike roll. "I guess," she added grudgingly as she pulled a handful of dough off the end of it, "it wasn't so hard to do after all."

"I guess," he agreed, putting the fist-sized mound of dough into the iron pot, which he had set directly on the fire.

"I guess," she continued, without looking at him, "it could be a handy thing to know."

"Could be," he conceded, tamping down again on the ever-ready smile that wanted to break out at the sight of her discomfiture warring with her curiosity and bravado. "You'll never starve as long as you've got a pinch of salt, baking powder, and five pounds of flour handy around you somewhere."

She tossed him the last circle of dough and watched him pop it into the iron oven, cover it, and set it on the coals. "I have such a feeling of accomplishment," she murmured mockingly. "I saved the morning, didn't I? My efforts are going to feed us. I learned something new."

He poked the fire under the pot and looked up at her, his black eyes inscrutable. "You did *not* save the day, Lizzie, and I'm beginning to wonder about that sassy tongue of yours. I'm not even sure I should share these."

"But *I* made them!"

"But it takes the fine hand of the cook to render them edible."

"Galt, I'm full of this godawful floury stuff, and I'm starving," Elizabeth said humbly, holding up her hands, poised to smear them all over his clean shirt.

She was sure her expression was guileless, certain he couldn't infer her intention from her submissive words. "I'm glad to know it, Lizzie. Why don't *you* start for the water first, front of me, please, and don't get any funny ideas, because I'll have the coffeepot in my hand."

*   *   *

136

It was noon before they broke their camp and the well-rested oxen lumbered their way slowly out of the clearing and back onto the track. Elizabeth sat perched at the edge of the wagon seat, a leftover biscuit in one hand, her hat in the other. She took a healthy bite of the doughy pillow and chewed contentedly as the wagon bored back into the unknown wilderness and found, within fifteen minutes, the rutted road.

God, her biscuits were good! She still had another one squirreled away in her lap to eat later, and she could not get over, an hour afterward, the sensation of biting into the first one that came out of the pot.

He had watched her, too, with a funny little smile curving his mouth, and then he had taken his own, tasted it, and nodded approvingly, and she had felt like a student who had learned her lesson properly and tested well.

Even now there were still faint traces of flour dust smeared on her skirt, and remnants of it coating her fingers, and she found herself wondering about his unexpectedness.

She shook off the warm feeling. She was still clamped to the armrest of the wagon seat; she was still just as much a prisoner. Every time she found herself bending toward him, she had to remember that. There could be no gradation of feeling here. Nothing had changed except that now she could whip up a pan of biscuits. A skill like that did not wipe away the questions, the periodic terror.

"You're thinking too hard, Lizzie." His voice broke through her restive satisfaction with herself. "Let it go, it will work out all right."

She rattled her cuffed hand against the armrest. "I don't see how," she murmured caustically. "It doesn't go away, Galt."

"But *you* might," he rapped out shortly.

The tone of his voice silenced her. The outlaw tone. The don't-make-a-false-move tone. The one that was so adamant about keeping her with him that she found it impossible to find a rejoinder that would shake his resolve. Moments like this scared her, because there was a desperation in him that became subtly obvious in his urgency. Moments like this obliterated the striking sparks of camaraderie, and made her fearsomely suspicious about his motive for pursuing this course, with her, on this fool's journey.

Maybe there was more to it than he had told her, she thought as the miles plodded by; maybe there was a whole other story that had nothing to do with murder and chasing Lonita McCreedy all over the Kansas border.

But he had been in a frenzy to escape the Greenfields jail—that she was sure had been real. And maybe, she concluded warily, nothing else about him was.

Ten

"River Flats," Galt said, reining in and pulling the oxen to a lethargic halt at the crest of a small rise above the town. Below them, in the streaked orange light of the sunset, a daunting wall of wagons lined themselves up along the ferrying dock to their left. Beyond that stretched a horizon of dark water; farther away into town, they could see more wagons curbed up against the plank walkways, and a stream of people parading down the street.

And there was only one street, lined on either side, with rows of false-fronted buildings whose business it was not difficult to guess. Elizabeth was dismayed how small the town was. No safe haven here, she thought dispiritedly.

"Damn to hell," Galt muttered, pushing his hand back on his head and propping one dusty boot up on the wagon tongue. "The whole damn world is jumping off in River Flats this week."

"You never can tell *who* might show up," Elizabeth added disagreeably.

"*We're* here," he said mildly, "and I'm kind of amazed at that." He chewed his lower lip thoughtfully as he surveyed the scene below. What he saw was not good. Too many wagons meant a premium on space and the time it would take to ferry across the river. Too much activity in town too, though, on second thought, he mused, that could have its uses. He could nose out the going freight, and what it would take to move up the line. He had a grim feeling prices escalated as the sun went down and desperation increased. He could almost predict what he might hear, and he didn't like the thought. They had only so much money to spare, and not a lot of it either.

He had to go into River Flats. The question was whether to take Elizabeth with him.

He angled a pensive look at her sitting so primly next to him, her firm mouth set in a taut line. Her chin jutted out just the slightest bit upward, her pure profile silhouetted against the darkening blue of the sky. Her tawny hair, browned by the twilight, tumbled around her shoulders invitingly, and he felt a longing to reach out and touch it. He felt even more than that, sitting next to her in the sultry early evening air above the provisioning town that would take them who knew where and to what end, and he knew he couldn't give in to the urgency in him then.

He couldn't leave her there alone—his thoughts jumped ahead almost as if he consciously wanted to avoid thinking the forbidden. Easier not to, his mind backtracked just for an instant, before turning to the question at hand. He would have to take her with him; it was unthinkable to leave her bound with the wagon. Even more untenable to uncuff her and leave her to her own devices. There were too many people in town, too many places she could sink out of sight. She would never stay put, he knew her that well. She was still fighting, quiescent though she seemed. He sensed the fretfulness in her, the nervous thrust of tension; he was attuned to every nuance of her movements and expressions, and he knew.

She would come with him, manacled as she was, and he would devise some story to account for it.

River Flats by night was not a place for a woman alone, though there were ladies by themselves promenading down the brightly lit main street with an air of going somewhere and not seeking company for the night. Their movements of acquiescence were subtle, and with practiced looks and a dart in a doorway, they disappeared into the anonymity of one of the many hotels that were interspersed with saloons, gambling halls, and trading posts along the wide main avenue.

Elizabeth eyed the whole scene with a great deal of curiosity as their horses picked their way into town and wove around the sundry street walkers and wagons, coaches, and drays that crowded through the thoroughfare. It was almost as if the town were divided into two camps—the overlanding wagons and the itinerant travelers—and the emigrants were not the ones abroad in the street this night.

There was an air of recklessness about the whole scene, a scent of money. A sultriness that hinted of forbidden things going on behind closed doors. There was none of the hard hand of commerce this night. A wildness pervaded the atmosphere and a sense that anything was possible behind the false facades whose doors opened wide and welcoming to the roaming stranger.

Elizabeth could feel eyes on her as she obediently followed Galt through the teeming crowd: *male* eyes, curious and lustful, knowing and calculating, turning away regretfully as her straight-jacketed mounted figure never swayed an inch, nor her eyes to acknowledge their interest.

She hated being the focus of attention on even such a crowded avenue as this. Those men picked her out of the milling throng, assuming she was a chattel, hoping she was for sale to any of them. A couple of them followed alongside her, calling out to her, and she felt humiliated by their presumption and her obvious bondage.

Galt could not do this to her, she thought desperately, and get away with it. She had had no choice about coming to town—she knew that when he proposed it—and it had seemed reasonable for him to find out just what they were up against in terms of money. It didn't seem reasonable at all that she was still in handcuffs, and still being forced to go with him, to be subjected to lascivious scrutiny in a little border town that was presumably known for its wide open ways.

She had never thought to be taken for one of that kind of woman, yet here she was, treading meekly after her captor, and as open to the propositions of any of the men as any lady of the evening. And Galt didn't know, and if he did know he wouldn't care—she was sure of it.

It was even possible that was to be her ultimate end with

141

him: he would sell her to get the money he needed.

And she hadn't thought of that. A frisson of pure loathing shivered through her body. Didn't he just look like a man come to town to conduct some kind of business!

But what *kind* of business only he knew for sure. She kept her eyes resolutely on his ramrod back, ignoring her admirers, thrusting away the disquieting thought of his bartering her. She could outwit him—she would. Her chance would come, except that she had been sure by now he would have dismounted. But instead he headed out toward the ferrying dock where the emigrant families had made camp like the gypsies, awaiting the dawn and still another chance to make it across the water. Beyond the curtain of wagon tarpaulin, the Missouri River swirled, as dark as night and as mysterious.

And here, on the edge of the circled wagons, Galt reined in and waited for her to join him.

"You're going to throw me in the river," she mocked tautly as she came up beside him.

"Now what would that profit me, Miss Lizzie?" he answered in the same vein, and just for an instant she froze. "Who would make the damned biscuits tomorrow morning?" He swung off his horse and motioned for her to do the same.

"Can't you get rid of these things?" she demanded, holding up her wrists awkwardly. "I feel like someone's slave, and there are people looking at me as if I were."

His dark eyes narrowed in the dim flaring lantern light surrounding them; he hadn't thought anyone would notice, but he had not considered the fact that Elizabeth was a very noticeable woman. And she was not to be trusted. For all he knew, she had just made up that notion to rile him, and he couldn't take the chance. "No, I can't," he said, abruptly turning away; he didn't want to give in to the look on her face and the plea in her voice. Her expression went still as she gazed after him resentfully, and then slowly she went after him, trying to make her hands as unobtrusive as possible to deter close scrutiny.

He stopped by the campfire of the first wagon. A woman tended the fire wearily, her body bent over an iron pot that was suspended from a tripod hanger over it. There was something

142

visibly defeated about her, as though she were pushing herself onward, but given the chance, she might collapse exactly where she was.

Galt studied her for a moment and then stepped forward. "Ma'am." His rich voice startled her, along with the tone of respect it carried.

"Stranger," she said; her voice was cracked with fatigue and despair. "What do you want?" The question begged that he did not want anything.

"Where are your men?"

"Who wants to know?" she demanded, some life coming into her voice along with suspicion that superseded any bone tiredness she had felt two minutes previously.

"My name is Galt Saunders, ma'am, newly come into town, and looking to ride the ferry across as soon as possible."

"Good luck," she said, and turned back to whatever broth she was tending.

"Tell me why," Galt insisted, pacing slowly toward the edge of the fire. "Can I help you?"

"Why should I?"

"Because I'm not such a tenderfoot as to think I'm going to make it across that river just by waiting my turn in the line," Galt said softly.

"No, you ain't," she agreed harshly. "Smart man, no, you ain't."

"What will it cost me then?" Galt challenged.

"Your hopes and dreams," she muttered with an edgy brittleness that did not nearly betray the depth of her anguish. "And your woman's."

"How long you been here?"

"Long enough and too long, stranger, and what business is it of yours?"

Galt watched her hands as she stirred her potage. They clenched the long metal spoon with suppressed anger. It clanged against the side of the pot, and he wondered just how much food was even in it. Enough for her, he guessed, and her children if she had any. Her man was gone, that was clear, but whether he was just in town, or had turned around permanently, he knew she would not tell him. Her pride would

143

never admit a defeat even if her angular body already acknowledged it.

"We're new to town," Galt said again.

"You got money?" she asked hopefully.

"Not enough, I warrant."

She shook her head. "No, you ain't got enough. No one's got enough, stranger. You might as well park your wagon back of me, and go on into town with the rest of them."

"How do you mean?" he asked carefully, motioning to Elizabeth, who stood just behind him, too horrified to speak.

"I mean that word's come across that they built the damned railroad now fifty miles and more outside of Leavenworth, and every man going west is frantic to get there and get his pass to the Golden Promise, because he don't have to overland it no more, that's what I mean. The man that's got the most money is the man who gets over first, stranger, he's the one who gets the pickings on the first locomotive out."

"How much?" Galt asked harshly.

"A hundred today. Maybe more tomorrow. Ain't none of us got that kind of money, so our men have gone out to make it. I'll let you figure out how," she added bitterly, banging her spoon against the pot and setting it aside. "That answer your questions, nosy stranger?"

"Why don't you just pick up and head for Independence?" he had to ask.

"Got the same rush going on there, we figure, until the track is laid further inland. They say they're auctioning spots on the ferrying rafts, and we didn't hear that from the ferrying captain neither. We sent one of our own to scout it out. I'm telling you, stranger, you got the money, you get across, and ain't no one been killed yet because of it. But if they keep losing, those desperate men like my husband, I couldn't guarantee anything that might happen. You satisfied you know what's what now, stranger?"

"Yes, ma'am," Galt said, trying hard to keep the trace of pity out of his voice. "How long have you been at the end of the line, ma'am?"

"You varmint," she spat. "Two months and more. Now get out of here and don't come back." She reached behind her for her spoon and waved it at him. "Damn you, go away."

Galt turned slowly and took Elizabeth's arm to lead her from the circle of the fire. "Damn to hell," he muttered under his breath. "And damn again. Hell. The last damned thing I want to do is make my stake in some gambling hell in this hellhole town."

Elizabeth wrenched her arm from his grasp. "We don't have to go to Kansas," she said pointedly. "You don't have to go anywhere."

"It makes it damned hard for me to lose myself in Dodge or wherever the hell you think I should be going with a price on my head," he agreed mockingly. "However, I have a yen to cross the Missouri River with you, my dear Miss Lizzie, so make a stake I will, with you as my good luck charm."

"Don't you sound full of yourself. What makes you so sure we won't still be here two months from now?" she asked crossly.

"With you bent and defeated over a watery stew," he amplified. "What a story you'll have to tell, Lizzie; it won't matter a hoot by then who killed whom or why. I look forward to it. Maybe I'll see to it I lose a few times before we get started. The thought of you in humbling circumstances is positively inspiring, the stuff of melodramatic romances."

"She was pitiful!" Elizabeth murmured indignantly. "How can you make fun of her situation . . ."

"Lizzie!" His voice whiplashed across her words. "That won't happen to us. To me. We're going across river tomorrow, I promise you. And if I can, I'm going to find a few dollars for her too."

"You felt sorry for her, fine. I hope you can make the few extra dollars. But you're telling me you're going to take whatever money you brought with you into one of these gambling dens and parlay it somehow into a hundred or more dollars, and *I* think you're crazy," she fumed. "And what do you plan to do with me while you're playing 'men's' games?"

"I told you, Lizzie, you're going to hang over my shoulder and tell *me* exactly what to do. Now up on your horse, woman; we've got a long night ahead."

Which of the men hanging out in front of which of the gaudy

gambling houses could be that broken woman's husband, Elizabeth wondered warily as they cantered back into town and Galt found a likely spot to hitch the horses. It seemed like the town had filled up with even more people the half hour or so they had been gone. The sight was mesmerizing, a constant stream of men in and out of each of the brightly lit doors lining either side of the street. Piano music played counterpoint to the drone of wagon wheels and horses' hooves. Laughter punctuated the heated air, and the odd gunshot. Loud voices beat a background rhythm against the ears. The clump of boot heels against the plank walkways was the only reassuringly normal sound.

A sweet-looking woman made her way toward them. There was nothing painted or obvious about her. Her dress was plain and well made, and her face was pretty in a vacuous sort of way. She cast a speaking glance at Elizabeth and turned to Galt. "New to town, are you?"

"Yes, ma'am," Galt said, his eyes gleaming with a mischievous jetty light that Elizabeth missed completely because she turned her head away from him. It wasn't possible this person was going to say what Elizabeth thought she was going to say. She looked like a *nice* woman. It wasn't reasonable at all that she had scooted across that horrible street because she wanted to accost Galt, of all people, who was only one of many men she could have approached.

And yet that was exactly what she wanted. Elizabeth clenched her teeth as she heard the woman murmur softly, "Care for some *good* company," with the insinuating accent on the word *good*.

Elizabeth's chin went up and her spine stiffened. The no-good bastard; what *would* he say to that proposition?

"I thank you kindly, ma'am." His rich voice rippled over Lizzie and that faint trace of amusement incited her fury as she realized that he was talking to *her* and not his would-be lady of the evening. "But Lizzie wouldn't hear of it, would you, woman? Lizzie has first approval of all the ladies I bed, ma'am, and she's in a temper tonight, so I don't think she'd be happy at me going off without her."

"Now—" The woman started to back away, sending him an

146

edgy, distrustful look that enlarged the whites of her eyes in pure fear.

"Now you," Galt called her back gently. "How many men *have* you gone for tonight?"

"None of your business," she said, keeping her distance. "Enough to help with my stake, if you have to know. Now you leave me alone." She skittered away in the opposite direction as she saw he made no move to detain her.

Elizabeth whirled on him. "You scared that poor thing to death."

"And you, too, I warrant," he said grimly, staring after the creature.

And me, too, Elizabeth thought, consciously admitting her fear that the woman's overture might have been attractive to him. And how the thought of what might have followed was torturous to her.

She turned to look at him but his coal hard gaze was fixed on the woman, who had already preyed upon another likely man, her hand gently touching his arm, her eyes staring into his as if he were the only man on the street. Desperate or not, Elizabeth thought, she was the kind who knew exactly how to get what she wanted.

And she, Elizabeth, knew nothing.

"This town is trouble," Galt said, biting out the words. "That woman is selling herself to make her stake. And how damned many others?"

"Just think," Elizabeth said lightly, bitterly, *"you* could sell *me."* Oh, why had she said that? She had only been thinking about it for this past hour. And that woman—and her fear . . .

He turned on her. *"I* could *strangle* you at this point, you vixen. You've got a runaway tongue, Lizzie, and one day you're going to spit out one word too much, and then you'll see where it will get you. At that, you're damned lucky I need all my wits tonight, because I'm *aching* to show you how you'll wind up if you stick me with those words again."

"It was a possibility that crossed my mind," she said stiffly, staunchly. And she wasn't about to back down from it. Anything could happen. Even though she didn't sense that desperation in him, she felt his frustration could be a greater

147

danger to her. She was not about to relax her guard with him in the midst of a nightmare where anything or anybody was for the taking.

"Well, it didn't cross mine," he returned sharply, yearning for just one minute to lay his hand on her. God, she was exasperating. And antagonistic. An opponent one moment, fascinating the next.

He steered her past a knot of curious passersby. Sell her! "Damn, Miss Lizzie, that wouldn't even be a gentlemanly thing to do."

"No," she agreed sourly. "Just practical."

And he saw it then, as he propelled her from saloon to saloon, curiosity giving way in an instant to pure lust in the eyes of strange lecherous men, who hung over bars and assessed every newcomer, male and female. It was the handcuffs, which, though she held her hands unobtrusively, were still visible. And it was her attitude, haughty, disdainful, faintly incredulous. She was a woman and she was fair game, and if he held the key, they wanted him too. He could have given her to any and all of the men ten times over and pocketed a small fortune, enough to get him to Rim City and maybe even to California.

"You see?" she murmured triumphantly at one point.

"I don't see," he growled in her ear. "And I especially don't see what I most want to see—a damned game that needs a damned fifth."

"You *sound* in such a lucky mood."

"I make my own luck, woman, and don't you forget it."

"I don't intend to forget one moment of the time I have spent with you," she assured him trenchantly.

"And I don't intend you to either," he retorted, pushing her into yet another overcrowded smoke-filled bar. Every eye in the place shot right to them and immediately centered on Elizabeth.

She faced them down, her contemptuous gaze sweeping over them, hardly seeing them, her scorn pulsating from every pore. This was what this man had brought her to: brash voices shouting unintelligible obscenities across a dim room in a rowdy saloon on the way to nowhere.

148

She was his entrée, she perceived suddenly; no one would have been interested in him if she had not been with him. He would find his game all right, because someone in that crowd would be hopeful she would be part of the ante. She felt sick. She didn't have to wonder whether that had been his intention to begin with. Of course he wouldn't think of selling her—yet.

How clever he was with words, she thought as she watched him angle back to her from across the room, and nod his head imperceptibly.

She felt the searing eyes on their backs as they exited the place, and she heard the low insinuating whispers that followed her right out the door too clearly.

Morality didn't exist in River Flats, she thought; and Galt Saunders had crossed the boundary. She was totally unprotected now. Only his lust for money and her own formidable wits stood between her and who knew what degradation.

They walked briskly down the long plank sidewalk the same direction they had come, until they reached a place where he hauled her briskly across the teeming main street to the opposite side, and a nondescript building that was occupied by a gambling parlor thronged with men hanging around its front porch, and a fair number of customers pushing into and out of its swinging doors. By comparison to the rest of the street, the activity here was low-key, almost as if the clientele were striving for some anonymity.

Nonetheless, all eyes hewed to Galt's tall figure and Elizabeth's blatantly feminine one as they mounted the plank walk and pushed toward the entrance to the hall.

He seemed to know exactly where he was going. He propelled her purposefully through the crowd of onlookers and would-be gamesters up a flight of stairs to a room at the far end of a long hallway, and knocked briskly on the door.

"You do what I say, now," he cautioned her in a whisper. "You're going to stay with me, and watch me, and if you so much as betray by a sound or a flicker of an eyelid what you see, we both will be in big trouble."

Her eyebrows lifted slightly. "Don't worry." But then, she

149

was sure she would never be permitted in the room as an onlooker, and she wondered just how Galt was going to handle that problem. He would probably handcuff her to the banister, she thought wryly, and then wondered whether that was a worse fate than whatever he had planned.

The door opened. A grizzled face appeared in the crack of space. "What's your business?"

"I hear you're looking for a fifth," Galt said easily.

"Might be."

"I got some money to spend."

"Ain't that nice." The door moved forward. "We ain't got nothing for you here, stranger."

"Lamar says you do."

"Did he now?"

"Lamar said there was *serious* playing going on up here."

"Yeah, serious. Let's see your stake."

Galt hesitated a moment, looked at Elizabeth meaningfully, and dug his hand into his shirt near his belt and withdrew a bulging buckskin pouch, which he opened up to show the man behind the door. "That's good green, mister, and I hope to make it better."

The grizzled gambler parted his thick lips in a gap-toothed grin. "So do we all, stranger." He opened the door a tad wider, and his sharp blue gaze settled on Elizabeth. "Who's she?"

"My sister."

"Go on. We don't play with women."

"She's not playing; she's in my custody and I've got to keep my eye on her every minute."

"No women."

Galt turned to look at Elizabeth, who flashed a message to him with her icy green gaze: give it up. He lowered his voice. "She's crazy. She's man-crazy. Family sent her from home; she's going to Seattle, as far away as possible so they don't hear about her escapades. All I've got to do is keep her quiet and get her to Leavenworth. She's contracted to be married to a man there who is on his way to Oregon. If I leave her by herself, she'll go hog-wild, and we'll never see her again. So she stays with me."

"I don't like women in a game."

150

"She'll behave," Galt assured him, ignoring the warning lights in Elizabeth's glittering look. "If she doesn't, I'll forfeit my stake." He stared back at her, daring her to say something, or make a wrong move.

She felt, for a split second, like a character in a novel being moved around in a strange dislocated way by the writer. For Galt to bet his stake on her conduct, after describing her in that thoroughly despicable way! And the way Blue Eyes was looking at her, he *wanted* her to do something untoward, he looked as if he might make an offer for her himself. He swung the door wide open, and motioned them in.

Damn Galt. Damn the situation. And the bastard was going to cuff her to the damned chair where he sat too. He pushed her into a seat that Blue Eyes pulled up behind him, gave her one more warning look, and seated himself around the rough-hewn table.

Three other men were seated around the table, over which hung a dusty kerosene two-bracket angle lamp. Blue Eyes pointed to each of them in turn: "That there's Moffat, Smoot, Cox, and I'm Ingalls."

"Saunders. She's Lizzie." Elizabeth punched his ribs with her free hand. "Gentlemen: let's play," Galt said, ignoring her and laying his stake on the table.

Ingalls dealt the cards, and Galt picked his up. Elizabeth peered over his shoulder. Five draw, no wild. And Galt's hand was not too terrific. She felt a hard moment of panic. Everything was on the line now, all on Galt's shoulders and capabilities.

She knew nothing about his facility with cards either, and she knew her little foray into playing with him was no measure of his skill. She skimmed a covert glance around the table. What she saw did not reassure her.

Moffat, directly to Galt's left, was a smooth one, with tanned skin and well-matched clothes, who handled his cards with a feral precision that was almost suspicious. She knew Galt saw it; she sensed his eyes raking in every movement at the table, settling next on Cox, directly across from him, in whose eyes she herself recognized a familiar fevered look that was at variance with the ready smile on his thin lips. He was well dressed and well mannered, although something guarded had lurked in his eyes as she had entered the room, and remained there still as he waited for Ingalls to define the play.

He was a man who handled his cards carelessly and his money disdainfully, and Elizabeth was sure he was an inveterate gamester, one who wouldn't know when to stop and who was wildly superstitious, which accounted for the glittery look of hostility he kept sending her. She knew the look, and she knew the signs. Her oldest brother had gone through two seasons of heavy gaming and heavy losses when he couldn't stop himself from being seduced by the lure of the gaming table. Her father had seen to it that his urges were restrained and finally repressed. He had sent him, she remembered, to college up north.

She wondered about Cox as she assessed Smoot, who seemed as sharp as Ingalls, sharper, eagle-eyed, roughly dressed as if he didn't care what he wore. Older, with a beard and those piercing eyes which were the first noticeable thing about him. His eyes spoke for him, and his eyes shot antagonistic sparks in her direction. He didn't like women, he didn't want her there. He wanted Galt's money, and preferably without her presence. He was short, this man, and grizzled, and he looked as if he had worked hard all his life. His hands were hard, callused, and ingrained with dirt. He might have been a miner, she thought, a man who had amassed some money by dint of his own sweat and who was now looking to multiply it endlessly in the easiest way possible.

They were dangerous men, she concluded, schooling her expression as play began and hell-for-leather sums slapped on the table as each man anted up. Ingalls dealt the first round, and Elizabeth trained her eyes over Galt's shoulder, where she could just see the set line of his jaw, and his not too prepossessing hand.

They were greedy men, she thought as the others made their play. Galt discarded three, and took up the three cards he was dealt. His expression was totally bland, and Elizabeth's hands grew cold as she considered the possibility that he had been steered to this game because his contact thought he was ripe for plucking, a pigeon among some very hungry cats.

152

He had to have known that and yet, as she watched him lose steadily for the first six rounds of play, she couldn't believe he knew anything. And she couldn't look at the others. The atmosphere was too clogged with the air of their collective feelings of satisfaction.

Galt couldn't help but sense it, she fretted. But not a muscle moved. His hands held his cards steadily, and his money insolently, as if the losses meant nothing, and Elizabeth watched in horror as his pile of money dwindled at an alarmingly fast pace.

It was all a farce, she thought, everyone acting as if winning or losing meant nothing to them, and all of them knowing winning meant everything to at least one of them, and a stake to better things for a stone-faced open-handed stranger, who probably was one of dozens who had hopefully occupied that same chair, and had probably walked away wounded and broke.

Not Galt. The words whipped through her mind as she began to consciously make sure her eyes did not move from Galt's cards. Not Galt.

Confidence? she asked herself. She couldn't see his eyes—how could she tell what he was thinking or what he knew? No, she couldn't see him slinking away from any challenge that required skill and outmaneuvering an opponent.

Galt knew something. She felt just the faintest shift in his lounging body that was not betrayed at all in either his face or his hands. He didn't escalate his bets; he didn't change his stance or his posture. He discarded in each successive round, and he said next to nothing in that rich expressionless voice of his, and yet, she sensed something coming. And then he won. Once.

They let him, she thought. But no—Cox would not look at him like that if it had been an agreed thing, to lull his suspicions. But Cox would not be able to bear losing anything to anyone. He leveled that same cutting look on everyone else when his hand did not pan out. There was something even more inimical in his pale eyes, and she couldn't define it, couldn't risk looking at him long enough to try to define it. Eyes down always, she reminded herself, lest anyone accuse *her* of giving away the game.

153

Galt dealt the next round silently, expertly. Elizabeth concentrated on the way he held the deck and how his long fingers flicked each card with a fine precision right in front of its intended receiver. She remembered having thought, on that long ago afternoon she had played with him, that he was a man who took his card playing seriously. Now the evidence was before her. He knew what he was doing, and even more. She felt herself relax as he picked up his cards and fanned them out tightly.

Her muscles felt cramped but she didn't dare stretch or make a move even after all this time spent hunched in one position, looking over Galt's shoulder, which, she had to admit, had its fascinations. But not at the expense of the growing ache in the small of her back and the crick in her neck.

The air in the room had thickened increasingly to the point where it was almost claustrophobic. Rank distrust permeated the atmosphere as Galt gave his full attention to what must have been close to the hundredth spread of cards he held in his hand again. Beside him, the little pile of silver had multiplied steadily over the hours he had been playing, but she was hard put to guess how much time had elapsed since she and Galt had entered the room.

And it didn't seem as if any end was in sight.

In all those hours she had no perception that Galt's attention had flagged one minute. But neither had his adversaries. As nervewracking as the play had become, she had no sense either that it had affected Galt, and it was obvious to her that the rising tension among them was meant to unsettle him.

But there was not a nuance of change in his stance. If anything, his movements took on a kind of impudence as he made several audacious bluffs and won two hands with seemingly extravagant good luck.

"That ain't luck," Smoot muttered under his breath as he threw down what he had been sure was the winning hand and Galt drew in the second of the two large pots he had won.

Galt's hand stopped in mid-motion. "Are you suggesting

something, Mr. Smoot?" he asked coolly.

"I didn't say nothin'," Smoot said hastily, his pale eyes fixed on the money. Galt resumed moving the pile of silver toward him, not unaware of the speaking looks Cox was throwing his way. Cox was angry, thwarted, disbelieving of Galt's stunning upset with a hand that was as unlikely as snow in summer.

Galt looked him directly in the eye and smiled. "Next hand, gentlemen."

Smoot reached for the deck eagerly. "You ain't gonna find another full house like that in any cards I'm dealin', mister."

"I would never expect to," Galt said smoothly, laying his hand casually over the first card he was dealt. "You had every right to think a queen over ten in house would take the pot. However, I hardly feel like apologizing because I happened to have an ace-king combination in mine." He grinned at Smoot, a cold warning, daring him to take the matter of his win one step further. "I promise not to count on your generosity this time." He picked up his cards, and at that moment, Elizabeth straightened up slightly to ease the throb in her lower back.

It was almost palpable, the way all four men's eyes shot right to her, full of suspicion and blame. She scanned their faces in a split second and lowered her eyes in almost the same motion. The force of their resentment was aimed wholly at her, and for the first time that whole night, she felt scared, for herself and for Galt.

She closed her eyes in despair. Galt was good, so very good, but he couldn't possibly turn the trick against a clutch of men who had expected to relieve him of every last dollar he had come in the room with.

They were watching him very carefully—and her, as if they thought that every shift of her body or movement of her eyes were a signal to him somehow, and she couldn't figure out how. She could see nothing but the line of Galt's profile, and the glaringly bad cards he now held in his hand, as Smoot had promised. She could just see the corner of Galt's mouth stretch into a sardonic little grimace as he arranged and rearranged the five cards, and discarded two of them. She wanted to see Smoot's face as he dealt Galt the succeeding two cards in the deck, but she didn't dare raise her eyes.

155

Galt slid the two cards over in front of him, but did not pick them up. Instead, he folded his three other cards on top of them and slouched back unconcernedly in his chair.

Elizabeth took heed; something was going to happen. Galt was acting a little too casual, throwing dollars on the table as if he had fielded a flush instead of the measly deuces that comprised his hand before he discarded. She pinched him in exasperation, and he didn't move a muscle, didn't pick up his cards.

The only sound was the clink of silver being tossed into the pot. Tension mounted as each man eyed the closed cards in front of Galt suspiciously.

Finally, after several long tight moments, Galt picked up the cards and spread them out slowly, deliberately cupping his hand over them. Elizabeth cringed. He held four deuces and a five of diamonds. The taut silence roared in her ears. The enmity surrounding them was palpable. She felt the successive sharp glances of his opponents as if they were piercing darts lancing against her skin, and again she didn't dare look back.

This was the moment. Galt would either lose everything or walk away with the pot—and a bullet in his back.

"Gentlemen," he said easily, and with no trace of trepidation in his voice or in his hand, which held his cards with just the right nonchalance.

He had to be mad, Elizabeth thought, her cold hands clenching the spindled back of the chair. Mad, or reckless—or both.

"You got nothin'," Smoot growled, tossing another handful of coins into the pile.

"I got nothin'," Ingalls said, a note of menace coloring the outward geniality of his words. He folded his cards and slapped them down in front of him and slowly looked around the table.

Elizabeth sensed the full weight of his gaze come to rest on her bent head. Dear Lord, she thought, there was something else operating here, a thread underneath the atmosphere of danger and money, a cohesiveness somehow among their adversaries that even as she got the impression was belied by the rising antagonism directed at Galt's too casual attitude.

"I want to see them," Moffat demanded, his voice even and

unrevealing as he added to the pot.

Then Cox. An attenuated pause fraught with something like desperation assaulted Elizabeth's senses. She knew instantly when his hot eyes slewed her way; his voice was tight as he said, "I'm in," and threw his money at Galt. "I call."

Only then did Elizabeth lift her head, her eyes jolting immediately against Cox's rabid eyes. She shivered. This man was more than an enemy; there was something unnatural in the fervor with which he looked from her to Galt, waiting with some kind of heightened emotion to see what Galt's cards would reveal. This was a man, she thought uneasily, that believed in omens and portents and was superstitious as hell, judging from his avidly negative response to her presence.

And Galt had a spread of deuces.

He was crazy.

They were all crazy. They had thought Galt was someone they could play with, their prey, carrion to be picked over. And yet—four deuces . . .

"Show 'em, stranger," Ingalls said in that same pleasant menace-tinged voice.

"Read 'em," Galt said, matching his tone. Very deliberately he spread the five cards down in front of him—two, two, two, two, five. He looked up and smiled benignly, ignoring the electric shock that coursed from man to man around the table.

Moffat shrugged and threw down his cards. Cox, drained white, laid his cards down carefully, precisely. Smoot cursed and threw his on the floor.

"I thank you, gentlemen," Galt said, leaning forward to draw in the mound of coins and bills. His jetty gaze never left them as he stood up and added, "We will call it a night." He had the key to Elizabeth's cuff in his hand, and he bent to unlock it. Cox's voice made him bolt upright as her hand came free.

"We will *not*." He brandished a small pistol in Galt's direction and Elizabeth froze.

"Surely you're not going to accuse me of palming a pair of deuces," Galt said calmly.

"We play another hand," Cox said, letting the flickering overhead light glint off the gun barrel.

157

Galt shook his head. "I made my stake fair and square, gentlemen, and I'm leaving."

Cox waved the pistol at his cohorts. "It was the woman, it was the woman. I demand the right to recoup. You hear? Gentleman me all you want, stranger, but you'll honor my right to recover my losses—and without your accomplice whore in the room."

Galt's eyes narrowed. Smoot and Moffat could be pushed to Cox's side very easily, he perceived, as Smoot grumbled his agreement.

He turned to Ingalls. "You watched my sister; she didn't move."

Ingalls returned his look blandly. "I couldn't swear to it."

"Son of a bitch."

"Sit down, stranger. One more hand, win or lose, and you can go."

"The hell—" Galt broke off as he stared down the barrel of Ingalls's revolver. He sat.

"The girl goes," Cox said.

Ingalls fixed his pale blue gaze on her. "The girl goes; I'll fix 'er up outside, stranger; she won't be going nowhere, and no one'll interfere with her—or you."

Elizabeth didn't move a muscle; she was stone. If they thought she was inanimate, they would overlook her and not do what Ingalls said. But he stepped forward, took her arm, and forced her to her feet. His imperious grasp propelled her forward, out of the door and into the hallway. Her eyes widened as he led her to a bracket gas lamp that hung low on the wall, and took her cuffed hand and fastened her to the bracket.

And then, to her horror, he turned and walked away, leaving her in the dimly lit dank-smelling hallway, attached to the wall, with only her imagination and fear between her and the door he slammed shut against her avid eyes.

Eleven

Her arm ached. She lifted her elbow tentatively, amazed that she had the wherewithal to do even that much. Her arm felt numb, the time stretched to a point where she had no sense of it at all, only the unremitting pull on the enforced awkward position of her left arm.

There was noise: the hallway echoed with it, its narrow confines magnifying the sound of the piano, the hollow laughter, the voices down below somewhere, and perhaps, somewhere else along this corridor. But no sound at all issued from behind the doorway across the hall.

Deadly men, she thought in horror; Galt could be dead for all she knew. Cox had been so strung up, he would have been perfectly capable of killing once they were alone. Cox . . . his eyes. Deadly. Her thoughts didn't help. She couldn't conceive of any reason Galt would have thought he could leave a game like that alive and with money in his pocket.

But he had thought it. And not without reason. If it hadn't been for her presence. She felt muddled. She would not have wanted to stay at the wagon alone, nor would she have thought he would let her. If only he had decided that River Flats was *her* final destination, he could have gotten his stake and been away across the river by now.

None of it made sense, least of all her hanging by a handcuff in a sleazy gambling house hallway, waiting to see if the man who had abducted her would survive a crooked poker game.

She was losing her sense of humor. She couldn't figure Galt

out, and she didn't want to think of anything extraneous concerning him and her reactions to him. He *had* to rethink this enforced captivity if he walked out of that room alive and solvent. Or just alive for that matter.

He'd get across the river, she was sure of it. The man was too inventive not to find a way, barring he could win the money. He would get away altogether. It was inconceivable at this point that Edgar Healey was searching the river towns to find a petty murderer. His reasoning was at fault. He had only to go over, and he would be free.

She wondered acrimoniously how his vaunted honor would uphold him in that stuffy room filled with potential killers. And what, her thoughts asked her, would they do with *her* afterward?

Never! Her green gaze sliced upward to the bracket lamp that burned steadily with dim energy inside an etched glass shade. She could remove the shade. She could cause trouble, she thought speculatively. She might be burned badly, but they wouldn't want her then. And that might be just as well.

She touched the shade. It was burning hot from hours of absorbing the heat of the gaslight.

Damn him! If only he had left her at the McCreedys'! Edgar would have gone there eventually, she thought. He would have been bound to search everywhere for Galt, and not just assume he had hightailed it out as far and fast as he could.

She might have worked herself free. Or not.

Her head whirled with the force of all the "if only's" crowding around in her brain. Galt was in that room at risk of his life and hers to win a stake to cross a river to find a woman who might or might not know who had killed her husband and why, and who might or might not be where he thought she was going.

This is insane. The words formed on her lips and in her mind. There was something else. He was rabid to follow Lonita, so sure, so dedicated. He was betting everything at this very instant on the turn of a card so he could clear his name, and he had her with him at great cost to his freedom and mobility, and he claimed it made sense.

It made no sense.

She listened hard to try to distinguish anything among the loud sounds filtering up into the hallway. If he walked out of that room, he would have lifelong enemies dogging him. She was as sure of that as anything she had ever known. She had seen those kinds of faces, traipsing through the woods behind her home in the war. Nakedly violent, desperate, taking everything, righteous in their invasion, the many against the one.

She had had strength then; only at the end had she given way, and that had been to Martin Healey's importuning. The jolting rejection afterward had been a relief, she knew that now, and she had survived all of it.

And for what?

So some arrogant overseer's son of a cowboy could spirit her away on some stupid fool's chase and leave her trussed up in a fetid hallway and growing more hysterically impotent by the minute.

What could he be doing to save himself in there? What if he held the high cards, and they took their revenge rather than letting him leave?

She beat the wall behind her in terror and frustration. How *could* he win, with a prospective wild-eyed murderer sitting across from him trigger happy and edgy as a bobcat? Lord, lord, and devil damn; if he got away with it . . . if!

And if he got away with it, he *would* go on alone, she swore. She didn't care about his story, or whatever he was hiding— what he *had* to be hiding. She would get away from him—or them, as the case might well be. But if they hurt him—

If they left her there—

If they took her with them . . .

Time stopped, and she made her mind a blank. She had to conserve her energy instead of wasting it on useless speculation. The end of her waiting would come when it would come. All she had to do was prepare to be ready.

And in the end, the door opened, and Galt walked out of the room alone, his hat held carelessly in his hand, without looking back. Beyond him, she saw Ingalls at the door, and behind him

161

Cox, straining to follow Galt and being restrained by Moffat. Moffat the pragmatist, she thought. Moffat knew how to win and Moffat would know how to lose.

And Galt? Her jade gaze slid to his impassive face.

"Don't move," he cautioned her in the merest whisper, his lips barely moving.

She froze, her eyes fixed on his face to take her cue from him and what he would want her to do. He motioned her to crook her free arm, and very carefully he set his hat into it. She didn't dare look downward. Its weight was enough to tell her Galt had retained his stake—and maybe even won more.

As he grasped her left arm to free it from the wall bracket, something inside her heaved and let go, and the tightness seemed to shift downward in her. It wasn't relief; the thing wasn't over yet. It was just that—he was all right.

Yes, he was all right, she defined it to herself as she relinquished his hat and followed him very carefully down the hallway. And he had come for her, and now she could put an end to this craziness.

Down the stairs they went just as warily, Elizabeth preceding him now and aware of his reassuring presence behind her, which, without warning, leaped forward and pushed her violently against the landing stairwall as a shot rang out above them and Cox's overwrought voice shouted after them, "You won't get away with it, Saunders. I'll be after you for this. I'm coming to get you. You watch out behind you, man, I'll be there to get my money back, you hear? You hear?" Another shot heaved into the air, high over them, crashing into the ceiling, then Ingalls's rough voice, and the sound of fists hitting flesh, hardly audible over the inexhaustible piano that just kept right on playing.

"Oh my God," Elizabeth breathed, her mouth against the flaking paint of the cold wall. Galt's body still pressed against hers, blanketing her in full protection, inch by inch aligned with hers in a way that slowly imprinted itself on her consciousness as she became aware of him and not the danger.

No. She didn't say it, but her whole body rejected the radiant heat of his pressuring hers, constraining her from making a move to rebuff him.

She wriggled her shoulders and he stepped back, and the heat dissipated in the smoky air.

"Quickly now," Galt whispered, guiding her forward again. And quickly they ran down the remaining stairs into the saloon to become two of a hundred late-night faces populating the bar, male and female both, lounging and circulating, playing the desultory game of poker or monte if they were really feeling reckless with their money. The door, only a dozen feet away, took them endless moments to reach through this motley crowd, and then they burst through the swinging doors and out into the clear early-morning air.

The street was teeming with idling and itinerant vagrants looking for a game, a handout, a job; a tenderfoot to fleece; a bed for the night.

"Damn to hell," Galt muttered, "damn town never sleeps."

An elegant carriage rolled by, filled with satin- and paint-bedecked young girls who had no qualms about calling out to the men.

Elizabeth stared after them. That could be her fate too, she thought. Anything could happen between this moment and the dawn. She almost had the sense even Galt didn't know what he wanted to do next.

Nonetheless, he grasped his hat and her arm, turned in the opposite direction from the gambling hall, and led her firmly through the loiterers, into the street to mill with the walking throng that seemingly paced from one end of the avenue to the other looking for excitement.

"Galt—"

"Not now, Lizzie. That damned reb can still draw a bead on us from that second-floor window. *Don't* look back." Instead, he increased their pace as they threaded their way through the crowd and dodged behind one or two hacks before backtracking across the street and in the direction he had tethered their mounts.

"You're crazy," she panted, running to keep up with him.

"I think I am," he grimaced, grabbing her hand so she wouldn't lag behind him. "We got our stake, and we're going over tomorrow, Lizzie. I told you."

"Devil it, you told me . . . Damn it, Galt . . ."

163

"We can't talk now, Lizzie. Keep going."

"Somebody probably stole the damned horses and sold them," she grumbled.

"They're nags, not even worthy of the term *horseflesh*," he contradicted, turning his head slightly to get a fix on where they were in relation to where they had been. He stopped walking, and she crashed into him.

"We're okay, Lizzie."

"*We* are not okay," she said crossly. "*Where* are the damned horses? And what do you *think* you're going to do next?"

He smiled, that crinkly right-to-his-eyes crooked little smile, and he shrugged. "You know, Miss Lizzie, I don't have the foggiest idea."

He fed her. That, she thought, was the least he could do. There was always someone overlanding, he told her, who would be willing to sell a bowl of soup and some bread, as good as any restaurant or hotel. And he wanted to find that lonely desperate woman whom they had first encountered in the camp.

It wasn't easy to find their mounts and then, under cover of the noise and chaos of the street movement, transfer his winnings to a saddlebag. From there, they made their way back to the wagon camp, bought themselves a bowl of steaming soup, made from vegetables culled, said their hostess *pro tem*, from the best gardens along the way down from Independence, where they had no hope of financing the crossing fee. Her husband, she told them, was a creditable cardplayer and an even better scavenger, owing to the exigencies of war, and she herself could make do with straw and still make a meal of it.

"I know what you mean," Galt agreed. "I'm mean in the fields myself. We had to learn to make do every bit as much as you, ma'am, and sometimes with less. It's a tasty soup, worth every cent you asked."

Her face softened toward him in the crackling firelight. "You're welcome to another helping."

"I thank you, ma'am; I *would* like more." He turned to Elizabeth, who was looking at him with a jaundiced eye over

164

her bowl.

"But not your lady?" the woman questioned sagely.

"She isn't hardly used to trail cookery, ma'am."

"I'll have more," Elizabeth interpolated coolly, throwing Galt a venomous look. She held out her bowl. It was hot after all, and chunky with vegetables, salted, and boiled to a fare-thee-well. She couldn't help it if she preferred something a little more full-bodied, or that the stock tasted watery. The bread helped, and she wasn't sure, were she the cook, that anything she concocted would have tasted much better.

She smiled at their hostess. "It's hot and nourishing and that's what counts."

The woman smiled back, and doled out another ladleful, noticing for the first time as she did so Elizabeth's cuffed wrist. Her warmth turned uncertain as she slowly gave the bowl back to Elizabeth. "You—um—in trouble or anything?"

Galt followed her eyes. "No, ma'am. We had a run-in with a gang of card sharps. They—ah—"

"Didn't like women sitting in on their game," Elizabeth finished smoothly, sending him a smug glance. "Women are *real* trouble hereabouts, apparently—"

"Truly," Galt muttered under his breath as she continued, "And Galt only just managed to—" Whereupon he broke in, ". . . intend to finish the job back at our camp."

"They shot at us and everything," Elizabeth added with relish, seeing the woman devouring this quasi-true tale avidly.

"But didja win?" the woman demanded.

"I bought your victuals, didn't I?" Galt said, lifting his spoon again, not even looking at Elizabeth as he uttered this blatant distortion.

"Where's camp?" the woman asked offhandedly, turning away to stir the kettle.

"Up aways above town," Galt answered, setting aside his bowl. "We only arrived here earlier on. I wish someone had warned us."

"So did we all," the woman commented darkly. "That be it for tonight, stranger? You gonna try to make it back to your camp?"

"We're going to try."

165

"Anything else I can help you with?"

Galt shook his head.

"And how you gonna see where you're going?"

Galt grinned. "How *am* I, ma'am?"

"I'm gonna sell you a lantern, stranger, and some matches, and you'll make it back right and tight." She rummaged around the base of the wagon and came up with a smoke-clouded chimney and a bail-handled holder with a spring to clip the chimney to the base. "This'll do it." She held it up.

Galt restrained a smile. "And how much is *that* going to cost me?" he asked, his lips twitching.

"I ain't a robber, stranger," she said defensively. "And you do be needing something on that steep trail." She paused, gauging how far she could push him. "Five dollars, with candle and matches."

Galt nodded, and counted out the money.

"So we're all square now, stranger."

"That we are, ma'am, and I thank you for your hospitality and concern. Now we'd best be making our way back." He held out his hand to Elizabeth. She grasped it, and he pulled her up. "'Evening, ma'am."

"I'll be seeing you, stranger," the woman called after them cheerily.

"I'd bet on it," Galt commented in an undertone as he led Elizabeth to their horses.

"And why didn't you ask her about that other lady?" Elizabeth asked curiously.

"She wouldn't have told me. Everyone's out for their own survival here, Lizzie, couldn't you see that? She's tickled to have gotten such easy money tonight. She wouldn't have told us if she knew the other one; she would have wanted to keep everything for herself. And so would our friend from yesterday." He lifted Elizabeth onto her mount. "We'll find her—tomorrow most likely when we make for the ferry. We're going over, Lizzie, just like I said."

The night folded around them like a shroud once they were clear of the town. Elizabeth felt all at once like talking and not

166

talking. The events of the past hours were like some nightmare, and she knew the dream wasn't over yet.

She felt fear—fear of the vastness of the night, of the sense of her smallness and loneliness in it; fear of what was to come; fear of her secret knowledge of what he aroused in her, and fear of going it alone without him if she should be able to get away from him.

But the night's events had proven to her just how necessary that was. Whatever might happen to her, she knew it was a man's world on the ragtag frontier; they had no use for women except for one thing, and she reckoned, as she followed Galt edgily up the steep trails outside of town, she could do laundry as well as anyone.

"What would you wager someone's made off with the wagon?" she called out testily as she tried to see his bulk ahead of her in the darkness. "And why don't you use the damned lantern she sold you? I feel like my horse is going to tumble head forward at any minute."

"There isn't much of a candle here, Lizzie." His voice sounded closer to her as if he had stopped and was waiting. She felt his hand take her horse's reins, still all in the blackness, and somehow she felt reassured. She didn't like feeling reassured.

"No one deals fair in this devil-town," she grumbled, sensing him next to her. "I don't know how you made it out of that room alive."

"Honor among thieves, Lizzie. Knowing when a man's looking and when he isn't. Knowing when to lose and when to pull in the pot. I spent a lifetime of days playing poker with desperate men, Lizzie, and I know most of the tricks. Cox and Smoot are crazy, but they have a skewed kind of honor."

"I know it; it involves using a gun when you don't like the outcome."

"Then that's how it is," he consoled her gently. "We're well away, and one step closer to Kansas."

"*You* are," she contradicted, her voice expressionless.

He noted the flatness in her voice. "I *knew* I saw that look in your eye when I walked out the door, and I mistakenly thought you were glad to see me."

"Oh—that too," she conceded sardonically.

"I'm so glad."

His rich voice was so gentle she wished she could see his eyes. She felt a little pang as she went on resolutely, "You don't need *me* to slow you down now, Galt."

"Surely, Lizzie—"

"And what happens at the next crossing, or when you need to refinance yourself again? You do realize you could have swum across the river at any point if you hadn't had the wagon or me."

"Oh yes," he agreed, a mocking note in his voice now. "But that's my concern, isn't it?"

She stiffened in frustration. "Of course; nothing to do with *me* or how you're dragging me all over Missouri, *and* a good part of Kansas I'll wager, in handcuffs. Absolutely no reason for *me* to have an opinion about the whole thing."

"Just as I keep telling you," Galt agreed mildly.

"Galt—" Her tone threatened mayhem she couldn't possibly carry out.

"Rest easy, Lizzie. I'm not going to leave you here."

"I *want* you to leave me here!"

"Nonsense; the night's events have worn on your nerves. You're losing your sense of humor, Lizzie."

"I never thought this was funny."

"Nor I," he said gravely. "I want you with me."

She had no answer for that. She drew in a deep breath and tightened her body to prevent herself from saying anything further. She never would convince him except by taking action. And she was willing to do anything to get away now. Once she made it back to the town, she was sure she could find some turnarounder willing to take her back to Greenfields.

But what for? her waspish little inner voice asked, echoing the question Galt had asked, and another of the things she did not want to examine too closely.

To get away from *him,* her tormented sane self retorted.

To what?

Normalcy.

There hadn't been normalcy in Greenfields. There had been routine. There had been a modicum of security. There had

168

been no excitement, no looking forward from day to day to what *might* happen. She had known what would happen very well because every day was the same.

Except one day, when Galt took her captive and almost punctured her throat and scared Edgar out of his wits by threatening to scar her forever.

A flash of light startled her. Galt, striking the match, lit the candle, and the glow dimmed down as he doused the fire and the wick caught.

The thin eerie light exposed shadows and turned rocks and bushes into threatening monsters ready to leap on them. Nothing looked familiar to her, and yet Galt proceeded with a surefooted certainty before her now, threading his way among the rocks and trees, holding his lantern high so that tenuous fingers of light guided her way.

No doubt he had trailed his way through many darknesses during the war, she thought. Men did have the best of it; they knew how to survive by wit and by action, and women had to make do with the best they had at hand: themselves. But she never could have survived this black wilderness without him, she thought, and she couldn't understand how he knew—or thought he knew—exactly where he was going.

But he did. Slowly, dark looming shapes in the distance turned distinct—the wagon, the oxen, the sheltered clearing where they had been secluded.

She had never felt more relief; even the thought of their makeshift bed was welcome, including sharing it with *him*.

She was tired, and she felt desperate. Her heightened emotions scared her, to the point she feared that, when he lit the lantern hanging by the wagon, her anxiety would be reflected plainly on her face. If only she could lie down—if only she could think. . . .

"Lizzie?"

She started as she realized he was speaking to her, and she hooked her leg over the pommel of her saddle and slid off her horse. She watched him deftly uncinch and remove the saddle in the flickering light of the kerosene lamp, then rub down both horses briefly and water them before motioning to her to climb into the wagon.

He was right behind her, lamp in hand, and he hung it onto its accustomed hook just near the wagon gate, and reached for her hand just as she was about to sink onto the mattress.

"Oh Galt—no!"

"Oh Galt—yes," he mimicked, taking her unresistant hand and snapping the empty cuff around his own wrist. "It's too dangerous, Lizzie. I see it in your eyes."

"I see. You know card tricks and you can read minds. We're a traveling medicine show."

He started to say something, and stopped. His good intentions meant nothing to her now. She was dead tired, wary and feisty all at once, and perhaps a little scared. Yes, scared; Cox had frightened her beyond description, and not with his wild gun either.

But they were well rid of him now, they had money, and barring bad weather, in the morning they would cross over to Kansas, and then, he thought, settling down next to her rigid body, maybe, just maybe, he might feel secure enough with her to finally put aside the handcuffs.

She awoke with a start minutes before dawn. She didn't know what it was that made her open her eyes so suddenly. She had fallen asleep with that same suddenness, bone weary and totally unable to cope for another minute with her fantastic situation.

Galt slept soundly next to her, his body slanted just that little bit toward her which she could feel by the weight and heat of his body. Everything was dark, silent except for the occasional insect or the low whickering of one of the horses.

She lay perfectly still, listening to the sounds and to his deep breathing. She was afraid to move, afraid she might awaken him with the merest shift of her body.

She didn't want to wake him; she needed to think. The scene seemed intensely familiar, and it took her long moments to realize why: she was in exactly the same position as the previous night when she had fantasized about stealing the key to her cuffs. Yes—she went over it in her mind briefly. His body was angled beside her just right; his breathing was so deep and heavy, and she knew, in her mind, just what she had to do.

She moved, just the flicker of a wriggle, and waited, her feelings divided as she made her plans, astonished by her initial sensation—she didn't want to leave him—which was followed by the resolution of purposeful determination fueled by the sense of opportunity.

There was no other choice: she could not go on the way she was, and she surely could not ferry the river with him without knowing the truth. And even if he had told her, she thought, as she began to lift her upper torso inch by inch slowly, languidly as she might have done were she asleep, she would still have had no recourse but to try to escape him. Whatever his truths, or his mission, whatever he was seeking or why, he was still better off without her, and she—without a doubt—would get along perfectly fine without him.

She shifted her cuffed arm the barest bit to lever the weight of her body against her elbow. And she waited.

He stirred slightly and she caught her breath. But no: he realigned his legs and buried his head more firmly into the bedding.

She waited, and she thought about exactly what she would do. She would get away from him, and she would take water, and one of the horses. Maybe some of the money—why not? She could secrete herself in the underbrush nearby, and since he would not discover her defection until daylight, she thought she might be capable of eluding him, since she would know whichever way he tried to search for her.

Assuming he would search for her. Maybe he wouldn't.

She waited.

She hoped he wouldn't. Or did she? No, no—that, as everything else, made no sense either. She shoved the thought away and began, by small degrees, twisting her body toward his, uncomfortably aware of the heat emanating from him even as he slept. So damned unfair all that burning warmth exuding from one lone man, like forbidden fire, inviting the touch, seducing her into its wanton heat.

Her hand moved, as if to brush away her wayward thoughts; she could not let herself be upended and deterred by fanciful delusions and virginal yearnings.

171

I know too much and have experienced too little, she thought, reaching out her hand with grim purpose now toward the long lean line of his flank. Damn it, and where was his bottom and that deviled damned back pocket?

Her hand descended and touched his body lightly, hesitantly, and she waited to see if he was aware of the presence of her fingers resting delicately across the span of his lean hip.

Nothing; his breathing remained deep and even, his body stretched in minuscule increments periodically, and shifted now and again with whatever dark vision pervaded his dreams.

She skimmed her fingers across the rough denim stretched across his hip toward his buttocks, the pads of her fingers seeking the seam of the back pocket with attenuated little movements, and—ah—here, the edge of the pocket opening. And she paused. *Did* she dare? *Really* dare?

Her hand slipped, of its own volition, under the pocket rim, her fingers subtly probing for the short thin tube of the key that she would extract with breathtaking finesse and . . . God, all she could think about was how firm and rounded this portion of his body felt, even beneath his well-worn denims. And horror on top of that—the key was not there.

Her heart pounded wildly as she inched her hand back up out of his pocket. Devil damn him: he had seen it in her eyes—he had even said so. And he had moved the key because of it. Damn, damn, damn . . . but where?

She paused a long moment to get her agitation under control, and to ascertain that he still slept. Her hand rested once again on his hip as if it were a compass point to the rest of his body. And it was. *Where* would he have put the damned key, where?

She listened intently to the sound of his breathing; she couldn't even tell, in her trepidation, whether anything had changed. There was a quality of anxiety in the air around her now, hers, that she might fail and he might find her out.

She took a deep breath. He hadn't had time to secrete the damned thing anywhere else but on himself. Another pocket—gingerly she leaned forward, taking care not to jar the arm that was attached to his, and skimmed her fingers over the outside of his left back pocket, a feat that required an ingenious twisting of her body so as not to touch him or realign her own body next to his. She felt like killing him when her explorations made it obvious the key was not there either.

Games, she thought suddenly. All games. He thought he was so smart, he knew her so well. He thought she might try tonight while they were still camping on the Missouri side of the river. Or maybe he had thought she might try tomorrow, when they had crossed to Kansas and she could get away to Rim City by herself, where she *would* be sure to find employment and the real possibility of return.

He was a fox, she thought as she waited that long extended moment until she was sure her movements had not aroused him. Wily. Sure of his prey. Yes. She had only to outfox him.

Her hand snaked under his right arm to his chest on the off chance he wore the key around his neck, and brushed upward toward his neck. She felt nothing beneath her fingers but the solid pulsating wall of his chest, and then suddenly bare skin that jolted her whole body as if she had been burned.

Ridiculous. There was nothing about a bare hairy male chest—this bare hairy male chest—that should make her jump a foot in the air just because she had inadvertently touched him.

Still, she hesitated a moment before she moved her hand again. He was an extraordinarily strong sleeper, she thought edgily, or she had an inordinately delicate touch. She couldn't credit either theory, actually, as she traced the line of his body downward now, trying to sense where the front pocket was as her next recourse.

Her questing fingers lit on his hip once again and she slid them toward her, across the taut stretch of material that defined his hipbone, to the line of his front pocket opening.

This time she didn't hesitate. The minutes were ticking by with exaggerated speed in her mind, and some inner clock prompted her to hurry. Or fear. It was not that far from dawn.

She plunged her fingers into the narrow gap of the pocket opening. Nothing. And still nothing as her hand inched still deeper, and she mentally consigned him to the devil for understanding her too well.

And then her hand froze.

173

She had come in contact with something all right, something hard and long—tubular, she thought on a rising feeling of panic, not daring to even flex one finger.

And yet—there was no sign that he was awake. Only that one tangible part of him moved almost as if it had a life of its own, and nudged her rigid fingers.

She caught her breath. Images flitted through her mind. Feelings. The sense of him, and his overpowering maleness. The things she kept pushing out of her mind, burying, refusing to examine—recognize.

His manhood pushed at her fingers again.

The key, she thought, paralyzed. He had to be awake. He *had* to. If she moved her hand now, she would have to touch him. And if she touched him . . .

No key. The bastard; he had known exactly what she would try to do. She hated him. She hated the whole thing. It had been a trap. But for what? For what?

The portentous stillness almost sent her into a fit of screaming. The sense of his throbbing manhood an inch from her fingers unnerved her totally. She itched to move her hand, and she didn't dare.

She remained rigid beside him, holding her body tensely, still braced against her elbow, aching all up and down that arm, her wrist twisted awkwardly in his front pocket.

She couldn't conceive of just how she had managed to put herself in a posture where if she moved her fingers one way, it would be tantamount to an open caress; and the other, she would surely awaken him and put herself in an even more precarious position.

Obviously, the best thing to do was *keep still* and wait until his lusty organ had calmed down. . . .

Not so obvious. She could have sworn *she* hadn't moved a muscle—but his rampant manhood seemed to have elongated to a point where it just grazed her fingers, almost as if it were reaching for her.

She caught her lower lip between her teeth in vexation and terror. She had no idea what to do; she only knew she didn't want to be caught with her hand in Galt Saunders's pocket, looking for all the world as if she were seeking the one thing she wanted to avoid. And she didn't know if she could hold her body angled that tautly long enough to extract her hand gracefully—and without his knowledge. . . .

Not possible.

"I think," he spoke into the darkness finally, his rich voice gentle and just the faintest bit amused, "you have found what you're looking for."

She swallowed hard, letting a heavy beat of silence go by before summoning up the nerve and wit to answer tartly, "An empty pocket? Not hardly." She wrenched her hand away from him and let her body fall backward in grim relief. No key, and a price to pay, she thought, ignoring the pounding pain in her right arm.

She knew, she could feel, that he had propped himself up on his elbows next to her, too close to her, and he was pleased as a polecat that he had foiled her. "And where *is* the devil-damned key?" she demanded imperiously, as if she had a right to know.

"In the *safest* place, Miss Lizzie," he answered, a smug note in his voice now, which made her want to pinch him. "Which I'd be pleased to show you, since you've evinced so much interest," he added, and it was impossible to mistake his meaning or the humorous note just under the tone of his words.

"I beg to differ with you," she rejoined acerbically. "*It* showed a great deal of interest in *me.*"

"What did you expect when you go rooting around in a man's pockets?" he asked reasonably.

"I expected to find the damned key," she answered huffily.

"I, on the other hand, expected some loyalty from you in repayment for everything I've done for you."

What?" she sputtered, jerking upright at the sheer brazenness of his words. "What *you've* done for *me? Done* for me?" She choked on her indignation. "Tell me *one* thing you've *done* for me!"

"Now now, Miss Lizzie, you know darned well you're grateful I got you out of that damned-to-hell town . . ."

"At the point of a gun . . ."

"To a life of travel and adventure . . ."

"In handcuffs . . ."

175

". . . teaching you how to survive along the way . . ."

". . . in handcuffs . . ."

". . . cook . . ."

". . . in handcuffs . . ."

". . . those biscuits . . ."

"In handcuffs . . ." she ended grittily, absolutely certain that he could feel the steam spuming out of her ears by this time, and still he continued into the darkness: ". . . risked my own life to make us a stake . . ."

"With me handcuffed outside the door, damn you!"

"And you show me damned little gratitude for what *I've* done; all you want to do is steal the keys and run away somewhere."

"Your mind is skewed if you think *that* version of your story washes anywhere but in a salt creek."

"Be that as it may, I've got the key, so—"

"Let me make myself very clear about this then. I—do—not—want—to—go—to—Kansas—with—you."

"Nonsense, Lizzie. Of course you want to go. You're here, aren't you?"

"Galt—"

"Lizzie—"

"Don't call me Lizzie."

"Don't make threats," he said mildly, and the bland tone of her voice was all the more shocking to her as she comprehended the words. He *meant* them. It was the outlaw again, overlaying the man with the munificent humor.

"I expect you thought I'd fall right in with your plans," she added, wondering why she was pitching headlong onto dangerous ground after that warning.

"No doubt in my mind."

"I'd just shrug and adapt."

"Don't be silly, Lizzie—I never thought you'd just *shrug* it off."

"I see. You just thought you could haul me all over the Missouri border in handcuffs. Simple, really, when you get right down to it."

"Lizzie—" The warning note crept back into his voice again.

She plunged ahead, ignoring his tone. "You could travel a

lot faster, and a lot cheaper, without me, especially after you cross over; you'll be only twenty-five or so miles from Rim City, and you could make that in a day on horseback."

"And you?" he asked silkily. "What would you do?"

"I'd do *laundry*," she said fervently, "until I could get a wagon going back inland. I'd be fine. I *would*."

"You'd rather do laundry than come along with me?" Again, his tone was deceptively mild as he phrased his questions. "You'd rather do *laundry?* And wait for God-knows-what to get you back to Greenfields? To go back to *nothing?*"

"To go back to some kind of routine and sanity," she contradicted him. "To get out of these damned handcuffs, and forget *you* ever existed."

The deadly silence that followed that statement scared her.

"You won't forget me," he said at last with a sure finality. "And if you think you're just going to walk into River Flats and take the laundry trade by storm, you're sadly mistaken. There's only one thing that will happen to you, Miss Lizzie, and I tell you now, you're better off with me."

She rattled her cuff. "Really? Tell me about it. Maybe getting paid for being mauled is better than being handcuffed and—"

His mouth stopped her uncontrollable flow of words; he just covered her lips and pressured them right back into her throat. His body shifted over hers, and his hands surrounded her head with such command that she did not protest when her cuffed hand lifted with his; she clung to him almost helplessly as her body tried to thrust him away and she wrenched her head from his kiss.

"Oh no, Miss Lizzie, you talk too damned much."

"And you . . ." she started to say, but he would not let her get another word out.

"Lizzie, shut up."

"Don't—" she moaned, but he did. And he did it so well she felt for one instant that she had been waiting for it, and that everything between them all these miles and these several days came down to this: the feeling of his lips tasting hers, and his body settling down on her with that same molding familiarity that both scared and exhilarated her.

177

She could never give in to him this easily. If he meant to show her what she might expect in River Flats, he could have conserved his energy. She knew already, and she was sure— she was damned sure she could resist the lures and fend for herself. But he couldn't have known that, and she wasn't naive enough to think he wanted to save her from herself.

No, he meant to conquer, and he was no different from any other man in this regard, and she had to demonstrate to him that his soft coaxing kisses, and his long hard body seeking her in that subtly impassioned way, could not seduce her . . .

. . . could seduce her . . .

. . . had the strength to force her . . .

And almost as if he sensed the direction of her thoughts, he eased the pressure of his mouth against hers. "Lizzie?" he murmured against her lips.

"*What?*" she snapped.

"You're coming with me."

"Of course I am; I have no choice. Just like I have no choice about what *you* want to do now," she said tightly, trying gamely to turn her head away from him.

His free hand immediately guided her mouth back beneath his. "You always have a choice, Lizzie," he said softly, touching her lips with his.

"Then I choose not to respond to your seduction," she whispered.

"And I, my dear Lizzie, choose to keep trying."

"No!" Panic swamped her, and she knew why. And so did he, as his next words proved. "You're scared then, Lizzie. You and I both know damned well what I can make you feel."

"I can feel nothing when I'm coerced and in handcuffs," she lashed out, lifting her manacled arm and thumping it back down against the mattress in frustration, in lieu of thrashing it into the face that was so disconcertingly close to her own.

"That is a definite point to consider, my Lizzie of the sassy mouth," he said thoughtfully. "Let me even the contest."

She had no inkling from his tone of voice what he intended to do; she was shocked to feel the steely constraint around her wrist suddenly unhinge and fall away.

She acted on her first impulse: her body lunged upward,

178

twisting and wrenching away from his restraining hand.

He reacted the only way he could have done—he pinned her with his body, an instinctive movement, born of his field training years, and his intense desire to feel her beneath him again.

Her hands automatically shot out and grasped his arms as she felt herself falling backward. She felt like killing him. "Devil you, you certainly have given me *some* advantage, haven't you?" she hissed at him as she felt his right leg twine around hers.

"If only you knew," he murmured whimsically, surrounding her flaming face with his huge hands again. Gently, he fit his mouth against hers, softly testing, tasting the texture of her lips, and her willingness.

She bit him, hard, and without conscience.

"Lizzie . . ." he growled, pulling back abruptly to nurse his lip.

"Just get it over with," she spat. "Why do you go through this charade of pretending you have a moment's concern for my feelings, or my needs? Just—do it."

"Oh, Lizzie," he sighed, touching his bruised lip with one finger. "I can see the only thing left to do is keep that trenchant tongue of yours very very busy."

"Galt . . ." she whispered in terror as she felt him lowering his head toward her.

"Lizzie, I *hate* the feeling that the only thing I ever say to you is shut up; but—shut"—his mouth grazed her unresisting lips—"up . . ." His mouth settled purposefully on hers, dominating, provoking, seeking, not allowing her to deny him.

Her body twisted under him rebelliously as if to make the statement her captivated lips could not. She felt the darkness intensely, and the weight of him as he sought the intimacy of her body in concert with her mouth.

She knew she could not successfully battle the ravishment of her mouth. He was too well aware of how to entice her response, and she was too well aware of wanting to give in to it. It was easy to consider giving in to it, to be swamped by luxurious feelings that would escalate into that wild honey-moist feeling that came from nothing else and no one else. Too

179

easy to surrender, just as it was becoming too easy to accede to him.

She couldn't, she *couldn't*—but then his tongue began its leisurely exploration of her mouth, licking her lips lightly, defining their shape, darting lightly against her clenched teeth, tasting the delicate inner skin of her mouth, and nibbling with firm determination on her recalcitrant lips.

"Galt," she groaned against this provocative onslaught.

"You taste so good, Lizzie," he murmured, taking instant advantage of her protestation and sliding his tongue deep within her mouth, seeking hers, tasting it, duelling with her as she attempted to avoid him, and finally removing his mouth from hers to murmur against her lips, "Kiss me, Lizzie, *now.*"

"You're crazy," she groaned, still fighting the inevitability of her surrender. "You're crazy; I'll fight you."

"I'm not and you won't. I'd never hurt you and I won't take you by force . . ."

"What do you think you're doing now?" she cried.

"You will come to me, Lizzie; it's the only way."

"Not now then."

"Now," he said firmly, sinking his hands into her tangled hair, to hold her still more tightly. "I won't do anything you don't want."

"*Anything?*"

"*Anything*, Lizzie. But I promise you, you'll want."

She wanted to refute even that, but she couldn't; his hands buried deep in her hair were gently rubbing her scalp in that circular coaxing way of his that already made her insides feel a kind of molten cave-in to his ministrations. Just that motion summoned up the remembrance of other feelings, other sensations those same hands could summon with some innate knowledge of her that she didn't even have of herself.

"Kiss me, Lizzie, willingly now," he commanded, his mouth a breath above hers, waiting, letting her feel his ardor in the note in his voice, a certain yearning to feel her lips on his that he wanted her to hear. "Put your arms around me, Lizzie; come . . ." he whispered, importuning her with his need. And when she didn't respond, he touched her lips with his, demanding her answer.

180

"There are no choices," she hissed as he removed one of his hands from her hair and firmly pulled her left arm around his neck.

"Sometimes not," he agreed calmly.

"And you only *want* this," she added edgily, "because you know I'm half naked under these damned clothes anyway. I wish you'd gone with that woman."

"Damn to hell, Lizzie," he growled, and swooped down on her mouth like a predatory animal, the anger in him, already so close to the surface, unleashed by her ferocious words. She did *not* want that, and he knew it; no matter how much she protested, she wanted him, and what he, and only he, was able to make her feel.

And now there was no question of anything except surrender to endless sensation; she knew it, and maybe she had invited it, but she had no time to contemplate her folly. It was all one, the sensation—his mouth and tongue delving into hers, his hunger unabated, lengthening the caress, tasting her, demanding of her, giving to her until her other arm, of its own volition, crept around his neck to draw him closer. No space between them, even to think. The odd notion flitted through her bedazzlement that the captor was now the captive, but even that did not settle anywhere real in the lush yearning that took over all reason and sense.

It was her body; her body remembered the sensations, and her body wanted the replay of those feelings that it had never known before. *She* wanted to experience those feelings again, and she never wanted to admit that to him. But she would have to make the demand. His hands, still pressing into her hair, did not move. His mouth, joined intimately with hers, made her feel frantic to have his hands caress her. His own need was there, and obvious, as he thrust his hips lightly against her; it *had* to be a matter of indicating somehow . . .

Her body spoke for her, arching upward to meet his tenuous thrusts eagerly, yielding to his voluptuous kisses ardently. Her hands began their own sensuous course over his shoulders and arms, and back up around his neck, to brush the stubble on his cheeks and play lightly over his face.

She felt his body tense at her tentative touching, and

181

wondered at his reaction. Her hands moved again, up, down, around, sliding past his shoulders to the long taut line of his back—and farther—

No, *no;* she wasn't supposed to *feel,* to *want* this much. *Even* this much.

Constrictions warred with desire. She wanted to know more and still more as his luscious kisses sent shimmering tendrils of need like molten silver through her veins. But the want was more elusive, harder to pin down. Her body quivered with it, ached for some kind of end to its creamy sensation like the explosive frenzy she had experienced with his hands. Yes, that. *That.*

Her pliant body churned at the thought. *That.* Her hips gyrated with experimental movements as an enticement to him to relinquish her mouth and concentrate elsewhere.

She needed no words; he heard her smoldering demand in the straining of her aroused body.

His lips moved from her mouth across her cheek to her neck and upward to her earlobe. His right hand slid downward to cup her face, to hold her close to his mouth as he explored the delicate shell of her ear with light flicking movements of his tongue that were countered by the soft scrape of his mustache.

It was almost too much to bear. She pulled away and he eased her back to him, and only the silence spoke between them. Her agitation begged for the repetition of all those things he had done before, and somehow he understood. He rolled to his side, cradling her against him with his left hand, and began the sensuous exploration she yearned for.

His mouth captured her willing lips once more as his questing hand traced its bold path downward, to feel the fragility of her collarbone under the open neck of the rough shirt, to lie flat against the wall of her chest, at the very swell of her breasts, which, could she define it, craved his touch.

He knew, as he seemed to know everything, that she wanted him to cover the firm mound of her breast with his hand. As his palm closed over it, her whole body shuddered violently as the heat of his hand permeated every pore of skin beneath her clothing that came in contact with his hand.

And then her need escalated; she hungered for him to

remove the clothing, to bare her straining breast with its taut nipple to the exquisite stroking of his long fingers. Everything in her centered on her desire to feel him caressing her naked breast until she thought she might scream from the tension of her yearning.

And he must have known, but he chose not to undress her just then, just there. He reached still farther downward to cup her buttocks, and pull her up against his long hard length, letting her feel the response that she alone could command from him.

She remembered it; she could feel the dark deep sensual sense of his heated maleness envelop her. She wanted to touch him, to know that hidden part of him that pulsated with such strength and voluptuousness. She wanted to rip off her impeding clothing and lie next to him naked and open to whatever he desired.

"Yes, Lizzie," he whispered, removing his relentless mouth from hers for just that instant. "Yes." The sibilant sounds of his words sliced through the darkness and the compelling thick heat between them.

She reached for him then, unable to bear his lips away from hers for more than the space it took for him to utter those words that echoed in her mind. Yes. It was so very simple. She wanted him and he was there for the wanting. And she wanted to know the answer to the final ineffable mystery of her sex, and the answer was there for the taking. She had only to ask, as he had said.

Did it matter what she did or what she said with him? In the end, if she ever got away from him, no one would ever know what did or did not happen this night in a wagon on the edge of nowhere on the Missouri River.

In the end, she could be as bold and vocal as she had to be and damn his surety that she would come to him. It didn't matter; nothing mattered but the culmination now. Her intelligence took second place to a wanton primitive drive that impelled her at breakneck speed along her curious path to fulfillment.

Curious, yes; her mind phrased it that way while her body commanded his caresses. Her desire went against everything she knew, everything she had been taught; everything she felt about him.

But if she had this ultimate knowledge, she thought somewhere in the recesses of her mind, how much safer she would be.

But it was more than that, she realized as she felt his hand finally make contact with her skin, somewhere beneath her skirt and her undergarments, and she groaned with a purely female appreciation of the sense of its heated imprint on her body. It was also that she loved the sensations she was feeling. And that was dangerous.

And not to be dissected at the moment his fingers flirted with the moist edge of her provocative femininity.

She shifted her hips to meet his torrid caress; she felt him questing deep within her satin heat, and deeper still, and she wanted more. There *had* to be more. Even she, as unknowledgeable as she was, could *feel* it.

Her own hands moved, brazen and urgent; she tore away her confining shirt, tore away the underclothes; she reached for his shirt, pulling at each button with the ferocity of an untamed tigress, running her splayed fingers over the hair-matted wall of his bared chest and his burgeoning male nipples, clinging to his mouth with wild tumultuous kisses.

Nothing mattered but that sense of filling her feminine core to the utmost with the ramrod length of him—and only him.

And another moment to release his rock-hard manhood from its confinement, into her eager hands that grasped him with delicious avidity that was echoed by the lusciously wanton noises she made in the back of her throat.

In the blindness of the dark, she examined every elongated inch of him. She felt his body shudder as her audacious hands stroked him up and down his granite length, imagining it within her, filling her.

She was hardly aware when he pushed her onto her back, and pushed away her confining clothing to expose her breasts still further. The broken kiss went on endlessly in her mind, impelled by her bruised lips, and by the licking pulling sensations at her breasts, first one and then the other, before he settled his hot mouth over one taut hard nipple.

184

He wanted to keep on doing just what he was doing, to have her caressing his throbbing thick length, to lick and suck at her nipples, to caress her deep within, but some degree of practicality intruded: he wanted her, all of her, willing and yearning for him. Reluctantly he withdrew his hand to tear away her clothes, not caring she hardly had more; not caring about anything but having her then, perfect with a wild wanton desire, and naked to feel every caress.

Yes, her mind and her body reverberated with approval as he ripped away the remainder of her clothing with one purposeful flex of his hand. Yes, as he centered himself over her, and began an upward course from her womanly core to taste every feminine inch of her up to and surrounding each breast with the wet slide of his tongue until he came to the succulent taut-tipped peak that invited his moist exploration with great attention to each luscious nipple.

Yes, to his mouth which sought hers once more after he left her breasts reluctantly, at the urging of her enthralling hands which had never let go of his hard male length. And as his tongue met hers avidly, she gave in to him and gave herself to him, without a word and without loss of pride.

He didn't need to hear the words, nor caution her of the hurt. He had a fine understanding of her now; to that he had added a wondrous knowledge of her body and her capacity for sensuality. He moved with firm surety between her legs, spreading them with his knees, and poising his body over hers at just the right angle.

He tasted her just one more time before he pulled away from her lips, and heard her confirming words: "Don't stop."

"Lizzie?"

"You win," she whispered, reaching for him again. It didn't matter; nothing mattered except that he complete the act with her now.

But even her overwhelming desire did not prepare her for the sensation of that brief stabbing pain. He entered her with a long throbbing pause and a quick lunging thrust that settled him deep within her while she assimilated the pain and wondered at the power and strength of him.

His lips assuaged the ache within her so gently, so

considerately, that she had time to feel, to separate each moment of awareness and define it so she could treasure it, and the awesome feeling of being connected to him in a hitherto undreamed-of way. How perfectly he fit within her! Nothing in her experience could have conceived of the magical excitement of this joining. Nothing. All her vile sentiments about him dissolved as she experienced the sense of his elemental maleness united with her pristine femininity.

Everything primitive in her responded to his virile masculinity. As the memory of the pain ebbed away, she felt an urgent seeking overtake her senses. This fusion of their bodies could *not* be all there was to it. And how long would she have to wait to find out the rest, she wondered, shifting her hips restlessly.

"Galt—" Her plea permeated her uninhibited calling out of his name, and he responded as she hoped he would, with a slow deliberate thrust of his lower torso that drove his manhood into her in a long provocatively sensual slide of sensation that almost reduced her to tears.

This—this was the feeling she was seeking, the one that led inevitably to the explosion in her that she ached to experience once again. Her body knew it; she heaved against him, demanding more. Perhaps her unruly mouth had been brazen enough to demand more—she never knew. He took up a rhythm without further coaxing that excited her beyond what she imagined it was possible to feel.

Her body rocked against his, wild with her need to take everything he was willing to give. She craved every thick stroke, every shimmery cascade of heat that slithered through her veins. Every part of her body reached to touch his, to wrap around him, contain him, to enfold the dark mystery of his manhood deep within her and experience it to the fullest.

And he meant for her to know every secret of her provocative sex. Her eagerness and urgency heightened his pleasure and fueled his desire. Her hands, the hands he had watched for so long from a jail cell window, now stroked his body with compelling need. Her body writhed beneath each slow driving thrust of his hard length, seeking more from him and still more. Her desire was building now, her body tensing

186

to meet his powerful strokes with a subtle voluptuous answer of her own.

And the sensation billowed upward, almost unbearably, with each potent surge of his body. His maleness was the center of the world to her in that torrid moment when all feelings thickened and expanded almost unbearably just before the elusive explosion became volcanically real, fathomless, radiant and devouring all at once, a cataclysm of her body and soul impossible to ever define. And so slowly, like molten gold, the culmination twisted and spiraled through her blood, her body, her femininity, her heart.

And what more could possibly be left? There was hardly time to have the fleeting thought before his mouth covered hers once again, as intimately as his body covered hers, and the thrusts became hectic, tense, as though his body were gathering every ounce of strength, constricting it like a spring for that one last ferocious plunge into her satin heat. She braced for it, the lunging plunging surge that heaved his wracking relentless release within her very core.

Drenched with his desire, and satiated beyond words, she nestled wordlessly beside him, her eyes wide open, her mind teeming, and wondered just what she had done.

Twelve

What *had* she done? Her eyes shot open to ivory-shrouded daylight. She was on the mattress, naked, and covered. She had dreamed it.

No, her imagination could *not* have invented what she had experienced. She sat up, clutching the thin cover to her breast. Something was missing. The cuff! He had really removed it, and he hadn't, sometime in the short hours between culmination and dawn, clasped it back around her wrist.

She felt dislocated without this familiar pinpoint of contention. And burdened with unfamiliar feelings about Galt Saunders that she did not want to complicate matters more than they were already complicated.

But she had made her bed, she thought humorlessly as she felt around for the remnants of her clothes. They were gone as well.

So what had she accomplished by her rash submission to the dictates of her passion? she wondered, wrapping the cover tightly around her and crawling to the wagon gate, where the aroma of boiling coffee assaulted her senses. Her eyes slewed downward to her bare waist. There was no difference; she was as much a prisoner now as she had been before she had surrendered to him. He would take her with him just the same, and now perhaps he would take her as well when he would.

Nevertheless, the coffee smelled good, the day was fine and warm, and Galt looked particularly appealing as he sat on a rock across from the campfire punching a needle through a shirt—hers or his, she couldn't tell. She hovered just beyond the wagon curtain, watching him, wondering if he were aware she was awake, her stomach growling as she inhaled the enticing scent of the coffee.

She was hungry, and just a little wet from the residue of her night's exertions. But she could hardly bear to face Galt after her shamelessness; she had had no thought about consequences. She had truly seized the moment and savored it.

She felt a wave of heat suffuse her body. She had wanted him, and she had let him know it. What would happen the next time? She was hardly safe, as she had thought last night; rather she was in more danger, for now she knew the depth of her sensual capabilities.

And it scared her. To think of all that passion and emotion buried deep inside her to be released in that one way with that one man. And what might he demand of her next?

Or she of herself?

The worst thing was, she couldn't undo it, couldn't take back her brazen response, or retract her goading words, her moans of encouragement, her body's total capitulation. It all belonged to Galt Saunders, and not to her, and it was all something she could never bestow on another man again in quite the same way.

If she really thought about it, she could hate herself endlessly for this folly, and him for taking advantage of her. But she couldn't even accuse him of that when she had participated as eagerly and ardently as he had predicted she would.

She shuddered. It was those feelings, those devil-damned bone-melting feelings that had made her lose her sense of self, her wariness of him. And he knew all about those feelings—*all* men know about those feelings. Hadn't her brothers told her? Yet those feelings had made her so addled that everything had flown out of her mind when *he* had touched her and she had lost all control of herself. She'd remembered nothing of warnings, regrets, or resolutions.

No—she wrapped the cover more tightly around her. She didn't want to explore that notion any further. She needed something to conceal her nakedness; she wanted something to eat.

Their clothing supply was so meager. He had nothing; she had the one other skirt of Lonita's and the second of Buck McCreedy's shirts. She knelt down and pulled them out of the dresser drawer as she let the cover fall away. Her breasts brushed her arms as she bent over to close the drawer.

She straightened up and looked at them curiously. Those small taut rosy-peaked mounds of flesh had driven both of them into a frenzy last night. She cupped them and held them. Commonplace parts of a woman's body. Felt so good when he held them, caressed the nipples, drove her wild when he kissed them . . .

Her body reacted to the memory of his hands and mouth; she made a little sound somewhere deep in her throat. She was shocked by her response to the thought alone. It was inexplicable, undefinable. It was moreover too much to think about.

The aroma of the coffee beckoned to her. It was the only thing she had the strength to consider. She thrust her arms into the dank-smelling shirt, and wondered how she was going to approach the campfire, look Galt Saunders in the eye, and take one steaming cup of coffee that might warm her conscience as well as her trembling hands.

She made a rather ludicrous figure climbing out of the wagon twenty minutes later wearing a shirt that was a foot too long for her, though it provided a perfectly respectable cover. Under it, she had wrapped a portion of the sheet to shroud the rest of her shapely legs and bare feet.

Galt hid a smile and bent his glinting jetty gaze back to the shirt in his hand, but his hand shook just that little bit as she approached the rock where he sat.

He watched her pour the fragrant coffee into the dented cup, and sink slowly down on the ground near him. Her face looked drawn, her leaf green eyes remote. She stared past him into the dancing flames without saying a word.

He watched her covertly for a moment or two. She had burned her tongue on the first hurried sip, and kept licking her

190

lips with an uncomfortable motion of her tongue, trying to ease the stinging sensation.

"You can't drown your sorrows in hot coffee, Miss Lizzie," he said mildly as he observed these fascinating machinations.

"I might drown them in the river," she retorted, feeling tense and too aware of him and the possibility of repercussions. She didn't trust him, she didn't, and now she felt she could hardly trust herself.

"I must see that you have the opportunity," he said helpfully, pulling a thread upward with a meaningful look at her. "Do you want to submerge yourself dressed or undressed?"

"Why—what would it matter now?"

"My dear Miss Lizzie," he chided, sending her a reproachful look. "You surely wouldn't want to be pulled from the river in a buttonless shirt. *What* would people think?"

"They would think I couldn't sew," she snapped, banging down her empty cup. "And *is* that my shirt? You mustn't trouble yourself."

"No trouble, Lizzie."

"*You're* trouble," she shot back, her eyes starting to blaze as she jumped up and stamped over to him, her hand outstretched.

He smiled, that infuriating crinkle-eyed smile, as she grabbed at the shirt in her fury, and pulled. He pulled in opposition, marveling at her strength which, as he knew it would, ripped the shirt right in two. He held up his half. "The wisdom of Solomon, Lizzie."

She stared at the half she held in her hand, and then at him, not understanding.

"Neither of us can win, Lizzie, unless we both win," he amplified. "But I expect," he added, balling up the material and tossing it aside, "you probably did that just to avoid learning how to stitch on a button."

"So imaginative of me," she murmured, defeated.

"It's what I like best about you," he said with a faint smile. "Come, Lizzie; no recriminations. I made some small repairs so you can get dressed while I fry up some bacon. It's all we have time for this morning." He tossed her the skirt and undergarment that had been in shreds last night, and watched her head into the wagon.

She hadn't protested; no, she had given in a good deal too easily, even she thought that as she unwrapped her makeshift skirt and hurriedly dressed. The truth was, he had disarmed her; she had been prepared to do battle for whatever was left of her honor, and he was busy sewing buttons. She didn't know quite how to deal with that.

She had to concentrate on how she might elude him. She pulled another strip of sheeting off her makeshift cover and wrapped it around her waist, then bent to shimmy her feet into her socks and boots.

He was insane if he thought she was crossing that river today. She jabbed her tense fingers into her hair and groaned; it felt tangled and knotted almost beyond reclamation by a mere comb.

She needed a good hot bath, some *real* food, some decent clothing. And she could find all *that* in River Flats. She grabbed for her comb and mirror and then, as an afterthought, felt around the bedding, not feeling a bit ashamed that she was overtly looking for some of the money he had won and cleverly hidden somewhere. But not under the mattress or anywhere easily discerned by *her*.

If only she had fifty or so of those golden dollars, she thought, vaulting over the wagon gate, lured once again by the aroma of cooking food, she surely would have the wherewithal to survive for a week or two in River Flats.

She propped the mirror up on the rear wheel against the side of the wagon, and stared disgustedly at her image. Daylight made her look worse, and she was sorry she had even taken the damned mirror from its place. There were shadows under her eyes and her face was pale. Her lips looked bloodless and slightly swollen. She did *not* look like a woman who had been made love to. She looked like a woman doing battle.

Oh, and she was. Against her instincts, her unexpected—though intermittent—feelings of liking for him; against her unreasoned feeling that this whole charade had very little to do with what he was telling her; against her resentment of being kept prisoner; against her insensible, incomprehensible, overwhelming, awakened passion. All of that. No wonder she looked so well used.

She swiped the comb through her hair. Painful. It dragged and pulled, and brought tears to her eyes as she kept at it, a punishment for her indiscretions, her debauchery.

"Lizzie."

Galt's quiet voice behind her was almost her undoing. He took the comb from her hand.

"No." She heard herself protesting, but it had no effect. He began gently combing through the tangles, and she remembered the first time he had done it. The first surrender, she thought, holding herself stiffly against the gentle tug of his hands. But it was all the same. He knew exactly what to do to command her submission. And she *would* yield, not with her mind but with her body, because her body craved the sensation with a need that had nothing to do with thought or logic. It just existed, and all because of what he could do—with his hands, his body, his words.

It was so beyond her understanding that she felt herself being left helpless in the wake of its force.

She could no more combat it than she could escape it. She leaned into his clever hands that made love to her with such knowledgeable familiarity, and she pushed away the danger.

She watched him covertly in the mirror. He wasn't watching her this time; his face was intently focused on what he was doing, and his firm fingers briskly worked out each little knot and tangle with a brusqueness that belied the sensuality of his handling of her hair. Each long stroke of the comb became a caress, the manifestation of what she had physically experienced in the dark. She understood it now, and her eyes closed in voluptuous abandonment to the realization that she was as much a prisoner of her own carnality as she was to his abduction of her.

His hands ceased their erotic play in her hair abruptly, so suddenly that she almost fell forward at the shock of it.

She opened her eyes to see him tossing the comb over the wagon gate. His voice was calm and commanding as he issued what were tantamount to his orders. "Time to eat, Lizzie. We can't go over on an empty stomach. Get the plates; take your last cup of coffee because I'm tamping out the campfire now . . ." He broke off as he noticed she was just staring at him. She was so beautiful with her heavy tawny hair fanned out over her shoulders, and her eyes glowing with deep verdant lights, but her mind was obviously elsewhere. Where? he wondered as he threw a handful of dirt over the smoldering embers of the fire. What plots and plans were hatching in her fertile imagination now that she had the mistaken notion he had freed her?

He dished out her bacon and poured her coffee and handed them to her. She took them with an abstracted air, and put a piece of bacon in her mouth without even tasting it.

He watched her with covert amusement as he served himself and settled back down on the boulder.

"It won't work, Lizzie," he said after a while, when he had set aside his plate and was leisurely sipping the dregs of his coffee.

"What won't?" she asked innocently, dumping the remnants of her partially burned bacon into the heap of dirt that had been their campfire. "*Your* schemes? *Your* stories? *Your* chasing after fool's gold?" And why did she detect just the faintest flicker of shock touch his face when she said that? She raised her tin cup to sip the last drops of cold coffee, and observed him curiously over the rim. But the moment had passed. His face schooled itself back into the same cynical lines, with the same maddening quirk on his lips that was just barely visible under his mustache, which badly needed a trim.

He rubbed his large hand over his stubbly chin and sent her that crinkly-eyed smile that she detested because it was so infectious, and shook his head. "*Me*, Lizzie?"

"*You*, Galt Saunders," she mimicked. "I'm still waiting, you know, after almost a week, to hear something from you that makes *some* sense."

He shrugged. "You've heard it; we're crossing the river today, Lizzie, and that makes a lot of sense to me."

She almost threw her cup at him. His damned impervious answers! She held up her hands. "Why this?"

194

"Why not?"

"It doesn't make *sense!*"

"Now Lizzie, it made sense last night."

"Nothing made sense last night," she shot back.

He straightened up from what he was doing to look at her. "That's a damned lie. Now why don't you take care of those plates, while we're talking about sense, and then we'll get going. And don't tell me you don't want to go."

She picked up both of their plates and cups and sent him a scathing look. "I can't think of anything I want to do *more*," she said nastily, watching him uncork the water barrel and empty some of it into the iron oven for her.

His jetty eyes lit up as he handed it to her. "*I* can," he said imperturbably, and left her, for once, without anything to say.

From the rise above the docks, they could clearly see the chaos and the mechanics of ferrying the wagon across.

"Damn to hell," Galt muttered, surveying the scene, which, because of the height from which they viewed it, looked like the backdrop of a painting on which the myriad of complex details had to be viewed separately to understand the coherent whole.

The focus of attention was a man at the dock gate, which was bounded by what looked like a toll booth on either side. Beyond the gate was a long horizontal dock that hugged the shoreline, which had, at intervals, massive pylons reaching up ten feet in the air. Appended to each of these was a pulley and rope system that stretched across the churning river into the distance, which must have seemed to the onlookers like the very horizon.

Midway across the river, a flatboat was simultaneously being pulled and rowed across the river with its heavy burden. It wavered from side to side dangerously, tilting into the swells of the river one way one minute, swirling crazily around a different way the next. One man wielded the long paddle that steered it with the currents. If there were passengers aboard, a faraway onlooker could not tell.

"That's *it?*" Elizabeth demanded in disbelief.

"I reckon," Galt said, not a little dismayed himself. His opaque black gaze rested on the toll booth. There was a lot of activity there already, centering on the man at the gate. It looked like bidding. It looked like grim war.

"A person could drown," Elizabeth said, daunted by the fragility of the flatboat and how easily it was buffeted by the waves. "Maybe they've all drowned."

"They're sitting on the flatboat floor, and the wagon is anchored to the sides. They take the wheels off, you know," Galt said, his thoughtful gaze still resting on the activity at the gate.

"I didn't know, and it doesn't reassure me."

"But I'll be with you."

"That doesn't reassure me either," she said darkly, scanning the river as a bulky shape came into view. "Another boat—look. Someone coming back—fast, I'd wager."

Galt sent her a skeptical look. "Not so fast at those prices, Lizzie. It's time for us to strike our bargain."

Our, she thought as the wagon began moving forward down the rutted trail slowly. Our. Two horses, two oxen, a load of useless pots and furniture, pounds of flour, salt, and beans. A pair of handcuffs that have suddenly disappeared, and he says *our*.

She could just tumble off the wagon seat someplace near town and have done with him. She could.

The damned thing jounced and jolted her very bones. He had to be cutting through this roughly marked path to foreshorten the time it would take them to get themselves into the fray. As they came closer to the line of wagons, it became obvious that a lot of shouting was going on; there was a lot of anger in the air, the scent of a thwarted mob of people who once more were being prevented for lack of money from having what they most desperately wanted—passage across.

"They're being held up," Galt said suddenly, jerking on the reins, "as surely as if someone held a gun to their heads."

And it was true. Without the money, they couldn't get across the river, and staying on this side, they could not get to their fool's heaven—virgin acres welcoming them with outstretched fields begging for cultivation. Towns to be built along the railroad. Money to be *made* if only they could get there.

Galt edged up the line of wagons, searching for one particular one, the worn tired woman who had almost given up hope.

She wasn't the last on the line today, and she was seated on the high perch of her wagon watching the crowd with resignation written all over her face. If her man had managed to eke out a little money the previous night, it was obvious that today it was not enough.

"Ma'am," Galt called across to her.

She turned her head stiffly. "You!"

"Yes, ma'am." His rich voice again held that respectful note which seemed somehow to soften her face just a little.

"Make your stake, stranger?" she asked after a long pause, almost as if she couldn't bear to ask, couldn't bear to hear he had been successful where her man had not.

Galt hesitated, and then said, "Yes, ma'am, I did."

She nodded. "Good luck then."

"Thank you, ma'am. But I'm sure I'd be more successful if I had some extra clothes if you could spare them."

Her spine stiffened and her face hardened. "You don't need to do that."

"No, I don't," he agreed. "I need that extra pair of pants and a shirt, ma'am. I left with but one, and two pairs of levis, which are going to get mighty wet on this crossing."

Her grim face lifted. "How come?"

Galt paused again, wondering how much to tell her. "We left town real fast," he said finally.

A knowing look flashed into her deepset eyes. "I bet you did. All right then, stranger. I won't scruple to take money from a wanted man. I believe I can find a couple of extra things that'll do you."

She turned and climbed into her wagon. They heard low voices and things being shifted around before she reappeared with the items he had asked for. "I reckon these'll fit."

Galt surveyed the worn workshirt and the wrinkled denims she held up, and he nodded. "That's fine. Take them, Lizzie, will you?" he requested as he handed a wad of bills across to

197

the woman.

Her fist closed around its thickness, and her eyes widened just a fraction. "You sure you want to pay this much?" she asked disbelievingly.

"Necessities come dear when they can't easily be had," Galt said gently. "Can I ask your name, ma'am?"

She studied him for a moment and then said, "I'm Ada Rudd."

A name, Elizabeth thought as she folded the stiff, washed clothing, that was appropriate to this rough unschooled woman with her monumental pride. She acknowledged his sketchy introduction of "This here is Lizzie" with a pleased-to-meet-you nod of her head; it was not the place to argue his use of her name or her place in his life. And hard to tell what Ada Rudd's washed-out blue eyes comprehended as they bid her good-bye and nudged their way upward on the line. She didn't know what to make of Galt's action. He had wanted to find the woman and help her, and he had, and the way he had handled it confused her even more.

She sat very quietly as the wagon pushed closer and closer to the dock, where the next overland wagon was being prepared to ferry over.

She watched, fascinated, as everything was taken off the wagon in preparation to removing its wheels and loading it onto the flatboat.

Directly before them, a swarm of men massed themselves in an impenetrable line between the two tollhouses. Above them, the gatemaster swayed on a ladder, shouting at the crowd, a plank in his one hand, a piece of charcoal in the other.

And still they inched closer. By this time, the axle bolts had been removed from the wagon wheels, and the front pair of wheels were off, and the wagon slanted forward like a toboggan on the crest of a hill.

The crowd milled and shouted as the second pair of wheels were taken off, and six men rushed forward onto the loading dock to pull up the waiting flatboat into a position where they could load the wagon onto it. The voices died down as the workers surrounded the wagon, and almost in one motion, crouched, grasped, and lifted the enormous weight of the wagon and shuffled it to the edge of the dock and onto the undulating flatboat.

And then the arduous job of loading the wagon again began.

"How many a day at this rate?" Elizabeth whispered, leaning close to Galt's ear so he could hear her clearly.

He shook his head. "Ten—maybe fifteen if they use all five pulleys and off-load as efficiently on the other side. Damn to hell, I had no idea it would be this time-consuming." He looked at her with a rueful little smile. "It's going to cost us, Lizzie."

"*You,*" she mouthed silently as he turned his eyes back to the activity, which now centered around the family's loading their possessions back onto their wagon, and the dock workers helping, and then tying down everything to make sure it was secured, and throwing over all a rubberized tarpaulin for protection. They worked with the precision of a clock mooring the tarp to the floor of the boat, and then roping and tying together the family's livestock to be towed across behind.

At the end, the family—four adults and three children—were instructed to board and sit on the floor around the wagon; two of the dock workers boarded as well with their oars, and the gatemaster lifted a hand, and a signal sounded forth from the horn of still another waiting man. A breathless moment later, the pulley moved and the boat glided forward.

Ten minutes later, the flatboat Elizabeth had seen crossing back from the Kansas side of the river mounted the dock and was grasped into its moorings by the ever-efficient dock workers.

There was not one wasted moment as they began off-loading wheels, furniture, pots, pans, mattresses, after removing the drenched tarp from around this wagon load of returnees.

The crowd was even more silent, watching. Who had come back, and why? They weren't always turnarounders. Yet not one of the milling crowd shouted out the questions they were all thinking. They didn't want to know the reasons; they only wanted to hear the positives. The grim faces of the returnees bore witness to the fact that what they would hear might be something they did not want to know.

It took an hour to reverse the loading process, during which time no bids were made for the next crossover. Everyone watched until the last moment when the axle bolts were tightened, the possessions were fitted back onto the wagon bed, and the tight-lipped emigrants climbed onto their respective perches. Then, almost as if it were biblically ordained, a wide path opened up for them to pass and the silence continued until they slowly made their way through the passive waiting crowd and along the lined-up wagons and on into the main street of River Flats.

The wall of humanity closed in around the gate as the departing wagon disappeared from sight, and the gatemaster stared after it, calculating the dollars lost by virtue of what the expression of the emigrants' faces had told the crowd.

But then, just as quickly as the noise and commotion had died down, it swelled up again, the excitement of the possibilities beyond the watery horizon catching the imagination of the milling crowd once more.

The gatemaster did not have to say a word. Disparate voices, confident with energy, shouted at him, the words mingling and lost to definition. But he heard; he heard something, because he lifted his board and began scrawling something on it.

And then he lifted it to show the crowd.

"One hundred fifty, silver," Galt read slowly. "I'll be good goddamned."

The crowd fell back in shock. The ante had gone up fifty dollars in the space of time between the settlers' leaving and the returnees' arrival. Their collective turbulence turned murderous. Violence was in the air, primed to erupt at a moment's notice.

"One-ten," a bold voice shouted over the restive movement of the crowd.

"Can't do," the gatemaster shouted back.

The crowd roared.

Galt cursed under his breath. "The bastard." Elizabeth tensed. She could feel the escalating rage of the crowd echoed in Galt's taut posture as he leaned forward to assess the confrontation, as if, she thought, he might do something about it. Even so, a hundred and ten dollars silver—and the rate rapidly on the rise on the whim of any given moment the gatemaster felt like increasing it—

And then Galt stood and shouted over the noisome throng, "One ten or no one goes," and Elizabeth's eyes widened at his audacity in the face of the crowd's desperation.

"Say *what*, stranger?" the gatemaster yelled, as if he hadn't heard. But he had heard, and the crowd had heard. The noise died down, and Galt shouted back fearlessly, "One-ten or no one goes."

"Who says?" the gatemaster demanded, looking around, his expression wily. He could read a crowd. They wanted over, and the best price would buy the next crossing in five minutes.

So he waited. The crowd shuffled, and Galt stood where he was, in the perch of the wagon, with Elizabeth edgy with nerves beside him. What a chance he was taking, she thought, assuming that anyone in this mob would figure out the gatemaster would cave in if no one met his price. She tried to look at their faces, to define what they were thinking, but the faces around her were either blank or looking up at Galt, scared witless by his foolhardiness.

The silence lengthened, with no one coming forward for the next shift over. "Well, gentlemen?" the gatemaster shouted. "We're ready to move. Who'll go first?"

The crowd shuffled and no one moved. The silence lengthened. The sultry air of explosiveness permeated the atmosphere. Something—or someone—would have to give.

Minutes passed. Maybe a half hour, it was hard to gauge. Galt hadn't moved a muscle. Elizabeth sat still as a statue, not even daring to turn her head and look back at the long line of waiting wagons. Not one of them, she thought in amazement, had contested Galt's statement. She was dumbfounded that he would be backed up so unanimously.

But then there was Ada Rudd, for whom the price of crossing was forever out of reach. She and the others, Elizabeth thought, they would have now some small means of controlling their destiny. They might just get over, the prices might just come down. She knew Galt didn't care how much or little the price was, that he was fuming because they were being held up by the gatemaster's pettiness. And he would wait as long as he had to to bring down the crossing fee.

They all waited. The silence became deafening, and after a

while, a small ripple of resentment began coursing its way over the crowd. But no one came forward at the stated price. No one wanted to be the first.

An hour passed, in which the gatemaster lost one hundred and ten dollars that would not make it across the river that day.

He wavered for a moment, and then set his shoulders and waited. They all waited; he could not miss the message that no one wanted to pay his price, and that if he waited much longer, he would lose yet another hundred and ten dollars.

"One twenty-five," he shouted suddenly, and the crowd moved slightly, first forward, then back.

"One-ten, or no one goes," Galt shouted back in the same adamant voice, and the gatemaster looked as if he wanted to kill him.

The gatemaster waited. He sensed the surging impatience of the crowd. They wanted over; they felt murderous about the first wagon that had gone over at one hundred dollars' fee, and had a half day's start to Kansas City and Leavenworth. Someone was on the edge of offering the hundred and twenty-five the gatemaster demanded.

Galt sensed the increasing agitation. "One-ten, gatemaster, or no one goes over this day," he called out again. "That's a lot of money to lose to gain another five hundred dollars."

An assenting murmur swept through the crowd. They wouldn't be lining their own pockets, not yet. Sentiment swayed back toward Galt's position. They would wait. Whatever they lost, they would only lose it to one family, one wagon, who could not possibly conquer the whole of the Kansas territory opening up with the railroad. One-ten, one-ten it was, and maybe less on the next day. Maybe they could jack it back down the same way, and still more the day after. A rush of hope calmed the violence in the air, and they waited, just to see what the gatemaster would do.

He waited too. Another flatboat arrived bearing livestock and a herder, quickly off-loaded and swallowed by the crowd. The gatemaster didn't know what the going rate was across the river, but he knew finally he was going to lose three hundred and thirty dollars on just the boat he had waiting if he did not reduce his fee.

"All right, stranger. One-ten today, just for you. And who goes first?"

Galt pulled out his pouch of silver and held it up. "I do!"

Elizabeth watched as the dock workers unloaded the rocking chair, the mattress, the dresser, the sacks of flour and sugar. Then came the water keg, which Galt refilled from a nearby tank the gatemaster had set up for just such use, (and ten dollars to do that, she thought with resentment), the meager store of pots, their slab of bacon, tins of coffee . . . what did it look like, this skimpy assortment of possessions that belonged to neither of them—except the ludicrously dangling bonnet which had belonged to Galt's wife. Oh yes, Galt's wife. The memory of that, and her feelings about it, seemed almost a lifetime ago.

Did it matter? Her expression did not change as the wheels came off, and the body of the wagon was shunted onto the flatboat, and the same procedure was repeated in reverse. Galt, who had disappeared behind some bushes, reappeared wearing Ada Rudd's cast-off clothing, and tossed his own into the wagon before the tarp was fastened to it.

He tied the leading rope to the horns of the oxen, secured the horses' tow rope to the boat, and turned to look at her.

Elizabeth's expression was blank as he came to her in a way that told her he recognized her perturbation, and that he discounted it. She had come this far, after all—as if she had had a choice about it—and she wondered what he might say to dissuade her from taking the monumental step of parting company with him. The crowd would support her, she was sure, if she made a scene about being held against her will.

Or when his back was turned, she could duck into the crowd and he would never see her again.

But she could have done that ages ago, she thought, feeling skittery and wild as he approached her.

What could he say?

He held out his hand. "Stay with me, Lizzie."

And he gave her the choice.

203

Thirteen

The blunt prow of the flatboat battered the swelling waves into submission as it plowed its lumbering way across the river. The shoreline drew closer and closer, and not soon enough, Elizabeth thought, shivering in her spray-drenched clothes. Beside her, equally wet, Galt knelt forward, ready to spring into action, to do what Elizabeth could not conceive. Their steady oarsmen did not need their help, and though the opposing shore looked very close, she knew it was impossible to estimate the time they would dock.

All told, it seemed as if the trip across the river were taking forever, and it left her too much time to think. She still did not know what had compelled her to take his hand and follow him on board without a word of argument or protest, and her attempt to understand it was becoming a wasted effort. Something had shifted in her feeling about him, and she could not pin down what it was—the intense experience of the night before, or just her realization that she was better off going along with him than trying to make it back to Greenfields.

Or the idea she *never* wanted to go back to Greenfields.

She slanted a curious look at him but his snappy black eyes were on the horizon—on what was to come.

Oh, and what was to come? she wondered. Unanswered questions, a curious quest, a man wanted for murder who wanted to prove himself innocent by apprehending a witness whose story everyone had believed to begin with. She hadn't forgotten any of that, or his challenge to make up a better story. But the man in the jail and the man Greenfields whispered about was not the man beside her in the unsteady flatboat.

This man had a tenderness and a humor—and a hunger that, if she examined it, might have been the things that reached out to her on the dock this afternoon. Just might. But she steeled herself, even as the boat veered downstream with a frightening little jerk, not to respond to this facet of him; she was aware of it, she knew he had guile, but he was every bit as much the schemer as she. She couldn't let down her guard for a moment. He was up to something, and that was all there was to it. And she was going to discover what it was.

The boat lurched again and the wagon behind them shifted agonizingly forward. Galt immediately shifted his position and leaned his body backward against it. Every muscle in his body tensed like a coiled spring, and he sent Elizabeth a rueful little smile. "Thinking awfully hard again, Lizzie. Regrets?"

"Surely not," she said caustically. "I will especially have much to thank you for if I come down with something awful because I almost froze to death in these wet clothes. But— don't trouble yourself about *that*."

His eyes crinkled. "I won't, Miss Lizzie. I have every reason to know you can take damned good care of yourself. *You* wouldn't let that happen to *me*."

And that was the other thing, she thought, his neat way of twisting everything around on her. She had a feeling once they really were on the trail of his quarry, she would be privy to even less information than he had imparted thus far. And she hated him for it, the meaningless assurances which hid secrets only he knew the answers to.

She looked up at him, fuming, her green gaze deepening with the resentment his comment aroused in her.

But he was not looking at her face. His jetty eyes were focused on her body, on her wet, clinging shirt that outlined her taut-tipped breasts as naturally as if she were wearing no shirt at all. And then his glittery black gaze moved up to meet her jade-sparkling eyes, and he smiled at her. "It's really all right, Lizzie," he said with a note in his voice she could not define. "You made the right decision."

*　　*　　*

Once they had reached shore, it took still another hour to pole their way back to the loading dock—because the treacherous river had propelled them a half mile downstream —and unload the wagon and their possessions. Elizabeth wrapped herself in the other of Galt's dearly purchased chambray shirts and set about keeping herself as busy as possible, hauling their goods to the wagon, and ultimately, hitching up the oxen, an accomplishment which had the dockworkers standing around and staring in admiration at her.

Galt held up his hand as he met her defiant stare. "I know, I know; you used to hitch the teams to harness the plow back on the plantation."

"Something like that," she said noncommittally, refusing a leg up into her perch in the wagon. One foot in a high spoke of the wagon wheel was impetus enough to vault her into her seat. She settled herself in with smug satisfaction, and wrapped her arms around her wet body. Her outer shirt was damp through and through as well. Her efforts had warmed her, and the soft evening breezes began to cool her down once again. She couldn't wait until they made camp.

"How many miles today?" she asked as Galt climbed into the wagon in much the same manner as she had.

He took the reins briskly and strapped them down lightly on the rumps of the oxen. The wagon lurched forward with a sickening jounce and then moved jerkily off the dockside and onto firm ground.

"Till we get tired," he said, looking around at the meager crowd that awaited a return trip across the river. Far away, on the water, he could see the second of the flatboats plying through the waves with no little difficulty toward the shore. "The second ferry's on its way, Lizzie. I hope they held the bastard up for all he was worth."

She swiveled her body to look out at the river. "How did you know that would work?" she asked curiously as she turned around to him.

He clucked to the team, and whacked the reins again. The pace picked up a notch as the team found the path which looked as if it led straight into virgin forest.

One of the drovers called after them, "Town's about three miles upstream, stranger," and Galt waved to him before he considered Elizabeth's question.

"I didn't," he said finally. "The crowd has a lot of power, Lizzie, and they can use it violently or they can use it constructively. They could have attacked the gatemaster and accomplished nothing, or they could have stood back and told him by their actions that if he didn't compromise, they wouldn't take his ferry. And you see, money spoke louder than brute force. I don't doubt he would have rather been beaten up than lower his price. But now, because of his greed, he's going to have to take less and less, because they'll pass the word on, all of those who don't cross over this week or this month."

"Who is he, anyway?"

"Someone who got to the right place at the right time, I reckon. He probably owns the land, and he figured out how to get them across the safest and most efficient way, and he probably pays a cut of his take to the town. Or the town pays *him* to raise the prices. I'd be hard put to guess which feeds off of which."

"It was ugly," Elizabeth said.

"Yes it was," he agreed. "But after all, Lizzie, you had me to protect you—"

"—who knew all along just what he was doing," she interpolated.

"Never doubt it, woman. And so here we are, over the river and hot on the trail."

"Yes," Elizabeth said slowly, "I've been meaning to ask you about that."

"Damn to hell, Lizzie, haven't I given you enough time to figure it out?"

"The trail's pretty cold by now," she pointed out, trying to keep her tone as normal as possible. "And I still don't get it, so maybe you have to explain it to me one more time."

"Nothing else to explain, Lizzie. I didn't kill Buck McCreedy, and Lonita knows it, and we're going to find her and she's going to tell the truth," he said noncommittally, focusing his attention on steering the team around a large rut in the dirt track. "Simple."

And what else, she thought. There had to be much more; she had so many questions. "Why?" she asked abruptly.

He scowled. "I told you why, Lizzie."

"And I told you it didn't wash, and that you don't need me hanging around to accomplish any of it. Besides which, I don't see Edgar Healey hot on *your* trail."

"Can you say for sure?" he asked, his tone at once kindly and infuriatingly smug.

"Can you?" she retorted.

"Well, you think on it a little more, Lizzie. I expect you've worked out the part about my not being a murderer"—he slanted a humorous look at her—"and the rest is probably none of your business anyway."

But I'm making it my business, she thought angrily, touching the long-ago-healed pinprick spot on her neck.

The brief movement of her hand did not go unnoticed. His expression darkened perceptibly and his disapproval pervaded the silence between them.

Was she not to remember that violation? she wondered, seething herself at his cavalier dismissal of what she had suffered when she thought he might at any moment murder *her*. Was she supposed to have been grateful that he had removed the handcuffs and given her a choice—which when it came down to it, wasn't much of a choice? And on top of that, was she supposed to accept half-truths as legitimately making sense?

"I haven't forgotten either, Lizzie," he said.

"But why would you remember?" she asked stubbornly. "I was only a means to an end, and the resolution still isn't at hand. You're still running, still chasing after some elusive proof, still seeking something that is so shapeless that it defies description. And you remember such a small incident as that?"

A grim little smile forced its way across his mouth. "Yes, I do, Lizzie. Yes to all of that. And I will accomplish what I set out to do, as undefined as it may seem to you. But as I said," he added darkly, "it doesn't concern you."

"I see," she said slowly. "That makes less sense than anything else."

"Maybe," he said expressionlessly, "that makes the most sense of all."

*   *   *

208

She was tired of trying to sort out the puzzles, so when he drew the wagon off the road and into a small clearing, she was happy to have something else to occupy her thoughts.

Her clothes were still damp, but they did not cling to her as she climbed down from her perch, and she found it very easy to commence the myriad chores that had to be done for them to make camp for the night.

"You're being mighty helpful," Galt said at one point as he watered the horses and oxen.

She held up her hands. "By choice," she said meaningfully, and continued gathering the twigs she needed to build the campfire.

He was amazed at how efficient she was now that she had no reason for rebelliousness. The fire was laid and lit, the coffee set over it immediately to boil. She carved off several rashers of bacon and threw them into the frying pan along with the remainder of the dried apples and put a potful of beans to soak for breakfast.

She never noticed that Galt had disappeared, or that he was gone for a long time. She was feeling hungry and a little frenzied and the bacon could not cook fast enough to assuage the rumblings in her stomach. She watched over it like a mother hen, until she could fork one crispy piece out and into her mouth.

She almost choked when Galt popped unexpectedly out of a clump of bushes behind her, his arms full of green things and a shirt dangling over his shoulder.

"Oh, God," she groaned, "they'll be after us for theft. What on earth is all *this?*"

His jetty eyes danced. "Vegetable soup, Lizzie. Come and look—potatoes, and turnips, carrots, corn, another shirt . . ."

"Plucked off the vine?" she wanted to know as he spilled his goods into her hands. "What do I do with these?"

"Empty the frying pan and get out the oven. And the rice. We're going to boil it up till the rice is done and have us a feast. Lord, vegetables at last. C'mon, Lizzie. Eat up that sour old bacon and let's make ourselves a treat."

She emptied the frying pan's contents onto a plate, and drained the beans and set them in the frying pan. Galt crawled into the wagon for the rice sack, while she filled the oven with fresh water. He doled out two heaping cupfuls of rice into that, and she put it on the fire. He in turn began scraping and peeling the vegetables into the second plate, and when he had done with that, he added them to the rice and water.

The coffee had begun boiling by then. Elizabeth put in a pinch of salt and some cold water so the grounds would settle, then poured a cup for him and one for herself.

Galt settled himself down close by the fire to stir the soup and eat some of the bacon and apple.

"I wonder you didn't find us some meat," Elizabeth said from the opposite side of the fire.

"I'm damned lucky I was able to swipe that much. And the shirt. You ought to change into it, Lizzie, and let the other two dry. We're not far out of town now; we'll stop over and restock tomorrow."

"Which town?" she asked idly from within the confines of the wagon as she took his suggestion. "We're nowhere near Rim City."

"Nope. A little river town called Drover's Landing. And ten mile or so beyond that is Rim City."

"That quick," she commented, more to herself than him, as she slid on the freshly washed well-used shirt. It was yellowed from washings and usage, with streaks of white here and here, under the arms, around the shirttails, to give clues to what color it had been.

She climbed out of the wagon and sat herself down across from him. The sun was lowering slightly now and the aroma of the boiling vegetables permeated the air. There was an atmosphere of companionship growing between them that was just a little unnerving. Again she had that nascent feeling that she was starting to like him too much, and that was over and above his irritating refusal to give her explanations.

Across the campfire from him, in the twilight, she felt as if that brief aggravating conversation they had had enroute had never happened.

The silence became close and comfortable, underpinned by a faint bubbly sound from the boiling water. Galt leaned forward to stir the concoction and to taste the rice. He grimaced as the steaming liquid scalded his mouth. "I reckon you'll be scavenging the stores next time, Lizzie. Making the soup is nothing, just another something to add to your repertory."

"I believe I can say I'm grateful for your instruction in *some* matters," she agreed smoothly, and felt herself skewered by his flat black gaze.

"Watch that runaway mouth, Lizzie," he warned in a tone that was neither considerate or humorous. "There are always penalties."

"Yes," she said gravely, "that I do know."

Another silence settled down between them, which did not discomfort her in the least.

But his question thrown casually into the simmering silence did. "What about your brothers, Lizzie?"

"Whatever made you think of *them?*" she demanded, astonished.

"Thinking about the way you handled the animals today, and set up camp. How you handled the trip across the river. How you've been accommodating yourself to the situation without the usual feminine vapors. You're an unusual woman, Lizzie, and from what little you've said, I gather you had an unusual upbringing."

"You could say so," she concurred flatly.

"Tell me about your brothers." His rich voice was gentle but there was that steely note under it. He wanted to know, in his own good time, just like he wanted anything else—and got it, she thought.

She shrugged. "There were three of them, all older. I was a late child of my parents, so I was rather spoiled by all of them. And then when the war came, they all went off to serve. And they all died."

He considered this bald recitation silently. Spoiled! Lizzie!

"You were in the field," she added defensively. "You know."

"I know," he said. "How much do *you* know?"

"They wrote to me," she amplified. "Some. Father left it all to me to take care of, and Ellis—he was the oldest—tried to help. I knew a lot, of course . . ."

"You were out in the fields," Galt guessed.

"From the time I was a child, I went with Father, or Ellis when he would take me. But the war . . . Ellis went first, Lucas and R.B. shortly after. And toward the end, Father volunteered. He was killed first, and my mother never recovered."

"Everyone left . . ." Galt prompted.

"Everyone left, and it was just me, Mother, Rilla, and Verdine. And Jonas, who was Verdine's husband. And Ellis's letters, which got to be more about hell than help. And then"—her voice broke—"they stopped."

He let the silence comfort her memory, and after a bit she went on, "It nearly killed my mother. Father, and then Ellis. Ellis was . . . I loved him very much, and I tried to emulate him as best I could—until the gambling. Well, anyway, whatever he could do, my brothers would want to do, and therefore, I wanted to do. And I did. Ellis thought it was amusing. He used to say I had plenty of time to cultivate the womanly graces. He called me his shadow, and I went with him wherever and whenever I could. Or I snuck around with R.B., who was kind of in the same situation as me, being the youngest of the boys, the baby. Two babies . . ." Her voice trailed off. "He was but nineteen when he died. Nineteen. I was sixteen, and I had been running the farm for two years prior, when Father left. So you see . . ." She paused, bemused. "That is all about my brothers."

"I see," he said.

Her eyes flickered in his direction. Oh, he saw nothing, nothing. Not the pain of loss, or the burden she had had to bear, and the inheritance she had ultimately lost. *Her* honor, she thought, to keep it for her children. And she had failed. *Why* had he brought up the past? She had thought that she'd successfully buried her ghosts in Greenfields.

She wondered if he had buried his.

The soup was hot, and watery, and the taste had been altogether boiled out of the vegetables. However, the rice was palatable, and the change in their diet considerably refreshed Elizabeth, who was feeling testy and resentful at Galt's nosiness by the time the soup was ready.

She tossed the last piece of browned bacon into the liquid and sipped it slowly, along with her coffee, ruminating on the oddity of her past that had brought her to this situation.

The second year that Ellis and her brothers had been gone was when Martin and his renegade brigade had invaded their hard-won serenity. She had managed by that time to decrease the crop to a manageable size to cultivate and to feed them. But just barely. The rest had to come from their own efforts, and Verdine had not been loath to show her how to tend a garden, milk the two cows they had left, and develop her chicken coop.

At that, they were more fortunate than their neighbors, and marauding soldiers, gray and blue, heard about it, but were hard put to find them, as they were situated on a rise off a dirt road and beyond a concealing little forest.

She had always loved that isolation, until Martin Healey decided he needed her provisions and he was going to find her come hell or high water. And he did.

And she did not know what to make of him. He had buckets of charm on top of extravagant good looks, which were not diminished by his makeshift uniform and two weeks' dirt coating his face and body.

And he was on a mission, leading a group of irregular volunteers from a border state that did not have the guts and spleen to make a stand, he said. She had to help.

She helped. His men took over Longview for a period of two weeks, and they ran reconnaissance forays into the Virginia border counties that were resisting secession.

She knew why; his unspoken assignment was to foment dissension, to bring public opinion over to the Confederacy. She didn't want to know about it. She wanted nothing to do with the war by that time.

But she wanted him.

Or she thought she did. He was the commander of operations, and he ran things from the front parlor at Longview. He was there, with her, everyday. He worked alongside her as she tilled the soil, and set his available men to work for her as payment for usurping her home. She was in a perfect location for him, well off the known roads, in the western arm of the state, close enough for day incursions by his men.

And she was beautiful, even in calico, with dirt-encrusted hands. He fell madly in love with her youth and beautiful face, and her capabilities. And she thought she had fallen in love with him.

When he left, he could make no promise as to when he would return, only that he would.

And when he did, he found her in the hands of her creditors, her mother disastrously on the edge of death, her crops decimated by the weather. His gentlemanly instincts came to the fore. He wanted dearly to rescue her, but he could only make promises.

He gave her money and swore that when he got back to Greenfields, he would send for her. She must sell Longview and come to him.

By the time this was possible, her mother had died and her creditors had taken the house anyway. He sent her the money for the arduous trip west. She came by stage through Illinois, and across. And by that time, she hardly remembered Martin Healey. She was grasping for a lifeline to some kind of salvation. He was handsome, and he had a life somewhere other than the destitute South.

Later, she knew she should have stayed.

Or maybe not, she amended in her thoughts, as she regarded Galt Saunders across the rim of her tin plate. She wondered what set of peculiar circumstances had brought him and the wife who hadn't wanted to come to a place like Greenfields. She had a sudden jarring intuition that there was more to his story that he had not told her, just as she had withheld things from him.

The mystery wife, the wearer of the ugly bonnet who died in questionable circumstances. Had he loved her? she wondered. Had he made love to her, her unruly thoughts intruded, the way he did to you?

Her body twinged. She thought she had shoved all that into some nether region that was not going to be allowed to remember it or yearn for it.

And what was the twinge? *Jealousy?* Surely not. Her pensive green gaze raked his long lean body as he hunched by the fire eating his watery soup with relish.

He felt the touch of her eyes and looked up at her with a rueful little smile. "Now Lizzie, the rice is done at least."

She girded herself against that smile and his sweet self-deprecation. Too likable. *Too.* "It's no better than that lady's soup we bought in River Flats. I surely thought *yours* would have some culinary inventiveness. I'm positive I could have figured out how to do that much by myself," she added for good measure.

"I believe you could have," he agreed, "but it's hot and it's nourishing and—" He broke off his paraphrasing her words to the woman in town. "Who's *there?*"

Elizabeth froze. She hadn't heard a sound. Indians, her first thought. Galt coiled himself upright, tensed and waiting. The etiquette of the campfire demanded that he offer hospitality, but no one came forward at his words, and he moved slowly to Elizabeth's side, and knelt beside her.

"It could be anyone," he said in a low voice, his hard gaze scanning the surrounding clearing which was rimmed with trees and bushes. "Settlers on turnaround, miners, Indians . . ."

"Which?" she asked tremulously. Indians! Who had thought of Indians?

"Sioux. Osage. Kansa. Some Cheyenne. They don't make war on the border though. They're traders, and they're damned curious about the white invaders. But they don't attack settlers coming across the river. At best they might want food and maybe our horses."

She let out a hard breath. Indians. Stories of death, raids, and destruction filtered through her brain, read or heard somewhere in the years she had spent in Greenfields.

She listened to the eerie silence. Night sounds as the dark closed in on them and the flickering fire danced in the shadows.

They waited. Galt dished out another helping of soup and made her choke it down, then took some himself. "That's the last of it, Lizzie. We'll try to do better next time." His voice was even and steady, normal-sounding in a situation that was not normal. A visitor who meant no harm would have shown himself already.

215

Elizabeth's nerves tightened unbearably as she strove to maintain the semblance of routine that Galt's attitude conveyed. Her hand shook slightly as she lifted her plate to her lips to sip the steaming liquid.

The sense of threat surrounded them. The anonymity of the oncoming night turned menacing.

A shot rang out behind them. Galt leapt up and wheeled toward the direction of the report.

"Hold up, stranger," said a deadly calm voice behind him.

Galt whirled. Shadows—only shadows. The voice stood beyond the light of the flame. The voice had a gun, and by Galt's estimation, he had a compatriot somewhere in the trees behind them.

"Show yourself," he commanded, tensing his body like a spring to jump, aware of Elizabeth's terror and his own stupidity for dispensing with a weapon.

The shadows moved; Elizabeth gasped, feeling faint. Cox, the dandy, his smooth face triumphant, his edgy eyes searching behind them, moved into the light.

Fourteen

"Welcome to the *real* reckoning," Cox said suavely, motioning for Galt to sit back down again. Galt sat, and Elizabeth looked at him with glimmering eyes.

"Aincha gonna kill 'em?" a rusty voice demanded from behind them. Smoot!

"I'm going mad," Elizabeth muttered. "Where did you say that gun was?"

"Damn to hell, Lizzie; I wasn't going to use it on *you*," Galt whispered. "It's well and truly *buried* . . ."

"Shut up!" Smoot's gun barrel nudged Galt's ear. "We gonna kill 'em?" he demanded again, hopefully.

"Not until we get our money," Cox said, his pale eyes focused on Galt, trying to read what he knew Galt would not tell him. But the stranger was a consummate poker player too. He showed nothing, damn him. "I have a feeling it is not going to be as easy as searching their possessions." Yes, now the stranger reacted with a satirical smile. "Well, it appears to me, stranger, the least you can do is offer us some food before we get down to business."

"We have no business," Galt said calmly, and Elizabeth wondered at his self-possession when she was grappling with hysteria deep inside herself and trying with every ounce of energy not to let it show.

"We kin kill 'em," Smoot interrupted. "We don't need no cooperation. We just need the time to find the money."

"A last resort," Cox said, never moving his eyes from Galt's

217

face. The threat did not even dent the man's composure.

"Make it look like Injuns," Smoot went on, ignoring Cox's words. "I know how to kill like them Injuns." He grasped a handful of Elizabeth's hair. "They'd whack it right off, girl, for the least little reason. I could do a good job of it . . ." His voice tailed off as he perceived Cox's pale eyes glaring at him.

Elizabeth sat like a stone beneath his hot violent hand; a waterfall of images cascaded through her numbed brain, all of them ending with the picture of her body crumpled at Cox's expensively shod feet.

She couldn't let herself give way to the fear that gushed through her veins. She turned her concentration on Galt, damn him, who didn't show a single sign that these masked threats were in the least meaningful. The ultimate bluffer, she thought tensely. Faced with death, he would probably pretend it had all been just another sham.

"Or maybe not," Cox amended thoughtfully, his pale eyes moving to Elizabeth's face and dissecting it with the finesse of a surgeon's knife. "Maybe her—first."

His eyes slid to Galt, who stared right back and shrugged.

"She ain't worth all them dollars?" Smoot demanded in disbelief.

"Not to me," Galt said, and Elizabeth swore she would shoot him for the equanimity in his tone as he answered the question.

"Why you been hauling her all over God's creation?"

"I told you; she's going to Leavenworth, and after, I'm done with her."

"I don't believe 'em," Smoot said definitively, waving his gun.

Cox hesitated. "I want the money; I don't care about the woman."

"You ain't gonna get the money," Smoot said with maddening surety, seemingly unaware of Cox's fluctuating emotion.

"He's right," Galt interpolated, still in that calm no-nonsense voice that showed no emotion whatsoever.

"You're crazy." This from Cox. "We'll kill you and take everything."

"Help yourself," Galt said provokingly.

Elizabeth could not even turn her head to look at him. How could he risk aggravating Cox's already unstable state of mind? What kind of man would follow them all these miles, across a treacherous river, to steal back God knew how much or little money? Fear clutched at her again. It must have been a damned *lot* of money, she thought in anguish, if it had the potential to cost them their lives.

"There isn't much here," Galt went on. "Got a couple of horses, some beans, some worn-out saddles, and worn-down oxen. Wagon isn't anything much. There's a dresser inside, a rocker, some goods. Pots. You're welcome to 'em. I didn't rightly expect to be killed for a ten-pound sack of flour, but that's the chance you take."

Cox choked, and Smoot said, "Ain't he funny. Like he don't have all that money somewheres around here."

"There's about ten pounds of bacon strapped onto the other side of the wagon," Galt said helpfully. "There's no soup left, but you're welcome to a couple of rashers of bacon. Lizzie'll be glad to fry 'em up for you."

Elizabeth sent him a murderous look and Cox said, "That's a good idea; let's carve up some of that bacon. Let the girl do it. Get up, lady. Smoot, you shoot if she makes a wrong move."

"Good ideas you have," Elizabeth whispered savagely as she got to her feet. Galt quirked his eyebrows at her. "Just get the man his bacon, Lizzie. A man can't think straight on an empty stomach."

"This isn't funny," she hissed, stepping over him and resisting the urge to kick him.

She stepped in front of Smoot's itchy gun, and shot a covert look at Cox. Cox wanted Galt. Hate radiated out of his entire body. He wanted Galt and he wanted the money, and he couldn't decide if killing one was worth the other. He was hoping Smoot would find it somehow. He was praying, she thought, that Galt had hidden it in some unlikely place like a side of bacon.

Good lord. She walked forward gingerly, with Smoot following, his rusty cracked voice in her ear like an unpleasant refrain. "You're a beauty, you know it. Cox can't appreciate no

219

female beauty when he's het up about his gamblin'. I got a knife you kin use, lady. Don't cut much good, but it'll get through that fat and we'll take a look at whatcha got in there."

He nudged her arm and pushed a small ebony-handled knife at her. "You ain't gettin' much else, lady, so start cuttin'."

Elizabeth clamped down on her quaking nerves and took the knife from him. "There's hardly any light," she said shakily.

"We'll do it by feel, lady. You just make the cuts, and I'll do the talkin' and the lookin'." He settled himself next to her, his weapon perceptibly by her ribcage, and she crammed the knife into the meat and began slicing.

The damn blade was dull and it took a little effort to move it through the thick fatty meat of the remaining haunch. Like cutting into flesh, she thought, and amazingly, her nerves steadied and calmed and something focused inside of her. She had a weapon in her hand, and she could use it against Smoot, *if* she were steady and cool and remembered what she had been taught about using a knife.

She felt Smoot's wiry-muscled arm snake over her shoulder and his thick fingers feeling through the cuts she had made. "Good. Keep going, lady. That's fine."

Her heartbeat slowed perceptibly as Smoot removed his arm. She took a deep breath and jammed the knife into another part of the meat. Just practicing, she thought mordantly. His skin would cut just like that. She had only to find the right time and the right angle, and . . .

She had to do it quickly. *She had to do it.*

"Hold it, lady!" Smoot hissed over her shoulder. She felt his arm, heavy, odiferous, dangerous, his fingers sliding into the slashed meat in a way that almost made her retch to think of her ever eating it again.

"Go on."

His words sent a chill down her back; his frustration was becoming very evident. He had expected to find something, expected that Cox had been shrewder than he in guessing a possible hiding place. And there was nothing, and his patience was fast diminishing.

There wasn't much left of the haunch of bacon. She hesitated a moment before attacking the next section, which she determined by feeling the greasy surface.

"*Lady* . . ." His ragged whisper terrified her.

"Yes—I . . ." She didn't even think; she pivoted on her right foot, pushed with her left, and lunged at him. The knife plunged into his midriff easily. Too easily. He made a startled sound and lifted his gun arm. And tried to wrench the knife from her hand. And slid, slowly, to the ground, his blood seeping out of the wound in a hot wet clot all over her hand.

Her fingers relinquished the hilt stiffly as he crumpled at her feet, and she stifled a scream. No time for the vapors, for hysteria. Only time to grasp the knife and pull it from his body, and to feel for the gun which was not in his hand, damn it, damn it; somewhere on the ground where she could not take the time to grope for it.

She had only the knife and whatever residual skill she could call up to use it to save Galt. And she didn't think twice about whether she wanted to save Galt over trying to succor the limp body of Smoot slowly bleeding his life away at her feet. He would not have given her even the mercy of a thought had he been the successful attacker.

She wiped the blade on her skirt unheedingly, and biting her lips, she crept forward slowly, inch by inch, around the corner of the wagon to where she could just see the firelight, and the shadows beyond it.

And heard Cox's bellow: "*Smoot!*"

Oh God, she had no time to plan. Any moment, Cox might come looking for his partner. She fingered the blade of the knife. Cox had turned as he called out, and now was in her direct line of vision; she could just see Galt, still hunkered down by the fire, which Cox with his innate acumen kept between them. She had to get the gun out of Cox's hand. Simple.

She angled her body slightly to get a better view of his hand. His steady steady hair-trigger hand. He looked itchy, prickly. Galt was obviously rattling off his impervious answers and Cox was getting very nervous. He wasn't a killer, she decided. He was an obsessive gambler who went after his prey no matter how much or little he had lost. What was it about Galt that had compelled him to follow them all this way?

She watched him for a long moment, positioning the knife, aiming, thrusting, testing her wrist and the way it would snap the knife when she released it.

She listened a moment; the voices were distant, garbled. Cox spoke and Galt refuted in that unflappable way of his, and it didn't matter what they were saying. She could see Cox getting hotter and hotter with suppressed anger. Obsessive. Superstitious. She remembered she had thought those very things about him from the moment they had walked into that hotel room.

He had come after them because of *her,* she thought with a sinking feeling. She had been the bad luck, the omen, the reason why he'd lost, and now Cox would take it out on Galt whatever the outcome.

She held the knife up in front of her eyes, lining it up with Cox's rock-hard grip on his gun, poising her fingers at the point of the blade. She raised her arm and lowered it slowly, slowly, so she could pull back if the moment weren't right. And slowly until Cox was in her sight, and slowly—she released the blade with a quick explosive movement, and watched as it sailed unerringly from her hand through the air.

And into Cox's arm just above his wrist, knocking the gun out of his hand, startling him so that he lost his balance. As he fell, Galt leaped and vaulted over the campfire onto his prone body, rendering him unconscious with one well-placed punch.

She came into the clearing as he lifted himself off Cox's body. He turned and smiled. "Hello Lizzie," he said lightly. "I knew you'd come and rescue me."

"He's not dead," Galt said as he bound up Smoot's gaping wound. Elizabeth bent over Smoot's body to retrieve the sheath in which Smoot had kept the knife.

"I will keep this," she said, tucking it and the knife into her boot. "And what do you plan to do with him?"

"We're going to send him on his way, Lizzie, nice and tidily trussed up on his horse, with his friend tied up behind him. And you better hope they make it to Drover's Landing or else Smoot is done for."

"I don't care," she said callously. "The only person whose

death I didn't want on my conscience was yours."

"So nice of you to say so," he said, lifting Smoot's bound body over his shoulder and hauling him back into the clearing where he had already tied and saddled Cox. He slung Smoot's unconscious form over the cantle, and began winding him into an intricate set of knots that were subsequently attached to Cox's bonds.

Then he led their mount out of the clearing, pointed it north, slapped its rump, and sent it on its way.

She came up behind him, an eerie shadow that almost matched his height by firelight. He held out his arm and pulled her close to him. "That was a very knowledgeable throw, Lizzie."

"Yes it was," she said, wriggling away from him. "Can we bury that bacon, do you think? I could never eat another slice of it."

"You sure you want to?"

"Why, *is* the money hidden there?" she wondered.

"Now, Lizzie. Actually, that was an interesting assumption on his part—an army kind of assumption. Maybe from someone involved in undercover work."

"The money isn't there," Elizabeth said, waiting for his confirmation or denial, and knowing he wouldn't tell her. "Where *is* the money, Galt?"

"Now, Lizzie . . . let's bury the bacon instead of burying me with useless questions you know I'm not going to answer."

"It *was* a lot of money, wasn't it?" she demanded as they unstrapped the side of bacon from the wagon and lowered it into the shallow hole she had dug.

"The money's safe, Lizzie. And the wolves will dig up the meat, so it won't go to waste," he added as they tamped down the dirt.

"And I've got the knife," she put in, not a little smugly.

"Someone has to protect me," he agreed silkily.

"Since your legendary gun is still a legend," Elizabeth finished neatly. "Trust me, Galt."

The moment the words were out, she felt the tension shift between them. Galt held our his hand to her—again. "*Can* I, Lizzie?"

"*Can I*, Galt?" she asked in turn, touching his hand lightly with her fingers and removing them just as quickly. She turned away abruptly and walked back to the campfire. Dangerous moment, she thought, sinking down beside the dying embers. A moment she could almost have capitulated to him, damn him. She felt exhausted in all ways. A pair of would-be murderers *and* Galt were too much to deal with in one day.

She reached out to touch the coffeepot. It was cold. She felt cold, cold and drained. Empty. She lifted the soup pot and turned it over to drain. Empty.

Endless space around her, dark, menacing. And empty. She pushed a little mound of dirt onto the embers with her foot, got up slowly, and turned to the wagon, picking her way toward it in the dark.

And Galt within, leaving her to find her own way. But after all, what could he have said after her damning question when everything that had happened so far proved nothing other than he was a far different person than the one who had abducted her? His actions and his treatment of her still explained nothing, still mystified and tantalized her to the edge of frustration.

She climbed over the wagon gate by feel and crawled over to the mattress. His presence was palpable, but when she touched the bedding, she was surprised to find that he had sprawled out on the farther side of the mattress. Trust? A test? She arranged herself in a sitting position on the edge of the mattress, her knees drawn up against her chest.

She felt too unsettled to try to sleep. Her arms, wound in repose around her knees, shook just a little. Her hand could still feel the heft of the knife; her mind felt the thrust of wielding it.

And her body now felt the aftershock of having actually wounded a man. Or possibly killed him.

"You didn't kill him," Galt said quietly, sensing what she was thinking.

"So you said." He could have lied, she thought, to reassure her. But why should he? He knew nothing would reassure her except to know the real reason why he was on this fruitless search. His ardor to go on had not abated that she could tell. His frenzy had diminished somewhat, but he was still adamant about pursuing his course, and that was inexplicable when, at

Affix
stamp
here

ZEBRA HOME SUBSCRIPTION SERVICES, INC.
P.O. BOX 5214
120 BRIGHTON ROAD
CLIFTON, NEW JERSEY 07015-5214

Get a Free
Zebra
Historical
Romance

a $3.95
value

——— FREE ———
B O O K C E R T I F I C A T E

ZEBRA HOME SUBSCRIPTION SERVICE, INC.

YES! Please start my subscription to Zebra Historical Romances and send me my free Zebra Novel along with my first month's Romances. I understand that I may preview these four new Zebra Historical Romances Free for 10 days. If I'm not satisfied with them I may return the four books within 10 days and owe nothing. Otherwise I will pay just $3.50 each; a total of $14.00 (a $15.80 value—I save $1.80). Then each month I will receive the 4 newest titles as soon as they come off the press for the same 10 day Free preview and low price. I may return any shipment and I may cancel this arrangement at any time. There is no minimum number of books to buy and there are no shipping, handling or postage charges. Regardless of what I do, the FREE book is mine to keep.

Name _____
　　　　　　　　　　　(Please Print)

Address _____ Apt. # _____

City _____ State _____ Zip _____

Telephone ( ) _____

Signature _____
　　　　　(if under 18, parent or guardian must sign)

Terms and offer subject to change without notice.

11-88

MAIL IN THE COUPON
BELOW TODAY

GET FREE GIFT

To get your Free ZEBRA HISTORICAL ROMANCE fill out the coupon below and send it in today. As soon as we receive the coupon, we'll send your first month's books to preview Free for 10 days along with your FREE NOVEL.

ACCEPT YOUR FREE GIFT
AND EXPERIENCE MORE OF
THE PASSION AND ADVENTURE
YOU LIKE IN A
HISTORICAL ROMANCE

Zebra Romances are the finest novels of their kind and are written with the adult woman in mind. All of our books are written by authors who really know how to weave tales of romantic adventure in the historical settings you love.

Because our readers tell us these books sell out very fast in the stores, Zebra has made arrangements for you to receive at home the four newest titles published each month. You'll never miss a title and home delivery is so convenient. With your first shipment we'll even send you a FREE Zebra Historical Romance as our gift just for trying our home subscription service. No obligation.

BIG SAVINGS
AND FREE HOME DELIVERY

Each month, the Zebra Home Subscription Service will send you the four newest titles as soon as they are published. (We ship these books to our subscribers even before we send them to the stores.) You may preview them *Free* for 10 days. If you like them as much as we think you will, you'll pay just *$3.50 each and save $1.80 each month off the cover price. AND you'll also get FREE HOME DELIVERY.* There is never a charge for shipping, handling or postage and there is no minimum you must buy. If you decide not to keep any shipment, simply return it within 10 days, no questions asked, and owe nothing.

Zebra Historical Romances
Make This Special Offer…

IF YOU ENJOYED
READING THIS BOOK,
WE'LL SEND YOU
ANOTHER ONE

FREE

a $3.95 value

No Obligation!

—Zebra Historical Romances
Burn With The Fire Of History—

Rim City, he could just board a train and disappear into the wilderness.

"Obviously nothing will prevent you from your fool's quest," she added snippily.

"Nothing," he concurred.

"I still don't understand it."

"You understand everything, Lizzie. I'm only afraid that now you're going to use that knife on me while I'm sleeping."

"I'm too tired tonight," she retorted. "I wouldn't have the strength to push it in."

"But would you, Lizzie? In other circumstances—have the strength . . . ?" He pushed himself upright as he spoke, and leaned toward her.

"We do what we must," she said insolently, barreling into the situation with a breathtaking lack of consideration, aware he was close and coming still closer. She caught her breath. She had said it, and he was most definitely going to accept the provocation.

"Indeed we do," he agreed softly, and he was right beside her, tangible, touchable. She sensed him leaning over her, his mouth coming closer and closer. The note in his voice changed as he murmured, "You *never* disappoint me," before his lips touched hers, testing gently as first in spite of their harsh words, savoring the mouth that issued such brazen taunts. Hers. *Her.*

She was overwrought, she thought bemusedly, moving into his arms as though he drew her there by his sheer will. He wanted her there, and she came, to be enfolded by his warmth and his desire, and perhaps, she thought in the brief moment she could stand outside herself and assess her own response, she wanted it too.

Why, the nervy little inner voice demanded as she opened her mouth to him, wound her arms around him, let herself feel his ardor and arousal. You hate losing control, you hate being at his mercy. Or did she? *Did* she? She was willingly in his arms now, and she knew the consequences of that. Oh yes, the repercussions . . .

He sensed her uncertainly. "Lizzie?"

"You're crazy," she whispered.

"You keep telling me. But this is not crazy." His mouth

225

dominated hers again, devouring every soft edge, seeking deeply, taking her once more by storm. This is not crazy. A seduction by his mouth, an assault on her senses solely with his lips and tongue, his hands never touching her, never moving downward from the expanse of her shoulders. Moving upward instead, to her neck, to her face, to fit his mouth even more tightly against hers, to cradle her head and caress the length of her hair until she was utterly dazzled with the taste and texture and scent of him and all she could do was hold on to him.

She couldn't envision anything more sensual than the way his hands played in her hair, grasping it, stroking it, shaping it against her head and face, exciting her, enthralling her.

It was not enough. The words beat like a drum in her heart. Not enough, not enough. Not nearly enough. Her body was an entity apart from her mind crying out feverishly for something more. She writhed against his hard body provocatively, hoping to beguile his hands downward. Or his mouth.

More. Her body arched upward demandingly. Her breasts tingled with the imagined sensation of his touching them. He could just unbutton . . . she could unbutton . . . he could just slide his hand downward . . . her imagination heated up with images of what he could and could not do, what she was frantic to have him do.

And still he made love to her mouth only, in the dark hot passion-scented confines of the wagon that felt as if they would burst with the outward force of the desire he aroused in her.

Her need was becoming almost unbearable. Her body shuddered with it as her hands shakily began the hesitant removal of one impediment, hoping to entice his hands to her provocative taut nipples. God, should she, if she didn't . . . how would he know . . . but he knew; he relished every tantalizing movement of her body as she made her subtle demand.

He knew she could feel his response to her titillating invitation. He could barely restrain himself from taking what she offered, but he held back, just another moment, and another, to excite her beyond endurance, to ravish her tongue once again, to push himself to the very limit to make her mindless with desire for him, totally abandoned to him; oh, he wanted it, he wanted her just like that, with his mouth and tongue and hands, and she was almost at that point.

Her shoulders moved, thrusting off her mended under-garment, baring her straining breasts with their luscious nipples, brushing their exciting tautness against his chest, branding their pebble-hard heat into his skin as she tore away his shirt in her passionate frenzy.

She tore her mouth away from him in agitation. "Touch me, Galt."

His lips hovered over hers. His tongue licked her lower lip. "Not yet, Lizzie." He took the soft curve of her underlip between his teeth and tugged at it. "Soon."

"Now," she breathed, reaching for his lips with a little thrusting movement of her tongue.

"We can wait."

"I *can't*," she cried, rising to her knees so that he had to release her, he had to move his hands. Her mouth closed over his aggressively, her upper torso writhing heatedly against his hair-roughened chest so he could feel the tumid heat of her hard thrusting nipples.

She felt like some exotic pagan woman offering herself with primitive abandon. Her clothing hung from her waist, and her naked breasts were just a hand's reach away from his touch as his tormenting fingers slid to her shoulders.

He was playing some kind of game with her, teasing her, torturing her by arousing her with his torrid tongue and sultry kisses. Her body wriggled closer, aligning her ripe femininity with the bulging tumescence of his groin. Her hands brushed his naked chest, seeking to provoke him with bold caresses, shamelessly fingering his pebbly male nipples with a brazen-ness that astounded her and brought him to the hard edge of his faltering resolution.

Move your hands, she begged silently, sliding her hands around the tips of his nipples wantonly, assaulting his mouth with her hot seeking tongue, sapping his determination.

"Oh God," he breathed, wrenching away from her marauding mouth and hands. "Lizzie . . ."

"Oh Galt . . ." she whispered tremulously. ". . . like that . . ."

He crushed her mouth this time, wondering in his own frenzy of feeling who was abandoning himself to whom. He wanted to consume her nakedness and devour her passion-swollen nipples. And yet—not just yet . . . not . . . yet . . .

He moved his hands, thinking of the lush soft-hard feeling of her breasts as he had held them the night before.

His kiss deepened voluptuously as he sought the soft undercurve of her yearning breasts. Her arms lifted and slid around his neck in a graceful beckoning motion. His hands moved on either side of her upraised arms to slide under the natural shelf of her breasts until they rested in his hands.

His hands were so hot, so dry. So right to hold her just like that, even though she was tumultuous with longing to feel his fingers caressing their taut tips. She could wait; she could wait for the erotic enveloping feel of his hands on her nipples. The torrid waiting coupled with the increasingly voracious demand of his mouth were as ravishing to her senses as actually having his hands on her.

Molten anticipation flooded every pore of her body. Her mind could almost re-create the feeling, but the re-creation demanded the satisfaction of the reality of it, when the reality was so close. So close, stroking the undersides of her breasts now, coming closer and still closer to the ripe succulent nipples, the exquisite motion of his fingers driving her wild with wanton greed.

Every one of her senses was aware of his moving stroking fingers as they sensuously trailed a path under and around her taut straining nipples over and over until she thought she would scream with frustration. And then his fingers settled on those rigid tips, and she almost screamed with the opulent pleasure that jolted through her and caved her body inward for the faintest moment of total surrender.

His mouth moved off hers the barest fraction. "Tell me, Lizzie," he breathed against her lips. Her answer was a low soughing sound of pure rapture. She had no words; there were none to describe the resonance within her at his touch. It was answer enough. His mouth closed over hers again, feeding on her carnal response, inciting it, intensifying it with the pressure of his knowledgeable fingers.

He knew her—and was still learning about her—with every delicate flex of his fingers against her skin. And she felt, as the honey thick tendrils of pure pleasure poured through her veins, as if her whole body might explode with the ecstasy of it.

And suddenly everything shifted. The rapturous constriction of his fingers was replaced by the lush heat of his mouth on her left breast, and his right hand eased downward to cup her buttocks, and to guide her body softly backward onto the bedding. His free hand worked off her skirt and underclothing, feeling the silken length of her leg and the womanly curve of her naked hip. His hand was like a kiss, trailing all over her body, dropping here and there in a fluttery exploration of some particularly inviting hollow.

She moved sinuously beneath his caress, and the succulent pull of his mouth on her nipple. Oh yes, she thought, or she moaned, as he transferred his ravenous mouth to her right breast.

There didn't have to be anything more than that, she thought, winding her hands into his thick hair and pressing him tighter against her breast. Sensations thickened within her, lush, luxuriant. She remembered them, reached for them, and reached . . . and his mouth moved from her breast, shocking her. She moaned in protest, useless, as his lips nipped the soft skin of her breast and slid wetly, softly, down to her midriff and lower, to the enticing tautness of her belly, and lower.

She felt a wet insistence at the gate of her femininity, grazing it with soft loving flicks, up and down, and then leaving it to slide over the sleek long line of her legs, and back again, to settle finally, decisively, at the juncture of her thighs.

She poised herself instinctively for the first surge of sensation, meeting it, undulating against it with a primitive intuition, urging his exquisite exploration. She lifted herself to meet it eagerly, moving with it, against it, letting the feeling on the edge build within her until rushing waterfalls of sensation cascaded through her the same and different, unquenchable, irresistible, relentless until they broke into a tumultuous convulsion of spiraling pleasure.

He held her until the incandescence ebbed away into a shimmery all-pervading radiance that suffused her body, and totally enslaved her. She had no words, for once. He wanted none. His lips brushed against her hair, her cheek, her shoulder, her breast, as his strong arms cradled her against his taut body. She could feel his heat, and the minuscule tremors of the desire he fought to contain. She felt the powerful seductiveness of his long lean body, she inhaled his scent, and she wondered when he would take his ease.

She touched him hesitantly, her hand trembling still from the force of her culmination, and she heard his sharply indrawn breath as she came in contact with the hot bare skin under his shirt.

What did he want? His body moved against her hand, almost against his will. He was resisting its demand, and she had to define it.

Her fingers stroked the flat of his stomach and his reaction, and its intense urgency, guided her to her ultimate destination. With no fear, in the blanketing darkness, she unfastened his trousers and grasped him in her hand. He responded instinctively, driving his ramrod maleness through the circle of her fingers, once, twice, three times, and then the sensation of her beautiful hands avidly surrounding his hardness brought him to a galvanic climax that came from his very gut.

She did not move her hand at the end. He cradled her closer, wondering what she was feeling, wondering what he could say.

He said nothing. She had fallen asleep beside him almost instantly, and he angled his clothed body toward her protectively until such time, in her sleep, she removed her hand from its precious position.

She awakened with a start, pushing at the blanket that covered her nakedness. Galt slept beside her, his arm folded over her hip, his body nestled against hers. Sometime in the night, he had put himself to rights again, she inferred, and had wrapped her up for warmth. His body was warm, the air was warm, and something had penetrated her pleasure-logged slumber and made her come awake.

She listened for a long moment. She heard nothing untoward, just the horses, and Galt's deep even breathing.

A calm morning, and dawn of their fool's journey to Galt's final reckoning. She shook her head impatiently, and gently moved his arm so she could lean forward and search out her clothing.

She looked at his recumbent body consideringly as she dressed. His face in repose looked younger, the deep carved lines smoothed out in the oblivion of sleep. His cheeks and chin were bristly as a porcupine, and she rubbed her own jaw ruefully, feeling in the light of day the scrapes and rawness from the excitement of the night before. His hair had grown longer too, she thought, and the gray strands were even more noticeable in the early morning light.

She lay down next to him to wriggle on her skirt, and was amused by the monumental differences in their bodies. Wonderful differences that, now she had experienced them, she wondered how she could give up.

If she were honest, she thought, sitting upright now to slide her arms into her shirtsleeves, she would admit that her fascination with Galt was not in a little part due to the raw sensuality between them. With him, she was not hesitant, not now, not scared of consequences. It was another dimension to that all-fired likableness that she felt so wary of. Could she let herself like him? Commit herself to seeing through this— search for Lonita McCreedy—to seeing through whatever plan he had that might or might not include her?

Yet how could she give up the pleasure of the nights? And the verbal duels of the day?

She held Smoot's knife in her hand as she thought this, balancing it, staring at Galt through the angle of the point. She would never use it against him, she thought, and he had always known it. She could wound a Smoot, but she could never find it in her to wield it against Galt. Never. No matter what happened. She believed him—he would never hurt her. She almost thought he liked her as well as she was coming to like him.

More than like him? Too easy; she had been willing to marry Martin Healey and she hadn't even known him a hundredth as well as she now knew Galt. She knew nothing about love, nor did she know whether what she was learning in Galt's arms had any relation to love.

After all, she had loved Martin Healey. No . . . she had planned to use Martin Healey to save herself. So instead Martin saved himself, and saved her the trouble. The thought of what life would have been like had he married her was impossible to consider. How lucky she had been. How lucky she was now. She was overlanding in the company of a man with a quirky humor, strong convictions, and vast experience in pleasing a woman in ways she had never dreamt possible.

How fortunate Edgar had taken Galt's threats seriously. . . .

Nonsense! She couldn't sit here thinking this way. Galt's sensual power over her must be exerting a tremendous pull if she was rationalizing that she had been lucky to have become *his* captive.

It was rather funny, in a way—

Her alert ear caught a faint rustling sound. She eased the knife into its sheath and strapped it around her leg before she slipped her foot into her boot. The other boot had been kicked toward the wagon gate. She crawled to it and swung herself out of the wagon before inserting her foot.

And she listened. Everything seemed the same. The cold mound of dirt that covered last night's campfire. The overturned soup pot. The empty coffeepot. The horses and oxen corraled by a rope ten feet away.

The wind rustling through the trees . . .

The sun beating down, already merciless in its intensity.

Elizabeth picked up the coffeepot, emptied the grounds and the dirt, and buried them.

A couple of miles more to Drover's Landing, she thought as she took the pot to the water barrel to rinse it. She uncorked the barrel, carefully filled the pot, swirled around the water, and dumped it into the bushes. A couple of miles more—it repeated like a refrain in her head. She wondered, as she filled the pot again, what answers she expected to find there. Or what—

A hand clamped over her mouth, a body shoved her against the curve of the barrel. The coffeepot went flying, her warning scream choked in her throat. An inexorable arm wound around her waist, and a superhuman strength lifted her from her feet.

In the space of a moment, her captor disappeared with his prey into the seclusion of the rustling bushes.

Fifteen

For some reason, he was dreaming of a waterfall. The rushing sound of the water was soothing, and he gave himself up to it willingly. It was sensual, mindless. A man could get lost in the sound of it and never return.

There was light beyond his eyes and he ignored it. The echoing water chamber dulled it. He wanted only to live in the peace of this rapturous self-contained repose. And he slept.

But he had a persistent sense suddenly of something missing. The light prodded his eyelids insistently. Outside sounds pervaded his peace: horses, he thought, rumblings—other wagons passing so early in the morning. Was it possible they had crossed over and were on their way at the crack of dawn? And then the tranquilizing sound of the water ... gone. . . .

He jolted awake as he strained to hear the waterfall, and his first conscious thought ripped into words: "*What* waterfall?"

And his empty arms! "*Lizzie!*" he roared as he catapulted himself upright and out of the wagon in one frenzied motion.

A resonating silence filled his ears. And a certain normalcy—but for the details: the trickling flow of water that dripped from the cask; the overturned coffeepot under the bushes. The missing horse.

And no Elizabeth.

Damn her.

He bent down and picked up the cork and inserted it in the water keg. Damn her. Even after last night, she had just seized the advantage and run out. Damn to hell.

He ran his hand over his face, his frustration knotting his stomach. He should have known. He fished up the coffeepot and looked inside, and was surprised to find it had been rinsed out.

Rinsed out and tossed under the bushes?

Why not? All of a piece with Elizabeth, he thought venomously, jerking out the cork again from the water keg to fill it. Even so, he had to tilt the barrel forward to get the water he needed for his coffee. All that water . . . puddled in a draining little pool at his feet.

Water.

He shook his head again. Something about water. He dug around for the coffee tin, and dumped the measured spoonfuls resentfully into the pot. What the damned hell about water?

Who had forgotten to cork the water last night?

He built the fire, his mind thick and sludgy with peripheral thoughts that had nothing to do with Elizabeth's perfidy. And that . . . the twigs caught . . . flamed, and he chunked the pot down on them . . . was not to be thought about before breakfast.

Elizabeth.

Water . . .

Coffee took too damned hell long to boil, he thought, and she had him, damn her, bury the bacon. : . .

Nothing the damned hell to eat, and all the goddamned water drained out; a clean coffeepot under a bush. A missing horse. No Lizzie. No food . . . and mystery water that flirted at the edge of his mind and wouldn't come into focus.

And eager loving Lizzie under the cover of darkness, plotting her wily way to escape. . . .

God.

He poked a foot at the overturned soup pot, and then tipped it over. Even the thought of a dull plate of rice sounded good to him this morning. He retrieved the pot, wiped it out with his shirttail, and emptied two cups of water into it, and a cup of rice, and settled it next to the coffeepot.

These small comforting actions calmed him down considerably, and enabled him to think more sensibly. He needed to finish dressing and washing. He damned well needed a shave—but that was irrelevant because of Lizzie's defection. He needed food, and he needed to tend to his chores with the animals. And by the time he had finished those, the coffee and rice ought to be ready.

He hadn't considered the time either, he thought, as he fed the few remaining dried apples to his stock. But now he was collected, he could see by the sun that it was much later than even he had thought.

He had slept like a damned sack of potatoes, dead enough to the world so that Lizzie could effect her escape and he never knew.

Damn. He tussled open the tin of salt and tossed a palmful into the boiling rice, and a pinch in the coffee.

As he settled down with his battered cup, he had an errant thought: Lizzie had taken nothing.

She had wanted to get out of there goddamned fast, his anger refuted smugly. And Drover's Landing was so close; the opportunity must have seemed irresistible.

He hadn't even searched for her, he thought, and the snide voice within told him it was perfectly obvious how fruitless that would have been. The horse was gone, Lizzie was gone, and there was only one conclusion to draw from that.

Besides, he had heard nothing.

He reached for the boiling coffee and poured some into his cup. Pour. Liquid. Falling liquid—falling water . . .

Water.

Fall.

He tilted the pot and poured the steaming liquid into a little puddle at his feet. Waterfall, he thought. Something about a waterfall. He set the coffeepot down on the fire, and his tortured eyes veered to the water keg. As he sipped the scalding coffee, he kept staring at the water keg as if it would volunteer answers to his questions.

Nothing made sense. He reached for the rice pot, hungry enough to eat it directly from the fire. It was done and it tasted deadly, but it would be filling. He forced himself to eat between swallows of the coffee.

He felt more coherent once he filled his belly. By the

235

position of the sun, he figured it had to be late afternoon. A far-off rumbling of wagon wheels seemed to confirm his deduction—another train of overlanders bound for Drover's Landing.

The thought of wagon wheels struck something familiar. He had heard them this morning. Or had it been morning? *He* had thought it was morning; *he* had surmised it was dawn . . . or in his half-waking state . . . there were dreams, he remembered suddenly. Something calm. Something about . . .

Water . . . fall.

He stared at the empty water keg. He had heard the water draining from the keg. He got up slowly and walked toward the damp patch of ground under the keg. The water had seeped into the soil. It could have been pouring out all night for all he knew. Except—it had been puddled up when he awakened, and the earth had absorbed the seepage very fast. If it had been draining all night, the water would have already been sucked up, he thought, stooping down to feel the quality of the soil. He crumbled a clump of dirt in his fingers. It felt as if it had been overwatered.

He wiped his hand on his leg and went back to sit by the fire. His coffee was cold, and he poured another cup while he considered what the wet patch of dirt meant.

It meant . . . Lizzie deliberately removed the cork and let it flow? And then took off? When she knew they had camped about a mile outside Drover's Landing?

She had washed the coffeepot first, and then . . .

If she had meant to escape him, why the damned hell would she rinse out the goddamned coffeepot . . .

And then toss it under a bush . . .

Waterfall. He remembered that much, and feeling comfortable, unwilling to open his eyes. The sound had been close and echoing, lulling. And then it had stopped, and he had awakened.

So. Lizzie had just gone off and left the water pouring out after she washed the coffeepot. Simple. Explained everything. He had been exhausted, no wonder he had slept so heavily.

Damn her to hell.

He felt muddled. What if she had been washing the pot, and

236

something had happened to her? Not possible. He would have heard something.

She had risen early, cleaned the pot—a gesture, an ironic gesture, that was all—said the hell with it, left the water running, tossed away the pot, and taken advantage of the situation. Period.

Or—she had awakened and dressed, fully intending to prepare breakfast. Cleaned the coffeepot—and something had happened—something that caused her to drop the pot and prevented her from corking the keg. Something that made her steal his horse and disappear without a trace from camp.

Exactly. It made as much sense as theory number one. Maybe it made more sense.

He threw aside his coffee cup and traced his steps back to the wagon. She had been standing at the keg, filling the pot . . . tossed it—threw it—dropped it . . . what would have made her drop it?

Something had startled her. Something that would precipitate flight. *What?*

She had seen something.

Or someone.

Who?

Or the person had—come up behind and scared her—grabbed her . . .

Oh God, *grabbed* her . . . and the pot would have flown out of her hands. . . .

Hell. It made too *much* sense. But *who?*

And then he had another thought: enemies.

And then he knew. Damn to hell, he knew, and he had a damned lot of work ahead of him before he could take up the goddamned chase.

Elizabeth forced her lips into a smug little smile. "Well, Mr. Cox?"

"He'll come looking, never you fear," Cox assured her smoothly from his position by the window which overlooked the rowdy main street of Drover's Landing.

"You're crazy to challenge him," Elizabeth said calmly, but

237

she was mentally gnashing her teeth at the thoroughness with which Cox had bound her to the nearby chair. There was a way of holding her wrists that would have given her some purchase to work her way out of the ropes, but she hadn't been thinking . . . she should have been thinking. But Cox . . . she was utterly astounded by his identity when he had finally revealed himself *after* he had trussed her to the horse.

"He was crazy to challenge me," Cox retorted smoothly. "I'm going to get my money, never you fear. One way or the other, unlucky lady, whatever I have to do to get it."

Elizabeth believed him. There was an odor of desperation about him which was in sharp variance with his calm demeanor. But he had already saved Smoot's life. Smoot now lay in the sick ward of the local country doctor, whose fee Cox had paid by selling the horse on which Galt had sent them to town. He had taken time to do that, in spite of his hunger for the money.

And then he had contained his impatience and waited until dawn to sneak back to camp with the sole specific purpose of luring her away so Galt would follow—and leave the wagon unattended for Cox's marauding intentions.

He was obsessed with the money, and he watched her and the street with equal intensity, waiting, and waiting, and in the end, after several long hours, his patience was ready to snap.

And Elizabeth sensed it, and goaded him. "He just might not be coming," she suggested coyly. "You might be stuck with me instead of money. How would that sit with you?"

"I'd kill you first, lady, and I'd get it anyway, one way or the other," he snarled, and effectively silenced her. He was wary of her now; he had a gun and he waved it at her often for emphasis. He turned back to the window. "I'll give you that he isn't eager, lady, but my guess is, he'll get here."

Elizabeth was torn between taunting him that Galt wouldn't, and assuring him he was probably right. Either way sealed her doom. All she could do was hope Galt had figured it out. But what clues had she left him? A cleaned-out coffeepot that had jolted out of her hands when Cox grabbed her. An uncorked keg emptying its contents into the soil.

Nothing. Literally nothing. And with her luck, Galt would

probably interpret that little in the wrong way. He would probably infer she had left him at the earliest opportunity as she had been threatening to do all along.

Devil damn it! Stupid fool's journey!

She cringed inside as Cox turned toward her with a menacing expression on his face, a man who had finally run out of patience.

It was as if she had disappeared into thin air, Galt thought grimly; no one had seen her along this line of stores and wagons edged up against the plank sidewalks. This was another of those towns where people elected to drop out of sight; likely, they said, she didn't want to be found.

Likely, Galt thought grimly, he was hiding out with her, probably in some seedy hotel. He hadn't the wherewithal to do much more until he could make his fruitless search of the wagon.

He headed toward the National Union Hotel, through a street thronged with overlanders, sharp-looking well-outfitted gentlemen seeking their next victims, curious redmen looking for a trade or a handout, and vacant-eyed children at the skirts of their bewildered mothers who were setting up camp right along the plank boardwalks in the center of town.

There were two hotels, he noted as he strode by, and probably that many more boardinghouses. Drover's Landing was that kind of town—a place with no middle ground. You either traveled on or you stayed, and if you stayed, you stayed for a long time, if not forever.

The desk clerk at the National Union wore a sullen expression that complemented an equally acrimonious tone of voice, informing Galt fifteen minutes later that what went on within the confines of the hotel was none of his business.

"You could not have missed her," Galt prompted, leaning over the scarred registration desk. "About so high, wearing a man's shirt and boots, long skirt. Kind of golden brownish hair. Probably with a gentleman . . ."

"Can't say if I have," the clerk muttered

"Can't . . . or won't?" Galt asked silkily.

The man's sleazy gaze rested on him for one contemptuous moment. "I didn't notice anything, mister." He turned away, but wheeled back sharply at the staccato ring of the desk bell, and Galt's proffering several enticing bills.

"A room for the night," Galt said flatly, laying the money out before the clerk and smoothing the folds with a hypnotic movement of his long fingers, daring the clerk to suggest he was intending anything other than renting a bed-down for the next twenty-four hours.

The clerk took the money, and grudgingly handed over a key with the room number 313 incised on it.

"I'll find it," Galt assured him, and mounted the stairs. The clerk's scornful expression followed him until he disappeared onto the landing. From there a long line of anonymous numbered doors marched down either side of the hallway, seven on each side, with nothing to distinguish whether they were occupied or not.

Damn to hell, Galt swore as he began the long-drawn-out task of listening at each door jamb. Once or twice he knocked. He turned knobs. His obnoxiousness earned him nothing. There was nothing likely on the second level, and no clues at all on the third floor, where he even went so far as to confront several irate "guests" whose assignations he had so brazenly interrupted.

He took the key with him as he left by the front door, staring down the clerk's skeptical expression as he strode out into the late-afternoon sun. Too late. Damned Cox could surely cover his trail this late. And it mightn't be a bad idea to head back to the wagon and head him off that way, he thought, veering toward the second of the two hotels, the River Vista. A homier place, as he discovered, family oriented, and set in the scheme of the town, nearer to the trail and the provisioning stops.

The clerk, too, was more accommodating, and he remembered the lady and the gentleman, the lady looking a might recalcitrant and a little travel-worn at that. They had stayed for several hours in 202 front, but then they had gone out—to eat, he assumed, or make whatever connections the gentleman had planned for the duration of his stay. He never asked questions, he told Galt, but he read faces, and situations.

"Could you allow *me* to 'read' their room?" Galt asked with a touch of irony, and was taken aback at the clerk's acquiescence.

"Well—she didn't look too happy, you know," the man excused himself, and gave Galt the key. "Besides, you don't look like you'd be telling stories on me anyhow, mister. You've got a real concern for that lady. I can see it in your face."

Galt palmed the key exasperatedly and made his way up to the second floor. The room was right at the head of the stairs, and he opened the door with a quick flick of his wrist.

It was empty. But he had expected that. What he hadn't expected was the complete absence of the sense that anyone had ever occupied the room.

There wasn't a trace of Cox or Lizzie, and the only clue that anyone had spent time there was the way the chair had been pulled over by the window from its place around the centered table, and the pulled-back curtain, as if someone had propped up his foot while he had been watching the main street. Just, he supposed, as Cox might have done had he been waiting for him to follow Elizabeth.

He returned the key to the clerk gratefully. "You don't suppose someone might have seen which way they went?"

The clerk considered for a moment. "Maggid might've. He's always hanging out front. Old miner, went so far from civilization that when he got back, he couldn't get enough of it. He's fixture out there, he is. Knows everyone and everything. Geezer with the stogie and the ten-pound beer belly."

Galt found him readily enough, but the crafty look in the man's beady black eyes stopped him for a moment as the man sized him up like a horse trainer ticking off a stallion's points at an auction. Then he nodded, stuck his cigar in his mouth, and pointed to the right. "'E tuck 'er to the trading post, mister. Lots goin' on thereabouts. They barter everything, mister, and I mean everything. Don't matter if yer red, white, orange, or brown. Always somebody there that wants the goods." His sly gaze swooped up to meet Galt's. "Them Injuns especially. They's great ones for the barter and the beggin'. No tellin' what yer man had in mind, but that there lady didn't look none too happy 'bout it. And they been hours gone, to boot."

Galt handed him a couple of dollars—"for a good smoke,

man"—and wheeled with tense determination in the direction of the trading post. He knew he was hours too late—he knew it. And the hell with the wagon and Cox; he could cut the damned thing to ribbons and chop it up, for all he cared. And damn him to hell for doing it. The only thing that mattered was Lizzie; what the goddamned hell could that bastard have done with Lizzie?

His name, they had told her before he took her from the trading post, was *Back from a River*—Heyóta—and he understood no English at all. What he did understand was that he had traded three horses for her to the paleskin who reeked of desperation and anger, and she was his to do with until the winter snows when he had a mind to trade her for the furs that would maintain his people for the succeeding two moons.

He was a formidable-looking man, in his breechclout and feathers, all bronzed and angular with deep-set black eyes that missed nothing in a man's face—or a woman's. The woman was scared, as she had a right to be when this paleface summarily handed her over to a redman for the price of three fleet horses, but nonetheless he tried, by gesture and guttural sounds, to assure her that he meant her no harm.

She had spirit as well, he perceived, by her response to him and the hatred that poured out of her directed at the spineless white man of the lily hands. The color of her hair intrigued him, and the changing moods of her eyes. She was not dressed traditionally either, and he did not know what to make of the fact that lily hands had the stewardship of her and could relinquish ownership with impunity. She was obviously with him under duress, and it pained him that he would have to bind her hands as well.

He did not trust the fire in her; hers was not a biddable personality. She must be mastered—or cornered. But she was also pragmatic enough to accept her fate. She came with him without protestation, and he felt amused at his passing thought that she might deem herself safer with a heathen Sioux than a lily hands of her own kind.

She lifted her chin as he consummated the trade and took

possession of her, and made known his name, Heyóta, by saying it, and pointing to himself. She repeated it, carefully pronouncing the accent, which pleased him and gave him her name in turn—Elizabeth.

He couldn't get his mouth around all the sounds. E—liz. A. Bet. E—liza-bet.

He had more horses, and he led her to his remaining string, pointing to one and looking at her questioningly. She nodded, and it pleased him that she was capable on a horse as she seemed to be capable in many things. Something shone in her eyes, an eagerness, a knowledge, a spirit—he came back to that word for want of something better to describe it. A willingness too to try to communicate. The fear was still there, but it had abated with his gestures of amity.

He had to lift her onto her mount as Lily Hands watched, suffused with some kind of triumph that was hard to define; he was reveling in this humiliation of the woman, and perhaps, Heyóta thought, he even envisioned the woman suffering physical harm at his hands. But the paleface would never know. He, Heyóta, was taking the woman to his hunting camp and Lily Hands would never see her again. He would dress her to walk among the little people, and when there was trust between them, he would allow her some freedom.

But not soon. He sliced a look at her set profile. No, the spirit had settled in her to accept and obey, but never to submit. He respected that. And he felt a quickening in him to learn to know her.

The camp was a half-hour's ride from Drover's Landing, but Elizabeth had no sense of time as their horses paced slowly in a circumlocuitous fashion toward their destination. Heyóta obviously wanted no one trailing them, and he had the patience to take the time to obscure their path. She bit her lower lip edgily; she was in no hurry to reach camp. She couldn't begin to imagine what awaited her there.

When they finally came through a natural stand of trees, she was surprised to find that they had finally arrived, and that this camp was nothing like she envisioned.

243

She faced a line of lodges, seven in all, constructed circularly of long lean saplings tied together and covered with buffalo hide. Each entrance faced east, she surmised, as the sun was slowly waning in the opposite direction, and one of the lodges was slightly larger than the rest.

Heyóta dismounted before the farthest lodge, and helped Elizabeth down. He motioned to the entrance, and she ducked under the opening covering and entered Heyóta's lodge.

It was bigger inside, and the smoke hole was at least ten feet above her. On the floor was a mat woven of cattail stems, and that was overlaid by more buffalo skins. She looked at Heyóta; he motioned her to sit, and he knelt to light the fire, to alleviate the darkness. He said something, pointing at the fire, and she repeated the word obediently as she settled her body as best she could against the crosspieces of the framework. She watched as the flame took and a little spurt of fire danced merrily among the twigs and lightened the small space considerably.

Then Heyóta stood and she was struck by his height and his impassivity. He said other words to her, words that sounded menacing, words that seemed to adjure her to stay where she was. He motioned to her, and she crawled forward as best she could to peer out the opening as he held the skin back for her.

Outside, and seemingly around the whole lodge, stood a contingent of braves, stolid and watchful. She looked up at Heyóta and nodded her understanding; she was not to try to escape while he attended to matters outside his lodge.

She crawled back to the warm space she had vacated and sent him a cautiously defiant look. He nodded, stooped over, and left the lodge, and she was finally alone with her thoughts.

And yet, her first notion was to take action. She immediately began twisting her wrists and working at her bonds. Her eyes focused on the fire and her heartbeat accelerated. Did she have the nerve, the resource in her, to lay her hands so near the flame that it would sear the rope? So near, it could possibly burn her, badly? Was the risk worth it?

She made a sudden movement toward it—and stopped. She had to think. She sank back again onto the buffalo skin. The risk . . . the risk . . . with those towering guardians standing like statues outside the lodge—it wasn't a safe course to take, to try to escape now. At night perhaps, or when Heyóta's suspicions were lulled somewhat, since it was likely he expected her to try something, she thought, just by the way he spoke to her and looked at her before he exited. It seemed more reasonable. At night, he conceivably might release the guard, he might leave her alone. By night, she might be able to work the ropes loose; by night . . .

She wrenched her wrists against the ropes in a fit of desperation. By night—she had the knife, she had the wherewithal to effect her escape if she could only free her hands.

Her eyes skewed toward the fire again. Even that. She would go so far as that. But not yet. Not yet.

She forced herself to relax. There had been nothing in Heyóta's treatment of her to indicate he intended to harm her. She had to give herself time, time to relax, to gather her wits and think clearly and calmly about the course she would take—time to plan and not make any mistakes, and not count on anyone trying to save her.

She was strong; she would save herself.

Heyóta returned a short while later, his arms laden. He carried a wooden bowl in his hands filled with something that emitted an appetizing aroma. Draped over his arms was a length of buckskin, and some black material, and crushed under his arm against his side were a pair of moccasins.

He set everything down carefully and deliberately, then pointed to the bowl and spoke to her.

That was clear; she twisted and lifted her bound hands, and he came forward instantly to cut the rope around her wrists so that she could eat.

And she didn't hesitate. Her willingness to do as he wished had earned her his quick approbation, and no matter how the pottage in the bowl looked, it did smell good, and she was hungry, and she attacked the boiled meat and hackberries with some gusto. He stood by the entrance and watched her with approval. She had a healthy appetite, this woman, and a lively intelligence. The food pleased her, and that pleased him.

And she sensed that. Her mind chanted as she chewed vigorously: stewed meat is stewed meat, berries are berries. She tried very hard to ignore the gamey odor emanating from the meat that was not disguised by the highly spiced liquor surrounding it.

What was enough? The hackberries had a sour taste, and the meat was half gone. She lifted the bowl and sipped the liquid thirstily, then put it down and set it aside with a gesture of finality.

He understood. He picked up the bowl and put it outside the lodge, then handed her the moccasins and materials with a guttural sound and an easily interpreted gesture of his hands.

She nodded, her eyes narrowing, and then audaciously, she motioned to him that he leave her.

She would have sworn his expression hardened, as if he were considering the ramifications beyond her request, that perhaps she was now formulating an escape plan. She could almost see his mind working step by step, his mind a map of possibilities that she might attempt. But she was a woman, after all, and how could she prevail against the might of his warriors, he concluded. Finally he spoke several words, and once again, he stooped to gain access through the doorway, and disappeared.

She walked cautiously to the skin that covered the entrance, and very slowly and slyly moved it aside so she could just get the merest glimpse outside.

He stood there, lofty and inflexible.

She stepped back jerkily and swallowed the sudden tightness in her throat. No prospects there. She wished heartily she could see out the back way, and then she had the sudden realization that she could. She unsheathed the knife strapped inside her boot, and stealthily crept to the opposite side of the lodge. Slowly and with great care she slit the skin that covered the poles, and peeked out.

She could see very little, yet there was enough breadth to the cut for her to make out men—not surrounding Heyóta's lodge, but going about their business in a casual way, and in a deliberate manner that made it obvious they were watching not so casually for any irregularity within or without.

Heyóta's voice shouted something from beyond the skin

walls, and Elizabeth jumped. "No!" she cried involuntarily in a panic, feeling for her boot, and the sheath, nicking herself in her hurry and terror that he would duck into the lodge the very next moment.

But the fear in her negation must have communicated itself to him; he said something else, but he did not appear.

Hurriedly Elizabeth scooped up the materials he had dumped on the floor near the entrance and held them up, first the buckskin, which turned out to be a skirt, and the black length, which was a long rectangle of some kind of cottony material. A covering? To be wrapped around her upper torso? He wanted her to wear these somehow?

She took a deep breath. And where would she hide her weapon? she thought, dismayed, staring at her boots which she must remove to don the moccasins. Devil it, damn it. She started undressing with cold hands that were weighted with fear: boots first. Unhook the sheath—oh God, where could she attach it so that it would not be seen? Drop her skirt over it— just in case Heyóta slipped into the lodge unexpectedly. Unbutton the shirt.

She stared down at her underclothes as she slipped her cold feet into the stiffness of the moccasins. She could . . . her hands reached for the thin material almost before the thought was completed in her head, and she ripped two holes in it side by side, and threaded the sheath belt through them.

Still acting instinctively, she reached for the skirt and thrust it over her head, wriggled herself into it, and smoothed it down over her hips.

There was no sign of the knife, which dangled from its hiding place between her legs, at the point where the material flared out to just barely cover her knees.

She took a deep breath and picked up the black rectangle. Now how to wear this? she wondered, draping it this way and that over her now soiled chemise. She could make no sense of it, and finally she exasperatedly wound it around her midriff and breasts and crossed it over her shoulders and tied it around her neck. She couldn't imagine how she looked, with the primitive skirt and covering and her lacy-edged chemise straps bared over her shoulders.

She jumped as Heyóta entered the lodge suddenly, and she whirled to face him, her hands groping for the back wall for support against the momentary flash of admiration in his dark eyes.

And what next? she wondered, poised, crazy with fear that he would touch her, and worse, that he would discover the secret of her hidden weapon.

He motioned to her to turn around, and it took all her control to do it without revealing the terror that coursed through her. She was hardly safe from him or his warriors now, she thought wildly, as she felt him grasp her wrists again, and the rough scrape of the rope as he began to tie them.

And so much for trusting her. She shook with fear. No, she couldn't give way now—she had to find just enough presence of mind to clench her fists, and hold her hands . . . just slightly . . . oh God, out—he wrenched the damned rope so hard, almost as if he were reading her intention, and the trick that her youngest brother R.B. had taught her, when the two of them used to be tied up by Lucas in the guise of game playing, but in reality as a malicious ruse to keep them away from him for hours.

R.B. had figured it out. A jut of the wrist, a flex of the arm one way or another, and he could get just the smallest purchase to work his way free—admittedly hours of working his way free—but he used to do it, and he showed her how to do it.

She had to control her terror; she had to *think*.

He pulled one final time on the rope, whirled her around, and held her by the shoulders. He said something, a sound that had no malevolence in it that she could tell, and pushed her lightly into a sitting position by the fire, which was now a heap of glowing embers.

He stood over her, talking to her, gesturing, encouraged by her furrowed brow that seemed to want to be able to somehow interpret his words. He made a satisfied sound finally and motioned for her to lie down.

She obeyed, her heart pounding. What if he meant to lie with her? What if all the words had been a preface to . . . he stopped beside her and touched her hair. She pulled back involuntarily, swallowing a scream, and her fear.

He spoke slowly, reassuringly, threading his fingers through the texture of her hair that was so unlike anything he had ever touched before. Then he rose and left her without speaking further, and she cowered against the frame of the lodge and wondered if she would come out of her captivity sane—and whole.

Two days later, Galt stealthily crept into camp by the light of the moon. Two damned endless days fraught with imaginings that were too gruesome to go beyond the merest whiff of thought in his mind, until he had found the tracks and settled the direction, then carefully followed, wiping away every trace as he went, which slowed him down even further.

He knew how to do it, since he had tracked sounds in bushes, and footsteps in mud through the thickest brush and forest; he knew, and he knew what he was dealing with, the desperate little people who were being forced back from their lands every day by the government agents they called Heavy Eyebrows, who coveted their hunting grounds to sell to the settlers who still poured overland into Kansas because the railroad was laying tracks still deeper into the wilderness.

The greed of the government was astounding, and the innocence of the natives appalling. And now they were hampered by their possession of a white woman. His woman. And what they intended to do with her, he could not guess. It was imperative that he find her and that was the only thing he allowed himself to think about.

And now, as he moved with minuscule increments through the forest that shielded their camp, he was wary of how easy it was to approach them. In a way, he would have preferred the difficulty, for it would mean they were aware that she could have been followed and they were hiding her. For all he knew she might be dead from the dearth of warriors attending the hunting lodges. All was silent, except for the eerie stillness that alway worried him.

He ducked into a bush within sight of the line of lodges, always a line because the little ones were always symmetrical, according to their beliefs; never a circle. Easier for him, if it came to that, to scout around without being seen, going from one to the other and back to the haven of the darkness between forays.

And no mercy if he were caught. The little ones were a big people, fearsome, living on the edge of hopelessness, distrustful of the white man, who kept insisting he was doing only what was best for *them*.

And what were they doing to Lizzie? He refused to consider it. Lizzie was alive, untouched, in one of those lodges.

But which? He forced himself to stay hidden while he considered the question. She was a woman, after all, and without a doubt none of the hunters had expected to have to house her. There might be, at most, two of their own women in the party to cook and do for the men. They wouldn't keep Elizabeth with their own women. She would be separated, but still, she could be in any of the lodges.

Damn to hell. It was so silent; there wasn't even the whisper of a breeze to stir the leaves which, miles beyond the river, thinned out into the flat endless prairie. He felt instinct warring with his native caution, impelled with a shot of unfamiliar emotion. It made him want to throw all caution aside; experience reined him in, and forced him to move with the utmost care and forethought.

He would start at the farthest lodge and work his way back toward where he had tethered his mount. Bending low, he moved slowly and deliberately through the bushes that ringed the camp, meticulously aware that every step could have repercussions.

He pulled back abruptly as he spotted movement. A guard— one of the hunters, or the brave who had traded for Lizzie. Damn. Every time he thought of it . . . His eyes narrowed as he plotted out the man's progression from lodge to lodge as though he were checking—what? There was no way to tell if he were making a random verification or if there were a pattern that would give a clue to Lizzie's whereabouts.

The hunter disappeared, and the darkness enshrouded the camp once again, the moonlight bright above, filtering through the trees.

Galt made his move then. Bending low, he sped as sleek as a

250

panther through the bushes to the westerly side of the last lodge in the row, and then hunched over, waiting.

Silence reigned. He pulled out a knife, which he had had the good sense to purchase at the trading post, and slit through the buffalo skin covering with one easy slide of the weapon. He pushed aside the halves and peered in. There was darkness within as well, alleviated some little bit by the glowing embers in the campfire in the center of the lodge. Shadows populated the interior. There could have been five people lying on the floor asleep—or none.

He waited, his eyes becoming slowly adjusted to the dim light. And then suddenly, Elizabeth's sharp whisper came at him. "Who's there?"

A dark mound struggled upright, and then he could see her, bound in black, her arms behind her at an awkward angle, her hair knotted and tangled, pushed out of her face for convenience. "Who's there?"

His skin prickled at the tone of that whisper. He pushed aside the curtain of the slashed wall and slipped inside.

"Devil it," Elizabeth growled, "what the hell are *you* doing here? I was doing perfectly well by myself."

Sixteen

"Delightful to find you all in one piece," Galt returned lightly, not fazed one bit by her ungracious welcome. He knelt beside her, and began cutting away at her bonds which she had already worked appreciably loose.

"So you didn't need to come rushing in here like some hero to rescue *me*," Elizabeth hissed resentfully, twisting her wrists impatiently as he slashed through the rope. "I would have been out of here in an hour, and now—who knows?" She rubbed her raw wrists, wincing with pain.

"Now you may have to rescue *me*," Galt whispered back, tucking his knife away. "Come on, Lizzie. There *is* someone patrolling out there, and we have no time at all for these pleasantries."

She got up hurriedly, and he was taken aback by the sight of her standing with her buckskin skirt, black-wrapped bosom, and her legs—her legs were painted yellow.

"Galt—!" Her pleading whisper jolted him into the present. He pulled aside the gashed buffalo skin.

A sound behind them—a roar: *"Hauh!!!"*—as Heyóta strode into the lodge, his face like carved stone, two of the little ones' hunters behind him. He pointed at Galt. *"Nika-shah!"*

Galt froze, his hand on Elizabeth's arm. "He says, white man," he mouthed in an undertone, barely moving his lips

Elizabeth fastened her eyes on Heyóta, forcing herself not to show the horror that wrapped itself around her like the night.

Heyóta's braves disarmed Galt, and swiftly bound his arms

252

behind him and pushed him onto the floor. He fell heavily and Elizabeth did not dare look at him. The two hunters left them alone, exiting the lodge with minimal movement and without a word.

Heyóta spoke, and his words were filled with fury. He was unconscionably angry with this woman he had named in his mind Spirited Eyes. She reeked of fear now, but still she opposed him; she did not try to run away or escape her punishment, and he did not know if she knew this man. But she must. There could be no other reason for his presence in this place.

His words grew harsher, and he could see she understood the import if not the sense of them; his fury communicated itself well to her, and he was satisfied that he fed her fear. She would respect him more now, and she would not try to repeat this folly.

He grasped her arm and jerked her toward him. More words; he could not help the words, and it was not something he liked in himself. He twisted her around and grasped her arms to tie her up once again, and pushed her to the floor in much the same fashion as his braves had done Galt.

And then his glittering eyes fell on the white man, and the jolt of feeling he perceived emanating from Spirited Eyes almost devastated him.

His anger intensified as he pondered whether to separate them tonight. He decided against doing so; he would give them the remainder of the night to talk as an act of mercy before he saw this meddling white man to his justly deserved death.

"Well, now look what you've brought me to," Galt said, rolling onto his back and levering himself up to a sitting position clumsily.

Elizabeth, who had been staring at the curtain entry fixedly after Heyóta left, turned to look at him and choked. "Me? *Me?* And who had the stupidity to walk right into the situation without one moment's thought that maybe, just maybe I might be able to get out of it myself?"

"I reckon that was me," Galt drawled, "but I didn't seem to

253

see you making progress here, Lizzie. You can't fault me for that mistake, now can you?"

"Well it *was* a mistake," she told him roundly. "I would have gotten away tonight perfectly well without your help."

"I sincerely apologize then for botching up your well-laid plans, Lizzie; I just can't think why I came haring after you when I know you have the ability to take care of yourself."

She ignored the tone in his voice. "Exactly."

"Especially against bounders like Cox."

"He caught me by surprise," she said defensively.

"And traded you for three lousy horses."

"I was assured that was a handsome price."

"From a buck who would as soon trade you off again as bed you, and he probably will," Galt muttered.

"He has feelings about me."

"Well, I told you. So he'll bed you first and *then* trade you off. No difference."

"Somehow it sounds vaguely familiar," Elizabeth said tartly.

"Lizzie, there is a damned difference."

"I'm waiting to hear it."

"I think you damned know it, woman."

"And I think you have a damned lot of explaining to do." She glared at him across the dimming light between them. What a damned coil; and what a place to prise confessions out of him, when neither of them knew if they would survive the night. She wrenched her roped wrists futilely.

"Lizzie—" The note in his voice stopped her frenzied movements.

"Yes, Galt?"

"We have to get out of here tonight."

"I *know*," she hissed through gritted teeth, her frustration mounting. For the first time, she felt real fear and not for herself. Galt was the one in danger, much more than she. They would kill Galt without a moment's hesitation, unless they felt they could use him—damn him for interfering! Her fury escalated in concert with her desperation. If only he hadn't come . . . if only he had trusted her . . . if only and if only . . .

And if they managed to get away . . . then what? She knew

what: he would continue his endless mindless pursuit of Lonita McCreedy and he wouldn't give her one good damned reason why he wouldn't give it up.

She stopped her furious manipulating of her ropes suddenly. They, the two of them, were on the the edge of some kind of reckoning. She had a weapon, and only Galt knew the truth. If she were going to die, or he—or even if they engineered an escape, she could not continue further with him without knowing his real motives.

She looked up at him with narrowed eyes, and was interested to see he was watching her with the same intensity reflected in his jetty gaze.

"What do you want to know?" he asked curiously, resignation edging his tone.

"Maybe *you* want to know what *I* know," she retorted, angered that he had divined her thoughts, and that the nature of his question cleverly put limits on his answers.

"And what is that, Lizzie?" he asked gently, sensing her roiling vexation.

"I have the knife," she said quietly, tamping down on her rising temper.

"You—have the knife," he breathed reverently. "Lizzie, you are a wonder. *Where?*"

"We talk."

"Damn, Lizzie, we don't have time."

"*I* have time," she said suggestively, and was rewarded by his exasperated scowl.

"God . . . where do I start?"

"Start with this senseless chase after Lonita . . . and me . . ."

"Can't I be getting us free while I'm talking, Lizzie?"

"Can I trust you to tell everything?"

"Even if there are things *you'd* rather not know?"

"Me? Absolutely. Start talking. I attached the thing under my skirt."

"Jesus. All right. Wait. I'm going to move over, and you lie down on your side against the wall, and I'll . . ."

"You look like a snake," she commented, watching his unwieldy efforts to slide over to her that were fraught with his

255

frustration and urgency. "I think you *are* a snake, Galt Saunders. Start talking."

"Damn to hell," he grunted as he slithered his body backward against hers, his head toward her feet. "Can you manage to slide your skirt up a little?"

"I'll try."

"I'll work the front . . . just . . ." He wriggled his body again to align his body more accurately against hers, his hands grasping the skirt and pushing it upward in concert with his movement. "Better. Damn, it . . . takes so damned . . . long . . ."

"I'm listening . . ." She reacted involuntarily as his seeking hands brushed her uncovered knees. She knew he could feel the steel of the blade against his back, and she moved her body in opposition to his so that he could maneuver his hands as easily as possible once they came in contact with the sheath.

"Damn to hell, Lizzie . . ." He moved again, cursing his limited capacity to reach and grasp. The muscles in his arms were killing him from the exertion and the awkward angle. "All right . . . Buck and I were mining lead . . . and he was extracting the silver. Partners. No one . . . knew . . ." He pulled at the sheath, cursing that she had buckled it so tightly to her undergarments. "No one suspected . . . that far from St. Joe—but—Buck knew; he forty-nined before he settled in . . . Missouri . . . Lizzie, I have to either pull this damned thing out or just get the knife, and you buckled the damned thing *in*."

"Do what you want; just get *on* with it," she hissed.

"We were storing up the silver . . . to get a reading on what kind of profit we could expect . . ." He pulled on the leather sheath and rolled forward to stretch the material to which it was fastened, pulling with as much strength as he could muster. Pulling—one more roll and he would tumble into the embers of the fire. . . . He pulled on the sheath and worked it upward as if it were a pulley, and finally the material gave with a satisfying hiss of a tear and came free in his hands.

"Lizzie!"

"Yes . . ." She rolled forward until she touched the sheath. "Wait . . . wait . . ." Her hands, her body squirmed forward

256

until she could grasp the handle and feel the little buckle that held it in place. "Devil it . . . all right, I've got the thing now; I just have to get it out. You talk."

"She knew about it, somehow. She had a lover, Lizzie, and it wasn't me."

"That's hard to swallow."

"You think about it. Just why do you suppose Martin Healey left you at the altar? Hell, Lizzie, he had been carrying on with Lonita for months before he knew you were coming. He didn't have a choice about it when you agreed to marry him. He did ask you."

"Yes, he did," she confirmed stonily as she picked at the buckle and the ache in her wrists increased with every revelation. It weighted her down, his telling her this now; futility moved her fingers, and nothing more.

"And he was bound to honor his commitment to you, damn him. So he went, and my feeling is, Lonita had found the silver by then, and he was on his way to stake out a hideout for them."

"And you could have told all this at the trial, and saved us all a damned lot of trouble," she muttered through clenched teeth as she missed one chance to unhook the buckle.

"Who would have believed it, with Martin gone all that time and Lonita starting to play the devoted wife; please, Lizzie. That's about when she started on me. And the sheriff."

"*What?*"

"I think once she got word from Martin of his whereabouts, she started planning to kill Buck and make off with the goods. I expect she figured to pin it on me, but she lured the sheriff into it. I don't know how, but he was a fairly frequent visitor at the ranch while Buck and I were doing the extraction, and I figure she had to have had him on her side by then. Damn it, Lizzie, what the hell are you doing back there?"

She pinched his wrist. "*Keep talking.*" She constricted her fingers around the haft of the knife and tugged at it, just to do something to relieve her feelings. It jammed against the little strap. She pulled again, testing, wondering if she could stretch the belt just the littlest bit to give her purchase to manipulate it more easily at the awkward angle at which she worked.

257

"She set it up," Galt went on, his voice getting hoarse from edginess and desperation. "Edgar happened to be there real nice and handy. One minute Buck was arguing with me about some missing goods, the next he'd drawn his gun and Lonita pressed hers on me. And then, bam, he was gone. And Edgar damned walked in the door. And you know the rest."

"No, I don't," she grunted, pulling at the little strap, damn little strap that she could hardly feel with her fingers, but it was coming now, coming, easing out of the buckle right on her fingertips practically, and if she didn't lose concentration, or let her anger interfere with her determination, she would have it, have it—she pulled at it delicately, finely, almost losing her spider web hold on it—it was coming, on the tips of her fingers, and finally, finally, it was out, and she let out her breath.

"Lizzie?"

"I have it. Just a second and I'll . . ."

". . . let me . . ."

"No . . . I—have it now; hold still, I'm going to start cutting through. And you can tell me why you think Lonita is headed toward Rim City." She felt for his bonds, and inserted the knife upside down, by feel, between his wrists.

"Lizzie!"

"I can do it. *Talk.*" She moved the blade in a sawing motion against the rope, cursing Heyóta, cursing Galt in her mind, blaspheming the circumstances that had brought her to this. And she could slice his wrists open right now as easily as she worked the blade against the rope. And she wondered if she didn't just feel like doing that.

And, devil damn it, it was damned slow work. "*Talk!*" she commanded again, poising the blade, moving her wrists in short staccato bursts of energy that totally enervated her.

"She talked . . ." he said slowly, feeling but one strand of the hemp give. "Lonita talked about Rim City. She wanted Buck to take her there, and he was in the middle of the processing. He found some new way to do it, and he couldn't or he wouldn't go. He didn't give a damn. Lonita was right: she was second to the lure of the metal, and I was around the damned ranch house more damned often than I should have been. And I expect that's why she got those ideas."

258

"And we'll never know if you gave them to her or they just came to her right out of thin air," Elizabeth interpolated caustically. "Fine."

"Hell, Lizzie . . ."

"I'm cutting; keep talking."

"A man has a hell of a lot of time to think in jail, Lizzie, and the way I figured it is Lonita had her eye on the goods. She got Martin out of the way so she could get Buck murdered, and frame someone else for it. Then she planned to join Martin and hole up till her pigeon got sent up before she returned for the stake. I think she picked me because she wanted my share, and I'm thinking she got Edgar to do it by either promising him a share or her body, and I wouldn't care to take a guess which."

"And then I got in the way," Elizabeth prompted, her voice dangerously soft, the edge of the knife deceptively close to his life's blood.

"Maybe you did, maybe you didn't," he said noncommittally.

"I'd love to know *which* maybe," she said, and she ceased cutting.

"Maybe both," he muttered. "Damn it, Lizzie. Don't stop!"

"Pull your wrists."

He pulled, and again, flexing his muscles and wrenching then with all his strength, just enough. Just enough now. Another moment . . . his skin felt raw, he pulled—and the rope loosened and he roughly pushed the confining coils from his hands.

He rotated his body, and grasped the knife from her. "No nonsense now, Lizzie; we've got to get out of here." He sawed away at the ropes around her wrists, and she was free in a hundredth of the time it had taken her to release him. "God, Lizzie, why did they paint your legs?"

"The women do it," she shrugged, watching the quick neat movements of his hands as he sliced through the rope at her ankles.

"All right, listen. Break off one of those crosspieces from the framework . . ."

She nodded her understanding before he finished the sentence and had it thrust into the embers before he finished

259

cutting through the rope that bound his ankles.

"All right. It's . . . damn . . . not taking; keep at it." He moved over to the rear wall to the gash he had made in the skin before he entered. He pushed it aside cautiously, the knife at the ready, and peered out into the darkness. "Damn to hell, there's a goddamned army of them out there. Lizzie!"

"It's flaming," she said steadily as the sapling caught. She lifted it and held it to the crosspiece over the entryway. It fired up immediately, and she watched it in fascination for a moment, until she realized the flame was eating its way down the branch she held with alarming rapidity. She threw it against the skin wall, and backed up against Galt. He wrapped his free arm around her as they heard shouting behind them.

"The first Indian through the back way is a dead Indian," he swore, and pushed through the opening. One man stood guard, and as he rushed them, Galt caught him with the knife, and he fell noiselessly.

"Nice diversion, Lizzie," he whispered. "Now *run!*"

They spent the night huddled in the bushes, covered with a blanket that Galt had had the forethought to purchase at the trading post. He held her tightly, waiting for the aftershock of her realizing how narrowly they had escaped death, but her indomitable strength held, and she was only appalled by what she could see of her appearance in the dull light of the dawn of the next day; she had not seen herself in naked daylight, nor realized how fully the buckskin skirt bared her legs and revealed the hideous ocher color they had been painted.

Her face was streaked too, Galt told her, and she seemed to remember it had been done, or perhaps her mind had blanked out the whole thing altogether—she didn't know. She only knew she was desperate to return with him to their wagon, and she welcomed the bit of beef jerky he handed her as he threw the blanket over her shoulders and lifted her onto the horse.

She sagged against him when he swung up behind her, and let him bear her full weight as he carefully guided their mount through the treacherous woody area which had concealed them so completely through the night.

They moved silently as shadows away from the little ones' camp, away from danger and darkness and toward other threats, other shadows.

The sun rose finally, and they found a clear stream where they assuaged their thirst before going on.

"And what do you think Cox did when he couldn't find the money?" she asked him, and Galt shrugged. "He probably tore the wagon up and left. I wouldn't put it past him to destroy what he could, but there's nothing of worth to him except the oxen, and it would take a damned lot of patience that he hasn't got to get them to the trading post for sale."

They continued on, slanting a horizontal course behind the town line as they approached Drover's Landing, circling wide of the branching dirt streets that were starting to make incursions into the surrounding wilderness, and heading south toward the river. And then finally they rounded a narrow bend, and Galt veered right and pulled up abruptly.

He had no doubt in the world that this was where he had left the wagon. But the clearing was empty. There was no sign of wagon, oxen, tamped-down campfire, anything.

"Damn to hell, Lizzie," Galt whispered, awed, "the son of a bitch stole our wagon, and made it away without leaving a trace."

They rode the back track into Drover's Landing. "Don't want those ladies gossiping about you, Lizzie. They don't take kindly to squaw clothes. We'll get a hotel room, and I'll get you some clothes."

"And a bath," Elizabeth put in, too drained to argue with anything he said, and feeling faintly defeated by Cox's bold move to counteract their possible escape.

She huddled in the blanket while Galt made his arrangements, and then spirited her up the back stairs of the River Vista Hotel, whose desk clerk had been so helpful his first visit.

It was not the same room; he whisked her farther on down the second-floor hallway to a large corner room with a large iron-framed bed and sturdy walnut dresser and chifforobe. "Lie down, you look exhausted. I'll arrange for your bath. Go *on*, Lizzie. There's nothing you can do now."

He was so right. There was nothing she could do. She put her head down without the least show of reluctance. She did need to rest. She did need sleep.

And she needed to think. She couldn't even assimilate half of what he had told her in the lodge while she was so frantically working to free his hands. *What* was that story?

Her mind drifted. Her legs. Her dress. He had said, squaw dress? He had been working a mine—lead? And he had said Lonita knew? Martin had been with Lonita and they had plotted to steal Buck's goods and kill him and that was why he hadn't married her. Was that clear? Had he proposed? She was sure . . . but then . . . so of course he had to abscond. And all that silver. Simple. Galt a pawn in the game of a desperately bored adventuress, fine. Just—he was there, so he had admitted. But her? Where did she fit? Maybe? Maybe not? *What?* Her head whirled.

Why *her?* She had gotten in the way.

Maybe, maybe not. He was thinking that Lonita was on her way to meet Martin. They were all going to meet in Rim City. *All*.

What if Martin saw her? She wondered passingly what he might do . . . say hello? Ignore her? Kiss her? Kill her . . .

But—how else would he know where to find Lonita? No, it was a gamble he would see either of them in Rim City. He would have to search every room, every building, every . . . but then he had Lizzie. No. That didn't make sense. Devil it, nothing made sense. He had supposedly told her everything, and it still didn't make sense, except . . . the possibility her presence with him might smoke out Martin Healey. *That* made sense.

And if Martin was *there* . . . it just meant Lonita *might* be there. Or she might not. She might have double-crossed Martin as well.

She drifted off to sleep, a small pinpoint of pain like a dot of light searing her brain: the possibility existed that Galt had used her, and she hadn't just "gotten in the way."

* * *

262

"Lizzie."

She felt him shaking her and she resisted just for a moment before she opened her eyes to see him sitting on the bed beside her.

"Good God, Galt!" She struggled to sit up.

He rubbed his newly shaven cheek and sent her one of those rueful crinkly-eyed smiles. "Cox didn't get our stake, Lizzie— just the wagon. We can make our way in some comfort from now on. I parsed out enough for a shave and a clean shirt, and a robe for you until the post opens later."

"Truly civilization," she murmured, swinging her yellow-stained legs over the opposite side of the bed. "Are we civilized enough for privacy?"

He stood up and faced her across the bed. He had the sense that something wasn't right, that sometime in the night she had become wary again; the scent of her fear grated on him. She did not trust him for some reason, and he had no handcuffs to hold her now. But he had determination.

"I think not, Lizzie."

She caught the tone in his voice. "Back to beginnings again, I guess. Fine. Please hand me the robe."

"I've seen you naked, Lizzie."

"I hope you remember it," she said sweetly, holding out her hand. God, the steaming copper tub looked so inviting. She closed her fingers around the rough material of the robe. She wrapped it around her defiantly and turned her back to him. It was damned hard undressing under its tenuous cover. The moccasins and skirt were easy. She had to unwrap the black cloth from around her neck and body, and remove her undergarment, and she accomplished that by draping the robe over her head to give her the needed leeway to move her arms. She was sure Galt was laughing at her, but when she faced him finally, she had divested herself of all her clothing and the only thing that showed beneath the hem of the robe were her feet, which contrasted oddly with her yellowed ankles.

She paced regally to the tub, and raising the skirt of the robe daintily, she shot Galt a look of triumph and stepped in. The water was gorgeously hot, just right to sink into, and she yearned to drop the robe over the side and give in to the seductive heat.

But there was Galt, arms crossed, with that amused smile now on his lips, his jetty gaze pinned on her as if she were a specimen of some kind whose behavior he was studying.

"Well, Lizzie?"

"Devil you, Galt Saunders," she snapped, then flung off the robe and dove into the water so fast that he only had a brief glimpse of her long legs, and the lush nakedness of her body.

He knelt beside the tub. "You need help, Lizzie."

"A bar of soap and maybe a cloth and some privacy, and I'll do fine," she said, holding out her hand imperiously.

"Lye soap," he said, tossing a large block of it into her hand. "A cloth—which you will need, especially for that dye on your legs." He reached behind him again. "Several towels, a brush, some lemon water to rinse your hair. Let me see . . ."

"Oh, stop being so damned thoughtful," Elizabeth said crossly, immersing the cloth in water and soaping it up.

"Beg your pardon, Lizzie. I'll just watch." He leaned backward and positioned himself on his rump, his arms around his drawn-up knees. "Now you see, we're just eye level, and I can't see a thing."

"Hogwash," she said succinctly, reveling in the feel of the water cascading over her head as she wet her hair.

"It's a mess, Lizzie."

"I'm in a mess, Galt." She began rubbing the soap over the tangled strands.

"Care to elaborate on that cryptic comment?"

"Maybe, maybe not." She worked the soap into her hair vigorously, dismayed by the snarls and the oily feel of it.

He said nothing as she rinsed her head, and reapplied the soap to her hair. And still nothing as she rinsed it again, and then requested the lemon water for the final dousing. And nothing as she began soaping her body, his imagination running riot when he could not see her hands.

"The damned dye won't come off," she said finally, lifting one leg over the edge of the tub.

"Shall *I* scrub it for you?" Galt asked, not moving a muscle. He felt suddenly that something critical was in the air, something that, coupled with her mysterious "I'm in a mess" statement might catapult her feelings in a direction he very plainly did not want them to go. She did not trust him. He felt that as if it were her hand touching him.

"I suppose so," she said grudgingly, handing him the cloth.

He rolled up onto his knees and then his feet. There was a chair by the table at the window, and he appropriated that and positioned it next to the foot of the tub before he sat down. From this angle, he had a completely unfettered view of her nakedness beneath the water, and he was aware of every inch of her alluring femininity as he grasped her right leg with its bruising color and began scrubbing as hard as he could.

The water concealed nothing. She became sensible of it suddenly and panicky. In spite of his brisk application of the wet soapy cloth, he held her leg like a lover; and an undercurrent of feeling flowed between them, undefined, edged with a nuance of violence, rippling like the movement of the water when she moved her hand beneath it.

He reached for her other leg and began scrubbing it, his hand tense, his face set, his inscrutable eyes fixed on the long line of her limb until he reached for the little pitcher that had held the lemon water, and dipped it into the bath to rinse her legs. The color poured off into the water, leaving her legs with just a faint yellow cast as if they had been discolored by an injury.

"They're ugly," she mourned, as it became obvious the yellow could not be completely washed away, and neither could the feeling of his large hands that now held her by the ankles in such a commanding way. Excitement trickled through her as he did not move, and his glittery black gaze assessed the emotion in her face.

"They're beautiful," he contradicted huskily, and the tension screamed through her veins. Would he move his hands, would he stroke her—did she want him to . . . she wanted him to; his blazing black gaze caressed her, a living feeling touch all over her nakedness under the water that hid nothing from him. It was that same awareness that led to that blinding mindless desire that enslaved her. And she knew she should be more wary, defend herself from it somehow, but what defense was there from the consuming flame?

She felt both vulnerable and powerful and her body sloughed aside her mind's objections, and began little arching seductive movements under the water almost of its own volition.

Such danger, she murmured to herself, and the ripples . . . and then his hand moved purposely down her right leg, honey warm on her dry silky skin, and a little spiral of desire deep in her stomach circled its way slowly downward to attack her vitals with new sensations, new demands. It was all reflected in her face, which he watched with a lover's intensity, absorbing every subtle change. What she felt was written in her expression more clearly than if she had spoken words out loud, and she knew it. She had to beware, and yet, as his other hand moved along the line of her leg, feeling its contour now, exploring, gently flexing his fingers against the line of it, the length of it, she knew at some point she must remember it— but not now; not now.

This, she thought, drove every other thought out of a woman's head; so many ways a man had to bewitch a woman, ensnare her, so many enticing places on her body to be ravished by just the touch of his hands; her face was still with the rapture of her feelings as his hands moved just on her legs and so slowly up and down and back up again, tracing a line toward the water, and stopping just short of touching her beyond that point.

She wondered how much of *his* body was so susceptible to her touch and she thrust the idea right out of her mind. This was not going to go any further than her enjoyment of his hands playing on her legs. No further.

His fingers grazed her skin under the water where the line of her thighs dipped temptingly toward her ripe femininity, and slid back up toward her feet, trailing a thin streak of wetness, which cooled her heated skin as it dried.

His hands grasped her feet and held them tighty. She felt it, behind her closed eyes and her rapt expression, she felt him swallow her feet with his hands, and a score of new sensations spumed through her body when he rubbed the ball of each foot with his thumb.

The water cooled and she never noticed it. Her whole body

felt thick and rich with a voluptuous urgency that overset all rationality.

She wanted more, that much more, all the more, the culmination now that his hands and his eyes promised her. She implored him with her eyes soft as spring leaves, and he let go of her feet, and took her outstretched hands and pulled her from the water and into his arms.

He crushed her slick wet body against his, and ground his mouth down on hers in a fury of unassuaged hunger. She clutched his arms, his shoulders, his neck. Her hands couldn't get enough of the feel of him; her body could not get close enough to him.

He lifted her up against him, holding her just under her buttocks, pulling her tightly against him where she could feel the ardent arousal that surpassed her own.

So gently, still holding her against him, he moved her to the bed and laid her down, his arm still supporting her from behind, and came down with her, over her, bearing his weight on his free arm so that he could look into her face.

"Elizabeth," he murmured, and his voice called to her while something in her tried to struggle past the sensual call of his voice to remember another time in this bed when her mind had been occupied with wholly different thoughts.

Yes, the thoughts—a possible explanation, something she hadn't liked at all, that made her suspicious and distrustful—something that chilled the heat of her skin, and made her push him away abruptly and grab for the blanket that covered the bed to cover her nakedness.

"Lizzie!"

"Sorry," she said briskly, feeling as if she had been doused with the cold water in the tub. "Would you mind getting that robe for me?"

He moved slowly off the bed, bewildered and slightly disoriented. "Miss Lizzie, you are a one, leading a man to temptation like that." He tossed her the robe.

"Didn't I?" she muttered, wriggling her way into it. "I need clothes, Galt, truly I do."

"Yes," he agreed, "but I have to leave you alone here in order to purchase them. What the hell do I know you'll take it

267

in your head to do while I'm gone?" He sat down heavily at the foot of the bed facing her.

"I agree it's a chance you'll have to take, but I'm not likely to go far dressed like this," she said, pulling the ties into a bow with an emphatic jerk. "On the other hand . . ."

"My feelings exactly, Miss Lizzie. It does give a man pause. Why the hell did you stop me?"

"I felt like it."

"Damn to hell you did. I'm waiting for the words, Lizzie, and this time they'd better be good."

She drew up her legs to her chest and huddled against the curlicued iron headboard. "It's nothing mysterious. When I'm in danger of letting myself forget certain facts, I tend to remember them at the oddest times. I was thinking about that business about my abduction, and since I still don't understand what I'm doing here . . ."

"You know what you're doing here, Lizzie."

"Let's say perhaps that now I think I know what I'm doing here."

Galt stood up abruptly to quell his urge to throttle her. He hated when she spoke in riddles, and it obviously had to do with the turnabout he had sensed in her. He walked slowly to the window and stared out at the roof overhang that covered the walkway entrance to the hotel. It was like a little porch, he thought; she could climb right out and shimmy down a post and he would never see her again.

He turned to look at her, calmer now that he knew what to expect. "So what do you think you're doing here?"

She was astonished he wanted to hear; she would have thought he would try to talk her out of telling him. Damn, she would never understand how that man's mind worked. "I think you thought that if you could get me to Rim City, there was a chance that you might use me to smoke out Martin Healey and get to Lonita that way."

He smiled, not a pleasant smile, and she hated him for it because it confirmed what she had been thinking. "Aren't you the smart one? It was a slim chance, Lizzie, but yes, I had that at the back of my mind when you came sashaying into that jail cell."

She stared at him, appalled that he admitted it. "Well then, now it all makes sense," she said lamely, mentally cursing him for confessing all and leaving her without another word to say.

"And just think how it would have sounded if I'd told you that back in the McCreedys' cabin."

"I said you're crazy; I haven't changed my mind."

"Except once or twice since, Lizzie, but I'm not counting."

"You just get me some decent clothes, damn you."

"Only if you promise not to climb out the window and disappear," Galt said. "Otherwise, we'll sit here forever."

"Oh no, I want those clothes, and I promise I won't try to leave by the window until at least tonight."

"Sassy Lizzie. You and I aren't done yet, you know."

"I don't know what I know, Galt Saunders, except I need some decent clothes," she interrupted wildly, casting about for something to throw at him.

"And I need some decent appreciation, Miss Lizzie, for rescuing you from a life of sheer boring hell. Maybe we're even," he added, ducking out the door as she flew off the bed and grabbed the bar of soap. It hit the door just as Galt slammed it behind him. She heard the scrape of the key in the lock, and her expression froze.

She stared at the door for a long moment, and then turned and strode to the window to push the curtain aside to ascertain the possibility of escape by the window. She was startled to see the little porch roof appendage directly under the ledge. No wonder he thought she might disappear. It was very tempting just to think about hopping out the window that very instant.

But no. Galt Saunders could stew for a while, wondering just when or if she might do it. And she would. But not just yet.

She dropped the curtain thoughtfully. Soon.

Very soon.

Seventeen

She had to be grateful for the brush. It was the first time in days she had been able to comb out the tangles, and her ever-lengthening golden brown tresses felt clean and smooth under her hands. She yearned for some combs to pin it up, but the best she could manage was the long neat plait down her back which she secured with a strip of the black cotton she ripped from the material that had clothed her.

She wondered idly what Galt would come up with to clothe her. It didn't matter. She didn't need anything fancy; the same shirt, skirt, and boots would do. She hardly thought any more about the luscious silks and lace she had worn with impunity before the war. That seemed a lifetime ago. Even Greenfields seemed years behind her. Galt wasn't far wrong, she thought humorlessly, setting the brush aside and going to the window again. He *had* saved her from certain boredom, a certain life that she herself had almost decided to reject.

But for what? The seemingly irrational fool's chase now had a point. Galt's point, but still a point. He had invested time and effort and he and Buck had obtained results, and Lonita had manipulated Buck's murder in order to profit, and had hidden the goods. He wanted his share, and obviously so did Lonita And he wanted vindictation. She could understand that, even though it had less to do with his much-vaunted honor than it did his desire to reclaim what was rightfully—she supposed—his.

All that now was clear in her mind, and she could grant him

that it was reasonable that he had to escape certain imprisonment and try to find Lonita and salvage his reputation and his hard-won wealth.

The rest was questionable. He had used her as a decoy to legitimize his escape, and had dragged her in handcuffs across two states already, put her life in danger twice, and her emotions in danger even more times than that, and he now expected her to be perfectly amenable to becoming the bait with which he might lure Martin Healey out of hiding and so find Lonita.

Incredible.

It was the silver; it all came back to money, always. A new lead strike, Galt said, and a new process to refine the silver from the ore. A lifetime of wealth up for grabs now, among Galt, Martin Healey, and Lonita, and Galt did not hold the winning hand: he was still wanted for murder.

But how much could that count in Drover's Landing, Kansas? Or when they reached Rim City?

They?

Why was she thinking *"they"*?

Why was she thinking anything at *all?* Her part was finished as far as she was concerned; Galt was going on alone from here, whether he believed it or not.

She would not let him seduce her again, not with words, not with his sensuous hands, not with any appeal he could make. What appeal could he make?

The idea piqued her curiosity. It was so easy to make up stories—and hadn't he encouraged her to do that very same thing early on?

In point of fact, she thought, he needed her no more. He would find Lonita with her or without her, and he would settle the question of guilt or innocence, and he would go back or he would stay, but he would do all that without her.

He was so avid to find Lonita McCreedy, she couldn't find it in her heart to hinder him.

But . . .

What if that fervor concealed still a different purpose altogether? No! She couldn't consider it. But her mind ranged around the possibilities as the thought snaked its way into her

271

ruminations. Anything that fit the facts was viable. Nothing so far had been anything like what it seemed. She had been pushed and pulled Galt's way with Galt's explanations as he chose to give them to her for a couple of weeks now.

There was always more than one way to write a story. He had said so himself.

So . . . what if this was all a plan between himself and Lonita, rather than Lonita and Martin? What if Martin had no part in it, if his name were just a smokescreen to lure her, Elizabeth, to come with him? Perhaps he thought she still loved him. Perhaps Galt really was in love with Lonita McCreedy exactly as she had said he was.

And they were going to hide out, in one of those lawless Kansas towns, until they could go back for the silver, just as he had said Lonita and Martin were planning to do.

Oh God.

Inconceivable.

Too conceivable.

She wrapped her arms around her waist and stared out the window blankly, shuddering with the force of just how imaginable such a theory really was.

And now he saw her as she really was, tricked out in a gown that was approachably fashionable down to the swooping hoop-stiffened hem that was decorated with green velvet braid that matched the curlicues on the jacket front. She moved her arms experimentally, as if they were unused to the fine crape fabric of the underblouse against them. She fingered the lace edging the finely ironed pleats that scored the bosom, and slanted a considering green glance at him from across the room.

He was too perceptive by half, she thought, her pleasure at full odds with her intuition. How could she be angry about *this*? He couldn't have guessed more tellingly what would delight her after so many months of having made do with used garments, or shirts and pants borrowed from her brothers' wardrobes. And none of the five plain gowns she had brought west with her could even match this one in quality or sophistication.

"Thank you, Galt," she murmured, twirling experimentally, revealing the modest cotton bloomers beneath and the practical buff boots, which were useful for negotiating the dusty street in town but hardly a match for the outfit.

"They do tell me," he said conversationally, "that some of the ladies are even wearing skirts that go higher than the undergarment. They say it's more convenient on the prairie, and for riding."

"Of course," Elizabeth broke in, "since we don't expect to be riding in the near future, I think you made the right choice . . . for me." She adjusted the collar of the blouse once more in the mirror. Oh my. She didn't say it, but the words tremored all through her. Why did he do this? And what did it matter, after all, that he knew all these intelligible things about women's clothing and underwear, and *just* what she would like.

On the bed lay another set of underwear, a divided skirt for riding, a coarse cotton shirt—her size, or as near to it as he could approximate—a buckskin vest, a jaunty bandanna, and a straw hat. These items pleased her as well, even though their very nature told her that he fully intended to have her traveling farther with him, and he had, in fact, provided himself with appropriate additional gear as well.

Galt lazily watched her as she touched the shirt and the vest and then went back across the room to preen in front of the mirror. So beautiful, he thought, and elegant in the graceful modish gown. Here was Miss Elizabeth to the core, the one who had been the pampered young daughter of aging parents; the one who had had the steel in her backbone to take over men's work when her own went off to war. The one Martin Healey had fallen in love with.

And she had been the imperious Miss Elizabeth when he returned to the room not an hour ago, changed so subtly yet again from the sensual creature who had denied him her bed.

Which Elizabeth was she? he wondered. The mercurial change in her was unsettling; he wanted her as an ally so badly. And now, he was back to watching her, to confining her with figurative handcuffs. He could not let her go. Nonetheless, even he did not know how he was going to proceed from here with the extra burdens of finding a way to get to Rim City and keeping an eye on Elizabeth. They needed transportation, supplies, horses; he wasn't sure his stake would stretch that far with what he had spent on ferrying them over, and Elizabeth's clothes.

He was of a mind to move as soon as possible. He unwound himself from the window where he stood watching her, and reached for his hat.

She watched him in the mirror, her glowing green gaze heightened by the color of the gown. "You're leaving." A statement, filled with a kind of suppressed pleasure, the implication of which he did not like.

"*We're* leaving," he said firmly, grasping her arm and directing her toward the door. "I do believe I would like to show you off, Miss Lizzie. You're looking particularly— fetching."

"Wretch," she muttered under her breath, yanking her arm from his tight grip. "You're going to drag me with you everywhere now, aren't you?"

"Why Miss Lizzie, I wouldn't do anything so ungentlemanly as *drag* you," he said easily, pulling open the door. "A gentleman *accompanies* a lady, I seem to recall, since she needs to be chaperoned at all times. Wasn't that how it went?" He motioned her to precede him into the hall.

"That's not how I'd like it to go," Elizabeth said plainly, pulling at her hand now, which he had caught in his own as he locked their door.

"Nonetheless, Miss Lizzie, you're a practical woman. You're still better off with me, no matter what nonsense is roiling through your overactive imagination." He tucked her arm through his in a thoroughly gentlemanly fashion. "I promise it will come out all right." He said it with a great deal of conviction, but she lifted her chin and shot him a baleful disbelieving green glance.

"But for whom?" she demanded stonily. "For whom?"

The noon sun baked the gritty main street in a hot luster. Every slow-moving passing wagon threw off a cloud of dust and dirt that looked like steam rising from the ground. Wagons already lined either side of the plank walkways in a manner similar to River Flats, and anyone who had hoped to do business this hour had taken shelter instead under one of the lean-to roofs that fronted the shops and the street.

Galt muttered under his breath as he and Elizabeth made their way laboriously through the loungers that had collected along the walkway fronting the hotel. The keen appreciative eyes of travel-weary overlanders followed Elizabeth's graceful figure as they passed, and Galt was acutely aware of the interest.

He glanced down at her. Even her walk was different; she held her head high and her shoulders were set, her back was ramrod straight, and the skirts of her dress swayed with every step. The epitome of Miss Elizabeth, strong and unalterably proud, he thought, from another world that he knew nothing about. He might have shoved through the crowd, but Elizabeth would not. Elizabeth was gracious and graceful, patiently mannered to even the rudest idlers who blocked her way.

When he was able to take her arm again, he directed her toward a cabin situated down near the trading post, which had a crude sign overhanging it that read *Eating House.*

Elizabeth looked at him questioningly. "You're going to feed me too? Here?" The question dripped with disdain.

"Unless you'd like to starve, Miss Lizzie, this indeed is it," Galt said, pushing open the door and holding it for her as she marched in with that off-putting preemptory air.

The interior was a surprise, clean and well kept to an extent that even Elizabeth had not expected, with rudely constructed harvest tables set up in three rows front to back so that the cook could feed as many mouths as possible from the limited menu, which seemed to specialize in soups and stew. The temperature inside was several degrees higher than without.

Galt motioned her to the one end of a table that butted a window and she seated herself daintily on the makeshift bench opposite him.

He ordered stew, which was simmering in a huge iron pot on a cast iron stove in the back of the building, and two bowls of it appeared in record time in front of them, brought by a grizzled-looking woman who was dressed plainly in calico, with a white apron covering her dress, and a white triangle of cloth over her head as well.

"M' name's Allura," she said, holding out her hand. Elizabeth took it first, and then Galt. "Came west in '49. Lost my husband in the rush, dang it, and stopped by coming home, and never left. Laundry first and then food. People got to eat," she said cheerily, waving at them to start eating. "I'm back there if you're wanting anything else. Four bits in the bucket. No one's cheated me yet." And off she went to stir her stew pot.

Galt dipped his spoon into the bowl. "I wonder if you'd come to that, Miss Lizzie," he said speculatively, "seeing as how you're so eager to take in laundry instead of coming on to Rim City with me." He took a mouthful of stew to avoid her telling look that flashed over him like wildfire. If he had met it, he thought, he would have been burned to a crisp.

"What now?" she asked after a long beat of silence, during which she sipped at the liquid in her stew.

"Damned if I know, Miss Lizzie."

"Galt . . ." She stopped. She wondered if she had even an inch more patience to deal with him. He thought he was so smart showing her what Allura had come to, and her own possible fate. He thought he was so smart about everything, and she was willing to bet that as much as he protested, he probably had a very good idea about what his next step was. What she really wanted to know was what *her* next move was, and in her mind it was not to go with him.

"No, Lizzie." He said it before she had phrased her question, and she disliked him intensely for being able to predict her responses.

"Nonsense. Why not?"

"Because you wouldn't wind up in a cookhouse, Lizzie, judging by the way those itinerants looked at you. There's a perfectly proper-*looking* boardinghouse in town that would take you in like a shot when you got desperate enough for money, and sell your services to all comers. Now, Miss Lizzie, I couldn't possibly let you descend to that kind of life by agreeing to leave you behind, could I?"

"I just love how you look out for my interests," Elizabeth

said snippily. The damned man had an answer for everything, she thought in frustration. And he always presented it to her in such a calm and reasonable manner that it left her no room whatsoever for argument. Unless she wanted a confrontation. She wondered if she did.

"My pleasure," Galt said, tipping his spoon at her. He felt such an indefinable satisfaction sitting across a table from her, eating a real meal, with her dressed in women's clothing and looking every inch the lady. She ate with gusto, but in such a genteel way that he felt a moment of awkwardness about his own manners. But Lydia had taught him well; when he had married her, he had been untutored—in everything, wild but principled. Her family had been in dire straits and he was there, almost like a knight in a Scott novel, to save them. The delineation between their social status had been very easy to wipe away with the respectability he offered. And in time, a very short period of time, Lydia had trained him in his manners and his clothing, and in holding back his very real explosive emotions.

He remembered all of it too well. She was too fastidious for the carnal bed, too well bred to work her own land. And her family supported her, leaving him to bear the burden. He had thought at the time the only thing to do was get her away from them; he felt stifled by their impractical gentility and their clinging to times and customs that did not exist anymore. He had thought if he could make a new start with his wife . . . and without the webs and walls her family erected around her . . . there might be a chance their marriage would survive.

But then later, it had become obvious he had made the wrong choice and Lydia was not loath to let him know it. She had never wanted to move away from her family. She had a boundless supply of words to castigate him for his imprudence. He was a boor, a dolt, a damned farmer and nothing better, always and ever the overseer's son.

And when he demanded his marital rights and she conceived their child, he became a brute, an animal, a rutting bull, insensible of anything but his own lustful desires.

And when she lay in childbirth, her life's blood seeping away along with that of their child, she swore before witnesses he had murdered her. Buck and Lonita McCreedy had been witn him that night.

The rumors had started shortly after that, and it had been easy for him to become reclusive and hostile, particularly with Lonita casting her lures while she was talking behind his back.

He wondered whether Lydia's accusation was the starting point of Lonita's subsequent plan; how likely it seemed now, a year after the fact, and almost two months after the murder, the trial, and his imprisonment.

Except now there was Lizzie, who had all unknowingly saved his sanity and his life; Lizzie, who was two different people and one of them was the woman who was raised to live and believe all the things that Lydia had believed, who was as much a lady if not more than Lydia, who had it in her to become that woman once more in another place with another man.

His mind fled from the thought. She scared him. The woman across the table from him terrified him, and he almost thought that she was exaggerating the differences between them for just that purpose.

He felt a keen desperation to get her back to the hotel room and turn her back into *his* Lizzie of the oversized men's shirts and the long hoopless riding skirt.

The dress, a gesture, had turned into something more futile for him. It had brought her social station to life for him in a way he could never have envisioned in his imagination, and it blotted out everything else about her that he was coming to want as the embodiment of everything Lydia was not. The dress made them sisters under the skin; it gave Elizabeth an identity she had not heretofore had. She was not a rootless, impoverished woman without ties and history.

He saw her suddenly as Miss Elizabeth Barnett of Lexington, Kentucky, among a loving family and her elegant home. It flashed before him like a photograph, complete in all its detail, the family group intact—the brothers, the father in all his honor, the delicate mother. The overseer's shack was far beyond the white-columned plantation house, and even now, too far beyond his dreams.

All he could hope for was vindication of his name, and the means to start over.

And all that lay just as far beyond his reach at this moment as Elizabeth herself.

He rubbed his hand over his eyes, as much to gain a moment's respite from conversation as to clear his vision and try to bring everything back into perspective again.

Elizabeth watched him curiously; he had been so far away in his thoughts, and his face had gone taut with some indefinable feeling that reflected what he was thinking. Once again she felt that reluctant liking for him because of that forthright vulnerability, and the sadness she felt in him.

But it mattered, damn it, it mattered how he had used her and if he was indeed plotting and planning with Lonita. It mattered to her, and she could not allow herself the weakness of being seduced by that unguarded emotion that tamed those outlaw eyes. If she gave in to it, he would have yet another way to get to her, and it was hard enough for her to deal with the unexpectedness of her own voluptuous response to him. There was no guarding that, no taming of the wild flaming hunger he could arouse by merely touching her.

She steeled herself against his eyes and the power he had to infuriate her and pique her all at the same time, girded herself to ask him the questions she needed to have answered.

She pushed her half-empty bowl away from her and set her spoon down beside it, a little nicety that he took in avidly as he followed suit, leaving his own spoon in the bowl.

"You are still determined to push on to Rim City?"

"There was never any question of it," Galt said easily.

"Do you intend to walk?"

"Now, Miss Lizzie, what do you mean by all these questions about *me?* We're both going, and I'm pretty well sure there's a place we can get hold of a wagon and team for hire. It occurs to me a place like Drover's Landing would do a brisk business in hiring out transport as well as selling supplies. Our problem is solved, and we will be in Rim City by sunset."

"*You* will be in Rim City by sunset."

Galt shook his head. "Lizzie, I'm *not* going through all that with you again, and I swear I'll handcuff you again if I have to,

279

but you *are* going to Rim City with me and that is final."

She got up abruptly and carried her bowl to the front counter where the pay bucket stood, its copper bands shiny with care. Galt set down his bowl beside hers, tossed the coins into it casually, and took Elizabeth's arm with a meaningful grasp. He called out their thanks as he propelled her out the door and onto the still crowded walkway, then turned left.

"We're going to the trading post," he told her, and her head snapped up.

"And how do I know *you* don't intend to exchange me for your viable means of transportation?" she asked cattily.

"Watch your mouth, Lizzie. Even I, for all my patience with you, can only take so much." And he didn't know how much more, he thought, his body tensing as he compelled her forward onto the dusty street, toward the store.

"*Your* patience with *me?*" she shrieked in disbelief. "*You* are some piece of work, Galt Saunders. And don't you think your finding a beautiful gown in this godforsaken provisioning town is going to make things better between you and me. You're holding me against my will right now just as much as if you had me in chains."

"You're right," he agreed lightly. "Can't argue with you there, Lizzie. When you are right, you are most definitely right."

Her teeth snapped together in her rage; he had done it again, ripped her justification right out from under her with that even calm tone of his, that unflappability that was going to drive her to attack him. Even now, she felt an animalistic urge to bite him, just to get some kind of reaction from him beyond his smug imperturbable *surety*.

"I'll be damned," he said suddenly, breaking into her train of thought. "I do believe that the lady in the wagon near the post over there is none other than Miz Ada Rudd."

"No—how could it be?" Elizabeth turned to look, distracted from her mental diatribe against him.

"Let's find out," Galt said, a reflective note in his voice as he spoke. But he did not angle across the dusty street to where the Rudd wagon was hitched. Rather he approached it in a circular fashion, eyeing it with an interest far beyond that of a man

280

contemplating extending a mere greeting. And he moved slowly, as if he was waiting for something, and that something turned out to be Ada Rudd's recognizing them, and waving them over.

"Ma'am," he said deferentially as he removed his hat.

"Mr. Saunders," she said in that same tinny voice that had a clarity to it now that they had not heard in River Flats.

"You made it over," Galt said.

"We did. Coupla men desperate to come over was willing to pay me to take 'em. The dude paid the stake and enough left over to get me some provisioning. I'm a mite surprised to see you here, Mr. Saunders."

"I'm a mite surprised to still be here, Miz Rudd. Our wagon was stolen."

"Ain't that a shame," Ada Rudd commiserated in the tone of someone who has suddenly discovered she owns a valuable commodity and is about to make use of that fact.

"It surely is," Galt agreed smoothly. "Lizzie here and I were just about to make inquiries into hiring a wagon to get us to Rim City."

"Is that so?"

"Being as how it's only about ten miles upriver, we were even thinking a couple of horses would do."

"Mighty long ride though," Ada said thoughtfully, casting a shrewd and telling look at Elizabeth in her new green dress, which told her more about the state of Galt's finances than any bargaining they might do.

"Lizzie's tough," Galt said heartily, following the woman's train of thought as easily as if she had spoken out loud. "Nice to see you, ma'am. I'm glad you got your stake."

He turned away, pinching Elizabeth's arm for her to follow. She tore her fascinated gaze away from Ada Rudd's lined face and ran to keep up with his brisk strides.

"Damn to hell, Lizzie. What do you want to bet she brought over that damned Cox and Smoot? It sure to hell explains how they followed us over so fast. Hell. I'm getting to feel Ada Rudd owes *us*, damn it." He pushed in the door of the trading post with all the force of his anger.

And stopped. "Lizzie!" His sharp whisper brought her up

281

short. The place was crammed and crowded and not one person turned to look at them as they hurtled in.

She came to stand by his side as they surveyed the scene in the huge barnlike room. Everything imaginable in the way of barterable goods hung from the ceilings, the walls, the rafters, or lay on counters, floors, and over random lots of furniture, saddlery, racks, and even people if they happened to be in the way.

There was a slateboard between two windows straight ahead of them and on it were listed prices of items, needs of the various customers, wants, and advertisements of those not quite in such a hurry to negotiate.

In front of the board ran a long narrow counter that spanned almost the full width of the room, and behind this danced Trader Joe Musgrove, whose domain this was, eloquently orchestrating sales and deals with the finesse of an auctioneer.

"Lizzie."

She closed her mouth. "What?"

"I'm damned if I don't see that buck of yours skulking around the windows yonder."

"Devil it. Now what?" She couldn't even guess what; she felt as if an irresistible tide had caught her up and was taking her along with it, and she did not have the strength to fight it.

"I have to get some prices. You stay here."

She watched as he moved to the counter to consult the slateboard. He spoke to Trader Joe, a short cheerful man who spoke French and habitually wore a fur cap to cover his receding hairline. Joe's hands moved in Gallic hyperbole; Galt remained calm, low-key. A moment more and he had the information.

"Let's go, Lizzie."

As they reemerged into the sunlight, he was not surprised to see Ada Rudd right outside the door.

"Well, Mr. Saunders? You have success in there?"

"Some," he said noncommittally.

"Prices is high," she paraphrased, "when things come dear."

"Or when a man feels like being generous," he amplified.

"I take your meaning, Mr. Saunders. I'm prepared to offer

you a better price."

"I'm listening," Galt said, a little part of him amused and amazed at Ada Rudd's recuperative powers.

"Ten percent below the trader's," she said with finality.

"Twenty-five," he countered.

"Mr. Saunders . . ."

"Ma'am?"

"Fifteen."

Galt turned away and the wheeled back. "Twenty, ma'am, and you've got no place to go." He grinned at her. "that is, if you've got the room."

She considered for a moment. "Oh yes, I've got the room; I left Mr. Rudd at the gambling tables in River Flats. I'll do twenty for you, Mr. Saunders, because of your kindness, if you can be down here and ready to go crack of dawn."

"Agreed, and I thank you, ma'am, for your kindness." Galt reached up and shook her hand and turned to Elizabeth. "Lizzie?"

Elizabeth moved forward mechanically and took Ada Rudd's callused hand with a firmness that belied her bemusement. "You left Mr. Rudd in River Flats?" she asked faintly. Somehow she couldn't make the leap from Ada Rudd's hopelessness to her new entrepreneurial confidence.

"You betcha I did; and he don't even know it," Ada cackled. "Till the morning, Mr. Saunders."

Galt watched her saunter off. "Amazing what a few dollars' worth of success can do to a person," he murmured, catching Elizabeth's arm once again.

She pulled her arm away. "*What* are you doing?"

"I am trying to save you from the damned buck that's stalking us at the far end of the street. Look there, Lizzie, doesn't he just look like he'd like to steal you back again?"

Elizabeth shot a startled green glance down the long crowded street, which was now shadowed by the late-afternoon sun. And she caught just a brief glimpse of his buckskin-clad leg, his bronzed impassive face, before he disappeared behind one of the plethora of wagons that clustered in the street.

"Oh my God," she breathed. "Galt, he could be anywhere."

"Anywhere, my dear Lizzie, is where we're *not* going to be.

283

Walk slowly now, and carefully, and please be aware—he's not only after *you*."

She wasn't sure later whether that was good news or not. They had done an hour's worth of weaving and ducking among the wagons and in and out of the various establishments along the walkways, none of which were particularly savory, and all of which catered to the itinerant traveler who was not above shouting noxious comments at Elizabeth whenever she entered, in spite of the fact she was clutching Galt's arm.

"I just do not understand why they think every woman is for sale, or why if she is with a man, *he* is selling her," she muttered as they walked determinedly past the saloon, which was gearing up for the evening's entertainment and already housed a rowdy crowd that was spending its money freely on liquor, women, and cards.

"Oh, not just *every* woman," Galt assured her, and she glared at him. "You certainly could support yourself as a dance hall girl, Lizzie. You know, I never did think about that when we were talking about the remote possibility of my leaving you here."

"Shut up," Elizabeth said succinctly, again feeling that sink-her-teeth-into-him urge. But then—what the girls did seemed innocuous enough. They danced on a stage in abbreviated costumes, and they mingled with the men and perhaps coaxed them to buy drinks, and the rest was probably up to the girl, yes or no. Surely she was capable of saying no with some finesse.

"Oh Lizzie, you've got a look in your eye I do not like," Galt said in her ear as they spent a moment outside one of the saloons watching the goings-on over and through the swinging doors, as cowboys, farmers, drovers, and overlanders crowded in and out in a perpetual rhythm.

One of them buttonholed Galt. "Say, man, I'd give a hundred dollars to dance with that pretty lady."

"Would you now?" Galt murmured, his jetty eyes sweeping over to Elizabeth. He didn't say another word, and she looked at him defiantly and held out her hand. Her partner counted his money into it, and watched avidly as she tucked it into the bosom of her dress. He offered her his arm and Elizabeth took it, sending Galt a creamy little smile that said, I will handle this.

He watched them barrel through the crowd and onto the minuscule dance floor, and the man, an admittedly well-dressed man with some manners and perhaps some education, take Elizabeth into his arms and begin a bobbing kind of step around the floor in time to the music.

Elizabeth's face was a sight as she labored to keep up with him, and Galt was sure she was revising her initial positive feelings. But lord, maybe not. It would be just like her to come away from the dance floor and swear up and down there was nothing to it and she could see herself becoming a dance hall hostess at the drop of a hat.

He smiled at the thought, and then he felt an ominous prickling at the base of his neck, a sensation that was always an instinctive warning. Someone was watching him. Not the Indian. Some other one, hidden and menacing. Awareness danced along his nerve endings. He had to get Elizabeth out of there—fast. The feeling of danger escalated and he pushed his way through the crowd.

"Lizzie!"

Her expressive eyebrows tilted at him inquiringly as she continued pumping along the floor with her obvious admirer. He followed them determinedly, and reached for Elizabeth's arm to pull her from her partner's grasp.

"Galt!"

He whirled her into his arms, amused at the outrage sparkling in her eyes. And something else. "Damn to hell, Lizzie; I can just see you were on your way out the back door with that man, weren't you?" he growled in exasperation. He pushed her forward off the dance floor. "Why the hell can't you give that idea up?"

"It makes things a lot more interesting," Elizabeth said airily, wondering if her partner was going to demand his money back. "I gambled," she added tartly, "and I think that man deserves an apology from me for the ugly way you ended our dance."

"You looked like you were about to die," Galt said, "and you

285

don't fool me one damned bit."

He looked over his shoulder, and indeed, Elizabeth's former partner stood indignantly in the middle of the dance floor, watching them with a narrowed look that boded ill.

"Let's get out of here, Lizzie. We've got trouble, front to back." He ducked around a corner, pulling her with him, just as Elizabeth's partner started moving forward, having apparently decided he had not got his money's worth. "Hell!" Galt exploded, catching the man's purposeful pursuit out of the corner of his eye. "I'm beginning to think you are more trouble, woman . . ." He pushed her through an archway which led to a long, branching hallway, at the end of which was a window. "Let's go, Lizzie, and prepare to do some climbing."

He pulled her down the hallway. The window was not fortuitously open; it was locked. "Damn to hell," Galt muttered, yanking off his hat and thrusting his hand into it. One wallop and the glass broke as noisily as possible. He cursed again and knocked out the remaining shards of glass impatiently, and then swung through the window frame. "Ruined my damned hat, too, Lizzie. Come on! Never mind your dress." He reached his arms out for her just as she heard the thumping of boots behind her, and an incensed, "Hey! Lady!" behind her.

She scrambled out into Galt's arms, tearing her skirt as she tumbled through the window sash; he set her on her feet, grabbed her hand, and pushed her down to the ground. "Crawl, Lizzie!" he hissed, cramming his long length down next to her. She crawled—around the corner of the building—painfully, inch by inch on her knees, with him exhorting her to keep going, and keep going, and then suddenly she felt him grab her hips and thrust her forward into a bush and his whole weight come down on top of her. "Don't talk," he breathed in her ear.

"How can I, with all this dirt in my mouth," she grumbled, her words just barely intelligible, and her body reacting tangentially to the pressure of his, to the heat and hardness, his angular hips, and the rasp of his voice against her skin. What was it about him, she wondered with a sinking feeling as her body disregarded her will and began its own subtle little accommodations to the sensation of him covering her; and she

286

couldn't help it. Something in her sought to join with him whenever he touched her. It went against everything rational, her response to him. She should loathe him. She did loathe him.

"Didn't your mama ever tell you not to lie in the bushes with a man?" Galt whispered provokingly, levering himself upward slightly. "I think they're gone, Lizzie. Come on, we've got to *move*."

And then she had not time for reflection on her folly, or whether he had even noticed her seeking him. They ran, behind the buildings and skirting the edge of the encroaching dirt tracks with skeletal framework sitting and waiting for someone to complete them. They ran, as the sun slowly set and the sky darkened and the air became cooler, and finally he signaled her to stop, and she collapsed against a tree, totally out of breath.

"I can't tell you how grateful I am," she panted, "for this guided tour of the back alleys of Drover's Landing."

Galt sent her a speaking black look and removed his hat to look at it more closely. "I tell you, Lizzie, you can joke all you want about it, but that damned man was after more than just a dance with you."

She didn't look at him. She picked at her skirt and examined the damage, dismayed by the huge tear that gashed through the material. "All right," she said at length, "he probably was." She made a show of switching the dirt off the front of the dress as best she could. No way to hide the tear; she would have to hold the edges together.

"Thank you, Lizzie," Galt said gently, and went back to smoothing out the creases in his hat. He debated whether to tell her about his amorphous feeling of being watched, and decided against it.

Whatever the menace, they would be out of its reach by dawn. He crammed the hat back on his head and reached for her hand. "Come, Lizzie. We have much to do before the morning."

"Do we dare show our faces?" she breathed.

He smiled, the full-to-his-eyes smile she liked so much, and hated herself for liking so much. "Probably not," he admitted.

"But it's getting dark. I'm cheered to think no one will notice us."

But he wasn't so sure about that himself. The Indian was still in town, and the menace, whoever or whatever it was. It could be Cox; it could be Smoot. And it all could have been his imagination.

Very carefully and slowly, they eased their way back into town, silence between them, Elizabeth's hand clutching her torn gown, and Galt leading her almost as if they were a lady and gentleman approaching the ballroom for their first waltz.

Eighteen

"This dress is irreparable," Elizabeth said disgustedly, holding up her beautiful green gown, which was now streaked with dirt and grass stains in addition to the long rent down the side.

"Pack it," Galt said sternly, tossing his own dirt-stained shirt into the carpetbag he had placed at the foot of the bed. He glanced at Elizabeth's disheartened expression. "It *can* be cleaned and mended," he added encouragingly.

"It won't be the same," she said mournfully, folding it carefully into a small pillow of material. She placed it in the bag on top of his shirt along with the soap, washing cloth, towel, and brush he had provided her with. On the chair near the window, she had laid out the skirt and shirt he had bought her, and she was dressed in her underclothing and robe, having elected not to change her clothing for the evening.

He had already provided her with a sketchy dinner by somehow convincing Miz Allura of the Eating House to furnish a bucket of the stew they had eaten that afternoon, and some crusty loaves of bread. He had paid, he said, a handsome rent for the bucket, plates, and spoons, and Miz Allura expected them back that evening.

Elizabeth was overwhelmed by his ingenuity, and grateful for Miz Allura's perspicacity in figuring out—perhaps from the care-worn look on her face as Galt was negotiating for their dinner—that she was frantic to have some time to herself. Amazing, that woman's perception, she mused as she bolted down her food.

And she felt correspondingly wary. He had even kept her beside him when he slipped into the trading post to buy the aged carpetbag that now held what little was left of their possessions.

It could also hold her heart, she thought with agonized insight, if she stayed with him much longer. She didn't know if she could bear to find out that not only was he using her to flush Lonita from her hiding place, but that he planned to run off with Lonita as well.

Her pride might have saved her from the disgrace of caring, but her body was betraying her at every turn. Her self-respect held no sway over the touch of his hands, and this afternoon had only underscored her vulnerability even more emphatically.

But it was also obvious that he was still not willingly going to allow her to leave him. Not yet.

Yet *she* had everything she needed now—a weapon, money, and sufficient warning by example about the dangers of fending for herself on the frontier. She was sure she could make it back to Missouri with some turnaround family passing through—and soon.

Galt watched her devour her food, amused by the difference between the ladylike avidity with which she had eaten this afternoon, and the way she wolfed down her portion this evening. Tonight she was Lizzie, the woman who had toiled outside his jail cell window. She was the Lizzie he had watched so interminably all those weeks, the woman he had sworn to take with him. The Lizzie who was his equal.

He took her tin plate from her hand and placed it and her fork beside his dish in the bucket. Very deliberately, he opened the door of their room and set the bucket down in the hallway.

Her heart sank. He wasn't going to leave the room to return it.

He closed the door and turned back to her, a wry expression on his face. "Sorry, Lizzie. I arranged to have someone take it back. You just looked like you were raring for a moment of privacy, so how could I refuse the challenge?"

290

"Damned if I know," she muttered, and flopped down on the farthest side of the bed. "And we have to sleep together too, devil it."

He was tired. He sprawled out on his side of the bed, his arms and legs at all angles, so close to her screamingly tense body that her body shuddered from the strain of keeping as far from his as possible.

She was sure he was as wide awake as she, and not for the same reasons. Of course he was exhausted; he wasn't grappling with the complicated questions she had to contend with. He had no sense of betrayal, of being ill used. He didn't, she could swear, even begin to like her, in that same kind of mothering-a-stray way that she liked him. She couldn't figure him out at all, except that she knew she must still try to make an effort to get away from him; to do less was dangerous, to her, and she couldn't define why.

Even now, the powerful sensuality emanating from him was overwhelming, and it was proof to her how easily he affected her. She had only to lie next to him, or be touched by him, and every resolution went by the board. It was as if his potent masculinity robbed her of her will, and she hated the sense of being out of control.

There was danger if she stayed with him, and the danger was that she could come to love a man who was as good as a rogue and nothing more. She didn't want that; she didn't want him, and her stiff muscles told her a whole different story.

She lay awake beside him for what seemed like hours. The window was open, and a filmy moonlit iridescence flooded a little triangle of space by the table. Her clothing lay on the chair next to it. She had only to crawl out the window, just get that far . . .

Was he asleep? she wondered, remembering that the last time she had tried to test him, she had come out the loser.

Nonetheless, things were coming to a head now, and she did not want to stay around for the resolution of the events in Galt Saunders's life, not when the course of her own future had yet to be determined.

She moved an arm experimentally and then a leg. He did not react and she was emboldened to swing her whole body upright to dangle her feet off the edge of the bed.

And she waited. She felt free as though moving away from his overwhelming aura released her from its thrall. Her heart thundered inside her chest so loudly she thought he could hear it. But his large warm hand did not reach out to grasp her arm and restrain her. His breathing was deep, heavy, even, and she took heart that he really was asleep.

Slowly, almost inch by inch, she lifted herself off the bed and began creeping toward the window, stop-start, glance at his immobile form, start-stop, another cautious look, start-stop, and she was at the chair. She lifted the skirt and shirt from the back of it and tossed them out the window. Stop-start, she picked up her boots, and paused. Start-stop, she tiptoed to the window, and halted again. No movement, no sound except his steady masculine breathing. Start—she lifted her leg over the ledge, leaned forward, set down her boots on the overhang roof, and perched on the sill to swing her other leg onto the roof—

And she heard a sound.

She threw herself down onto the roof, her mind screaming, fully expecting to feel Galt's huge hand haul her up and pull her back into the room.

But it wasn't Galt.

It was a sound, a scratching at the door. She lifted her head warily. A consistent scratching at the door as though someone were trying to force it.

Devil it. *Who* would be at their door this hour of the night? She didn't stop to think beyond that. She swung her body around and back into the room.

Scratch. She shook him violently, and he awakened with a start. "Someone at door," she hissed, and bolted for the window.

Scratch. A creaking of springs behind her as Galt levered himself off the bed like an arrow out of a bow. She fell out the window, and he dived on top of her heavily.

They lay panting under the window ledge as the door burst open with a crack and one gunshot, and then two, reverberated in the room.

"Oh my God," Elizabeth breathed.

"*Shh.* Don't move."

She barely heard the words he whispered in her ear. He lay over her, on her back, his whole body covering her, protecting her. They lay silently, waiting for the inevitable when their visitor discovered there were no bodies in the bed.

Elizabeth thought she would die from the strain of waiting. Galt didn't move. His head was to one side of her, over her shoulder, and he kept whispering things to her, exhorting her to be patient, they were all right, nothing was going to happen . . .

But a killer! And two shots, two. He meant to get both of them. He *meant* it.

"Lizzie," he whispered, and she shook her head, shaking off the gentleness she heard in him. "Be still, nothing is happening."

"God," she moaned. *Two* bullets!

"He left, Lizzie."

"How?"

"I heard him. He left."

Why didn't the words reassure her?

"He didn't look? He's not in the room, waiting for us?"

"I heard his footsteps, Lizzie."

"All right." She swallowed the knot of fear in her throat. It was Galt's life as well as hers at stake now if he were wrong. "Let me up."

"*Shh.*" He shifted his body, and shook his head. "Turn over, Lizzie, I want to look at you. We're not going back in just yet."

She rolled over reluctantly, her fear dissipating against the stronger emotion overtaking it. "Why not?" she demanded, sparring for time to regain some equilibrium.

"Well," he murmured, settling himself against her again, "he might come back, and you might continue on your way. Either choice, *I* don't come up a winner."

"I gambled," she said tightly, pushing at the weight of his body.

"You saved my life," he contradicted. "Again."

"I wish I had thought twice about it," she muttered. She

293

could just see his face in the moonlight, and already she knew that the fusion of their bodies was acting on him—and her if she were truthful—like powder to a keg of dynamite. He was not in the least grateful-sounding for her good deed.

"Do you, Lizzie?" he asked prosaically, his hands wreathing through her hair. He tugged.

"No," she said reluctantly.

"I didn't think so, Lizzie." He lowered his head and fit his mouth against hers purposefully, sliding his tongue ruthlessly past her nipping teeth as she sought to stop him, to stem the fury of passion that welled up suddenly within him as her tongue boldly darted out to meet his.

She felt the uncoiling in him in the violence with which he took her mouth; it was an unleashing of the tension of the near-miss with death, and it was more. It was as if he wanted to imprint himself on her and in her through any means possible; where they were, who they were, didn't matter. Only the driving force of his tumultuous longing guided him with a keen desperation she sensed through his savage possession of her very willing mouth.

Her body responded ferociously to his power. She knew in an instant his body was hers, but she wasn't sure if she would surrender so quickly. And then surrender became arguable as his hands slid downward from holding her mouth to his at that very precise angle to her shoulders where he could feel the seductive straining of her body against him, and the demands she made without uttering a word.

She wanted . . . she wanted his hands now, and he knew it. His long fingers flirted with the neckline of her chemise inside her open robe, and he trailed little slides of molten gold all up and down her collarbone, neck, shoulderline, downward, and downward to the frilled edge that shrouded her breast, stroking the lush curve tantalizingly, sliding the material downward with a mesmerizing circular motion until her right breast was naked in his hand. Her body arched against him, willing him to continue his erotic caress, her taut nipple tingling voluptuously against the hard warm flat of his palm where he held her.

She felt him begin stroking the long side of her breast with that slow luxurious motion of his fingers; ever so slowly his fingers rubbed and massaged the curve of her breast from under her arm to a point just short of touching her lush straining nipple, and she groaned deep in her throat, wild with the craving to feel his fingers caress the throbbing peak.

He never touched it. Her body importuned him shamelessly, as she sought his explosive kisses over and over—*she,* brazen, provocative in her fluid, seeking movements against his hard male hips that met her undulating femininity with surging little movements of his own. *She,* ravenous for his mouth and the touch of his long knowing fingers. Her want was insatiable as if she could never get enough, or this were the last time she would seek his hands.

He felt her desperation as though it paired with his own. This unquenchable unbridled desire spiraled through him like a tornado until he could only reach and feel and take the sumptuous surrender she offered him. Her mouth was like honey, her breast a feast to be savored; her open wanton need enslaved him. This was his radiant Lizzie, willful, relentless, beguiling, sinuously winding herself around him, tempting him to lose the little control he still maintained as he fast lost the battle to take her with deliberation and intent.

There was nothing of that in his voracious kisses; his lusty hand explored every inch of her body in reach, without touching that one pure point of pleasure she craved. She tore her mouth from his in an agony of frustration. "Galt . . ."

"My Lizzie," he murmured, his voice barely audible, "I want you naked in my hands, Lizzie." Her bare breath of a "yes" sent a thrill coursing through him; these were words he could only utter in the dark of the night in a place no decent woman would be found with a man. They were words he never spoke in his marriage bed, words he never could have demanded of Lizzie in her green velvet braided finery. But she wasn't that Lizzie tonight. She was Lizzie of the pure naked need for him that she denied and encouraged all at once.

And he wanted her with a spuming primitive heat that consumed him with its volcanic passion as he held her body, lifting and turning it so she could bare every satiny inch of her body to his stroking, questing hands.

His perception of her needs was uncanny; his knowing

fingers explored her with tantalizing confidence and she gyrated her hips gently, inviting him to continue by lifting her leg and arcing it over his hip so her body was slanted just that much closer to his.

She curved around him like silk, all fluid movement in response to his long fingers; she wrenched her mouth away from his and pushed his head downward, toward her breast, explosive with the need to have him close his hot mouth over the taut hard nipple, and pull at the lush peak.

She felt the scrape of his mustache against that tender skin as he trailed a line of little nippy kisses all the way down to her chest, and finally rested his lips gently on the swell of her breast.

She rocked her body against him, against his knowing hand, and against his teasing voluptuous mouth that had stopped just short of tasting the swollen tip of her exquisite pillowy breast.

And then his tongue began its heated moist path slowly all over her breast, laving every inch of it, tasting the texture of her skin, licking and sucking at little intervals, driving her to a frenzied excitement that sent her senses whirling out of control.

His lips surrounded her pebble-hard nipple. He didn't touch it with his tongue; he didn't move. She felt his hot breath against the taut tip and she could have screamed with frustration.

Molten heat cascaded through her body, a volcano of sensation as she held her breath and waited for that one shattering instant when he would touch her nipple with his lips and tongue.

Her whole body heaved against him, her hands pulling at his waistband, seeking simultaneously the ineffable maleness of him that defined the female in her.

He answered her. His lips moved, constricting around the hard peak and covering it with his tongue, and she groaned at the sheer avalanche of sensation that rioted through her body, all thick and light, radiant with the heat he generated with his greedy mouth.

She tore at his clothing, avid to feel his skin next to hers, all hot and hard muscled and naked. His shirt gave first and her hands slid all over his hairy chest as he removed his lips from her breast.

"Lizzie . . ."

"Yes . . . ?"

He lifted himself off her for the briefest instant and released his virile manhood into her eager hands. He felt her hand grasp him and begin a wanton exploration that almost sent him beyond the edge of endurance.

He moved over her once again, nudging his way gently between her legs, which she parted joyously to welcome him.

Her arms wrapped around his neck and reached for his mouth hungrily and he poised himself for the long satin slide into her sultry heat.

Her hips thrust upward to meet him, a low animal growl punctuating the sheer pleasure of the infinite connection she felt at the moment of joining. He surged into her, filling her, enfolding her, his mouth covering hers, his virile masculinity potently and totally hers.

She undulated against him, seeking his rhythm, his essence, elegantly draping herself around him, gorgeous against his skin, fine and textured all at the same time in a way that his hands could not get enough of touching her. She felt them swooping down her hip and thigh, sliding under her buttocks, lifting her closer and tighter against him with a volatile need to embed himself within her as deeply as humanly possible.

She was utterly beguiled by the feel of the totality of his male root centered in her, wholly hers at that moment in a way it would never be anyone else's ever. She felt his inflexible male strength and the scorching heat of his desire, and she felt a voracious hunger for completion.

She circled her hips urgently, compelling him to move with her. She reveled in every thrust, every gyration; she could still feel the length of him imprinted in her hands and it was as if her hands held him as tightly as her feminine sheath.

Her all-enveloping sense of him shimmered through her veins, heightening the feeling, the voluptuous excitement, the oncoming explosion of rapture that she could sense her body was reaching for—and reaching for; nebulous, it was a feeling just out of completion, a moment more, another thrust, and another; he was reaching with her, their bodies rocking together in perfect timing, perfect awareness.

Another thrust and another, and the amorphous feeling thickened, becoming defined, certain, glimmering with promise; she opened herself to him, her pliant body demanding all he could give her.

She found the center. Her body rocketed against him wildly with each tensed surge of his hips. Once, then twice, then again, building to a pistonlike cadence, again, again, again, again—she knew, it came, it came, sumptuous, bottomless, hot, incandescent, golden pinpoints all over her skin, erupting into pure ecstasy within her.

"Ah Lizzie," he breathed against her lips, "Lizzie . . ." Her name became a litany as he plunged into her resonating femininity. "Lizzie . . ." His lips tugged at the softness of hers. "Lizzie . . ." For the Lizzie that didn't exist. And for the wanton Lizzie he held in his arms. And for the Lizzie who would not exist beyond this one wild night with her. And the Lizzie who existed in the green dress with the velvet braid who lived in the past and would be catapulted into the present soon—so soon. To dream of Lizzie, he thought raggedly, his body coiling for one last lunge, the last time forever with Lizzie . . . this . . . "Lizzie . . ." he whispered and drove into her convulsively, filling her then with the seeds of his hopes and dreams.

She held him tightly, her eyes open in the shrouding blanket of the night. The last time, she thought; tomorrow they would be in Rim City. Tomorrow all the ends would be tied up, and Galt would find his restitution, either in Lonita, or his treasure, or both.

For tonight—he had found it in her.

Nineteen

The aftermath was anticlimactic. They sorted out their clothing wordlessly, and Elizabeth, clutching her chemise and her boots to her breasts, climbed awkwardly back into the room. Galt followed, carrying her outer clothes and his shirt, which he dropped on the bed so he could light the kerosene lamp by the bed. He held it up to illuminate the damage.

Two burn-edged black holes were visible in the mattress. Elizabeth stared at them, motionless, the sticky wetness of his culmination trickling heedlessly between her legs, as if their wild coupling had never happened. Nothing existed beyond the threat of those two bullet holes. She looked at Galt and he shrugged whimsically. "Could have been worse, Lizzie."

He set the lamp down on the dresser and the dim light played over the finely defined muscles of his bare chest before he got down on his knees to forage under the bed for the bullets.

He found them. Elizabeth sank onto the bed as she stared at the two crumpled pellets in the palm of his hand.

"Someone meant business," he commented harshly.

"Who?"

"I don't know."

"Cox?"

"I don't think so." He closed his large hand over the bullets and jammed them into his pocket. Damned skulking bastard, whoever he was, damn his soul to hell, he could have killed Lizzie.

But then again—*she* had been on her way out the window . . .

299

Damn to hell.

She looked so forlorn sitting there. The shadowy light played all over her face and she looked tired, drawn. Regretful?

He muttered under his breath as he reached for his shirt and slipped his arms into it. "Get dressed, Lizzie. It's not long till dawn, and we're getting out of here *now*."

The trading post was open twenty-four hours. There, in the middle of the night, a man could get a cup of thick endlessly boiling coffee, a sack of flour, a box of ammunition, a gun.

Galt hefted a well-used Sharps rifle in his one hand, weighing it against the forty-four-caliber Colt revolver he held in the other. "They feel damned good," he said. "I'm of a mind to buy both. You never can tell what scum you'll have to deal with on the prairie."

He tossed the revolver to Elizabeth, and wasn't in the least surprised when she caught it deftly and held it up with both hands to sight him across the barrel.

He shook his head wonderingly. "You've surely had a proper education, Lizzie."

"Someone had to shoot game to feed us," she said noncommittally, lifting her arms and bringing them down in front of her eyes again. "I'm pleased to buy my own," she added, whirling away from him and then back, as if he had surprised her suddenly, and lifted the barrel to aim at him in a thoroughly businesslike way. "I like the feel of this."

"Lizzie . . ." He knew he didn't have to caution her, but she was something, in her skirts and straw hat and the damned gun dangling so assuredly from her right hand.

"Now Galt, if I had had a gun in my hand last night, there wouldn't have been two holes in the mattress this morning," she murmured just for his ears.

"I don't doubt it," he retorted wryly, setting his rifle on the counter. He motioned for Trader Joe to unpack another revolver. "I'm beginning to think we can't have too many of these damned things." He lifted the fresh revolver, approved it, counted the ammunition boxes, and put a wad of bills on the counter. "Lizzie?"

"How much?"

"Fifty dollars, ma'am," Trader Joe said, thumping down a box of ammunition for her.

She counted out the money, sending Galt a goading verdant look as she laid her bills down next to his.

He smiled, the crinkly smile, and she felt anger steaming through her veins because he was so calm and accepting, and let her spend all that money on just one weapon.

She jammed her hat back on her head and stalked out the front door, leaving him to follow with the carpetbag and his damned smug smile.

Light was cracking over the horizon, and Ada Rudd's wagon was parked right at the trading post as Elizabeth pushed out the door.

"Morning, ma'am," she addressed Ada dourly.

"Mornin'. Lizzie did he say your name was?" Ada climbed back into her wagon seat as she spotted Galt's tall form backing out the door. "You can make yourself comfortable behindways there. I made room along the wagon wall; you can use the mattress or stay by the wagon gate if you've a mind. Mornin', Mr. Saunders."

"Miz Rudd," he nodded, and went around to the back of the wagon to stow the bag. Elizabeth had climbed in and watched his progress through shuttered eyes as he threw the bag in the wagon and vaulted in beside her.

"Ready back there?" Ada shouted back to them, and at Galt's affirmative call, she lifted the reins and whacked them down on her horses' rumps. "Hyah! Yah!"

The wagon jolted forward and Elizabeth toppled against Galt's rock-hard chest. His arms surrounded her instinctively and she pushed him away impatiently. "Stay back, Lizzie," he cautioned, allowing her to put that distance between them, to put a curtain over the night they had shared and to act as if it never had happened. He had to. He had nothing to offer her except the little protection of his strength and determination, and lord knew, she didn't need that, not really. She didn't need a murderer stalking her either, or the amorphous promise of

301

some kind of future after he had resolved everything. She didn't need him at all, he thought ruefully, pushing his hat back on his head, grateful he didn't have to spell things out for her. She understood perfectly and she aligned her body against the wagon wall with alacrity and regarded him with her intelligent green gaze.

"What is it?" she asked curiously.

"He didn't stop to see what or who he hit," Galt said briefly. "I expect we're being watched, Lizzie, and now followed like as not."

"Devil it."

"Exactly."

An excruciating silence dropped between them as the wagon rolled briskly out of town and onto the north track to Rim City.

Elizabeth didn't know which way to look, so she fastened her eyes on the receding scenery; if she looked at Galt, she thought, she might capitulate altogether because of that damned bemused look on his face that was so appealing to her. She had to negate last night; she had to. She could come to need it too much, need *him* too much, and there was no future in that while he was still on the run. There was no love between them, only that explosive carnal passion that her rebellious body had already learned to crave. She hated herself this morning because of it, hated her need and her demand that he had fulfilled with such emphatic possession.

She stole a covert look at his guarded expression as his scout's eyes surveyed the forest. What, after all, did the outlaw know of love? she wondered idly. He must have loved—he had had a wife; there had been a child, for that brief moment it had existed. He had coupled with his wife at least once, she surmised grimly, and was surprised she did not like even the thought of Galt touching someone else the way he had touched her.

She couldn't allow that kind of emotion to creep up on her life that. What he had done before was no business of hers, and what he would do after was up to him. She had been caught in the middle, and she had not denied Galt her body, and she would have to cope with the ramifications of that when the time came.

302

And the time would be soon. The wagon jounced along at a disconcertingly brisk clip and Rim City was coming closer and closer, and Galt's jetty gaze never wavered from its hard surveillance of landscape.

He had that bad feeling again, and he couldn't let on to Elizabeth. Somewhere deep in the forest behind them, someone was following them, carefully, warily, with deliberate intent. His skin prickled with little alarms, intuition from three years in the field surrounded by enemies; he knew the feeling. In his gut. It took all his control to keep his hand away from the rifle, whose butt was sticking out of the carpetbag with such inviting power.

But Lizzie would know then, and he wanted to protect her as long as possible. And he wanted her as long as possible, just as she was now—with no past and no future, sitting across from him, and looking at him in just that faintly quizzical way.

The rifle stayed in the bag. Ada stayed on course. And Rim City was coming closer and closer.

Ada stopped so they could noon at a little wayside near the river, and generously shared her food with them, for which Galt insisted on paying her. Ada definitely approved of Galt; she continually addressed him as "Mr. Saunders," and Elizabeth as "Lizzie" with one of those cowing looks of hers. She wore the air of someone who has conquered defeat. Dollars rustled gratifyingly in her apron pocket and she would never want for anything again, even if she had to provide overland service from Drover's Landing to Rim City for the rest of her life. She knew how to make money now, and she didn't need a man to provide for her.

Her patronizing little looks at Elizabeth made it plain she didn't respect her at all. If ever a woman was being kept, Ada thought, it was this Lizzie, and that Saunders was being taken in by a pretty face and nothing else, because after all these weeks on the move, pretty Miss Lizzie was looking fairly travel-worn.

But that was his lookout. She liked him and his respectfulness, and she agreed that he and Elizabeth could ride up on the

303

perch with her as long as they were quiet. She didn't think Rim City was more than four miles beyond them now, and she was hankering to get there. It was a regular city, she told them; they weren't going to believe their eyes.

Three miles farther on, a trickle of rude wooden buildings heralded their approach to the town. Vegetation grew sparser and sparser, and the track grew into a wide dirt avenue that, a half mile beyond, rounded a bend onto State Street.

State Street. It could have been a typical commercial street anywhere, except that it ended abruptly at the shore of the Missouri River, which flowed just under the windows of the mercantile bank. In one sweeping glance, Elizabeth noted a stove and pipe fitters, a bookstore, a printing office, a photographer, a hardware store, a Singer sewing machine shop, stores that provided furniture, clothing, china, fruits, vegetables; a dentist, a restaurant, all crowded together on both sides of the street, housed in everything from crude false-fronted buildings, to brick- and brownstone-facaded structures with elegant ironwork detail.

Elizabeth blinked. Rim City, on the edge of everywhere and nowhere, was the most sophisticated place she had ever been.

"Well?" Ada's sharp voice cut through her astonishment. "Didn't I tell you?"

"You surely did, ma'am," Galt said evenly, hiding his own surprise. "The only thing I don't see is a hotel."

"Oh, they got 'em. There's one further on down—the Prairie, and one on Sequoyah Street, near the Best of the West Saloon, that's the Western Star. They don't come cheap, mind. If you're looking to conserve your stake, you can find a rooming house—along the back streets, there's signs, or you can chance it at the Shawnee. Your choice, I don't care to guess what you've got left of your money after you pay me." She tilted an inquiring birdlike look at him.

Galt smiled noncommittally and handed her the money. "Much appreciated, ma'am." He swung down from the perch, over Elizabeth's knees, held up his hands to her, and guided her down from Ada's wagon. Holding her hand, he walked to the back of the wagon to retrieve their bag.

Then he signaled Ada. She leaned over the side of the wagon

and waved at them. "I'm guesting with the Rookses," she called out to Galt.

"Appreciate it," Galt called back as she snapped the reins and the wagon moved forward slowly.

"Doesn't she like *you*," Elizabeth commented cattily, watching the wagon rumble slowly down the street and turn the corner out of sight.

Galt wasn't looking after Ada. He had that prickly feeling again, made worse by the fact they were clear targets as they stood in the center of the broad dusty sun-baked avenue that didn't even have the grace of a tree for shade, or cover.

He reached for the bag and her hand simultaneously. "Let's walk," he said, keeping his voice as neutral as possible.

"Where to?"

"Damned if I know."

"I love how you plan things in advance," Elizabeth said as they angled across the street and up onto the plank sidewalk.

"Oh, I don't know, Lizzie, I like a certain amount of spontaneity in my life."

Elizabeth grimaced. "I believe I *have* noticed that." She tried not to let his crinkly smile affect her, but it got to her nonetheless. For one perfect instant, they were in complete accord with one another. It was the kind of moment that raised hopes, became the foundation of tomorrows. She shunted it away, along with the urgency to know just what he intended to do about Lonita McCreedy now that they were here.

They walked.

They walked down toward the river, where the street slanted down to the docks on the right, and to their left, the newly constructed station of the Kansas Pacific Railroad, which had only just built its tracks as far as Rim City the previous year. Now travelers and speculators slept in the station, awaiting the next train out in order to be the first at the end of the line. Handbills posted on walls and streetlights advertised for construction crews; even as the speculators raped the land, the railroad was moving outward and onward to provide new fields for endeavor.

They could board a train right now, Elizabeth thought, and leave everything behind—forever.

But Galt had no intention of that. He was set on his course, and nothing would sway him. His lightning black gaze scavenged the shoreline expertly; their stalker could be hiding even now somewhere around the railroad station or behind the jumble of shipping containers down by the docks, and he was still feeling that sense of imminent danger.

He steered Elizabeth back up State Street, and down the first cross street on the opposite side of the avenue. Shadows enfolded them, welcome relief from the intense heat of State Street on the side away from the sun.

"West First Street," Galt read from a small porcelain sign nailed to a building wall. "Helpful to say the least."

"It's too quiet," Elizabeth said.

"I'd bet it gets livelier. This"—he paused at the next cross street—"is *not* Sequoyah. This looks like it starts the residential section."

They turned right and continued walking. Another small sign identified Jackson Street.

"Galt, this is crazy."

"You keep telling me, and I don't give a good goddamn. I want that woman, and I want my money and my reputation, Lizzie, and that's final."

"Fine, fine. But I'm out of it, Galt. You don't need me to track her down."

He stopped and looked at her. "I need you," he said quietly, and then continued walking, stifling his frustration at her continual desire to leave him.

They rounded another corner. "West Second Street," she read from the porcelain sign. "There's another cross street beyond State Street."

"Let's go," he said brusquely, out of patience with her, and himself as he began to think that perhaps he was on a fool's chase, and that it didn't matter, any of it, when he was on edge of everywhere and could easily make that new life that Elizabeth kept harping about.

They crossed State Street through a crowd of traffic, human and vehicular, as workers spilled onto the street on their way home.

"*East* Second Street," Elizabeth intoned as they passed the

306

next sign.

"Thank you, Lizzie."

And then, "Sequoyah Street," she announced. They gazed down Sequoyah Street, which was crammed head to head with buildings exactly like State Street. Best of the West Saloon was easily visible from the head of the street, and the Western Star Hotel. They walked toward it, and past it. Galt shook his head. "Too rich for us; they obviously cater to winning gamblers."

Farther down the street, they found the Prairie Hotel, again too luxurious, too dear.

"Never did ask her where the Shawnee was," Galt said.

"We'll find a rooming house then," Elizabeth said, her mouth watering as they passed an eating establishment with the namesake of a famous big-city restaurant.

"End of the line, Lizzie—East First Street." They were close to the water again.

"Not quite; there's the Shawnee," Elizabeth said suddenly.

"Sailors' haunt likely. Damn to hell. We can't do better tonight, Lizzie."

"I'm game," she said, but what she meant was she was dead tired and terribly upset with him. She never thought they would reach Rim City; she never thought he—or she—would have the tenacity to go on. She followed him into the dilapidated building resignedly. The rooms were cheap, just as Ada had said, and he registered for both of them and she did not protest.

The room was on the second floor again, and was as rundown as the building. Galt tossed the bag on the floor and looked at Elizabeth inquiringly.

She sank onto the bed without speaking. She had nothing to say. All roads led to Rim City, bustling, energetic Rim City, where a person could get lost on a street corner, and take the next train or riverboat out of town. Even if Lonita were here, Elizabeth would be happy to let Galt do all the searching. She just wanted to lay her head down on the lumpy mattress and sleep the week away.

Galt would not let her. He pocketed the revolver, which he dug out of the bag, and pulled her off the bed. "We will be tireless in our efforts," he said comfortingly. "Food for the starving soul is the first order of business."

"The restaurant we passed appeals to me mightily," she suggested.

"Me too, but we are neither dressed for it nor do we have the money—unless *you* would like to pay for our dinner?"

"Thank you, no. I'll settle for one of your eating houses, though I didn't notice any as we walked."

"We'll find one."

He sounded so sure, he was so sure; he ignored the telling look on the hotel clerk's face as he propelled her out the door into the street. They headed away from Sequoyah Street, along East First Street, past seedier establishments that supplied sailors' needs, a merchant shipping firm, a livery stable, a storage shed. They turned up the next cross street toward East Second Street.

"Republic Street," Elizabeth read from the sign.

It was lined on one side with rickety houses, and on the other side by businesses. A seamen's bank, another saloon, a delivery service, a printer next door to one of the two newspapers in the town. Handbills were posted on a board advertising entertainments and the arrival of new goods to the various establishments around town. Tacked over the upper row of announcements was an official-looking document with a drawing centered on it.

Elizabeth felt a frisson of foreboding as she and Galt moved closer, and she clutched his arm as they read: WANTED FOR MURDER—GALT SAUNDERS.

Twenty

Galt swore. "Damn to hell, the son of a bitch followed us all the way here." He moved closer to the billboard to read the particulars, then tore the notice off in a leashed motion of fury. "It was a lousy likeness," he said exasperatedly. "And how many the hell of these did that bastard post around town since he's been here, I wonder? And when the damned hell did he get here, and where the hell is the son-of-a-bitch coward?"

Elizabeth froze. "You think he's *here?*"

"He's here," Galt said shortly, staring at the crumpled ball of paper in his hand. It had been Healey, damn it, Healey following them, Healey's rifle, Healey tailing them on the way to Rim City. His presence changed things; Galt had hardly planned as far as their arrival in Rim City, and already that bastard was hard on his tail. It complicated matters, and it made him wonder why Edgar was so desperate to get him.

He was nothing more than a common murderer, sucked into a woman's web, jealous enough to take what he wanted and commit a crime to get it. So what warranted this hot pursuit by the sheriff whose sole responsibility was to deliver him into the hands of the circuit riders who would haul him off to the prison where he supposedly belonged.

Why had Edgar tried to kill them—if he had tried to kill them?

Why was Edgar after him?

"Let's see what damage the bastard has done," he said grimly as Elizabeth looked at him expectantly. He had no answers for her, and he already knew the answer she had for him.

They walked in silence toward Republic Street. There, on yet another billboard, was another poster. Galt pulled it off in disgust. "All over the damned town and who knows the hell where else."

"A wanted man doesn't have much freedom of movement," Elizabeth said derisively.

"That should liven things up," he retorted, unwilling to bend at all to the smug tone in her voice. Oh yes, she had told him, and it *was* crazy, just as she had been saying, and now look where it had got him: no farther than if he were back in jail in Greenfields. Edgar Healey's presence was going to control his life here as well.

Elizabeth bit her tongue to hold back the words just aching to tumble out. "I expect we'll have a lot of fun trying to outwit old Edgar," she said noncommittally, and her use of the word *we* was not lost on him.

He sent her a crooked humorless smile. "Or maybe old Edgar will outwit us."

They found a rooming house with lodgings that also set a daily table, and there they ate a silent beef dinner at an exorbitant two dollars a head amid a crowd of noisy guests whose curiosity Elizabeth fended off with her particular mannerly grace.

She was just as nice as she could be, Galt ruminated blackly, watching her adroit handling of the prying questions. Just the way her momma had taught her to act in company. Company manners—she didn't even need the fancy clothes. He felt a clutching of despair in his vitals. She was what she was, he thought, and in the end, her blood would tell. All this would become either some bad dream or some wild adventure to be relegated to the past. But he had known that, deep in his heart. The treasure in silver that he sought would still never equalize their status socially.

And when he had reclaimed that, he would lose her.

He signaled to her abruptly, and they rose simultaneously to exit the room. Curious stares followed them until they closed the door behind them and stepped into the cool evening twilight.

"Edgar could be anywhere," Galt said as he made a lightning survey of the surrounding buildings.

"Or nowhere near," Elizabeth countered. "So what now?"

"We find our enemies before they find us," Galt said harshly, "and we find them tonight."

"Tonight?" she said faintly.

"We're too noticeable by day, Lizzie."

"*You're* too noticeable," she muttered as he took her arm and steered to the right toward East Second Street.

"No one would ever recognize me because of that *picture*," Galt said scornfully.

"I thought it looked *just* like you," Elizabeth retaliated blandly, sneaking a guarded look at his obdurate expression.

Oh, he was intent now, she thought. Action and purpose were his watchwords; he needed a cause and he had one—a good one that gave him an excuse to go tearing after Lonita McCreedy. He didn't give a damn about Edgar except as he impeded his plans to find Lonita.

She was looking at the face of the outlaw—ruthless and determined to win.

Flattening themselves against the storefronts beneath the overhangs and in the shadows, they made their way toward the seediness of Sequoyah Street.

The avenue teemed with horses and wagons, pedestrians and ladies of the night, a gaudy contrast to the businesslike atmosphere that pervaded the street during the day. And everyone's destination was the Best of the West Saloon and the Western Star Hotel.

No one noticed them; no one would have noticed them even if they had crossed the street and mingled with the crowd. But for the lack of wagons lining either side of the avenue, it could have been the main street in River Flats. The aim and the ends of the crowd were the same: they wanted to gamble and drink and have a good time, and if they were lucky, find some

311

companionship for the night.

Galt pulled up suddenly, halting their stealthy progress down the opposite side of the street. His eyes expertly scanned the crowd, honed in to the sense that something was out of kilter.

How? How among this crowd? Unless their nemesis had been following them all along, ever since they had entered Rim City. Or someone else had picked up their trail. His skin prickled again, and he was swamped with the feeling of being alone and a target of an unknown stalker. Instantly he felt as if he were back in the field, with chaos and death imminent all around him. Every caution, every sense, was awake to some kind of danger he could not define, could not pinpoint. The noise receded into the background; he grasped Elizabeth's hand, and moving as naturally as possible, he pulled her with him in a steady advance down the street, alert to the nebulous threat that his instinct alone had intuited.

His sense of urgency increased as they proceeded down the street, and he stifled the impulse to duck and run. Someone was following them, gearing his pace to theirs, furtive as a mole in the shadows behind them.

Healey.

He felt it in his bones. Healey—but something else. They were way past the Western Star Hotel now, and the crowd was thinning, heading in the opposite direction. This part of the street was darker, the streetlights farther apart from one another, and yet they were more visible, more open.

He pulled Elizabeth to his side. "We've got trouble, Lizzie."

"I figured that out," she said dryly. It could only be Edgar, she thought, but how? Edgar had to have arrived before them by the evidence of the posters. Or had he? After all, it had been a wagon ride of a mere four hours or so for them; what might the distance between Drover's Landing and Rim City be on horseback? Devil it, devil it, and devil damn it. What if Edgar Healey had been their assailant the previous night?

Galt's grim expression told her that her surmises were not far from what he was thinking.

"Why would he want you so badly?" she whispered.

"He liked my company," he said mordantly, his hand going

312

to his revolver almost automatically as shadows moved behind them and across from them, menacing in their anonymity. He sent her one of those grim humorless smiles. "Just like you, Lizzie."

Oh no, she thought as they moved again with that catlike caution, she wasn't going to be drawn into denying *that;* she still didn't know why she was there and even *thinking* of being a part of his formless plan to recover a fortune and clear his name. Terror stalked her now, bird claws of tension digging into her neck, a soundless clarion call in her ear to run as far away as she could. Galt had the gun, and they slowly picked their way down to the less-populated section of Sequoyah Street, which sloped to the docks and the river.

It was eerie, walking in the shadow of the darkened buildings, with the light and motion above them, separated like heaven and hell. The threat was real; even Elizabeth felt it. The confrontation was coming. The air was thick with it, and Galt was deliberately inciting it.

They were almost at the juncture of East First Street. Without warning, Galt pulled her around the corner, thrust her into the first doorway, and backed into it with her.

The space was tight; it was the entrance to a consignment firm, and it was not meant to hold two people comfortably. Galt's body squeezed against hers as he cocked the revolver, and waited.

They heard nothing except distant sounds.

"Bastard," Galt muttered, easing his body out of the entryway just enough so he could see to the corner.

There was no one there.

He moved out, pulling Elizabeth with him. They ran. The Shawnee was directly in front of them. Galt pushed her into the lobby. "I'm going; I want the bastard."

"I'm coming too," Elizabeth said adamantly.

"No. *No,* Lizzie."

"*Yes,* Galt." She tried to push past him.

"*Why,* damnit?"

"To rescue you, of course," Elizabeth retorted with a confidence she did not really feel. She could not bear to let him go down that long dark street alone and then watch Healey—if

313

it was Healey—gun him down with intent to kill.

"He won't stop at killing only me," Galt warned, rounding off her thought as if he had read her mind.

She met his burning black gaze. "I know."

"Get your knife," he said brusquely; he wasn't going to argue. His Lizzie was as good in a crisis as any man. He watched dispassionately as she slipped it from its sheath within her boot, and held it up for his inspection.

She looked like a huntress, he thought, gauging the blade. He nodded. "It's not your fight, Lizzie," he added in one last attempt to dissuade her.

Her lips curved into a wry smile. "You're right, it's not."

He wanted to devour that funny smile; its humor, cynicism, and understatement were all part and parcel of *her,* the Lizzie who was his companion, his lover, the one in his forbidden thoughts. He wanted her with him. He had a secret thought as they crept into the shadows outside the Shawnee's entrance that it would be just if she were with him and he were to die, or if she died with him.

Morbid. The end was coming and it had nothing to do with Miss Elizabeth Barnett. When it was done, she would go her own way and he would head back to Greenfields. He pictured her pushing on farther west, maybe as far as California; he saw her in a city, surrounded by luxury, fashionably dressed, hurling her knife across a table as a party trick. They would love her. Who wouldn't love her?

Something metal crashed into the plankwalk far ahead of them, and Elizabeth grabbed his arm. "Well, ain't that something," he muttered. "He's talking to us."

"But what is he saying?" Elizabeth demanded.

"Damned if I know," Galt said, moving ahead of her cautiously. "Stay behind me, Lizzie."

"I wish I had my gun," she grumbled, letting him shield her with his body as they continued along the street, flattening themselves every fifth step against a building front.

"I wish you did too," Galt concurred, moving again. "I do believe it's possible we're being too cautious for the son of a bitch."

They heard another crash.

"Impatient bastard," Galt said as the echo of the metallic sound faded away.

"That fell," Elizabeth pointed out.

"He's not above us; I think he threw it over his head. Damned coward bastard . . ."

"Saunders!"

The voice roared out at them from a distance, deep and echoing as if their nemesis were in a tunnel.

Galt froze. "Hold it, Lizzie; that was too damned public to suit my taste."

They waited. The darkness and the night sounds enveloped them. Every noise reverberated like a shout all up and down the street.

"God," Elizabeth breathed as the minutes drummed by.

"Shh . . ."

He moved so slowly, a slither against the side of the building, and she shimmied after him. The livery stable loomed ahead, the only lighted building on this end of the street. Somewhere beyond that their pursuer waited.

"Time to smoke him out," Galt whispered.

Elizabeth couldn't tell a thing from the tone of his voice; she only felt the tension in him. He was coiled to react. She felt if she let go, he would catapult out of reach. He could—he might—die. . . .

Her thoughts cost her. He stepped brazenly out into the street. "Come and get me, Healey!" His voice echoed back to her as if she were hearing it from far away.

A shot rang out and he sprawled in the dirt. "Damn hell, damn goddamn hell."

Even Healey could hear him cursing, she thought. Healey. She still could not fit together a picture—Edgar haring after Galt so the circuit riders could do their lawful duty. Edgar stalking Galt so he could haul him back to the Greenfields' jail . . .

"Saunders!"

The shout came from a different direction this time. Galt, on his knees in the dirt of the street, twisted his body toward the sound "Damn hell . . . Lizzie! Get back!" He dove back into the dirt as another shot winged over his head.

Elizabeth covered her mouth to keep from screaming. A

315

second shot ricocheted off a metal sign. Without thinking, she plunged onto plankwalk and crawled forward, her heart pounding. Two guns, she thought; two men. *What* two men? *"Galt!"* she called out urgently.

"I know," he grunted, and she heard sliding sounds; he crawled toward her slowly and with some distress. Her mind envisioned the lean line of his body pierced by stones, and smeared with dirt and excrement.

"Who?"

"I could guess, but I can't fix a connection. Keep down, woman!" He shimmied his body to the edge of the plankwalk. "We're going to pull him out, Lizzie. And you're going to stay out of it. You stay back, you hear?"

"What are you going to do?" she whispered, reaching out for his hand.

"I'm going to make for the stable, Lizzie, and you've got to keep your head; one of them—or both—are going to follow."

"No—"

"I *have* to do it, Lizzie. They've got us cornered, and I'm going to find out what we're facing." He got up on his haunches and ran his hand over her face. "Besides, you might get another chance to save my hide."

She reared her head back. "It's your hide—but I can't say I'm not intrigued."

"I thought you'd see the possibilities. All right . . . I swear I feel Healey closing in . . . I'm going—now . . ."

She watched with mixed feelings as he doubled over and dashed around her and down the walk. She heard with a heart-wrenching feeling of horror corresponding footsteps crunching forward on the street toward him.

She crawled back into the shadows and stood up, her weapon gripped in her tense fingers. Somewhere behind her another threat moved soundlessly toward the livery stable. And in front of her, Edgar's bulky body hovered just at the edge of the square of light in front of the building.

Galt's shadow from within the stable cast a long dark finger of accusation right to Edgar's feet.

Edgar didn't move. Galt's body stood utterly still. Somewhere to Elizabeth's right, an inexorable form came closer, foot by careful foot. His boot steps on the plankwalk were audible now, and she pressed herself against the door frame of the building that shadowed her.

But he must know—Edgar must know—she was there; they had to have heard her talking to Galt. But Galt was their prey, not Elizabeth Barnett. For all they knew, she had been his prisoner all this time.

She smiled grimly at the absurdity of it, all of it, and at the thought that Edgar was in for a rude shock. Another notion flashed across her mind as she watched the cat and mouse game that Edgar and Galt were playing unfold: she was not scared of Edgar either. She wasn't so sure about the unknown commodity who was approaching the very doorway where she stood.

Her body tensed, waiting for the moment he would either pass her or perceive her presence and take her prisoner.

She counted his steps: one . . . two . . . three . . . her weapon hand twisted, and she balanced it against her hip, at the ready to stab him if he reached for her. Her body gathered her fear and her strength, coiling to thrust the whole of her weight, the moment she gouged with the kife. She stood poised— intent and scared.

And then he stepped off the plankwalk and onto the street and she thought she would crumple like a spent bullet.

But there was no time for that. Whoever it was, she had to disable him before he could reach Edgar. She steadied her body against the door frame and lifted the knife. Her hand trembled; she couldn't see the blade. She could barely see anything but black bulky shapes on the edge of the lantern light filtering out of the stable.

And somewhere inside, Galt waited for the precise moment to take Edgar's challenge; she couldn't fail him—or herself.

She closed her eyes, envisioning Galt's lifeless body on the threshold of the stable, using that devastating image to reach for the control that must supersede her fear if she were to disarm Edgar's accomplice.

The silence thickened as she felt a nervous calm descend over her.

"Saunders!"

Her eyes snapped open at Edgar's whiplash call.

"I'm waiting!" Galt yelled back.

"Good!" Edgar shouted, and to Elizabeth's horror, he lifted his rifle and fired. His accomplice instantly moved and Elizabeth's arm automatically lifted, took aim, and released the knife all in one instinctive motion.

The man screamed, and Edgar whipped around. Galt fired, and Edgar's rifle flew out of his hands. "Come get me, Healey," he roared, stalking out into the light. He fired again, and the bullet roweled a long channel right in front of his silent partner's disabled body.

"I'll get you!" Edgar shouted, waving his arm threateningly as Elizabeth inched toward the light and the prostrate man.

Cox.

Devil damn, it was Cox.

She stepped into the light and Healey made an involuntary denying motion with his hand.

"Elizabeth?" His voice sounded uncertain, as if she were unexpected. Well, he hadn't expected her, she thought. She wondered what he thought Galt had done with her.

"Move, Healey," Galt's deadly voice commanded.

Healey moved—backward.

Galt fired again; the bullet thudded into the ground in front of Healey's boot. "Move!"

Edgar stumbled backward into the shadows, shouting, *"Elizabeth!"*

Galt's revolver cracked out again.

Edgar ran; they heard his receding footsteps crunching dully on the dirt beyond their sight, farther and farther in the distance.

Galt emerged from the livery. "You all right, Lizzie?"

She pointed at Cox, shaking her head helplessly. "Look."

Galt bent to pick up Edgar's rifle and knelt to examine Cox's inert body. "Nice shot, Lizzie. You got his shoulder; I think he hit his head when he fell." He felt for a pulse, as Cox's blood seeped into the dirt below his shoulder.

"He'll live."

"But—Cox?"

"They probably met in Drover's Landing. Maybe Edgar was

318

asking questions. I wager he recognized something in the wagon, if Cox still had it. And Edgar probably figured he had surer shot two against one. Damn to hell. This bastard wanted my hide real bad if he figured to join up with Edgar would find me any faster."

"I guess it did," Elizabeth said dully. She could easily envision the scene: Cox coming to town with the stolen wagon in a frenzy of frustration over not having found Galt's stake, and Edgar nosing around the hotels and bar and probably the trading post, asking not terribly subtle questions, spotting, no doubt, the damned rocker, or recognizing McCreedy stock. He would not have cared where the stranger had gotten them, only that he had had contact with Galt. It was so easy to imagine them joining forces, Edgar stalking the one way, and Cox the other, hungry to regain his money and to take revenge on a man who had outsmarted him more than once.

Too bad she had only gotten his left shoulder, she thought vengefully, as she bent and retrieved the knife.

"You finished?" a voice quavered behind them.

Galt whirled, his revolver poised to aim, and then he lowered his arm disgustedly. "We're finished," he said, motioning toward Cox's immobile form. "Take care of this man, will you?"

The stable owner, a small balding man who wore a voluminous leather apron, crept forward and looked up at Galt with frightened eyes. "Is he dead? I'm not going to see to someone dead, you hear?"

Galt brandished the revolver. "He's unconscious. You take care of him."

"I will, I will," the stable owner swore, bending over Cox's body. If only they would disappear, he thought desperately, if they would just go away, he could pull the man inside and tend to the wound, and no one would ever know anything happened. He waited, his trembling hands examining Cox's body inexpertly just to have something to do until these two outlaws finally left him alone. The man looked fit to kill, and he watched everything with that flat black look of his; there was death in that man's eyes, the stable owner thought, his whole being shot with fear.

319

Galt looked at Elizabeth and she nodded.

As the stable owner watched, they melted into the shadows.

"What a stash: two rifles, two revolvers, one knife," Galt said disgustedly. "You'd think I was a damned wanted man or something."

Elizabeth sent him a baleful glance, settled herself against the headboard, and drew her knees up to her chest so she could wrap her arms around them and prop her tired head on them. "You sure accumulate enemies with a vengeance," she commented mildly. "Edgar isn't finished with you—and Cox—I should've pried out his gut, damn him."

"Such a bloodthirsty Lizzie," Galt murmured, regarding her with lively interest.

"You can just stop," she said sharply, disliking the expression on his face. "You can quit and go on and leave them all behind. I seem to keep saying that, but devil it, what you're doing makes no sense whatsoever. To lay yourself open to Edgar like that! And *still* come away determined to smoke out that devil-damned McCreedy woman—and you're not even sure she's here! It's hard to credit your sanity at this point, Galt Saunders. Or *mine,* for that matter," she added astringently, "especially after all that nonsense about honor and reputation. I'm finished, I'm done. I'm tired."

"We've got to move," Galt said, ignoring her tirade.

"*You* have to move." She turned her head away from him and propped it on her knees again. She couldn't bear to thrash it out again. It was still and all his fight, his quest, his *honor.* Her head lifted once more. "What more do you want, Galt? I got you to Rim City in one piece, didn't I?"

His appreciative smile—*that* smile—caught her unawares, and she laid her head down again. She was too damned susceptible by half to that smile, to that man, and it was becoming too devilishly hard to take a stand against him. She wondered how many times she had reversed herself. Every decision to walk away had been mitigated by circumstances or by her feeling she could not abandon him. And now, clearly, she could be of no use to him. None. She just wanted to rest and figure out what to do next.

Galt pushed away the wave of sympathy he felt for her. He needed her still, and nothing would dissuade him from taking her with him. The ferocity of his need was overpowering, and it had nothing to do with treasure or retribution, nothing to do with anything but Elizabeth herself, who in the world she would ultimately return to would never have had anything to do with the likes of someone like him. His intrepid Lizzie, he thought as he began loading ammunition to keep his hands busy and away from the overwhelming desire to touch her adamantly averted face.

It was almost tempting to pick her up and abduct her again, to run as far away from Lonita McCreedy and Edgar Healey as he could take her, and damn his betrayal, and his hard-won financial independence that lay buried now within Lonita's greedy grasp. What *did* it matter, after all? His determination had only put them in danger of their lives, and that was not over yet. Even now, Healey could be searching for them and he didn't want to bet what Cox might want to do to them once he was on his feet.

He had to resolve it. He couldn't walk away from it, he couldn't have the murder charge hanging over his shoulder for the rest of his life, and he could not let that damn-to-hell Lonita walk away with everything.

He sat down on the edge of the bed, hating himself for resorting to scaring Elizabeth. But he needed her. He *needed* her. "Listen, Lizzie, you know Edgar didn't run off to go to his hotel and go to sleep. You know he's probably looking for us right now. We've got to go."

She raised her head. "Go *where*, Galt?"

He reached for the first answer at hand. "We'll find Ada Rudd. She'll help us."

"She'll help *you*. Edgar wouldn't hurt me."

"He'd have a damned lot of questions, Lizzie. He'd want to know why you attacked Cox, why you didn't help *him*. Wouldn't he?"

"I imagine he *would* have a question or two," she admitted reluctantly. "Devil it, Galt, can't you do the rest without me?"

He smiled ruefully. "Oh no, Lizzie, I'm just beginning to find I can't do anything else without you."

Twenty-One

It didn't mean anything, Elizabeth thought as she wearily followed Galt out of the hotel the next morning. Nothing he said meant anything. She was the means to an end; she was useful; she was a lure to entice Martin Healey, if he was in Rim City, so Galt could get to Lonita.

And she had no conception of what might happen after that. She had a feeling he didn't know either.

The most she had been able to do was convince him she was not leaving their room that night, and he had sat most of the night by the window facing the door, rifle on his lap, armed with the certainty that Edgar was going to crash through the door at any moment.

She slept.

And perhaps, she had thought the next morning, Edgar had slept too. Galt had dozed in the chair, and his rifle had slipped to the floor. For one fractious instant, Elizabeth contemplated using it. And she had only the instant; some sixth sense awakened him just as she reached for the rifle butt, and he grabbed it from her hand with the force of a man fighting an enemy who had taken him by surprise.

She was looking at the outlaw face, and she dropped the rifle without compunction. "Edgar never showed," she said mockingly.

"No, you did," he countered with no expression in his voice, and she could not tell if he was angry or disappointed. He had wanted the confrontation, she thought, just as he had goaded

322

Edgar last night. He was roiling inside, he wanted some answers, he wanted . . . something.

Without another word, he handed her the second revolver —*her* weapon—and armed himself. The rifles went into the carpetbag with a brisk impatient thrust; nothing else had been removed.

"Let's go," his brusque voice commanded her.

So all the pretty words were meaningless, washed away in the heat of the morning as they stepped onto the street and began threading their way through the morning rush of pedestrians on their way to open a shop or enter one to do business.

This was a different crowd of people, the residents, the entrepreneurs who had settled in town by the railroad and had begun importing goods that voyagers on the river or by the train would want once they had settled inland. These were settlers who had come this far and stayed, seeing opportunities in the first frontier or jumping-off places that would not exist for them elsewhere. And their clientele numbered those who still elected to push on, and those who had chosen to stay.

The dissolute atmosphere of honky-tonk had totally dissipated. There was money to be made here all right, and the vendors were proud to purvey goods and services that had a reassuring solidity to them, a normalcy that spoke of other places which was also possible here, on the edge of the frontier.

By this time in the morning, wagon trains were trickling into Rim City, already clogging the wide avenues seeking provisions and just a place to rest their weary stock.

No one paid any attention to them as Galt and Elizabeth trekked up Republic Street toward the lodging with the public table. The sign was out for breakfast and they went in and assuaged their hunger with muffins, ham, flapjacks, and coffee along with ten others who were abroad that early in the morning. This table was not as convivial as the night before, but Elizabeth was in no mood for small talk either.

Galt was prickly as a porcupine, and she was feeling rather desperate herself. Neither of them knew where to find Ada Rudd.

She watched him covertly as he stolidly ate whatever was

323

put before him. His mind was somewhere else, the outlaw eyes narrowed blackly and forbiddingly against any light conversation.

She could hardly eat at all, but she forced herself. She was more than ready to leave when Galt signaled to her.

"I had a thought," he said abruptly as they stepped outside and he heaved the carpetbag up under his arm.

"I can't tell you how I would appreciate some thinking on this matter," Elizabeth said edgily, shielding her eyes against the fierce sun.

"*I* don't appreciate your lack of confidence, Lizzie." Galt strode down the porch steps purposefully and Elizabeth had no choice but to follow, mentally railing at his ramrod-straight back. He was nothing but trouble, she thought; nothing good could come from any confrontation in Rim City. She was tired of thinking it, tired of saying it.

But he seemed today to have tossed away all caution. He led her into the morning traffic without his usual circumspection, and they blended in with the pedesterians thronging the street as if they belonged there.

"What on earth are you doing?" she demanded when she caught up with him. "What if Edgar is up on some rooftop with a long-range shotgun?"

"I think not."

"And *that* is your famous thought?"

He slowed his pace a bit so he could look down at her with an oblique black look that hid too much. "You have no faith at all, Lizzie, and you don't deserve to hear it."

"Sorry," she said snippily. "I only saved your life."

He smiled slowly then, that smile that crinkled up around his eyes and she shook her head helplessly.

"Well then, Lizzie, to show you my gratitude knows no bounds, I'll be happy to tell you I think that instead of going into hiding, we should become visible."

"Another opportunity for me to hone my skills," Elizabeth muttered.

He ignored that. "We have to find Lonita *today*, and we can't do that by laying low."

"*You* have to find Lonita," Elizabeth contradicted. "And

324

you keep insisting she's in Rim City, and you don't have a shred of evidence for that conclusion, and you are getting *me* crazy now."

"She's here," he said definitively, taking her arm as they crossed over East Second Street and turned toward Sequoyah. "If Edgar's here, she's here."

"*Where*, if you're so smart?"

"Wherever Edgar is," he said simply, reasonably.

But they saw nothing out of the ordinary as they continued walking cautiously. No feeling of imminent danger assaulted his senses, no familiar face appeared among the pedestrians, nothing threatening happened until they were midway down the street and they saw another posting of the Wanted bill. Galt ripped it down with a disgusted imprecation. "He's not giving up either," Elizabeth said grimly. "You two could arrange a shoot-out on State Street." And at his exasperated look she added, "It would solve *something*."

"It would solve nothing. He knows why he's after me, and I'm coming to have a good idea. So it's a matter of finding Lonita because she is the only one who knows the truth."

"But you think you know the truth."

"I know I didn't kill Buck, and I know Lonita hid the silver, that's what I know, and there is no getting around that Lonita does know the rest."

"And you suppose she's just hanging around here, waiting for you to come find her."

"I think she was hanging around here either waiting for Edgar, or waiting for Martin. Or both."

Elizabeth felt a frisson of shock. "*Now* you tell me," she murmured caustically to cover it. "You mean Lonita killed Buck?"

"No, I mean Edgar did, and that's why he wants me so bad."

Elizabeth digested this in silence as they progressed down Sequoyah Street toward Best of the West Saloon. The activity there was frenetic in front of a mercantile store that was wedged between the saloon and several doors down from the Western Star Hotel.

325

"You could have told me this a hundred miles ago," she said finally, reprovingly.

"I didn't connect it until it was obvious he was our assailant. It makes sense, Lizzie. I told you he was right on the spot after Lonita shoved the damned gun at me. He walked smack in the room two minutes later, and she had hysterics, and he snapped those handcuffs on so fast . . . damn to hell . . . he let no one near me, and he wouldn't listen to anything I had to say, and that, Miss Lizzie, was just the way it was. And so here he is, and you tell me why he's traveled all this way just to catch up with me. To bring me triumphantly back to the Greenfields jail?"

"It appears not," Elizabeth said dryly, but she wasn't so sure his version was the right one either. It hinged on her believing that Buck had been mining the lead and extracting silver, that Lonita had discovered it, killed Buck for it, hidden it, and framed Galt all the while she was in cahoots with both Edgar and Martin Healey, and it included the fact that Martin had jilted *her* because of Lonita. It was quite a mouthful to swallow.

He watched her face as she made all the associations, but there was still a doubtful look shadowing her eyes, and he didn't know what it was that made her hesitate to concur with his suppositions.

"I believe you didn't kill Buck," she said at last, just as she and Galt simultaneously caught sight of Ada Rudd's weather-beaten face and gnarled form coming toward them.

She waved and Galt acknowledged her, and they waited until she came up to them and bid them good morning, her lined face alive with a peculiar kind of pleasure. "Good to see you this morning," she greeted them. "Didn't know if I'd of had another chance, and I know you got trouble here, Mr. Saunders. So since I'm on my way out late this morning, I'm wondering if I can be of some service to you."

"I thank you, Miz Rudd," Galt said gravely, "but we figure on staying here awhile and settling things. Where you bound?"

Ada cackled delightedly. "Oh, I got me a passenger that's wild to get out of town. And she don't know if she wants to go forward or back—she just wants to *go*."

Galt's senses prickled tellingly. "Appears to me you plan on

326

taking her around in circles until she does make up her mind."

"That makes me no never mind. She's got the money to pay for it, I'll ride her straight up and down State Street for the next whole week if that's what she wants."

Elizabeth started to speak but Galt checked her, squeezing her arm hard. "Gambling lady, you think?" he commented offhandedly.

"Scared lady, more like," Ada said, making a move to pass them, and then she stopped and looked carefully at Galt's impassive face.

Sharp old bird, he thought, giving up any thought of trying to deceive those shrewd old eyes. "Describe her."

Ada stared at him consideringly for a moment. "Genteel lady, with some rough edges, dark hair, blue eyes. Fragile-looking and tough as a steer hide inside. She had real ready money, and she wasn't just anxious neither. You know her?"

Galt nodded. "I want her," he said emphatically.

Ada's gaze skewed toward Elizabeth's stunned face. Her head lifted knowingly. She looked at Galt with an expression that said more than words.

He hauled out his money pouch. "How much, Ada?"

"Equal what she gave me."

"You're a thief, Ada. She couldn't have paid you a flat price without some definite destination. And you know you'll find another paying fare sometime soon this morning. So how much?"

"What's it worth to you?" Ada asked cagily.

"Not as much as it's worth to you," Galt retorted. "Don't try your luck, Ada. We'll get to her one way or the other, a little later than sooner if you insist on holding us up." He closed his pouch and made a motion to tuck it away.

Ada named a price. Galt reduced it by thirty dollars. Ada upped it by ten, and Galt lowered it by ten, and they settled amicably in the middle. Galt counted out the money carefully and ignored Ada's smug expression. She tucked it away with the speed of a magician. "How do you want to handle this? Will you ride in the wagon or follow?"

Galt considered for a moment. "We'll come. Lizzie?"

She looked at him blankly, feeling as if she were coming out of a trance. I want Lonita, he had said, with a devastating male surety that utterly unnerved her. And now he wanted her to come—to find out the truth? What truth, *his* truth? How fortuitous they had met Ada. *Did* she want to see the end of it all? To watch Galt and Lonita McCreedy ride away and make their own truth out of the hash of these last several weeks?

What did Galt want of her, after all the small humiliations he had inflicted on her—that she be witness to the final one?

Or did he really believe he could shake any truth out of someone like Lonita McCreedy, if all that he had told her about Lonita were true?

"Lizzie?" The gentle tone of his voice was undercut by just the faintest shade of urgency.

Ada turned and began walking back the way she had come. Galt held out his hand to Elizabeth, and she lifted her eyes to his. His expression told her nothing. It was her decision to make. Again.

She gave him her hand, and he pulled her after Ada.

Did she trust him, he wondered as they climbed into Ada's wagon one more time, or was it that she wanted to laugh at the pathetic conclusion to the whole adventure? There was nothing to say that Lonita would confess one minute of her deceit to *him* of all people, nothing to assure his vindication.

Once again he was caught in a bind of half-formulated plans and schemes that might just come to nothing. His sole strength at this moment lay solely in his determination. And Lizzie by his side, her expression noncommittal, her sassy mouth for once mute with the shock of the oncoming confrontation.

Ada turned to speak to them. "Eleven of the clock, Mr. Saunders, I am to pick up your lady on Jackson Street heading out of town."

Too much time, he thought, to sit and wait and think about everything he could say and probably wouldn't, and everything she could say and what she might do. And conversely, it was too little time to plan alternatives if scaring the truth out of her didn't work.

And over and above that, there was Lizzie, sitting there so calmly, too calmly; there was a frenzy centered in that outward serenity, and nothing revealed in her cool green eyes. Miss Elizabeth sat before him, as regal and self-possessed as if she were in a buggy on her way to a party. All her thoughts, all her opinions, were tucked behind her private face, in a retreat that withdrew the woman and left a shell. He hated the Miss Elizabeth who sat before him in that judgmental hauteur.

He felt as though he had no backbone to deal with either Lonita or Elizabeth. Everything hung in the balance—and nothing. The only important thing he stood to lose he had never possessed to begin with.

How singular that everything came down to Lizzie—and the money—and he wasn't sure even at that moment which was the more important to him.

But in point of fact, all his decisions had already been made for him. Elizabeth's leaving him was already preordained after all he had put her through, and her birth and breeding negated anything else.

Lonita would probably deny everything straight up and down, he thought, and he would have to plan what to do about that.

But it seemed simple after all, when he had ruminated about it for a concentrated few moments. He had only to draw them all back to Greenfields, and Lonita's greed and fear would do the rest.

His stone black gaze focused on Elizabeth, who was deliberately avoiding his eyes. Beautiful Lizzie. He would leave her, and not the other way around. It seemed easier that way too. If he handled it right, she might even be able to pick up a clue that would direct Edgar and Lonita to him. It was the only way to do it.

The only way.

He crawled forward to speak a few words with Ada, who sat stolidly on her perch awaiting the tolling of the church bell to signify the hour.

Elizabeth watched him with bleak eyes. She couldn't hear the conversation between him and Ada; she wasn't sure she wanted to. Her hands were icy cold, and she felt a peculiar

329

sense of fate as she waited for Galt to fold his body back into its niche opposite her, and for the wagon to move.

All the ludicrous events of the past several weeks would culminate finally on a much-used road heading out of Rim City, and nothing she could do would prevent it.

The clock struck eleven, and the wagon moved forward with its customary jerk as Ada shouted at her horses and strapped their rumps meaningfully.

"You nervous?" Galt asked.

Elizabeth shrugged. "Are you?" She really felt beyond nerves at that moment; she was heading toward some kind of cataclysm and she did not know what to expect. Neither, she thought critically, did Galt. But he had settled something in his mind. He exuded an air of purpose and a focused tranquility that made her almost envious.

"No," he said suddenly. "I'm not sure where we'll get with Lonita, Lizzie, but I am sure I'm going to prevent her from getting my share of the silver."

"I see," she said quietly, but she didn't see at all. The money was all-important then, and everything else be damned. Something gave within her that she had been holding tight and tense against her heart, something she perhaps would never have admitted—that she wanted him to choose her above all the convolutions of this search and where it was leading them.

But why should he? He had only been using her all this time, and she had known it. Nothing had changed, really. Her fretfulness coiled inside her into a tight spring of emotion that she was sure she might unleash on Lonita without warning.

Or Galt.

But no, she felt like attacking *him;* she felt like forcing him to see *her,* not as a means to an end, but as the companion of his quest and the woman she had become under his tutelage.

Yet what good would it do after all? He was still the outlaw, still on the run, still without answers. Still avariciously seeking a fortune that might or might not be rightfully his.

She stole a look at his adamant face as the wagon moved inexorably to the rendezvous. His jetty gaze glanced off hers,

330

opaque, revealing nothing. The lines in his face seemed to have etched themselves deeper; he looked weary and wary both, and there was a guarded set to his body, as if he was primed for any possibility.

Out the wagon gate, she could see the distance between houses widening. Her heart started pounding wildly as the moment of the showdown drew closer and closer.

Her composure almost shattered as the wagon all of a sudden jolted to a shuddering halt.

Galt's hand automatically went for his gun as they heard a rustling of bushes, and Ada's scratchy voice greeting his nemesis. "Morning, lady. You can settle your belongings in the back there, and we'll get on with it."

"Do you mind if I sit with you?" a musical voice with a husky undertone asked.

"It's your money," Ada said, and Elizabeth could just see her offhanded shrug. How well she played a part, she thought; how much of her crusty well-worn mien *was* actually an act?

But there was no time to reflect on that. Lonita's crunching footsteps came closer and Galt motioned Elizabeth back against the tarpaulin.

In another long suspended moment that seemed to take an eternity, Lonita McCreedy's sleek black head appeared at the window gate, lovelier and daintier than even Elizabeth could have imagined, but with a lithe strength in her arms that enabled her to swing her bags over the wagon gate with no effort at all.

She didn't see Galt, didn't feel the heat emanating from his anger that would have catapulted him out of the wagon if he hadn't been holding such a tight rein on himself.

"Lonita!" His voice whipped out behind her, and suddenly Elizabeth felt as if she were alone in the wagon; that somehow only the two of them inhabited the space between the wagon and where Lonita had stopped short, her breast heaving. She whirled, stared at the wagon, shrieked, "Goddamn you, Galt Saunders," and tore into a run.

Galt vaulted over the wagon gate and set off after her. He overtook her in ten steps and tackled her to the ground, wrestling her hands away from his face as he straddled her writhing body.

Elizabeth climbed out of the wagon slowly and stood watching them. Behind her, the wagon lumbered off down the track and she wasn't even aware of it. But Lonita was.

"Where is that bedamned woman going with my wagon?" she screamed, her desperation lending her an uncommon strength that even Galt's superior power and weight could barely contain.

"Son of a bitch . . . Lonita, damn you to hell . . ."

"Get off . . . of me, you bastard, you murderer . . ."

". . . thief, bitch . . . you'll tell the damned truth, you bitch, you . . ."

"Murderer . . . murderer . . . *Murderer!*"

"I could kill you . . . *Lizzie!*"

Elizabeth stared, fascinated by the spectacle. Had he called to her? Was she supposed to help him? Could he honestly expect *that,* devil his hide?

"*Lizzie,* damn it . . ."

She started. He *was* in trouble. Lonita fought him like a tigress and damned if she wasn't winning. She wondered if she wanted Lonita to win. Lonita could buck him right off and disappear into the bushes and that would put paid to all his scheming.

And then he would follow her because he was so determined to win.

Damn his hide, damn him.

She reached for her revolver, which was tucked into her shirt and waistband, and pulled it out. Tempting, she thought as she raised the barrel and then lowered it to take aim. She could just fire and eliminate both of them with one shot.

She lifted the barrel again, and fired into the air.

Lonita stopped struggling long enough to look at her. "Who is *that* bitch?" she growled, her glittering blue eyes sending messages across the space between them. Pure hate hung in the air, hate for Galt and the interloper who dared to stop her fight and her flight.

"My bodyguard," Galt grunted, levering himself off her.

She sat up disgustedly, one wary eye on the gun barrel that loomed over her. "What do you want, and where is that damned wagon?"

"You know what I want, Lonita, and the damned wagon is gone."

That little piece of information jarred even Elizabeth, but she held the gun steady, waiting, watching to see what Galt was up to, what Lonita would do, hating Lonita with a force of emotion that was totally alien to her.

"I don't know what you are talking about," Lonita said laconically. She started to get up, and some malicious instinct in Elizabeth made her motion the gun at Lonita to keep her on the ground.

Yes, on the ground she couldn't shift the power; on the ground Lonita was vulnerable, beaten.

"I guess you don't," Galt drawled, standing over her with his hands on his hips, feeling the frustration seep into his bones at her sardonic denial that no one could ever make her retract. "I guess I'm going to have to tear the mountain apart with my bare hands while you hightail it out of Rim City to who the hell knows where."

He saw the faintest flash of unsurety in her eyes, but a moment later she shrugged it off. "I still don't know what you mean."

"Fine, we'll leave it at that then," Galt said. "You go your way, and I'll go mine, and we'll see who gets to the silver first, won't we?"

Another flash of blue lightning in her eyes, and then she cast her eyes downward without commenting.

Galt pressed the point. "I'm pretty sure you took off without it. The way I see it, it's the only reason you've been hanging around Rim City, and the real reason you're heading back out of town."

Her head snapped up at that. "That's funny," she said tightly.

"All your cohorts are here, Lonita. All you have to do is outmaneuver them and head back to Greenfields. They'd be two days behind you at least before they figured out what the hell you planned to do. Two days. Twenty-four hours of daylight to arrange matters. Clever, Lonita, damned clever. Of course, Lizzie and I were down at the ranch for one damned long day. You'll never know what—if anything—we found there."

"You're bluffing," she said, her eyes sliding to Elizabeth's steady hand holding the gun just over her.

"We were there," Elizabeth confirmed, her mind reeling backward to the hellish night she had spent there with him. Everything . . . hellish, and now she was holding a gun over the woman who had accused Galt of murder. She felt topsy-turvy again, as if the things she did and the things he said had no relation to any reality she ever remembered.

"You found nothing," Lonita said.

"We found the truth," Galt contradicted.

"Such sincerity," she mocked.

"Such a liar," he said in kind. "What do you think, Lizzie?"

"It's your show," she said expressionlessly. And what a show, she thought; he knew just how to handle Lonita, just as he had known how to deal with Ada, and even her. Lonita was his adversary, but she had that same unwilling feeling of liking him as all the others, as Elizabeth herself. She could feel it pouring from Lonita, together with the reluctance and the supreme sense of self-preservation. Galt knew how to exploit it, too. He knew too damned much, she thought, as she had often thought.

"Is Martin here too?" Galt asked conversationally.

Again her eyes did that double take, and she looked away from him. "You said *all* my cohorts—you must know."

"I do," he agreed pleasantly.

"So you think you know everything now," Lonita said, goaded by his smug tone.

"I know everything," Galt confirmed, pacing away from her, his back to her, depending with his whole life on Lizzie's keeping the gun trained on her treacherous body.

Lonita surged to her feet, completely ignoring Elizabeth and the gun. Elizabeth's lips thinned threateningly, she aimed, and a bullet scored the ground directly behind Lonita's feet. Startled, she whirled around to face Elizabeth's glittering green eyes.

"Thank you, Lizzie," Galt said gently, so gently that Elizabeth wondered if it had been some kind of skewed test of her loyalty.

Lonita stood poised and unmoving, her face reflecting her respect for Elizabeth's skill. She really *looked* at Elizabeth for the first time, seeing beneath the layers of grime and ill-kempt dressing a purposeful kind of beauty and character, an elegance of stance in the line of her body. This was no cowtown ruffian he had with him. This was a lady who knew how to use a gun. And how, Lonita wondered, could *she* use *her?*

She focused her attention on Elizabeth, smiling self-deprecatingly with a little shrug that in other circumstances would have bonded them together against this smug powerful *man*. "You believe him?" she asked, tilting her head obliquely at Elizabeth.

Damn her to hell, Galt thought. He didn't look at Elizabeth; he couldn't guess what she was thinking. He felt Elizabeth's eyes flicker over him and then back to Lonita.

"I believe him," she said firmly, and he let out a breath.

Lonita perceived his tension. Such a good way to play for time, she thought. And what if she could convince this Elizabeth and turn her against Galt? It would be so easy . . . She smiled again, a faint knowing smile this time, and addressed Elizabeth. "I must admit he's good. He's real good at convincing people. You understand what I mean."

Elizabeth's expression hardened. "From what I've heard, so are you. I heard you did a real good job of convincing Martin Healey, for example."

Lonita stared at her. *This* was *Martin's* Elizabeth? The Barnett of Kentucky? The one whom he rued the day he had ever proposed to? The one from whom he had been hiding all this time? Bedamned, she thought gratefully, and he was well rid of that one; if he could see her now, ruined and in the company of Galt Saunders. How lovely, how ironic, especially since she hadn't heard the end of it for months, his abandoning Elizabeth, his guilt for trampling on all her expectations, and his leaving her at the mercy of his father and mother.

She turned to Galt. "What are you going to do with me? What can you *possibly* do with me? I will stand by my story no matter what, you know."

"I expect that of you," Galt said, still in that pleasant tone.

335

Lonita shook her head. "I feel sorry for you. You've come all this way, obviously with some idea of coercing some kind of story out of me, and you wind up with nothing. I can tell you nothing, and I'm sorry for that, and for the fact that Edgar would never listen to any kind of plea for clemency now. You're stuck with the conviction, Galt, and it hurts me that a man of your . . . ability felt he had to resort to murder."

"For *you?*" Galt said mockingly to keep her talking; he had a vague inkling now what he was going to do. It was already obvious that she did not have the money with her or she would be frantic to escape them and find Ada, who was in fact waiting for him at a prearranged distance down the road. All Lonita's bags were there to be searched—if Ada hadn't searched them first, he thought sardonically, since Ada had already perceived the lady had money. It didn't matter. She could not have been carrying the bulk of the treasure; he was sure of that, just as he was certain she was on her way back to Greenfields to unearth it without Edgar or Martin—if he were here—knowing it.

She was putting a good face on it, he thought, with just the right amount of calculated denial and righteous indignation. But he had known what a good little actress she was. He wondered how she would answer him; ostensibly he had been pining away for love of her, and had used the only means at his disposal to free her. The jury had believed it, Elizabeth had believed it.

Lonita sent him a fey little smile. "Oh no, not for *me,*" she said tenderly, slanting a sly blue glance at Elizabeth. "For the ranch, the property, the mountain; for Buck's security, Galt. You and I both know—you wanted it all, and you took the easiest way to get it."

Twenty-Two

Elizabeth's heart turned over, and something else inside her caved in to the realistic sense of Lonita's accusation. She felt twisted and turned every which way, and humiliated all over again. Every story sounded too reasonable, too possible. But on top of that, she sensed Galt's shock at Lonita's words, and she wondered why he should feel such an emotion if what Lonita was saying were true.

She gripped the gun as though it were a lifeline, almost ready in her agitation to turn it on Galt himself.

And he didn't deny it!

Lonita's lips curved in a faint smile of triumph directed right at Elizabeth. "That is really how it was, and if I had talked about that lead mine on the stand, every damned speculator from Greenfields to St. Joe would have descended on the ranch."

"Just think of all the money they would have offered you for the mining rights," Galt interpolated.

"They would have torn up the town," Lonita said defensively.

"They would have made us *all* rich," he contradicted, "but how like you not to think of anyone else but yourself."

"Go to hell, Galt."

"Oh no," Galt said easily, "I'm going to Greenfields."

For the first time, something flashed in her eyes that looked remotely like fear. Her body tensed, almost sensing she had possibly given something away, and she looked as if she might

337

make a run for it. Then she relaxed, and her face evened out into its former faintly derisive expression. "You seem to like wild-goose chases, Galt; I wish you luck."

Galt looked at Elizabeth, who stood still as a statue, her gun obediently trained on Lonita, and her eyes burning with green fire. He groaned inside. He had to leave her, and very soon. Too soon. She would hate him for it, and he knew it. But there was nothing else left to do. He couldn't take her with him this time. He was after speed and immediacy, and she would slow him down. More than that, he might wind up in jail again, and he surely did not want her with him there. Oh God, Lizzie . . . maybe he did. He wanted her with him anywhere, and he wished to hell he had never begun this obsessive odyssey.

She would not look at him either. Her scalding gaze was fixed totally on Lonita, all her resentment for the fact that she and Galt acted as though she, Elizabeth, did not exist pouring out at the woman who stood before her at the mercy of her gun. And no vindication for Galt either. He was a user, just as Lonita was. If she had been smart, she would have gone right off with Ada and the wagon and left them to each other. She felt wiser now, but no less in pain. This was the only possible outcome.

She fully expected Galt to make a deal, to ask Lonita to go with him. Two of a kind, they were, an outlaw and a jezebel. A wholly unfamiliar sensation knifed through her at the thought.

She stepped forward just to break the tension and intensity of feeling between Galt and Lonita, and Galt, after a moment, moved behind *her*, almost in a gesture of protection.

His hands touched her shoulders, and she wanted to shake them off. He had no business holding her like that, with that warmth and that seductive gentleness, aligning himself on her side as though they were some kind of team. She felt a furious indifference toward him now that was compounded by the ensuing silence and the reverberation of Lonita's mocking words.

And then he pushed her, thrusting her at Lonita deliberately and intentionally, and the two women toppled to the ground in a confusion of skirts and profanity.

The gun! Elizabeth scrambled to her knees frantically, feeling for the revolver—under her skirt, thank God—and she grasped it before Lonita could pick herself up, and taking one frenzied look around her to locate him, the bastard, damn him to hell, she raised the barrel and began firing wildly into the trees.

One . . . two . . . three . . . four . . . nothing. Lonita stared at her as if she were crazy; maybe she was—those four shots didn't nearly vent her rage at Galt, and left her totally defenseless, since all the ammunition was in the wagon. She blew at the smoking barrel of the gun, and stood up.

"Oh now, Elizabeth, wasn't that a stupid thing to do."

The voice startled her, and she saw by the look on Lonita's face that Lonita knew just who the speaker was.

So did Elizabeth. Edgar Healey walked around her silent stunned form and neatly removed the revolver from her boneless fingers.

"Well now," Edgar said, pushing his hat back on his head thoughtfully, "what we've got here is two little birds all helpless and flapping their wings and getting nowhere fast." He walked over to Lonita. "Howdy, Lonita; I reckon you ain't as smart as you thought."

"Reckon I wasn't," she murmured cagily, but she didn't seem surprised to see him. Not at all.

"And you let old Galt get away."

"Reckon I did," she agreed.

"And there wasn't nothing in that wagon except what you needed to cheat me out of my share, that so, Lonita?"

"If you say so, Edgar."

"I say so," he said with some satisfaction. "And you, Elizabeth, I'm damned surprised, *damned* surprised at you running around with that thief and murderer all this time, and then when you get hold of a gun, you wind up helping the bastard escape. I don't understand it, I truly don't. But that's already done and gone. Where's he off to?"

Elizabeth shook her head, wondering at herself for protecting him even now. Lonita sent her a shrewd blue look; oh, she understood everything, Elizabeth thought angrily, all the bitterness and ambivalence and mortification. She had the bizarre sense that those things never would have happened to Lonita. Lonita had the native canniness to hold her own against Galt Saunders, hold her own against anyone, including Edgar Healey, who was in a fine suppressed rage over her near-defection.

"Where do you think he's off to?" Lonita drawled.

"Shit," Edgar spat succinctly. "And you kindly foresaw his intention and rushed off to save the family jewels, eh Lonita?"

"Something like that."

"You gonna walk after him?" Healey asked sardonically, tamping down on his own urge to ride hell for leather after the bastard. He looked at Elizabeth. "You got some explaining to do, Elizabeth; you owe me."

"Do I have a choice?" she asked mildly.

"I don't believe you have," he said, and there was no mistaking the steel in his voice. "We're all going right back to Greenfields, ain't that so, Lonita?"

"I expect it is," she said, for the first time allowing both exasperation and the faintest urgency to creep into her tone of voice.

Edgar clamped them each on one shoulder and turned them back toward town. "It's gonna be mighty good to get home again," he said heartily.

Rim City didn't look any different in the late afternoon than it had when she had left it, but for Elizabeth everything looked different now that Edgar Healey had her in tow, and she was finally face to face with the formidable Lonita McCreedy.

She didn't like feeling stupid and gullible; she didn't like anything, including Lonita's sleek elegant looks that were hardly disheveled from her brief sprawl in the dirt.

Edgar was determined to lose no time. Galt only had a start of a couple of hours on them; they could make Drover's Landing by dark for sure. It was more than likely he wouldn't have gone over today.

"I'm not riding," Lonita told him with asperity.

"Oh my dear Miz Lonita, I wouldn't dream of dirtying your skirts," Edgar said with a touch of falsetto nastiness. "How about you, Miz Elizabeth, you got any funny fancies?"

"A bath," she said shortly.

"Heh heh, you always did have a strange humor, Elizabeth. Just don't think I'm forgetting your betrayal. You have a lot to answer for."

"So do you," she shot back. "Why don't you tell us how you plan for us to return to Greenfields?"

"Oh now, Elizabeth, I bet you're just waiting for me to go off and secure supplies and a wagon and leave you all alone."

"I was hoping," Elizabeth said caustically, but in truth, she had very little thought about it at all. Edgar held the reins now, and even if he disappeared at that very moment, she would still have no more choices than if he had put her in handcuffs.

"No, no, no. I did just what you gals did," Edgar said with some satisfaction. "I got me an accomplice." He turned and waved his arm, and they watched with a horrified curiosity as a wagon disengaged from the crowd by the mercantile store and slowly made its way up Sequoyah Street toward them. And Martin Healey was driving the team.

"Now ain't this cosy," Martin said as he settled back against the perch box, a gun in hand pointed straight at Lonita and Elizabeth, who were sitting back toward the wagon gate, strangely allied in their distrust and disbelief.

"Traitor," Lonita hissed.

"Aw now, Lonita, you know you were well on your way to a double-cross. You oughta thank Edgar and me for preventing it."

"Sure, he made it easy for Saunders to escape, and you thought you were so smart throwing in with him. See where it will get you, Martin. See where it will get any of you."

"Yeah, and you didn't help by talking a damned lot too much, lady," Martin snapped. "Saunders knew right enough where to find you, didn't he? I wonder what you offered *him*."

Lonita shrugged. "Let me tell you, there was more than enough to go around, but no damned man is worth it."

"Well, one damned man is gonna get his share, Lonita, never you fear, and it ain't gonna be Galt Saunders, either.

You stupid bitch—you probably told him every damned thing before you framed him. You probably had a deal with him too. You're a piece of work, Lonita; poor Buck's well out of his misery. I wish to hell I was, but I got a stake here, and I intend to collect."

"You'll collect nothing," Lonita said coolly. "Nobody knows anything, and I know everything. You stupid bastard men believe what you want to believe as long as it's a pretty face who tells it to you. The goods can sit forever as far as I'm concerned."

Elizabeth had to admire her. There wasn't a thing they could threaten her with. She could keep her secrets forever. The only thing she had to fear was Galt. Galt was smart, and he knew the lay of the land. If he were appreciably ahead of them, he would have unrestricted movement and time to find where she had hidden Buck's treasure.

Even *she* had to realize that, and Elizabeth marveled that none of it showed on her face. But her supercilious tone of voice and her bland expression irritated Martin to the point of explosiveness. His hand twitched as he held the gun on them; his face darkened with anger—little signs along with a frenzied impatience that seemed to consume him and drive him to goading her.

"The goods won't sit forever, I promise you. We'll tear that damned mountain apart, we'll tear the ranch apart; we don't need you, Lonita, and when you become expendable, we'll do something about it. But mark my words, Lonita, you won't come away richer—and maybe you won't come away alive."

"Maybe *you* won't," she retorted icily. "You gave in to your father right quick, Martin, there's no way I can trust a man who would do that."

"Daddy had a story to tell me, and I want to tell you, I was real interested to hear it after I woke up and found you gone, lady. Wasn't it a fool coincidence I ran into him five minutes after I hightailed it down to the livery to hire a horse? And wasn't it too bad Galt was on the loose and Daddy *had* to follow? Just think what would've happened if he hadn't known about the silver, hmm?"

"You stupid fool, he was working the mine with Buck; you

342

should have railroaded him faster, that's all. Edgar could have found a reason to get rid of him," Lonita snapped. "Incompetent fools."

"Yeah, but you see, he smartly got hold of Miss Elizabeth here, who unwisely chose to stay on where she wasn't wanted after she didn't have a prayer of getting married. Who do you want to blame, Lonita?"

"The lot of you are dull-witted idiots," Lonita swore. "It's too late for anything now. This bitch knows too much."

"I wish you had gone back the hell where you came from," Martin grumbled, directing his animosity toward Elizabeth now.

She faced him down, the hate smoldering in her eyes. He was a pawn and a beggar, and now that she was well over the shock of seeing him again after all this time, she couldn't imagine how she had been taken in by him. He looked the same—tall and faintly fleshy, almost as if his body were fighting off his nominal inheritance from Edgar. His dark hair was sun-streaked, and his raisin brown eyes, so like Edgar's, seemed to dull against the tan of his skin. He looked blurred and unfinished, the battle-honed soldier running to fat and hoping to live off the fat of the land—or ill-gotten gains. Maybe he had been living off Lonita all along.

"Too late for that now," she mocked, paraphrasing Lonita's last words.

"Not too late to get rid of you," he countered harshly, and she stiffened at the import of the words. "However, for the moment, you do have your uses. I wager that Galt Saunders will not hesitate to come running when he sees Miss Elizabeth Barnett in Drover's Landing."

So she was to be used to smoke Galt out of hiding when they arrived. How ironic, she thought, and how smart of Galt to have made it out of Drover's Landing before they came. But they still had the long wait for the ferry and the interminable boat ride over, which would be accomplished just before dusk and put them in River Flats just in time for the evening's carousing.

She felt as if they were solving a puzzle. A detail here, a space there, and soon the whole picture would appear before them. But not, she thought, the picture that either Edgar or Martin hoped to see.

Edgar fumed all the way across the river at both the circumstances and the excess fare because of his passengers. Once they touched shore, he had the further problem of locating food and a place for them to lay over in the wagon, all problems he was sure Galt Saunders wasn't having since Galt had at least a half-day's start on them, and no additional baggage.

In the end, he and Martin agreed they had no choice but to truss up their hostages to prevent them from getting any idea about escaping.

Several hours later, Elizabeth lay on her stomach in the dark, while next to her, a frenzied Lonita spewed an endless stream of curses at the darkened tarp wall, beyond which Edgar and Martin were somehow occupied. They had been fed, and their needs seen to, and now they were so much cargo until Edgard reached his destination.

So why was she thinking about Galt, Elizabeth wondered as she stared into the darkness. Why wasn't she protesting her return to Greenfields when she had the means to force her freedom with the knife that was snugly sheathed around her leg, and the remainder of the money, which was folded as tight as her skin beneath her heel in the opposite boot?

She had no sympathy for Galt, not after his abuse and use, and the callous way he had left her at Edgar's mercy. But still, something in her responded to returning to the places she had been with him, and that reluctant feeling of liking surfaced to blot out all other considerations. But it was ridiculous. Everything she had felt about him was mitigated by his leaving her, and the many possible endings to the story of which he had told her but one version—his own.

And whose was real, after all? They were all after the money, whatever form it took; they would kill for the money. Even Galt would kill for the money.

But Galt wasn't a killer. Galt was a man who knew how to use people; he was masterful at it, and wholly unlike the man who had been whispered about in Greenfields.

Who was he, really?

The question haunted her as she lay wide awake hour after hour, reliving the weeks she had spent with him. Nothing she knew about him jibed with the desperate man who had abducted her or the imperturbable companion on the trail.

Nothing had prepared her for her indelible response to him on any level. She couldn't shake it, even after everything that had happened, and she couldn't negate it. She felt swamped with this iridescent sense of him, as if he occupied a corner of her mind and body whether she willed it or not.

She had to see him again.

No! She pushed that stunning conclusion out of her mind. She never wanted to see him again. *Never.*

Oh, but when she did . . .

No. She had to plan to get away from Edgar long before they reached the outskirts of Greenfields.

Long before.

The landscape was familiar, or he kept thinking it was familiar, and that he had passed that way with Elizabeth, and that they had come upon that long field, and this quaint house, that particular group of plateaus, the farmer who pushed his herd of sheep along some well-worn track. He was sure they had seen it all, and yet some small part of him knew they had not come this way at all, and the thing he was feeling was a terrible yearning to share it all with her again.

And his imagination ran riot because he needed to fill that empty space within him that she had occupied: he needed Lizzie, and all he could ever have was the rejection of Miss Elizabeth.

He was so close to Greenfields now, an hour perhaps out of town, on a stultifyingly hot late Missouri afternoon, and he did not feel compelled to rush into town and out to the McCreedy ranch. He felt like turning back and claiming Lizzie.

But she was probably still in Rim City, making plans to restore some normalcy to her life; Ada had said she would check and send word. He had left Ada at the ferryboat dock, seeking passengers on foot or in distress to haul for a fee to Rim City. He had given her what she wanted of Lonita's sparse belongings, among which there was no clue to the whereabouts of the riches that he and Buck had mined.

And he had hired a mount in River Flats with the intention of getting away from there as fast as possible. He knew Edgar would follow, and Lonita. He didn't know who else.

They would expect to find him at the ranch—his or Lonita's—though most likely they would head for the McCreedys'.

He had at most a day to explore the territory, a day to find an inauspicious hideout where he could observe Lonita freely.

It could still come to nothing, he thought; he could still lose everything, and he wondered, as he topped a small rise that overlooked Greenfields, if he even cared.

The interior of his four-room house had been ransacked. Edgar, he thought disgustedly, bending to pick up the toppled kitchen table. What the hell had he expected to find? Even the beds had been torn up, and clothes strewn all over the floor in the bedroom. In the barn, the hay had been forked up and scattered every which way by human hand and by the breeze. The stock was gone, but he had expected that. And holes had been chopped into the roof and walls, and the one extravagance, Lydia's fancy sofa, had been extensively cut up.

He walked wearily back to the kitchen. There was no food, other than a tin of coffee, and he wished he had thought of buying some staples. Resignedly he washed away the dried-up crud on the coffeepot, filled it with water, and put it up to boil.

It reminded him of the night at the McCreedy cabin after he had escaped Edgar with Lizzie in tow.

Damn to hell.

Damned Edgar had stolen every damned thing.

It was time to take his revenge.

Three days later Galt rode cautiously into town, a growth of stubbly beard obscuring his face, his body encased in a

346

concealing rubber poncho.

No one looked at him as he dismounted at the general store; no one asked a single question as he purchased supplies and packed them up in his saddlebags. No one paid him any notice as he ambled down the plank-walked street, looking for some sign that Edgar was back in town.

Nothing seemed out of the ordinary.

He rubbed his cheek thoughtfully. He had a distinct feeling he was missing something. But he had had that notion for two days now, after searching intensively all around the McCreedy place and deep into the mine shaft Buck and he had forged with their limited means and time, and literally with their hands.

He angled across the street and headed toward the Greenback Saloon. It was a low-slung building located directly in the center of town, the place to go for idle gossip, speculation, or a night-long foray into a whiskey bottle. In the afternoon, only the die-hards were hanging out, along with the grizzled old timers whose luck had run out and whose well had run dry.

They sat in the windows, watching, and they knew everything that went on in town. They made a point to know it, and they weren't above selling their observations and information for the price of a drink.

Galt settled himself in at the window end of the bar, ordered a drink, and focused his attention on the group in front of him, their desultory conversation sounding at first like so much babble.

But gradually, as he concentrated, he began to make out what they were saying. Most of it concerned crops and horses, the local ladies of the evening and who had had whom the previous evening, this one's errant wife or son, and last month's drunken brawl, the details of which were commonly picked apart for at least three weeks after the fact.

And then his ears pricked up. He heard Martin Healey's name.

". . . yep, I seen him. Right back here in town."

"Heared Edgar brought 'em back."

"None such. They came together."

". . . and that McCreedy woman . . ."

". . . was going to marry her . . ."

". . . nerve of him showin' his face . . . just 'cause of his father bein' who he is."

". . . that purty gal that wuz helpin' out at Edgar's now, whut wuz her name?"

". . . that ole Martin was down at Flora's last night any to how, and that's how *I* know 'bout it . . ."

"Lemme tell who else was sweet-talkin' them ladies . . ."

Galt set down his glass carefully, not crediting what he was hearing. He beckoned to one of the men, a grandfatherly old man who was not familiar to him. "Buy you a drink," he offered.

The old man hooked a leg on the stool next to him. "What do you want to know?"

Galt motioned to the bartender. "Whiskey?" The old man nodded, and Galt ordered another round for himself as well. "What's your name, old timer?"

The man's shrewd old eyes assessed him like lightning. "Earl," he said. "Call me Earl. What can I do for you?"

Galt waited until they were served their drinks and took a meditative sip before he said, "You new to town?"

"New enough, stranger." Earl sipped slowly, letting the warmth of the whiskey curl through his body. "And around long enough to have an answer to your question.'

Galt smiled appreciatively. "You didn't know Martin Healey."

"Heard tell about him, though, and the town sure was talking when he came riding in with the sheriff day or two ago. They tell a lot of stories about him, I'm hard put to say which of them is true."

"I know them. Sheriff been gone long?"

"Couple of weeks, they say. Wife took over running of the jail, but there ain't much action in a town like this. Worse case managed to escape, I hear—murder, husband of that McCreedy woman they was talking about who came back with Edgar. I didn't know who the other lady was."

"*Two* ladies came back with the sheriff?" Galt questioned, keeping his voice as neutral as possible, ignoring the chord of fear that sounded deep in his gut.

"They say. I didn't see them, but the town's buzzing over the fact that they ain't guests of the sheriff. He's got them locked up as right and tight as any criminal."

"You don't say." God, he was amazed his voice was so calm. "And Martin just kind of slid back into place like he'd never been gone, it seems like."

"That's what they say, right down to visiting Miss Flora last night; they say he was a pretty frequent guest of Miss Flora, but I reckon you've heard about that." Earl sipped again, to give himself some time to figure which item of the information he had tendered the stranger was really after. He didn't know the man, and none of his cronies had identified him when he walked in. He was probably after Healey. From what he'd heard, a lot of people were after Martin Healey and would be damned glad to hear he was back in Greenfields.

He waited expectantly for the next question. Galt sipped his own drink a moment and then asked, "Do they say why the McCreedy woman is in jail?"

"They think maybe she was the one who murdered her husband." Earl shrugged. "They say. The other one—nobody knows; they say she used to live with the sheriff and do chores around the jail. Beats me, stranger."

"Me too," Galt murmured.

"Yeah, sheriff went after the convicted murderer who escaped, they tell me." Earl sent him a questioning look. "That's where the sheriff went. Dunno where he picked up his son or the two ladies. No one knows why he stuck them in jail, just the reason I told you, that's what they say."

Galt downed the last of his drink and signaled the bartender. "Another couple of rounds for my friend here." He clapped Earl on the shoulder. "Appreciate your being so forthcoming, Earl."

"My pleasure," Earl said, dumbfounded, never having expected to get more than the one well-topped-off shot of whiskey for his meager information.

It was interesting, Earl thought as he watched the tall man amble out of the saloon. The stranger didn't offer too little, and he surely didn't offer too much. He had a fine sense of the rightness of things. He had done nothing to arouse Earl's

349

suspicions except to make that impression on him.

He scurried back to his table to hear his cronies' speculations.

Galt contained himself, though he didn't know how he contained himself until he walked slowly out of the Greenback and onto the street, and then the blood started pounding in his veins, competing with the roaring in his head—damn him, and damn him to hell: Edgar had Lizzie right here in Greenfields in the goddamned jail.

He squashed down his first impulse to run to the jailhouse. Rescuing Lizzie would require a little more finesse than an outright attack. Edgar was smarter than that, but he wondered if Edgar were smart enough to throw her in jail just to lure him out into the open.

God. He heard the echo of his own hastily formulated plan in his assessment of Edgar's purpose. He hated it, he hated himself, and he had to get to Lizzie.

He forced himself to walk slowly down the street, forced himself to merely stroll by the jailhouse to get a fix on the situation, but no one was visible from the outside. It was just a squat little building backing a square with a tree and a horde of stray animals that Lizzie used to feed.

He edged in closer. It was too damned quiet, and Martin was abroad somewhere in town. He didn't think Edgar was cagey enough to recruit Martin to spy for him. He felt safe—there was no telling prickle at the back of his neck, no sense of danger as he roamed carefully around the outside of the building looking for signs of life, of guards.

It was suspiciously quiet, and too damned easy for him to scout around the building. Edgar was waiting for him, had made things as enticing as possible to lure him into the jail. He refused to bite at the bait.

He eased away from the building and angled behind Edgar's house, which was off to one side and set well behind the jail. Martha was nowhere about, and he cut across the little bit of property appended to the back of the house which led to a side road and back into town.

Without undue haste, he sauntered back down the street to where he had tethered his horse, and mounted slowly. What if *he* snared Edgar instead, he wondered, and led him off into the hills on a wild-goose chase along with his men? There couldn't be too many deputies watching over two women when there had only been two guarding him. Martin was a complication, but not one that would be so effective as to hinder him. Anyway, he would like an excuse, he thought, to vent some of his anger on Martin Healey.

Surprise was his best weapon. He was going after Lizzie this very night.

She still had the knife, Elizabeth thought, comforting herself as she sat stolidly at the table in the same cell from which Galt had escaped. It was a consolation. There was always a chance she might get to use it. For the moment, however, for the last two days, it was enough just to occupy this cell and experience the same things Galt had experienced, the same things he had felt. The frustration overwhelmed her even after that short period of time, and the sense of timelessness and isolation that was punctuated by the movement of the sun outside the jail cell window.

It was like being in a cage, with a keeper whose sole duty was to goad and patronize her and Lonita.

"Old Galt will come," Edgar kept saying with that smug condescending tone of voice, "and we'll pop him in that jail cell right next to you, Elizabeth my dear, seeing as how you've been pining away for him. And then Lonita and I will settle our little deal between us, won't we, Lonita? Or else Lonita will keep you company here while *I* continue the search, which I'm perfectly willing to do, Lonita darlin', and send you all off to prison for your dastardly crime. You might," he would add, "like to think very carefully about your decision."

Galt wouldn't come, Elizabeth thought, staring out the window into the light, into the dark, anywhere that she did not have to look at Edgar even if she did have to listen to his taunts. Galt didn't even know she had returned to Greenfields under duress with Edgar and Martin.

In any event, Edgar had to be bluffing. He couldn't be sure Galt was in town either. And he had nothing with which to make Lonita reveal her secrets except the threat of prison.

He wanted Galt badly and it had to be because Galt was the only one who could thwart his plans, the only one who knew that Edgar or Lonita had really killed Buck McCreedy, and knew the real reason why.

And all for the damned treasure in silver. All of them, even Galt, were after the wealth and nothing else.

Edgar couldn't be sure that Galt had not found it. Edgar couldn't be sure of anything, she thought. His self-control was probably riding a thin edge between tolerant patience and outright explosion. He couldn't control events; he could only sit back and hope his preposterous scheme would work.

And what of Martha? What was she thinking as she dutifully trudged back and forth with a tray full of ill-cooked fare for them twice a day? She never by look or word indicated anything of her feelings when she served Elizabeth in her cell, and what she must be thinking about Lonita's occupation of the other cell was anyone's guess. Her flat brown gaze never wavered, she never spoke to Edgar, and he never said a word to her.

Nor were there any recriminations for Martin as far as Elizabeth could tell. He had obviously moved back into the family home, and he, along with another deputy, Bryce, and Tex, whom Elizabeth knew, relieved Edgar in the early evening so he could have his dinner and a nap. He generally returned from that near midnight and then Martin left, and Bryce and Tex stayed on.

Tex often sent Elizabeth sad-eyed regretful looks as he checked on her every hour or so. Otherwise, he stationed himself down the jail cell hallway, at an expedient distance between Edgar's office and the rear door. He remembered right well the night Galt Saunders had escaped, and he had strict instructions to be on the lookout for anything unusual in and around Miss Elizabeth's cell. He didn't understand how Edgar could be stupid enough to think Saunders might return after he had so successfully gotten away, but then, he didn't understand what Miss Elizabeth was doing back in the very same cell. Edgar explained very little, which was fine with Tex, but he sure felt sorry for Miss Elizabeth, sitting there so lonely like.

Edgar was the only one who spoke and inevitably he addressed Lonita, threatening to reveal new information that would send her to prison, which had no effect on Lonita at all except to make her turn her face toward the wall.

It was insane, Elizabeth thought, and it was obvious something was irking him beyond the thought of losing the treasure.

She hoped he was wrong about Galt. She hoped Galt never found out they were back in Greenfields.

There was one place that was a perfect spot to watch the jail cell, and Galt found it easily accessible that night when he returned to Greenfields. It was a simple matter of sneaking behind Edgar's house, and climbing onto the roof then across to the porch which overlooked the office side of the jailhouse. When he lay down and flattened himself against the porch roof overhang, he could just see inside the building.

And he had the patience, from endless night watches during the war, to wait out the night, observe the routine, and calculate the risks. It became fairly obvious almost immediately that Edgar still maintained the barest minimum of personnel in the jailhouse. He saw Tex leave to have his dinner early on and then he returned with another man, and Edgar left for a long time and then finally he came back, and Martin Healey exited and went into town.

He found that schedule particularly interesting. Martin might go into town, probably to Miss Flora's, every night. As of now, barring he had not seen someone who was already inside and had not left for dinner, he calculated there were only the three men guarding Lizzie and Lonita.

One of them would be in the jail cell hall, one would probably be right at the entrance, and Edgar, as always, would be relaxing in his office immersed in the newspaper.

The time passed slowly. Martin did not return, and Edgar, as Galt could see through the window, had fallen asleep. One down, he thought interestedly. An hour later the deputy he did not know left the building, and an hour later he had not returned.

Nice odds, he thought, shimmying his body to the edge of the porch on the far side from the jailhouse. All was quiet under a waning moon which gave off no incriminating light. Silently he dropped from the rake of the porch roof and ducked into the bushes at the base of the house.

Nothing. Martha had to be a damned heavy sleeper, he thought, inching his way out, gripping his rifle and alert to every nuance of night sound.

He crept around the back of the house and slowly around the side adjacent to the jail. The light was still on in Edgar's office, and he waited, and waited until the moment was right to move forward once again, blending into the darkness in the shadow of the entrance.

He grasped the doorknob and turned it slowly by degrees until it released, and cautiously he pushed the door inward.

Silence greeted him. The jail was dark within save for Edgar's office. Lonita and Lizzie were undoubtedly asleep, but Tex might still be awake in the dark somewhere down the jail cell hall.

He eased the door closed and waited, then soundlessly he entered Edgar's office.

Edgar had heard nothing. His head rested in the circle of his arms on the desk, over the newspaper that was folded out to the center page.

Galt leaned against the door casually and waited for Edgar's keen sense of danger to awaken him.

But Edgar slept on.

Galt scanned the room for the keys to the cells. In all likelihood they were attached to Edgar's belt; there was nothing on the wall. He had to awaken Edgar, and he felt a pang of regret that he could not have just snuck Lizzie out from under his nose. He nudged the rifle barrel against Edgar's cheek and Edgar awoke with a jerk.

"Good morning, Edgar," he said pleasantly.

"Shit," Edgar said, reaching for his weapon automatically and then checking his hand as Galt cocked the rifle.

354

"Stand up," Galt ordered, and Edgar stood. He knew that tone of voice—it was the voice that had threatened to disfigure Elizabeth, and one that brooked no opposition. No one had ever tested the depths of Galt's ruthlessness, and Edgar didn't care to try. He had been caught in the trap he had baited, and now he could only try to salvage something.

"The keys," Galt commanded.

Edgar reached into his pocket and tossed them across the desk. "Come and get 'em."

Galt shook his head. "You pick them up and take me to Elizabeth."

Edgar moved his hand slowly across the desk, watching Galt's merciless expression. He grasped the key ring and edged his way around the desk toward Galt. Galt moved aside so Edgar could open the door, and jammed the rifle butt into the small of his back. "Don't try to shut me out, Edgar," he said easily. "I know every trick."

Tex!" Edgar roared, and Galt immediately lifted the rifle and fired into the ceiling. Tex stopped dead in his tracks.

"Drop the gun," Galt rapped out, and Tex's weapon clattered to the floor. "Get the light on."

Tex moved forward slowly to a wall sconce and lit it with an uncertain hand. The light flared in the chimney, shadowing the hallway, revealing Lonita huddled in the corner of her cell and Elizabeth grasping the bars of hers disbelievingly.

"Good evening, Miss Lizzie," Galt said gently. "I believe I'm supposed to rescue you."

"I believe it's the other way around," Elizabeth said mockingly, bending over and unsheathing her knife. She held it up so Tex could get a good solid view of it, and Edgar muttered, "Shit," and felt distinctly discomfitted by the fact he had not thought to search her, and because of that, she had had the wherewithal to threaten *him* all this time. He wondered why she hadn't.

"Get the keys," Galt directed Tex, who looked rather awed by the vision of Elizabeth brandishing a knife in a way that told him she meant business. He turned with that same jerky motion and held his hand out for Edgar to relinquish the keys.

355

Edgar dropped them disdainfully into his palm.

Elizabeth watched through hooded eyes as Tex shuffled through the keys to find the right one and shunted it into the lock with that same unsure movement.

What, she wondered, did Galt want with her? He had come full circle, and he was in a position now to at least recover something from this disastrous episode. Maybe he already had. She disliked the thought as much as she disliked how glad she was to see him.

She held the knife in front of her as the cell door swung open and she sauntered out. She motioned to Tex. "In."

Tex looked at Edgar, and Edgar muttered something incomprehensible. Tex slunk into the cell, deciding he did not wish to test the depth of Miss Elizabeth's desire to escape. He looked at Miss Lonita in her cell directly across from him. She was standing at the cell bars, watching everything, her blue eyes ablaze with hope as Galt jammed the rifle barrel into Edgar's neck.

"You too, Edgar," he ordered, and Edgar resisted.

"Not me, Saunders. Not me. We can make a deal. That bitch knows exactly where the goods are. We'll make her tell, between the two of us. She'll tell, and we'll split it."

"No deal, Edgar, when half is already mine by right. Move!"

Edgar moved; Galt shoved and he pitched forward into the cell and Elizabeth swung the door closed behind him.

"You no good bastard murderer," Edgar howled. "Damn you to hell, Saunders, when I catch up with you again . . ."

"Take me with you," Lonita pleaded suddenly. "Galt, please take me with you. I'll tell you what you want to know. I'll make everything right again, I promise."

Galt looked at her coldly, his eyes flat black and unrevealing. She was as beautiful as ever, and as much of a self-centered bitch. Her eyes held his, promising things, wealth and endless delights. It was so easy to read her.

And so easy to say no.

He pocketed the keys in a slow deliberate motion and turned his back on her, ignoring her desperate *"Galt."*

Edgar just watched as Galt took Elizabeth's arm and backed

his way to the door. "You'll never find it, Saunders, *never*."

"Neither will you," Galt retorted, reaching behind him for the doorknob.

The door jolted open behind him. *"Galt!"* Elizabeth shouted, leaping to one side and pushing him out of the way. He rolled and levered himself upright in a smooth fluid movement, his rifle at the ready as Bryce shoved his way into the building.

"Drop it," Elizabeth said harshly, thrusting the knife into his face purposefully. "Let it go. My friend here has a rifle, and you'll be double-barreled dead if you make one wrong move."

Bryce dropped it and Elizabeth picked up his and Tex's revolvers and tucked them into the waistband of her skirt.

"This is nice and tidy," Galt said, pulling out the keys. "Lizzie, you want to find the one to Lonita's cell? We'll give her some company since she's so hungry."

The last key slid in smoothly. Elizabeth looked up at Lonita, who was still hanging hopefully on to the bars. "Back, lady, or I'll shove this into your gut." Oh, she loved saying that. She loved wielding that power over Lonita, who had wielded her own power over them all for too long.

Lonita jumped back, nonplussed by Elizabeth's tone. The bitch *meant* it, and that damned Galt was enjoying every minute of her little speech.

He shoved Bryce into the cell with every evidence of pleasure and Elizabeth slammed the door behind him.

Edgar said nothing, only his glittering chocolate eyes revealing the volume of hate rising in his gorge. He wasn't through with Galt Saunders yet, by God. He would railroad him to hell and back when he got out of the cell in the morning. He would kill the bastard. Killing was too damned good for him.

He watched expressionlessly as Galt and Elizabeth backed out the door, a far different exit, he reflected in his growing fury, than they had made those several weeks ago. Damn him to hell, damn him.

Lonita watched his escalating frustration with malevolent interest. She felt calm, centered. She understood things now, and what she had to do. She had to lead Edgar on, distract him, focus his attention on Galt and away from the hidden silver. Galt had beaten him one time too many. It was enough.

"But isn't it obvious," she said at length, after watching Edgar's hand clenching the bars of the cell in such a steady rhythm it seemed as if he was ticking off the minutes.

"Nothing is obvious," Edgar growled.

"The fool is in love with her, Edgar. You get to him through her, just like you planned. You can make that murder charge stick. You can."

Edgar looked at her in shock, the information registering in slow degrees, filtering through to the ramifications. He could drag Martin into it too, the double-crossing son of a bitch. Serve him right too. They could say he went for Elizabeth again, and Galt came after him in a jealous frenzy. How convenient he had fallen for that sour old maid. How nice Martin didn't want her anymore. All he had to do was make a deal with Lonita, and he would walk away, innocent—and rich.

Twenty-Three

The flight through the night was too reminiscent of the night he had abducted her, and Elizabeth felt a shudder of uncertainty which communicated itself to him as he held her tightly against him and spurred their mount on. Talk was impossible against the wind as they sped through the eerie night, and he couldn't comfort her. She held her body taut, as far away from his as the awkwardness of sharing his saddle would permit. Ambivalence poured out of her: she didn't want to feel anything for him; she didn't want the contact with his body.

She didn't want to give in, she thought tensely, as she had every other time. But still her consciousness of him overrode the resentment. He had come, and if she was honest, she might admit that some little part of her had hoped he was in Greenfields, had hoped he would come for *her*.

But where was he taking her this time—to the McCreedy ranch again, or straight to hell?

Either way it wouldn't matter, she thought. She would follow him as willingly, and the realization was shattering. Her body went stiff and she almost lost her balance. Of all the damned stupid things, she thought angrily, pushing the thought out of her mind. She would *not* succumb to Galt Saunders just because she was happy to see him—this time.

He had his uses, especially when she was in trouble and he had the gun. She would be damned if she confessed to any feeling other than that.

She was not surprised when they drew up before the hulk of a low-slung building a long while later. He dismounted with a neat economical movement, and held out his hands to her. She came to him, sliding off the saddle into his arms, and she wriggled away before she was seduced by his heat and her own need.

She knew where she was; he did not have to tell her this was his cabin, his home, the place he had built for Lydia, shared with Lydia, and it was where Lydia had died along with his dreams.

And she followed him, up the steps and into a dark space, feeling the familiarity of the moment as if it were ordained to be repeated and set the way it should have been at the beginning.

He turned to her and took her into his arms, and his mouth found hers unerringly, hungrily, and she answered him with no less desire, her pent-up emotions spuming through her like a tornado as his tongue sought hers.

The darkness was a balm. She did not need to speak; he did not need to explain. Nothing was necessary but the fuel of their passion, and she had known it was inevitable, that her emptiness and her femininity yearned for him, and it didn't matter what he was and what he had done.

She wound herself around him, pressing her body against his, giving him her tongue, abandoning herself utterly to each lush sensation that only his mouth could evoke.

"Oh God, Lizzie," he whispered raggedly against her lips. "Lizzie . . ." He claimed her mouth again, drinking in her honey taste as if he had never experienced it before, and she savored the ferocity of his need.

Slowly and carefully he lowered her to the floor and shifted his weight onto her body, where she wanted it; she wanted him nestled tightly on her, in her, and without the elegant preparation of his lovemaking. She wanted something more elemental from him, something primitive and searing that she could remember for the rest of her life.

His seeking stroking tongue aroused her to a fever pitch; her hands reached for him, demanding his heat, commanding his touch. Her shuddering excitement was as explicit as words.

360

Her body arched against him in unmistakable supplication. Her purposeful hands pulled at his clothing, and worked frantically to free the taut shaft of his straining manhood until it was naked to her touch.

She was torn between wanting to caress his hard pulsating masculinity, and yearning to feel it inside her. Her hand flexed, grasping him tightly, moving the circle of her fingers up the towering ramrod length to the firm ridged tip, and his body heaved against her, demanding the caress.

His fingers cupped her breast, rubbing the underside of its fullness and finding at once the taut point of pleasure at its center.

She moaned ecstatically as his fingers surrounded her nipple and held it with the same throbbing tormenting touch with which she encircled his rock-hard tumescence.

"Now, Lizzie . . ." he breathed against her swollen lips.

"Don't move," she whispered as she floated on a thick cloud of pure sensation engendered solely by the feeling of his fingers encircling her lush pebble-hard nipple.

He stayed, for a moment, two, three, thrusting his hips against her fingers in pointed quick little strokes that were heated and urgent, and finally he relinquished his hold and his hand moved downward, pulling away clothing and undergarments until it touched her hot, trembling flesh.

She was ready for him, fierce in her response to his provocative touch, greedy for each sensation and for the final sumptuous joining. And when he knew, he lifted himself over her and plunged his lusty manhood deep into her sultry heat.

"Yes," she breathed, or maybe she felt it, that fullness, that bonding with him, all savage and sensual in a different way this time, voluptuous and white hot out of pure wanton need. In this shattering union, there was no tomorrow and no yesterday; there was only the sumptuous fusing of their two bodies, only the incandescent sensation that he stoked with each long potent stroke.

His tongue plundered her mouth, and she answered him with her own voracious hunger to possess his tongue with hers, his body with her torrid undulating movements and her bold audacious hands. She didn't want that rhythmic thrusting to

361

stop, didn't want it to build and build inside her all creamy and warm and enfolding. She fought it, fought the shimmering rapture that tantalized her just out of reach. She wanted the thrusting and the fullness to go on and on forever, her body quivering on the brink of surrender, whirling wildly beneath his firm rigid strokes, insatiable for every inch of his virile manhood.

She was keeping the culmination at bay, she thought; she *thought*. He drove into her forcefully again and again, in the same rhythmic cadence again and again, claiming her with his prowess and his fiery desire, holding back his own release with an effort of will that was nothing short of ferocious.

He wanted *her* climax, her complete insensate surrender to him and what he alone could command from her. She strained beneath him, provocative and exquisite all at once, all his, completely primitively his, and the exultation that he felt was savage and elemental.

Her body quivered; he felt the change, the subtlest vibration, and his body coiled and thrust into her with powerful relentless stroking, once, twice . . . again . . . again . . . and so close . . . and again . . .

And it broke over her, an unexpected eruption of pure molten sensation that racked her with glittering spasms spiraling gorgeously all over her body, never ending and unquenchable, melting into his erotic release as he surged into her one more time.

She cried. He felt the tears streaming down her cheeks and onto the backs of his hands as he tenderly touched her face and her swollen lips. She buried her silent sobbing in his shoulder as she pulled him down to her and he wound his arms around her to comfort her.

The darkness covered them, and just for a little while, they slept.

And this was Lydia's house, and Elizabeth was pumping water at the place where Lydia had pumped water to make fresh coffee in the early morning for Galt.

It was very early, the sun had barely risen, and Galt had

awakened her so gently, so lovingly, and helped her put her clothes to rights, and then, as if they were still on the trail, he had handed her the coffeepot and ordered her to fill it with water.

Outside, the house appeared large, larger than she remembered the McCreedy house, even though there were fewer rooms. The wide front room served as both parlor and kitchen, with the stove hooked into a flue at one end, and a cabinet, table and chairs, and a stone fireplace built into the other end, alongside which was a badly torn-up sofa, and a rag rug of indeterminate color. In the back of the house were two rooms, one a storeroom, and one Galt's bedroom, which contained the ubiquitous washstand, pitcher and basin, and a serviceable spool turned bed. Behind her, as she vigorously manned the pump, was the outhouse. And beyond the house were the barn and several outbuildings.

It was a small neat spread, meticulously built by Galt's own hands for a woman who had hated the life he wanted to give her.

Elizabeth straightened up abruptly, picked up the pail and the coffeepot, and made her way back into the house.

Everything had seemed different this morning. It was as if they were both pretending that their explosive union was some kind of dream. This morning, there was only time for practicalities, for surmises, for plans.

There was a divisiveness between them, and their deep pleasure in each other could not alleviate the source of the disagreement.

And Galt could not let it go, because it meant he had to make a choice, and he did not want to make that choice. He had worked for what Lonita had stolen, and he still wanted it all— Lizzie, his share, and vindication. But he was realistic enough to know that only one of those things was really possible; but he had to push, he had to, and as he looked at Elizabeth's beautiful face across the table from him, he felt that chord deep inside him, and he wanted her across from him at a breakfast table forever.

"When Martha releases Edgar this morning," he said slowly, "you can bet he and those fool deputies are going to

363

hightail it over here, Lizzie. I wish we could linger."

"Where will we go?" she asked calmly, her cool green gaze never wavering, never revealing what she felt this morning. She intended to shut him out, because the intensity of their joining last night was so devastating and still this morning he could make plans to salvage the thing that had been his objective all along. It was as if he thrust away that exquisite connection between them, relegated it someplace else, not to be bothered with in daylight. This single-mindedness was nothing new; she wondered why she had thought events might change the course of his determination.

"We're going into the mountains," he said calmly. "I came this far, Lizzie; I can't give it up now."

"You could give it up," she countered. "You could do anything you wanted to; you're free now. You could go anywhere. Edgar never could trace you from here. He might take the ranch, but so what? You hadn't expected to ever see it again anyway. This could end, Galt. Let them have it. It's not worth your life, and Edgar means to get you this tme, Galt."

He waved the notion away. "I mean to get *him*," he contradicted harshly. "And only one of us can win."

Even when she entered the jailhouse the following morning with breakfast tray in hand, Martha Healey's expression did not change when she saw Edgar and his two deputies locked up and sound asleep.

She set the tray down on Edgar's desk with a bang and retraced her steps to the house to retrieve the duplicate keys which Edgar never kept in the jail.

She shook him awake impatiently and he woke with a fulminating curse and turned an accusing eye on her. "'Bout damned time you got here, Martha. What do you mean, leaving me here all night in this goddamned cell. Nothing wakes *you* up. Damn it—get up, Tex. *Bryce!*" He shook himself and stalked out of the cell, followed a moment later, as Martha unlocked Lonita's cell door, by his two groggy deputies.

"Where in hell is Martin? Did that little bastard spend the night at Flora's? Damnation, a man can't count on his own

364

damned family these days. What's for breakfast? Seems to me I'm entitled to Elizabeth's since I spent the goddamned night in her place." He turned to Lonita, who was standing by her cell door looking bemused. "What's the matter, Lonita, you hungry? Think I can starve the information I need out of you?"

He strode into his office and picked up a piece of bread from the tray. Almost edible; anything that morning would be edible, he thought furiously. Damned Martha. Where the hell was that no good son of his?

He turned to find Tex and Bryce looking at him. "Go get some breakfast. Martha only knows how to cook swill."

Martha sent him a flat brown stare. "Do I feed the woman?" she said finally as she edged her way toward the door.

"I dunno. Leave me alone. I have to think. Lonita can wait an hour or so. Maybe more. Come back in an hour, woman."

He lifted the coffee cup to his lips as Martha obediently closed the door behind her. He sipped, spat it out, and sipped again. What the hell good was Martha if she couldn't even make decent coffee?

He had been looking forward to running off with Lonita. He still couldn't quite put together what had gone wrong. There was all that treasure that she had promised him for helping her get rid of Buck. There was Martin, whom she swore she was finished with. There was Galt, whom they had successfully framed, and then Lonita had run off without warning, without telling him, and put a crimp in all his plans.

And somewhere that only she knew, she had secreted Buck's hard-mined treasure, the means with which, she had assured him, they would make a new life together.

He had paid for it, he thought. He deserved what he had been promised. He set down the coffee cup and wandered back into the cell hallway. Lonita watched him, her blue eyes guarded, looking for the first time disheveled and faintly desperate. But she said nothing, because she knew Edgar had something on his mind, and she wanted to hear it first.

"You're probably right," he said conversationally. "Martha's cooking could kill a man—or woman."

Lonita shrugged. "It's not a situation calculated to give one

365

an appetite, is it?" she said casually.

"Well, let's see what we can do for one another."

"I can't give you Galt Saunders again."

"Oh, I'll get the son of a bitch, never you worry. No, I'm more concerned about our original little arrangement. I'm feeling mighty ill used, Lonita. I'm feeling, in point of fact, double-crossed."

"Well, if you thought about it," Lonita said, "what I did made sense. I got Martin to scout out a hiding place for us, and—"

"And you took off to meet him there, and wait till things died down so you could sneak back to Greenfields and sneak Buck's treasure out of town without anyone being the wiser."

"It would have worked too," Lonita said candidly.

"And my son-of-a-bitch son would have had my share," Edgar snapped.

"Your son-of-a-bitch son is free to marry me," Lonita retorted snidely, striking back with the first thing that came to hand. She never could have married Martin Healey either, because she never wanted to be stuck again with some low-down man who was solely interested in his own work, or her money. What she had looked forward to was the freedom to buy what she wanted, whether it was clothes, travel, or good company for an evening. It had always struck her, especially after all those years she had stuck by Buck, that money was the key to her living the kind of life she had dreamed about. She never thought she would be immured in a small Missouri ranching community with a man who was proud of her beauty and didn't want to show it off.

But when he had discovered the lead . . . oh then she had thought things would change. He had invented some kind of portable smelter and set it up right where he had started the dig. He was pulling silver from his strike almost daily, to the point where he brought Galt in to help him mine it, and to run his cattle while he extracted the metal.

And then it was never enough. Another day, Buck would tell her, another month, and just think of how much they could have and what he would have to show the St. Joe Mining Company, who would buy them out; they would be as wealthy as her dreams between his own stake and what the company would pay for the mineral rights.

He had it all planned, only not this week. Not this month. Maybe, he had said at one point, not this year.

Martin Healey was a welcome diversion; he was young, he liked to have fun, and he admired her tremendously. He had never told her about his fiancée in Kentucky—but later he told her he had never thought Elizabeth would accept his invitation to come west, and he got caught right in the middle. It was obvious the only thing to do was run away.

He didn't know by that time Lonita was making plans. Martin didn't have the belly to kill Buck—she knew that. But Martin did have the savvy to find the place she could hide, and she sent him west with her blessing to find their future home. He was to meet her in Rim City when everything was set.

And meantime, her eye lit on Galt Saunders, who was still grieving for his wife and wanted no part of her.

So be it, she thought, but she trekked out to Buck's little operation to watch Galt in action several times. A man could get greedy, she thought. Buck was too damned trusting.

Or a woman. She wanted Buck's stash, and she wanted to get away free of Buck and complications, and she didn't quite know how to accomplish that, short of sneaking out with it all one night. But she would never be free of Buck, she realized. He might or might not come looking for her, but she would still be married to him, and if she had all the money that his silver stash represented to her, she still would not have the freedom she craved.

She wished fervently that someone would kill Buck. She wished Galt would turn on him because Galt wanted all the treasure he had so painstakingly helped Buck eke from the mountain.

How could she make Galt kill Buck, she wondered. How could she murder Buck and frame Galt? How could she get the sheriff instantly on the scene so that Galt would be caught with the gun in hand?

What if the sheriff were part of the scheme? And finally, the last step, which occurred to her after a restless night of making and discarding futile plans, she wondered why the sheriff wouldn't be willing to commit the murder himself if she bribed him with something tempting—like herself.

And now she was telling him that had never been possible. He spat in her face and stalked away angrily. "You can starve, Lonita. I'll get myself over to the ranch. I'll find your damned hideaway, I don't need you, and I don't to hell need my turncoat son neither. Dream your dreams, lady. You can die in that cell for all I care."

She had to get out; she paced the small cell like a caged animal, spewing imprecations, helpless, hopelessly stuck in an eight-foot space that could barely contain her fury at Edgar's duplicity. All right, she had goaded him, and no man liked to be hit in his pride the way she had jabbed at him, but still . . .

He was free to search and she was not. And Galt, roaming around the ranch land he knew better than Buck himself—Galt might figure it out; Galt might find it, and then where would she be?

God. She wished to hell she had gotten away from Rim City sooner and never planned to come back to Greenfields. She could have just taken some of the stash and left the rest. She could have buried it in a thousand places where no one would ever have found it, but because she had hidden it in the heat of the moment and the instantaneous decision to leave on the heels of Martin's note summoning her, she had not been as careful as she wished she could have been. She was going to pay for it too.

It never paid to be greedy, she thought desperately. If only she had not been quite so avaricious, if only she had been content with Buck's death and someone else's taking the blame . . . But she had never been a settled kind of person; she had always reached and grabbed for everything she could get.

She needed to reach and grab now. She needed to think.

Edgar had gone, and whatever was on the tray had grown cold in his absence; he had eaten very little of it, and she would have given a good part of her stash to devour a small portion of it.

The deputies might or might not return. Martha was

supposed to check in with Edgar in an hour. Had it been an hour?

Not an hour. But how could she tell? She could tell because Martha had not come, and Martha struck her as a particularly punctual person, who was under Edgar's thumb totally. She wouldn't talk back, and she wouldn't dream of disobeying an order that Edgar had given her.

But would Martha help her?

Martha would help her. Woman to woman, she would appeal to Martha; there had to be some spark in her of sympathy for Lonita's plight. Edgar meant to steal what was hers, after all, and perhaps Martha could be bribed.

Perhaps Martha had wanted a totally different life from the one she had led in Greenfields. Perhaps Martha regretted marrying Edgar. Lonita could surely understand that.

The minutes ticked by with agonizing slowness and all she could think about was Edgar, alone at the ranch and up on the mountain, using all the time he had gained to search for what was rightfully hers.

The sound of the door slamming made her jump. She could just see Martha's stolid figure examining the contents of the tray. She grunted and picked it up, and turned as if to leave.

Oh my God, Lonita swore, she wasn't even going to check on her; she was going to take the tray and walk right out again. She grabbed the bars of her cell, pushed her face as far forward as she could, and called, "Martha," her desperation a mere thread underlying the conniving tone in her voice.

But Martha didn't respond, so she cried out, "*Martha*," and the urgency in her voice this time stopped Martha.

She let out a breath as she heard the tray being set back down on the desk and Martha's stolid figure appeared in the jail cell hall.

Elizabeth had not forgotten one detail of the grim ranch house where Galt had held her prisoner, and nothing, she saw, as they stepped inside the main room, had changed

She did not know why Galt wanted to start his search here. Lonita would not have been so stupid as to choose to hide her

369

treasure in such an obvious place. Nonetheless, Galt tapped the floorboards and walls, and went all over the furniture with his hands and a small sharp-bladed knife, checked the stove, even though he had cooked there, and tore apart the flue, searched behind the cupboard and under the table, and finally in the bedroom, where he slashed the knife through the mattress on the bed on which he had cuffed her, and still he came up with nothing.

She watched, and she said nothing. There was no desperation in him, only a hard clear purpose. He was going to find the silver stash first and that was that.

Both of them were aware, too well aware, that Edgar would be right on their heels, if not Lonita. And both of them knew that Edgar would be gunning for him.

"Wouldn't it be funny," Galt said at one point, "if the silver had been hidden in the mattress that Cox stole?"

"I hope it was," Elizabeth muttered as she kept an eye out for any sign of Edgar while Galt swooped through the ranch house. "What form is it in?" she asked curiously as he made another pass through the parlor area, cutting into upholstery calmly and intently.

Galt looked back at her and smiled mirthlessly. "Disks," he said abruptly. "The son of a bitch's joke. Liquid money, he called it, and he made a mold for it in the shape of a coin. Damn to hell, Lizzie, you know—he was a good man. Damn it all. There's nothing here. Nothing." He stood up abruptly. "Come on, Lizzie; we're going up the mountain."

Standing outside, waiting for him to mount and pull her up next to him, she could see the mountain in the distance, all hazy and purple with the morning mist. It was about a mile away and just beneath it was a rich verdant pasture where Buck and Galt had grazed their stock.

It took no time at all to reach it, and less time to climb to the plateau where Buck had built the entrance to the mine.

Just inside the timbered opening were a profusion of lanterns and a makeshift machine. "The smelter," Galt said, motioning to it. He picked up a lantern and lit it. A yawning hole gaped behind him, washed in blackness.

He swung the lantern around, pacing farther back into the

mine shaft, which did not, as she could see, extend that far back. "There's just nowhere Lonita could have hidden the silver in here, unless she dug into the ground," he said meditatively. "And I don't think she had the time to do it, or the will to dirty her hands that much. Now what the damned hell *could* she have done with it?"

Elizabeth remained mute, keeping her post at the entrance of the hole, alternating her gaze between the vista and Galt's tall form making its way carefully back and forth in the confines of what little Buck had dug into the cavern.

"Help me, Lizzie."

"I don't want to help you," she said stubbornly.

"I was safely in jail," Galt began, ticking off the salient points. "Buck was buried. Edgar was under her spell. And then suddenly she disappeared, and she went so suddenly that she could not have had time to convert the silver into money she could spend, nor would she have stayed five minutes longer than she had to in Rim City *if* that silver had been turned into spendable cash. But she had some money, because Ada said she had been paid well for the hire of her wagon, you remember. So she needed Martin's help to come back for the rest. Why *did* she need Martin's help?"

He paced around the small space edgily, stamping on the cave floor periodically, pushing the toe of his boot around in the dirt, seeking anything that seemed even remotely out of place.

Elizabeth felt like exploding. This was all so senseless, just as it had been from the beginning. She peered out into the blinding sunlight, hoping with some little part of her that she could see Edgar coming, because that would force Galt to abandon his search.

"Lizzie," Galt called out to her. She turned to see him standing behind the smelter. "Help me move this thing."

She moved behind it reluctantly. It felt as if it weighed a ton, and it looked like an old stove on wheels, topped by a beehive oven. But it had to be movable, if Buck had managed to haul it up here. She gave it a tentative push and nothing happened.

"All your strength, Lizzie. Buck had it pulled up here by wagon and mule."

371

"You're likening me to a mule?"

"Stubborn as one at any rate. *Push*, Lizzie."

She pushed, and he pulled, and the contraption did not budge an inch.

"Lizzie," he said exasperatedly.

"I'm *pushing*."

"Change places," he ordered.

She moved around the smelter and he took her place. "*Pull*, Lizzie."

"Why don't you put a harness around me," she grunted as she put all her strength into hauling the wretched machine forward; it scraped across the dirt floor of the mine just barely a foot.

Galt shook his head. Then he looked at Elizabeth. "Buck used to . . ." He didn't finish the thought. He knelt down and began feeling around under the stove part of the apparatus. Elizabeth began opening doors and exploring the chambers. "Lord, what are these for?" she murmured as her hand touched ash and slime.

"You melt out the metal," Galt said through gritted teeth, as though he had expected to find something and hadn't—yet. Damn. "It feeds through pipes inside those chambers through a purification, and then down into the cooling compartment— or molds. Damn, I can't get it . . . you find anything, Lizzie?"

"No." She ran her hands over the beehive, and felt around inside as far as she could reach into its retrieval door.

"It's here then, it has to be here," Galt growled. "She wouldn't have had time to do anything else. She put it in the likeliest place, damn it, and why won't this hellish thing open?"

"Maybe it's stuck," Elizabeth suggested sardonically.

"Maybe it's . . . stuck . . ." Galt repeated wonderingly. "Oh, Lizzie, you *are* wonderful. It *is* stuck, Lizzie. It's stuck, and you know why?"

"Why?" she breathed.

"Because she melted it down again, Lizzie. She melted it down. Damn to hell, she put it in the cooling compartment, and fired it up, and she went away. Jesus." He ran his hand over his streaked face. "I'll be damned. She probably couldn't calculate

372

the monetary value of the disks. She wanted something solid—and big . . ."

"And she needed Martin to help her haul it away."

"God, what an ending . . ."

"*Is* it the end?" Elizabeth asked quietly.

Galt got to his feet slowly and walked to the mine entrance. He couldn't answer her because he didn't want to admit this was the end of the quest. Nothing short of dynamite would retrieve that chunk of silver from the cooling drawer. A more fitting end, he thought tiredly, would be to blow it to hell altogether.

And then he stiffened, and shielded his eyes against the sun. Goddamn hell, Edgar was hot on their trail already, riding fast and heading just this way.

"It's not the end," he said regretfully. "Edgar's on his way, and who knows who else is following."

[faint bleed-through text from previous page, illegible]

Twenty-Four

They climbed over the side of the mountain, aiming for a ridge that overlooked the mine entrance just above it. It was hard to keep low, bending to blend in with the rocks and vegetation, so as to look, to some oncoming rider, like a critter scurrying for shelter.

The ridge provided very little shelter, but there was a hollow in the rocks where they could lie flat and observe what went on below over the edge of a flat-topped outcropping.

They could hear Edgar's heavy breathing and strenuous grunts as he began to climb up to the mine entrance plateau. "Saunders!" he shouted, and they heard that loud and clear. More crunching and grunting, and then Edgar shouted again, "Saunders!"

Silence greeted him, eerie and heavy with a sense of an intangible presence. He hated mysteries, and he hated being at a disadvantage. He drew his revolver and fired into the dark emptiness. The shot echoed deep inside the mine cavern. "Saunders!"

They could almost hear him debating how to use his slight advantage as he edged up toward the mouth of the mine step by slow step.

Then there was a heavy silence, followed by a volley of shots ringing against the mine cave walls as Edgar satisfied himself his nemesis was not hiding in the darkness.

They heard him scrambling inside, the scrape of a match, and his mutterings and mumblings as he searched the walls and

374

floor of the mine opening every bit as thoroughly as Galt had done.

"What if he figures it out?" Elizabeth whispered.

"Hell, Lizzie—he couldn't."

They heard him grunting as he attempted to move the smelter, and his curses as he gave it up.

"I'm going to get him," Galt muttered. "Damn it, he's there and he's alone and . . ."

"Galt—"

He ignored her, leaping up and over her before her protestation could be uttered, and sliding recklessly down the ridge onto the plateau ledge.

His rifle lay by her side. She picked it up as she heard Galt's rich voice shout, "Come get me, Edgar."

She heard a thud and a curse as he thrust himself forward and caught Edgar as he was moving toward them. She heard the clatter of a gun against something metallic, and the sound of flesh pounding flesh, grunts and more cursing, the rough scraping sound of leather on dirt. A body falling. A groan from the gut and the slam of body against body.

She stood up slowly and began the treacherous descent to the mouth of the mine.

And stopped. Far in the distance, heading toward the mountain like the cavalry on its way to rescue the settlers, she saw a clutch of hard-driven horses.

She ducked behind a copse of bushes that grew at a crazy angle from the rock-strewn soil on the ridge, and shielded her eyes against the sun.

She counted the riders—four of them, and two were women. Lonita surely, she surmised, and confirmed this as the riders came closer. But she was stunned to recognize Martha, bringing up the rear behind the two men—the deputies most likely. A curious combination to come haring after Edgar, she thought, checking the rifle to make sure there was ample ammunition. Accuracy counted today. There was no room for mistakes.

From below she could still hear Galt and Edgar having at each other, Edgar with a tenacity she would not have believed possible in him, and Galt with his deep determined desire to exact vengeance on the man who would have ruined his life.

The riders came still closer, and Elizabeth waited for the end to finally come.

"Edgar!" Martha's sharp unrelenting voice echoed into the mine cave. Tex and Bryce had dismounted and were scrambling up to the plateau. Martha and Lonita followed as fast as they could manage in their long skirts.

Elizabeth heard Tex's voice below her, commanding. "Hold it! Get back, Saunders. *Back,* you. Edgar, you all right?"

"I'm all right," Edgar muttered grudgingly. "You say Martha is down there?"

"No, Martha is here."

"What's Lonita doing here?" Edgar demanded.

"Lonita is going to reveal her secrets," Martha said, sounding businesslike.

"And you believed *her,*" Edgar sneered. "She ain't telling nothing, Martha, and you didn't have no call to get involved in this whole thing."

"Did I not?" Martha retorted. "Go on, Lonita. I think it'd do Edgar a world of good to see this treasure, and see *me* get a piece of what he coveted. Did you think I didn't know something was up, Edgar? Did you think I was going to stand by and just watch you run away with someone younger, prettier—wealthier? Oh my, Edgar. I am sure you never gave it a thought. Well, think about it now. Lonita!"

But what was Galt thinking, Elizabeth wondered as she carefully crept downward, carefully looking for footholds and a position where she would be in the best place to help Galt if he should need it.

"Bitch," Edgar spat. "Going back on our deal, throwing in with Martha, betraying me after all I've done for you."

"Oh please," Lonita protested prettily.

"So where is it, you double-crossing bitch? It ain't nowhere in this goddamn mine. You double-dealing my Martha too?"

"I promised Martha," Lonita said softly. "She deserves something for her suffering."

"Martha? Suffer? What kind of line did that witch hand you? God, Lonita, you got a line a mile long, and I wouldn't care to see who is tangled up in it. Poor Martha."

"Poor you," Martha muttered vindictively. "Go on, Lonita."

"Does everyone have to watch?" Lonita demanded petulantly.

"It ain't here," Edgar said, "is it, Miss Witch?"

"It's here."

"Get it."

There was a long silence. God, Elizabeth thought, pushing forward cautiously as she reached the plateau ledge. She couldn't see a thing beyond the timbered framing of the entranceway. She heard sounds—scraping, groans—but there was nothing to tell her whether Galt was unconscious or enjoying the scene being played out before him.

And what would happen when they realized the truth?

"There's nothing in this contraption." Edgar's voice, disgusted, out of patience. "It's a bluff. I'm starting to think there never was any silver. She made it all up just to get Buck out of the way."

"You're crazy," Lonita snapped, her voice sounding out of breath and just a little desperate. "I never would have planned anything like that unless I had money to go away with."

"Of course, she had *you*," Martha pointed out.

"And Martin," Edgar retorted. "You are something else, Lonita. Whyn't you just tell Martha what you did with your stash and let's get it over with. Then we'll plunk Galt here in jail and that'll be the end of it."

Galt laughed, and Edgar snapped, "Shut up."

"You won't get *me* this time," Galt's deep rich voice assured Edgar, and Elizabeth felt a hot wave of thankfulness that he was all right and he was amused. "There are a couple of witnesses here, Edgar. You haven't exactly been guarding your mouth, my friend."

"Yes, but they're *my* men, so see where that will get you."

Galt laughed again, an unpleasant sound to Elizabeth's ears this time. The tension thickened, and silence prevailed.

"It's in that machine," Lonita said at last, her voice thin with urgency. "I tell you, there's a kind of drawer beneath those compartments and I put the disks in there."

Elizabeth envisioned the scene: Lonita on the ground pulling at the underpart of the smelter and nothing giving to

377

her frantic yanks; Edgar, disbelieving and smug, making just a token effort to help her. Martha had to be watching with great satisfaction, her gun and perhaps the deputies' trained on Lonita and Galt. Oh damn, Galt—right in the line of fire, too, probably standing there and hugely entertained by the irony of it, and Lonita finally, for the first time, getting her hands dirty.

"It doesn't open," Edgar said at length. "There isn't any damned drawer under there, and there isn't any damned silver and this bitch has played us all for a fool."

No one said anything; no one, Elizabeth thought, wanted to believe his conclusion. And no one wanted to take the first step to make Lonita tell the truth.

And then, out of the corner of her eye, she saw a movement. Oh God—someone else, sliding carefully down the opposite side of the ridge, someone else eavesdropping and hearing the deadly truth.

She pressed herself back hard against the outcropped rocks as Martin Healey dropped to the ledge and took up a position right outside the entrance to the mine.

"So," Edgar said consideringly, "all your plans have come to nothing, Martha. You should have left her to rot in that jail cell. I think it's right considerate of all of you to have arranged to be in one place so we can pull you *all* back to jail."

"The silver is there, I tell you!" Lonita cried, panic in her voice now. "It's there. Buck had all the disks in a strongbox, and it was heavy. And then I couldn't figure out how much they'd be worth so I took a pouchful and I put the rest in that drawer compartment underneath. If they're gone—someone else stole them." There was a sound of her falling onto her knees again, and the desperate grunting of great stress being exerted.

"Let's all of us try," Edgar said helpfully, obviously trying to humor her.

What a viper, Elizabeth thought. He felt he was in command now because Lonita hadn't come through and he had two armed deputies to back him up.

"I think," Edgar said breathlessly after a few minutes, "we've given Lonita more than enough rope to hang herself."

378

"It's *there*," Lonita said stubbornly.

"Boys . . ." Edgar said.

"She's right," Galt intervened suddenly.

Damn, Elizabeth breathed. Why did he have to go get involved? They would kill him; Edgar was just looking for an excuse to kill him. She lifted the rifle and edged forward a step, two, watching Martin, whose attention was fixed on the awning mouth of the entrance.

"Well, well," Edgar murmured. "Now why did I think good old Galt might know something about it? So you got the goods, did you?"

"I'd like to say we all got the goods on *you*," Galt said maddeningly, "but I think it might be better if Lonita detailed the one step of the process she omitted to tell you all."

Again there was a deathly silence, and Elizabeth could just picture every eye skewing to Lonita, waiting to hear what her next disclosure would be.

Elizabeth could envision her shrug. "I fired up the smelter," she said at last. "I wanted just one big bar I could take to a bank and have converted into cash. I figured by the time I got back it would have melted and cooled and I could just lift it right out and take it up to St. Joe and get my money."

"So it's there," Martha concluded, relief in her voice.

"Go and get it," Galt put in helpfully, and Elizabeth damned his unholy humor. He did see the humor in it—it quirked in his voice, but what he couldn't see was Martin Healey all itchy and frenetic at the entrance of the mine, his face a mask of pure frustration.

"What does he know?" Martha demanded.

"I know the silver is there," Galt said.

"Well, damn it, let's pry it out," Edgar shouted.

"Better dynamite it out," Galt told him. "I figure it melted and overflowed, and then it cooled, and it cemented the whole underdrawer to the body of the smelter, and there is no way anyone is going to get it out—maybe not even if it's blasted."

"I don't believe you," Edgar said.

"I *told* you," Lonita protested.

"Damnation, let's look at this thing, boys. Help me tilt it over just a tad. I want to see this drawer, I don't believe a word Saunders said."

379

Elizabeth held her breath. They were so close to finding that Galt had told them the truth. Someone was going to have to pay the price.

There was the sound of multiple "ooofs" as Bryce and Tex took the weight of the smelter on their bodies, and then Edgar's voice sounding almost disembodied: "There it is." Elizabeth could imagine him standing there, fraught with disappointment and frustration, his one hope shattered, and nowhere to go.

"Melted to the sides and over," Edgar said, and it was obvious he was running his fingers over the sides.

"Chip it out," Lonita suggested.

"Set it upright again," Edgar ordered, and when that was done, as evidenced by a telling crunch of wheels against the dirt floor, he continued, "It's time to end this farce, boys . . ."

"It surely is," a new voice interpolated behind them.

Elizabeth's heart sank. She jumped from her hiding place, her rifle at the ready just as Martin Healey entered the mine cave, aimed his revolver at Lonita McCreedy, and shot her point-blank.

Edgar reacted instantly, the fear pumping through his veins giving him an uncommon strength, enough to shove the smelter forward, into Martin's chest, which gave him enough time and leverage in the confusion to escape from the mine.

And lo and behold, he thought, look at what the fates had put right in his lap on top of everything else.

Elizabeth stood there looking like some avenging angel with a deadly rifle aimed directly at his heart.

"Don't move, Edgar." And she meant it. He knew very little about her really, but he knew she could handle a knife, so he didn't doubt she knew which end was which on a rifle.

Her eyes swept the mine entrance behind him. The babble of voices told her nothing; Martin Healey lay in a crumpled pile in the shadows at the foot of the smelter, and where the hell was Galt?

"Turn around."

"Not likely, little girl."

"*Edgar!*" Martha's imperious voice distracted Elizabeth for that one critical instant he needed to jump her and pull her

380

down. But God, she was a tigress, her hands raking at him every which way. Still he was stronger, and he was desperate. He slapped her down and knocked her out.

When Galt emerged from the shadow of the mine entrance, he found his rifle lying pointedly by the smelter. Elizabeth was nowhere in sight, and Lonita McCreedy was dead.

"He killed Lonita," Martha said, her thick face set in stubborn lines. "He's my own flesh and blood and he betrayed his daddy and killed that jezebel, and he belongs in jail, and that's where he's going."

Galt didn't argue with her. Whatever pain she felt was not reflected in her face; it wore the same stolid expression as it always did as she watched Tex and Bryce push her only son into the cell that Lonita had occupied.

"I don't want to hear how she used him," Martha went on. "I don't want to know any of it."

"I have to find Elizabeth," Galt said.

"You have to get Edgar," Martha said, and her tone was a benediction. She wouldn't ask questions, whatever his methods, and she wouldn't detain him either. If he came back and told her Edgar was dead, she would accept that too, he thought.

But where *was* Edgar?

"He wanted that silver," Martha said suddenly. "He sure wanted wealth, and that woman, that damned prettified shell of a woman, is what he wanted."

"He doesn't want Lizzie," Galt asserted with a surety he did not feel. "He wants me."

"Yeah, he wants you," she agreed. "He killed Buck and he still wants you to pay for it."

"And Lizzie got in the way," Galt said ruefully, "just like today. Where the goddamned hell did he take her?"

He went back to the ranch. He didn't see he could do anything else. He felt drained and totally alone. He needed Lizzie. When he walked in the front door, it seemed to him that the air was permeated with the sultry scent of her.

381

He had no sense of homecoming tonight. Last night when he had walked in the door with Elizabeth was the only time he'd ever felt he had come home, and now he knew why.

Elizabeth was his home, and wherever she was, he could rest content.

The realization was stunning. She had entered his house freely and given herself to him freely and he needed all of that from her and more. He needed her companionship, her sharing, her wit and tartness; he needed her love.

But how? he wondered as he lit the kerosene lamps all around the parlor room. The diffused glow flaring from the wicks softened the barrenness of the room—and his heart. He felt a flicker of warmth—and of hope. How? How *did* the overseer's son convince the haughty Miss Elizabeth to share his bed and his life after all they had been through, and after all he had done to her in the name of vindication and greed?

And he had been greedy, a goddamned sin, and he had used Elizabeth shamelessly and abominably for his own purposes and had put her life in danger by putting her at the mercy of a man whose greed and violent nature outstripped even his.

Edgar's justice, he thought, was to kill and take, and his own was to take and be damned; brothers under the skin, he thought. He wasn't but a tad removed from the criminal that Edgar had become, and if Lizzie's life was on the line, he knew he could kill too. He would kill Edgar and not even think twice about it.

And Edgar was in a rage now. He had been thwarted by Lonita, his son, his wife, Galt, and even Elizabeth herself. There was no telling how he would vent his fury. He had lost everything, including the prospect of unlimited wealth.

They had all lost everything, every rapacious one of them, and a treasure in silver would be lost because it could not be mined from a smelter cooling compartment without blowing it and everything else to kingdom come.

And that, Galt thought, would be a damned fitting end to the whole business; he'd do it himself, and let Lizzie push the damned plunger.

The notion sat in his mind for a long time and he chewed on it tenaciously; it gave him a strange feeling of satisfaction to have thought of a way to put a tangible end to it.

But what if it wasn't the end? What if Edgar was just as determined to recoup that wealth? He was holing up somewhere, perhaps waiting for the very moment he could claim what he thought was reasonably his.

Hell, and Lizzie would be caught right in the middle of it. Damn to hell. Where could the bastard be?

One of two places, he would wager. Edgar was either at the McCreedy ranch or up the mountain. And then again, it was just as likely Edgar could be skulking around outside somewhere.

Galt levered himself upward abruptly and reached for his hat and rifle. He had the damned strongest premonition that Edgar was going after the treasure.

It was spectacular how one nightmare merged into another, Elizabeth thought as Edgar spirited her away at the point of his gun with a choke hold around her neck. Insane of him to hang around after all that had happened. But he still wanted Galt; he still thought there was a chance he could recover the silver.

She suggested with no little sarcasm that he might melt it down again and just pour it out and was not surprised when he looked as if he would whip her with the butt of his gun.

"Yeah, Miss Sass? And where do we get the equipment to handle that kind of heat? And the mold for cooling? You want to do it, you want to burn yourself to hell on that damned mountain?"

"You think you have a scheme that's better?" she taunted, well aware she was playing with an emotion that was right on the edge of cracking into a thousand pieces. "You going to blow it up, like Galt said? Or push it off the plateau ledge?"

"Ain't you the one, Elizabeth my dear. How about I blow the bedamned mountain sky high with you sitting right in the mine cave?"

His threat chilled her right down to the very bone, but she rallied enough to comment caustically, "I didn't expect you to do less."

"You got a mouth, Elizabeth. You're damned lucky there ain't no one to hear it in this forsaken place."

"Please—the first place anyone will come looking for me is

right here at the McCreedys', although lord knows, you've left little enough for sacking."

"Yeah, and I could leave you for dead, too," Edgar sneered as he paced up and down in front of the chair where she sat in familiar security, her arms tied tightly behind her, her mind bent on outwitting this captor as intently as she had sought to escape Galt.

But she would never run from Galt again, she vowed. She felt irrevocably bound to him, and never more so than when she was apart from him. This time it might be forever, but the warmth of her feeling for him wrapped her in an impervious cocoon that not even Edgar could penetrate.

He could not understand her foolhardiness in the face of his murderous desperation; he felt as if he were having a conversation with a pesky fly. He couldn't swat away her truths and she kept coming at him and coming at him.

"You don't want to murder me," Elizabeth said firmly, but she could see by his eyes it would not bother him one bit.

"You keep talking and I'll do it in self-defense," Edgar growled

"You could just leave here—tonight. No one would know, Edgar; you'd get away scot-free."

"I'd get away with nothing, *nothing*, do you hear? All that risk, all that planning . . ."

"You'd get away with murder," Elizabeth contradicted tartly.

That stopped him cold.

"That's *something*," she added for good measure.

Edgar shook his head. Even he was impressed with her thinking. "*You're* something, Elizabeth. You are some little thing. But I tell you, I don't care what, I'm going after that silver."

He left her alone for an hour or so in the early evening. She knew where he was going, he didn't have to tell her, but he was canny enough to bind her legs to further prevent any attempt to escape on her part.

"I know you, Elizabeth. You'd walk the four damned miles to town, you've got that much spunk, I'll grant you. But you

384

ain't gonna have a say in any of this, and you ain't getting a chance to spoil it for me."

"You're a fool, Edgar. You can't do it this way."

"Hell, Galt Saunders said so, why shouldn't I believe him?" He whipped out a kerchief and wrapped it around her mouth. "Keep you quiet, Elizabeth. It will be a pleasant change."

"*Mrmph*," she ejaculated angrily as he tugged it tight with a flourish.

"I won't forget you," Edgar said jauntily from the doorway.

"*Brphlt*," Elizabeth told him roundly—but he closed the door behind him before he could see the flaring determination in her eyes.

So here she was once again. He had not lit a lamp and soon she would be in darkness, judging by the oncoming twilight.

She still had the knife. That cheery observation was not uplifting. Trust her to have tucked it into the most inconvenient place to reach.

She hated the McCreedy cabin; it was dingy and lifeless. There had never been any life here except that engendered by a frustrated woman consumed with greed. Maybe the greed was in the air; maybe it was self-perpetuating. Whatever the reason, whatever the price, Edgar was willing to pay it. He would come back with the explosives just as he planned, and she was certain sometime during the night, he would take her back to the mountain and the mine.

Such a little mine, she thought, such a meager operation. How much *really* could Buck have recovered from his one-man strike?

There, she thought, was the real end of the story: that there was no treasure. That what had melted into the cooling drawer would total no more than a hundred dollars' worth of silver.

That Buck McCreedy's obsession was a worthless dream.

And what if it happened that way?

Edgar would never knew until he took the silver for conversion. And she would never know because in all probability, she would be dead.

Everything vital within her rebelled against this conclusion, but this time she was powerless to save herself.

She wondered sardonically why Galt never seemed to be around when she *really* needed him.

Twenty-Five

Galt dismounted a hundred yards away from the McCreedy house. There was one light burning, and an eerie stillness pervaded the air. He lifted his rifle out of his saddlebag and made his way carefully to a windowless corner of the building. Pressing himself against the wall, he edged his way cautiously toward the door.

He heard no sounds from within and a cold fear gripped him. He punched the door open with his foot and rammed his way inside—into a cold and empty room. A single kerosene lamp sat squatly on the table, the wick burning low.

Elizabeth had been here. He sensed it, he felt it, and he knew in his bones that Edgar had her up on the mountain.

And Edgar was going to blow the silver.

He leapt out the door, propelled by a deep-seated terror for Elizabeth's life. Edgar wasn't crazy yet. Edgar might get crazy if the smelter would not yield to dynamite.

He vaulted onto his mount and urged him toward the pasture. He could not see his objective at all in the moonless darkness. His instinct guided his hand, and he gave his horse its head.

The ride became a blur in his mind as the dire urgency to get to Elizabeth took precedence over everything.

It was like groping blind, trying to pinpoint something specific; he had no sense of distance, or time.

And then suddenly he saw the faintest glimmer of light far ahead of him, high up the mountain, and it disappeared. Edgar.

He knew it and he spurred his horse on, the flash of light his beacon and his milepost.

As he got closer, it became more distinct, a kind of dull flickering glow that a lantern gave off, placed, he reckoned, deep within the mine just near where Buck had intended to sink the shaft.

When he was within walking distance, he dismounted once again and continued on foot until he reached the base of the mountain, the dim glow eerily guiding him.

He climbed surefootedly along the familiar path toward the plateau and up toward the ridge where they had hidden earlier in the day. Had it been earlier, *and* this day? It seemed like a month ago, and that Lonita's death had been mourned and she had been buried.

But there was no one to mourn her, and she had died for a glittery dream that was about to be blown to hell.

He stopped abruptly as he heard Elizabeth's spirited voice.

He had the whole smelter rigged with sticks of dynamite, and since he couldn't move it back into the mine, he left it near the entrance where he had shoved it into Martin with that superhuman strength that had totally deserted him in the face of the leisure he had to achieve his goal.

"What if it flies into a hundred pieces but the drawer doesn't come loose?" Elizabeth asked with a touch of mockery in her voice.

"Damn, I knew I shouldn't have taken that gag from your mouth," Edgar snapped as he knelt to fix the final connection among the explosives. "That should do it."

"That should blow the whole thing to eternity," Elizabeth said caustically. "Which end do you plan to attach me to?"

"The end that will shut your mouth," Edgar retorted, pacing back into the cave to retrieve the lantern. "Let's go, lady. Maybe you get to stay alive another five minutes."

He pulled her out of the mine entrance with a jerk.

The crack of a gunshot caught him in midmotion, as he was about to set the lantern down. He pitched forward and the lantern flew from his hand onto the smelter, and flame

387

flickered dangerously near the network of cloth binders that he had only just finished tying.

Elizabeth panicked. Oh God—was he dead, was the thing going to blow—if he were alive, how the devil could she pull him out with her hands totally useless—and damn it, where was that damned Galt when she *needed* him?

She kept her eye on the lantern as she knelt next to Edgar to see if he was still breathing. There was blood everywhere; it was impossible to tell where the bullet had embedded itself. Damn his tying her up, damn the contradiction that his desire to restrain her might cost him his life. She couldn't tell if he were alive, but it didn't matter. She had to get him out somehow. She had to *try*.

"Lizzie!"

Galt! He burst into the entrance and took in everything in one sweeping black glance. *"Run!"* he ordered, bending to lift Edgar from the floor, not even checking if he lived, as the flame caught hold of the cloth. "Goddamn hell," he muttered, shifting Edgar's weight on his shoulder, feeling the burden down to his toes, and he hated the man, he hated him, and the glow of the firelight would help him save the man who would not have hesitated to sacrifice *him*.

But he did it. He scrambled out of the mine entrance and down the rocky path, slipping and sliding, just aware of Lizzie's stumbling figure ahead of him. Moments, mere moments they had before the explosive would ignite, and moments more before it blew.

"Lizzie!" His hoarse shout stopped her cold. "Duck!" He fell forward and rolled Edgar's body off his shoulder before he crawled to find Elizabeth sprawled in the dirt.

There was one long beat of silence as he covered her body with his, and then the dynamite blew with a blast of light that lit up the landscape like daylight.

They were showered with debris. The successive explosions ignited like clockwork. And then there was a long eerie silence that was punctuated by the crackle of the flames burning themselves out.

Galt shifted himself off Elizabeth's squirming body as he became aware her groping hands were not seeking him sensually. He helped her sit up, and sank to the ground next to her. He could just see her rueful expression in the dying firelight.

"I have a knife," she said defensively.

Galt resignedly reached for her leg. "You're a mess, Lizzie."

"We're all a mess," she said gloomily as he extracted the knife and efficiently cut away her ropes. She rubbed her wrists briskly and then cheekily grabbed back the knife and inserted it into its holder. "Is Edgar alive? Did you kill him?"

Galt crept forward to examine Edgar's body. "I didn't shoot him, Lizzie."

"Oh God," she groaned, inching her way next to him. "Is he dead?"

"He's barely breathing. We have no hope in hell of getting him to town unless one of us rides him there . . ."

"And the other gets to walk," Elizabeth finished.

"I don't like either solution, Lizzie, but we have to make a stab at it. I'll walk you to the McCreedy house; it's the best we can do tonight. I won't be able to go much faster with him astride either."

She looked up at the dying fire in the mine entrance, and nodded. It was the best they could do tonight. Tomorrow, she thought, they would do better.

Edgar died. Galt brought the news back the next morning. They sat staring at each other, Elizabeth looking fuzzy, disheveled, purely beautiful and utterly doubtful. "You didn't shoot him?"

"Never had a chance, Lizzie."

She hunched over her coffee, which was hot and smelled delicious, and couldn't take the chill out of her shaking hands.

"Would you have killed him?" she asked after a while.

Galt considered the question carefully. "Probably not," he admitted. "I'm not a killer, Lizzie, I told you from the beginning. You have to believe it now."

She smiled gently, filling her senses with the sight of his

389

weary body, and line-etched features which had no humor in them today. Even his hair looked grayer, as if the whole episode had taken something out of him that would never be replaced.

"I believe you," she said. "Someone set out to murder him. But damn it, Galt—someone could pin it on *you*." She had tossed and turned over that thought all night, and the warm light of morning did not make it any less feasible—and maybe the murderer had counted on that.

"I know. I thought of that too."

"So you're back to the same old solution—a one-way ticket out of town."

"I don't like that solution, Lizzie. I didn't like being on the run. I like rooting myself in one place at one time. I like finding answers to questions that bother me. I don't like being framed for murder more than once in a lifetime."

"Then who?"

"Either of the two remaining Healeys."

Elizabeth motioned that thought away with her hand. "Martin's in jail, and I could have sworn Martha was finished with the whole business after he killed Lonita."

"But Edgar had *you*. What do you suppose she thought about that? I bet she thought he'd make another stab at getting the silver."

"That's too much," Elizabeth said, "even for Martha. She couldn't plan down to that kind of detail."

"And maybe she could. Maybe Edgar's abandoning her was enough of a spark. I don't know, Lizzie. I just know I didn't kill him, and I'm damned tired of dodging accusations."

"So we accuse Martha?"

"No, we go up the mountain and see what Edgar's hand has wrought."

They rode together, and the way he held her was different, tentative, aloof almost. She gritted her teeth. A hard man, Galt Saunders, with all kinds of soft edges. She wanted to lean back against him and let him find solace in the strength of her body. Instead she sat straight and proud before him, with his arms wrapped loosely around her, holding the reins in a disjointed grip, and she couldn't keep her eyes from straying to his hand.

She loved his hands. The thought jolted her. Those hands could not kill—they could not commit murder and then touch her the intimate loving way he knew how to touch her.

She focused her eyes straight ahead of her. Too much was getting mixed up, too much was happening, one event on top of another. Their foray across Missouri and into Kansas and all that had happened there seemed as if it had happened a year ago, it seemed too far past, and that adversarial unity between them had died when he chose to return to Missouri to find the silver. If only he hadn't . . .

But she had not had the power to change his mind. He probably yearned for it still. No, she didn't know him, she knew facets of him, many sides to him, but she still didn't know to what depths he might descend for money.

She didn't know what he expected to find in the mine. Rock and metal were strewn all around its base, and it looked from their perspective below as if part of the mine wall had caved in as well.

They climbed carefully up the path to the rock-laden ledge. The mine entrance was obscured by a large boulder—the outcropping that had tipped over from the ridge above. Under it, the smelter lay in pieces.

"Help me, Lizzie," Galt encouraged, balancing himself under the rock and shoving upward. It gave, a little, and he flexed his arms again and it shifted slightly. "Can you see anything under there?"

"Not much. We should have brought a lantern."

"We can feel around underneath. Can you find the legs? I'm just interested in whether the cooling compartment blasted loose." He gave the rock another heave, and balanced it against his arms. "I can hold this another minute, Lizzie."

"I'm looking." She knelt beside the pieces and began groping for the legs and wheels. She found them, behind Galt, still in one piece, looking like the stove bottom she had thought it was originally.

"Galt—you'd better come see this."

Her voice rang oddly against his ear. He eased the rock down on top of the beehive portion of the smelter and hunched down next to her.

"The bottom is here—and the legs and wheels. The whole lower section is intact, Galt."

He stood up abruptly. "I know what you're going to say, Lizzie." And he did, he could read it in the set of her shoulders and the tone of her voice, and he felt a rush of frustration that almost choked him. "You're going to tell me the drawer got dislodged—just as Edgar intended, and I told him it would—and the silver is missing."

"Aren't you the mind reader," she commented, her disillusionment coloring her voice. "I have to wonder how much you had to do with it."

She had no choice but to go back to town. She couldn't stay with him; she couldn't let herself think about him at all. And she wanted to go to Martha; she wanted to see for herself.

Curiously, Martha didn't seem at all surprised to see her. "You're welcome here anytime," she said in her flat voice. "You can come to the funeral. We're burying Edgar tomorrow." Not a trace of emotion tinged her tone or her face.

"I'm sorry," Elizabeth said.

"Who was to blame?" Martha shrugged. "A man is greedy, it's going to cost him one way or the other." She turned away. "Your room is untouched. You can rest there until dinner."

Galt watched this interplay with a skeptical eye. Lizzie didn't want to talk to him at all. She wanted to walk straight into the lion's den and become a martyr.

But as she had pointed out, she had her knife, and she had some money, and she did not need him for anything else. And that was the way she wanted it until she knew better or he had proved differently.

He stayed until she mounted the stairs, never looking back at him, holding in her tears of vexation until she heard the door slam emphatically behind her.

A bath worked wonders for her disposition, even though she

392

had to haul the water that she heated on Martha's huge old stove. The process took two hours, the bath fifteen minutes, but she felt scrubbed clean afterward, cleansed of lies and murders and accusations, and she was missing Galt more than she had thought possible.

She lathered up her hair, taking that extra five minutes to thoroughly scrub away the dirt of days on the trail and in jail, the grime and the ugliness.

Maybe she had been mistaken. Maybe the thing had blown into the mine roof, and it was wedged someplace totally out of sight.

Maybe it had been Martha, she mused, but today Martha seemed so very like what Martha usually was. She never had had any great love for Edgar either; her reaction to his death was consistent with the way she usually behaved. She would not mourn, and she would do her duty and lay him to rest in a manner befitting the sheriff. Whatever he had been became meaningless in death.

Elizabeth dried herself off briskly and wrapped the towel around her nakedness. Her room was untouched, Martha said, and she opened her closet door to find it was true: her sparse wardrobe of dresses hung neatly one by one, all three of them, along with the pinafore she had habitually worn when she helped around the house. The clothes were clean, and she chose one—a plain serviceable brown cotton that had tiny jet buttons that ended in a belted waist. She found some underclothes and pantalettes and a brush, and she felt, suddenly, very much like herself again, centered and sure, purposeful and secure.

She dressed, brushed out her tawny hair, and efficiently plaited it into the convenient long braid down her back.

There was only one thing to do, and she wondered whether she had decided to return to Martha's house because she had intended to do it all along.

She had to prove Martha was the thief or the murderer—or both.

Edgar was buried the following day, with Martha, Elizabeth,

393

Galt, Martin, and the two deputies in attendance. Martha said nothing, listened to the eulogy, declined to speak, and led the way across the bleak cemetery afterward to where the pastor was to conduct a second service to lay Lonita to rest beside Buck.

That brief ceremony completed, she invited them back to the house to have a bite to eat. The atmosphere was funereal, she had to attend to incarcerating Martin once again, and Tex and Bryce had little to say to begin with, and they left shortly thereafter. Galt and Elizabeth were left alone in the cavernous parlor.

The taut silence between them exacerbated his temper. "Damn to hell, Lizzie," he exploded finally. "I don't suppose I've ever seen you without a word to say."

"Fine. I'll talk. I'm fine. Martha is fine. She is behaving just the way she always does. Nothing seems out of the ordinary. She isn't acting furtive or secretive. She hasn't been sifting money through her fingers, and she hasn't asked a single question of me."

"She's a perfect angel," Galt agreed caustically. "So what are you going to do, spy on her?"

She pretended to consider the suggestion. "That's an excellent idea. Maybe I can find out something."

"Hell." He stalked away from her to the other side of the room. "Lizzie—I need you."

Her insides churned at the naked emotion in his rich voice. But she couldn't back down now or she would never know for sure. She stood up imperiously, Miss Elizabeth to the core, and she said, "Yes, you've said that before, and I recall too well what happened after that."

He stormed out of the house, muttering under his breath.

Did she trust him?

Elizabeth sat alone in the gloomy parlor surrounded by congealing plates of food that was to have been served to an army of nonexistent mourners. Edgar had had no friends in death either, she thought. Martha had done all that was proper and still the only pallbearers had been Tex and Bryce, who had

394

ifted the heavy plain pine box into its final resting place.

She felt as if she were sitting in her final resting place. If she weren't careful, she would be back in this house doing for Martha what she had done for Edgar, and she would be trapped again.

And if she heeded Galt's plea . . . ? Could she trust him, or would she find out that in the course of presumably trying to save Edgar's life he had doubled back to the mountain and found what he had been seeking all these weeks?

Devil it, and why did she have to care about him? Did she want to prove Martha the culprit because then she and Galt might have some kind of nebulous future? He had said nothing about that, and his need, were she to examine it closely, might be nothing more than his having the convenience of her body in his bed.

Nonetheless, she had to do something; she felt severely angled by Lonita's death, and Edgar's following close on it, and the simultaneous funerals. The pendulous silence in the house was nervewracking.

The house was empty.

Martha had gone back to the jailhouse with Martin, and Tex and Bryce had disappeared to tend to other duties.

She had the house to herself.

She got up slowly and paced around the parlor, with its square heavy Empire furniture. The curtains were drawn with just a narrow parting line between them that let in a slender beam of light.

She walked in to the hallway. Across from her was the dining room, and behind it a pantry and the kitchen, and Martha's room, at the back of the house, which had been the second parlor. This was the place Martha had her desk, and a comfortable chair, and it was where Edgar's casket had been on view, with the pocket doors between the two parlors opened.

She was tempted to search there first, but she went upstairs instead. There were four bedrooms to be explored. Two were on either side of the house—one of them hers, that smallest one at the back over the kitchen. Martha and Edgar had not shared a room—they were across the hall from each other at the front of the house.

She went into Edgar's room first, which was sparsely furnished with a painted pine bed, a wardrobe, a dresser, and a washstand. There was nothing at all personal of Edgar's in the room; it looked like any anonymous boardinghouse room that was about to be let out to a stranger.

The wardrobe was empty, and so, curiously, were the drawers of the dresser. Where were Edgar's clothes? Martha had probably burned them already, Elizabeth thought wryly, but it seemed awfully fast. Edgar had been dead only two days.

Thoughtfully she made her way across the hall to Martha's bedroom. Here there was a fussiness that seemed uncharacteristic of the silent stolid personality that was Martha. Here the furniture was more ornate, with curves and applied moldings, flowery paper on the walls, overlaid with cheap framed lithographs everywhere. There was a whatnot in one corner filled top to bottom with trinkets, boxes, and a framed daguerreotype of a considerably younger Edgar dressed in a fine suit and posed stiffly in front of a backdrop with one hand grasping the edge of a chair. There was also one of Martha, much younger, with a milky complexion and a slender waist—Martha before the War, Martha before Edgar.

They had had some kind of life, Elizabeth thought wonderingly. They might even have loved each other at one time. She had never known what brought Edgar to a small rural town like Greenfields, or when he had come, but it was possible to speculate that he and Martha had wound up here for the same reasons Galt had, or she had: it had been an expedient place to end a journey.

She searched every surface thoroughly, inside the wardrobe and on top of it, in the drawers and under the dresser and the bed. She pulled apart Martha's writing case, and even checked behind the pictures, in her shoes, in the water pitcher, at which point she felt herself becoming frantic and a little lunatic.

She didn't have to find anything today. She just had to find it. Martin's bedroom was next, and it too, like Edgar's, was as spare and unlived in as a boardinghouse room, and there was nothing of his there except a meager two or three changes of clothes.

The clock in the downstairs hallway chimed; an hour had passed, and Elizabeth's heart started pounding violently. She had not been aware of the time, nor if anyone had come into the house. She darted into her bedroom to consider what to do next, and almost immediately she heard Martha's voice calling her.

She went to the head of the stairs to answer the summons. Martha, who was at the door and about to go out, turned abruptly as Elizabeth called her.

"Oh there you are," she said in her flat voice. "I was wondering."

"I was resting," Elizabeth told her. "Can I help you?"

"Why yes, I came to ask you whether you would. Mrs. Asburt has agreed to do the cooking until I can find someone more permanent. Would you be so kind as to deliver the afternoon meal to the jailhouse, Elizabeth?"

Elizabeth hesitated a moment. Martha's face was in shadow and she couldn't tell whether this was a deliberate attempt to define what Elizabeth's place was going to be in her household. Nonetheless, nothing bound her here, and she could repay Martha, for the time she remained, in this way.

"Of course I will," she said, coming down a step or two.

"That's fine. Tex and Bryce will be there. I have business to attend to, and I thank you for your help."

"What time?"

Martha paused on her way out the door. "One o'clock will be fine," she said, and closed the door behind her.

Elizabeth did not move. Another half hour. She took a deep breath, waited another couple of minutes to see if Martha would return, then darted downstairs and through the kitchen to Martha's room at the back of the house.

Here, more disappointment. The desk had been moved back against the window, and her rocking chair into a corner. There was one bookcase that was practically empty, and a rather nice Turkish carpet on the floor.

Four chairs were spaced in the center of the room in the configuration in which they had supported Edgar's coffin.

And there wasn't a single place to conceal a heavy bar of silver.

Elizabeth sighed. She would never have thought Martha was

397

so clever. She sat down on one of the coffin chairs and stared across the room and out the window, which overlooked the jailhouse.

How long was she to give herself to find some proof? she wondered. All the time it took, her adamant inner voice told her sternly. Two lives had been forfeited over that silver, and almost a third, if she counted the years Galt would have spent in prison for a murder he did not commit.

And all those weeks chasing Lonita and the truth.

What was the truth? She still didn't know. The truth was silver, hard and slippery, blindingly shiny, and intrinsically valuable for itself.

It would set Galt free.

The clock struck one and she reluctantly made her way to Mrs. Asburt's house, which was right next door. Mrs. Asburt was every bit as dour as Martha, but still she wore her long neat dark dress overlaid with a spanking clean white apron, and showed no shame that she was cooking for Martha for money.

Elizabeth took the tray and walked slowly to the jailhouse, where Tex opened the door with alacrity to let her in.

"Now, ma'am, you set that down on the desk, and we'll dole his share out to Mr. Healey here," Bryce said.

"Yes, I do believe that is a better way to handle it," Elizabeth said wryly. "I wish Martha had thought to distribute some of the food that's just sitting in the parlor right now. I'd hate to see it go to waste."

"Don't worry none, ma'am; Miss Martha is going to have Miz Asburt warm it up for us for supper."

"That's good then. How is Martin?" she asked curiously. He had seemed extraordinarily subdued during the funeral service, and he had not volunteered to help Tex and Bryce take the coffin from the funeral cart, or lay it to rest in the ground.

"He seems mighty quiet, ma'am, and not too hungry. It hits a man hard when his daddy dies like that," Tex said, removing bowls and covered plates from the tray. "Me, I never thought old Edgar was such a heavy cuss. Could of used Martin's help lowering the thing, but I guess he was too choked up."

Elizabeth edged a look over at Martin's cell. He was lying on the bunk, his face to the wall, seemingly oblivious to the conversation which he probably couldn't hear very clearly anyway.

"Yes, he did seem to be grieving," Elizabeth said, just to say something. In truth, she couldn't tell how Martin had felt this afternoon, no more than she could tell whether Martha was affected by Edgar's death.

She left as Tex was delivering the remainder of the food on the tray to Martin's cell. Outside, a certain sense of barrenness hit her: the main street of Greenfields stretched aridly before her, almost like the path to the rest of her life. She did not have to go back to the house. She did not have to go into town. She didn't have to do anything, and the prospect was daunting, even scary.

She cut across the adjoining stretch of grass and wandered into the minuscule yard of Martha's house. There was a small iron settee positioned under the one thick-trunked shade tree and she settled herself into it to think.

But she had not one creative thought. Her eyes kept straying to the house, skimming across the yard to the break of bushes that separated it from the road beyond. It was a newly cleared dirt road, barely laid out yet and it ran behind a bank of houses with the purpose of redefining the outskirts to town to provide more building lots with access to the main street. It was seldom used because no one yet had built a house along its parameters.

It was a desolate stretch, Elizabeth thought, a perfect alternate route out of town for someone who did not want to be seen. A good place to lie by and hide. A good . . . hiding place.

She got up abruptly. Could it be that simple? Could it? That Martha had just trotted home with the goods and somehow, without being seen herself, she had buried the silver right behind the house?

The thought galvanized her and she strode briskly across the yard and through the bushes.

The sun baked down on the dusty roadbed, which looked dry and parched. Untouched. Elizabeth paced toward Mrs. Asburt's house, where the road curved toward town, but it was obvious that anywhere beyond the Healey place would have been an unlikely choice because the road was more public there.

She turned and walked in the opposite direction, feeling like a black crow scouting carrion. But after all, wasn't that what she was doing?

The road angled away to the north just past Martha's house, as if the surveyors who had laid it out intended to develop an outlying district of town. The road petered out several hundred yards beyond that and every inch of it looked as dusty dry as the rest.

Elizabeth walked slowly down that length of the road, trying to assess the probability of Martha's having buried a treasure in silver in an abandoned roadway in the middle of the night.

She couldn't envision it.

How would Martha have carried it? She would have needed light, a shovel. Maybe she had help . . . who?

She stopped short as her eye fell on something glittering in the dust of the roadbed. She knelt down to take a closer look. It was a cross, a plain little silver cross that was nailed to the flat of a weathered piece of wood, and it was lying at the side of the road very precisely placed, and when Elizabeth tried to pick it up, she found it was attached to a stake that was driven deep into the ground.

A little cross appended to a stake by the side of a road going nowhere. Like a marker. Why?

She pulled at it and pulled at it and it remained wedged in the ground. So deep it couldn't be pulled up?

She needed something to dig with. She got up slowly and began walking back to the house, running over in her mind which implements were most easily transportable. Something for a garden. Not that Martha was much of a gardener—but Mrs. Asburt was, she remembered suddenly. Mrs. Asburt had an extensive vegetable garden, and yes, when she inquired, Mrs. Asburt had a trowel she could borrow, and a hand rake.

Perfect. Her hands were shaking as she walked briskly back to Martha's house under Mrs. Asburt's eagle eye. When *would* that woman close her door? Or had Elizabeth aroused her curiosity to the point where Mrs. Asburt would watch what she was going to do with the damned things?

Devil it—she was going to have to waste precious time skulking behind a tree because Mrs. Asburt was so nosy. And then, a moment later, she heard the satisfying click of a door gently closed, and she slipped around the tree and behind the bushes, which shielded her from any prying eyes.

Her heart pounded wildly as she got to her knees beside the marker. What if Martha saw her? Or what if Mrs. Asburt asked her why Elizabeth wanted to borrow gardening tools?

She jammed the trowel into the roadbed with all her strength. The parched dirt did not give easily, and she scraped at the surface with the hand rake, scratching away at the rocky surface with the frenzy of a madwoman. A marker with a silver cross—what else could it mean but the silver?

Martha had buried it in a place no one else would think to look, with an appropriate symbol. The earth broke under the rake, and she dug the trowel into the loose dirt and began scooping it out with her hand and the implement. Deeper and deeper she excavated, concentrating on one small hole right near the marker, sure she was going to hit something solid buried in a shallow pit.

She was still digging ten minutes later, and the hole was appreciably deeper and she still hadn't come up against anything.

She sat back on her heels and wiped the sweat from her brow, and then, without considering the consequences, she thrust her hand into the hole as far down as she could.

Her hand touched something—and it wasn't solid.

It was soft, cottony—some kind of material.

And then—horrifyingly—skin.

Devil it, she thought, where was Galt when she needed him? She surveyed her handiwork with a critical eye. It did not look as if it had never been touched, but it would. A day's sun would bake it dry. She nudged some rocks over the obviously darker dirt that filled the hole next to the marker . . . no, the tombstone, she amended. It had taken every ounce of guts in her not to react physically to her discovery, and to think clearly and calmly about the next step to take.

It was obvious she had to refill her little excavation and even that was hard to do, knowing she had to leave Edgar's body just where it was, and had to make it look as untouched as possible. And then she had to clean herself off so that when she

401

returned the tools to Mrs. Asburt, she would not look as if she had been in a mine shaft instead of genteelly working in the garden.

And with all that, she could not let her mind even think about her grisly discovery.

She could change her dress. She would have to change her dress. Did she have time? She had no sense of how much time had passed. Martha could be in the house for all she knew, and how would she explain her disheveled appearance?

Or was luck on her side? She crept cautiously back down the road and through the bushes, leaving the tools behind the tree out of sight of the windows in the house, and then scurried inside through the kitchen and up the stairs.

"Elizabeth?"

She froze. *Where* was Martha?

"Elizabeth?" Martha appeared at the bottom of the stairs, looking up at her questioningly.

Elizabeth shrank into the shadows. "Yes, Martha?"

"You were gone a long time. I've been looking for you. Would you be so kind as to help me with the food in the parlor?"

"I was just going to change," Elizabeth said, amazed at how steady her voice was and how she could respond so normally. "I took a walk and I'm afraid my dress got rather dusty."

"There's no hurry. I thought we might eat the remainder for dinner and take the rest to the jail."

"I'll be down in a half hour then," Elizabeth said, and darted into her room. She closed the door behind her, and leaned her shaking body against it.

And then she couldn't move. Her body trembled from head to foot and she could not take one step forward. If she could get to the bed, she thought wildly, she could just curl up under the cover and try to forget. . . .

But how could she forget? The feeling of that cold dank patch of skin would forever be imprinted on her fingertips. The gelid fear that enveloped her as she refilled the hole would always be in her bones.

Nonetheless, in thirty minutes' time she had to face Martha with some semblance of normalcy, even knowing what she did about Edgar, and she had to pretend that nothing had changed, and everything would go on just the same.

She didn't know how she was going to do it, when she now knew the final hiding place of the silver.

She did it. She dug deep into some reservoir inside herself and surrounded herself with the armor of knowing that in another few days she would never see Martha Healey again.

Her whole mind was occupied with planning how to remove the silver from the coffin. How deep had they buried it, after all? God, she needed Galt!

Mechanically she complied with all of Martha's orders, one of which offered her the opportunity to return the tools to Mrs. Asburt when she went to tender Martha's thanks for Mrs. Asburt's help. She did not answer the question she saw lurking in the woman's curious eyes. It was easier just to say good night and leave her standing at her door.

The last time, Elizabeth thought, as she helped arrange the cold food for the evening's meal and put it on two separate trays. But it really wasn't so easy as that. She needed to send a message to Galt, and then it might take another whole day before they could make arrangements to get to the cemetery. And they would need a wagon, since the graveyard was positioned well out of the residential part of town, down along the road to Galt's ranch; they would need light, and shovels. They would need a strong stomach besides, she thought wryly, to go digging up a grave in the middle of the night.

She was not going to be able to sleep this night. All her ruminations and plans could not shield her from the horror of her discovery this afternoon.

She wanted Galt, plain and simple. She wanted to tell him she had been wrong, and she should have trusted him—she should have known to trust him after all they had been through. She wanted him to protect her from the horror and the latent danger of Martha's discovering what she knew.

And all she had was the solace of Martha's company and later her own cold narrow and empty bed.

Twenty-Six

The clock struck ten and her eyes flicked open. She had slept; she must have slept because she was dreaming Galt was sitting right next to her on the bed, looking rakish and not the least bit apologetic in the dull glow of the turned-down lamp.

"Lizzie!"

Oh, she wasn't dreaming that urgent voice. That was Galt all right, and she reached out a tentative hand to touch him to confirm it. He was real, and he had not left her, and all she could say was, "Where were *you* when I needed you?"

"Where were *you*?" he countered, loving the look of Lizzie all muzzy and tousled from sleep.

"Oh," she said, nonplussed, and then she gathered her wits about her and struggled to sit up. "Where *have* you been? I've needed you."

He leaned over her, forcing her back down to the pillow. "I need you, Lizzie, I told you."

"But—"

"Lizzie . . ." He couldn't take much more. She fussed too much. He had been without her too long, and it had only been hours. His mouth closed over hers firmly, taking what was his, determined to take what was his no matter how much she might protest.

She offered no resistance. She needed that closeness at the moment, and she had not thought he would ever want to kiss her again. She pulled him down to her, reveling in the feel of his body as if it were the first time, drinking in his taste, reliving their last union, and yearning already with just these few delicious kisses for the next.

Just for a moment, his sensual presence and his luscious mouth blotted out everything else. He reached out one long arm and extinguished the wick in the kerosene lamp, and then lay down next to her to hold her and enfold her in his pulsating warmth.

There was a difference in her tonight. Her eagerness was restrained and she seemed to seek comfort as well as sensuality. He had the leisure to thoroughly explore the contours of her mouth, to play with her and duel with her pert tongue; to kiss her face and neck, her hands, her lips. The night was endless, and morning would never come. He could stay all night and kiss her and need nothing else.

"And where *did* you come from?" she murmured, her own mouth exploring the line of his jaw and the shape of his firm lips as if she had never touched them before.

"I hung off the roof, Lizzie." He licked her lips, answering her invitation, distracted by the sharp little flicks of her tongue that demanded his kiss. "You couldn't possibly have thought"—another long kiss, "that I would leave you here alone all night."

She shook her head. "I don't know what I felt." She lifted her face for the reassurance of his mouth. But she knew. She thought she had chased him away forever. She didn't deserve the hot wet caress of his mouth that excited her and aroused her.

"I came to get you," he whispered, seeking the sweet shell of her ear. "I've got a wagon and I want you to come with me tonight."

He took her mouth again before she could answer. He muddled her head with the lush movement of his tongue against hers, and his fierce desire that throbbed against her body without making demand. She could lie like this with him all night, and forever.

She had to pull away from him. "What if I told you I know where the silver is?"

He captured her mouth again before the words were hardly out. What did he care about silver if he had almost lost her because of it? His kiss told her what he could not, and yet she persisted, wrenching away from him and pushing their heated bodies apart.

"Galt, listen," she whispered urgently, and the note in her voice stopped him. He didn't want to listen; he wanted to make love to her all night with his kisses. He took a deep breath. "All right, I'm listening."

"She buried it in Edgar's grave. I found Edgar today. You understand, she buried the silver in the coffin, and Edgar—the road behind the house. There's a marker—no one would see it who was just walking by. It's wicked that she did that. She just can't come away with the silver, Galt. She *can't!*"

He stroked her hair gently as her body sloughed off its pillow of sensual comfort and relived the ghastly afternoon. "You're right," he murmured, "she can't. I'll dig it up. I'll do it tonight."

"Oh no," she whispered into the darkness. "*We'll* do it tonight."

It felt good to be able to take action. Galt appropriated the kerosene lamp and they crept silently down the stairs as the clock struck eleven. They needed before they left to find matches and two shovels, and Galt had no compunction about rummaging around in the kitchen, nor Elizabeth filching the needed implements from a shed behind the house.

Ironically, the wagon was parked on the old dirt road, just beyond Mrs. Asburt's house. Galt walked it up past Martha's house, past the marker which Elizabeth pointed out but which he could not see, down through the scrub that had overgrown the portion of the road that had been started but not completed, and out, in this roundabout fashion by the light of a half moon, onto the road that led from town toward the cemetery and Galt's and the McCreedys' ranches.

Fifteen minutes later, Galt propped the dimly glowing lamp up against a tombstone close by Edgar's grave and they surveyed the situation.

The earth was still loose on top of the grave. The partial moon suffused the whole cemetery with an eerie light that was just a little scary. The silence ripened into a kind of horror that any noise they made might be magnified a hundred times, and someone would hear it and come.

"Spooky," Galt muttered, and lifted the shovel. A mound of dirt came away easily from the grave. "Dig, Lizzie; we don't know that Martha won't be coming to claim her stash tonight."

Elizabeth dug, with a rhythmic expertise that came from a season of planting when there was no machine to till the soil— only human hands. *Her* hands.

Galt covertly watched her, admiring, as always, her unexpectedness, and her practical knowledge.

The night sounds kept them company; the cemetery had a life of its own. Once an animal startled Elizabeth and she dropped the shovel precipitately close to her foot. Too close.

"This is ghoulish," she muttered, picking it up.

"Keep going, Lizzie."

She watched him for a long moment, leaning her elbow on the shank of the shovel. He worked in a long fluid movement, bending, shunting the shovel into the deepening hole, and shifting the dirt out with an economical motion. He did not waste his movements or his energy.

"I don't know," he said, looking up, "whether we'll even need to excavate the whole thing. Maybe just enough to open it."

Elizabeth looked at him oddly. The grave was half empty of dirt now, and the thought hit her that maybe there *was* a body in the coffin. Maybe . . . no, it was too fiendish to contemplate, and Martha was not that diabolical. She took hold of the shovel and began digging again.

The flame in the lamp flickered and sent a dancing shadow across the dark hole. Elizabeth jumped as it touched her and died. She paused, shivering, the phantasmic atmosphere overwhelming her until the steady cadence of Galt's shoveling penetrated, and she shook herself out of it.

He didn't say a word. He hardly knew how to assess what had happened to her today. She had found Edgar: such a blunt blithe statement for such a gruesome unexpected discovery. What must it have been like to *touch* and not see—oh yes, Martha could not get away with such apathy even toward

Edgar. He hadn't deserved *that,* no matter what he had done.

His own growing bitterness fueled his final efforts and he dug the shovel into the grave with a burgeoning fury. What a way for it all to end.

His shovel struck wood, and they both jumped and then looked at each other. "I need the light," he said briefly, and he lit it and brought it closer to the dug-out grave.

The coffin was clearly visible, the unvarnished pine contrasting clearly with its dark confines. An easy matter to finish digging out the top of it. Elizabeth shook off the ache in her arms and bent to it until a good portion was showing.

Galt lay down flat on his stomach at the edge of the grave, and positioned the lamp so he could see clearly. "This is it, Lizzie."

She nodded mutely.

He reached his hands into the grave and felt along the top of the coffin. There were no locks, no impediments that he could tell. Slowly he pushed at the plank board cover, and slowly he eased it upward.

Elizabeth came around to his side to peer into the coffin.

She felt shocked, and she didn't know why she did. What lay within looked like a dull colorless oblong of detritus, a piece of debris that someone might have discarded as garbage.

"Not too prepossessing," Elizabeth murmured, kneeling down beside him to steady her trembling nerves.

"Damned heavy," Galt grunted as he tried to lift it. "Wait a minute." He pushed back further on the cover, and balanced it against the opposite grave wall. "I'm going in, and I'll hand up to you. It can't be so heavy that the two of us can't manage it." He swung his body around, slid down the dirt wall and into the box with a thunk, then crouched to give himself purchase to lift the silver. "Damn to hell, Lizzie. Damned drawer is still attached to the bottom."

"I'll come down."

"No. I'll work it up somehow. Maybe . . ." He lifted it up onto its uneven end. "Just—get the light closer . . ."

She moved the lamp and she could clearly see his struggle

with the weight of the object. Finally he got it to the edge of the box and propped it up against the wall of the grave. Dirt crumbled into the box. "All right, Lizzie. Move back. I'm going to give it one heave and try to thrust it up over the edge."

"And what if it falls on your head?" she demanded, scared that not even he had the strength to move it. But Martha had moved it. How had Martha gotten it away from the mountain?

He smiled crookedly. "You can bury me where I lay." He positioned himself carefully under the object, coiling himself like a spring so that all his strength would push upward with one intensive thrust. "Counting, Lizzie. Ready? One—two . . . three . . ."

It came up at her like a bullet, and fell heavily at the end of the digging. "Damn to hell," Galt said, rubbing his arm. "I need a hand, Lizzie."

"You sure you don't need an arm?" She grasped his hand and he levered himself upward, and they both knelt to inspect the object of all their machinations.

Elizabeth shook her head. "It looks like a piece of nothing."

Galt touched her face. "That's all it ever was, Lizzie. A hellish piece of nothing."

The faintest finger of dawn sketched across the sky as they turned into the barnyard of Galt's ranch house. He was coming home, he thought, home with Lizzie. And they didn't have much time. He didn't know what Martha might do when she discovered Elizabeth was gone. Maybe she would do nothing, but they couldn't take that chance; they had to make a decision and make it fast.

He untethered the horse and watered him down and fed him quickly, while Elizabeth drew water for coffee and a brisk wash.

She had the water up to boil by the time he entered the kitchen, and a full basin for washing. By the time he was finished, the coffee was hot, if a little weak. He hardly cared about that. He poured a cup while Elizabeth performed her perfunctory ablutions and he thought about what they had to do. He just wasn't sure Elizabeth would agree.

She sat down opposite him at the table, and took the cup he handed her. "Tired?"

"I am. I know we had to fill the damned hole back in but, lord, what a job," Elizabeth said. She took a hot satisfying sip of the liquid.

"We just don't know if she'll go out there today. She could be so fixated about the silver, she might check every day. But we still have to get rid of it. I wish I could blast the damn thing to hell, but there's no time even for that."

"What *is* there time for?" Elizabeth asked curiously.

"Maybe there's *just* time to pick up and go." He put his coffee cup on the table and looked at her. She was a wonder, his Lizzie. She looked fresh and hardly discommoded by a long hard night's labor in a graveyard. She had a faint smile curving her lips, and her eyes sparkled with some hidden secret that made them all green and soft. The hideous brown dress she wore took nothing away from her beauty. And he loved her all to hell and back and he couldn't find the words to tell her.

"And what do we do with the bar?"

"I've been thinking about that. The damned thing may haunt us forever. I wonder if I can smash it somehow." He got up and routed out a pickax from the barn as she followed, and he climbed up into the wagon and lifted it and swung it down onto the silver with all his might. It crashed into the bar and slivers of silver cascaded everywhere.

"This might work," he said. "I'm going to push it onto the ground." He shoved at it, using the ax as a lever and the thing dropped heavily downward.

"Stand back, Lizzie." He lifted the ax again, and swung, and swung, and shards flew all over the place, and he swung, and as if the night's labor had not been enough, he swung until the bar cracked and several pieces broke off and went flying across the barnyard.

"Hell." He lifted one up and toted it into the barn. The second piece he lugged into the bedroom, and the third, which was still cemented to the drawer, he pulled into the kitchen and propped up near the stove. Finally he sat down to rest.

"You know," he continued as if he had never stopped, "I built this house for Lydia. A pretty nice house by overlanding standards. She hated it. She never let me forget she had married beneath her. She came from a fine patrician home just like you did, Lizzie, and she despised what the War had forced her to accept. Still she thought anything was better than staying home with her parents, and dying without a husband. Even me. But not this." He gestured at the four walls. His eyes glittered blackly with hard memories that were still close, still raw.

"She likened me to an animal living in a cave, and she was too fine for that. She was happy when I started running Buck's cattle, ecstatic when he struck the mine. And she wanted to die when she found out she was going to have a baby." His face hardened at the recollection. "So she did. She had her moment of glory and then she was rid of me."

He sat very still as the words resonated between them, and Elizabeth wanted to put her arms around him and ease that haunted look from his eyes.

"I need you, Lizzie. I need you in a way I never needed Lydia. I can't take you to some way station and leave you to make a life for yourself alone. I want you with me." He looked up suddenly to find her standing in front of him. "I have nothing to offer you."

"You have you," she whispered, reaching out and touching his face. "All I want is you."

He pulled her into his arms and onto his lap, and buried his face against her neck and her sweet scent. He was home, and he would have to take a chance. And so would she, he thought. They would start out with nothing, and they might end up with nothing, but he saw in her face that she was pragmatic enough to understand that, and she patently did not believe it would happen.

But she knew something deeper than that; she knew that all the qualities that had made her so suspicious of him were the very qualities she valued in him. What did it matter in the end how their lives had collided? His integrity had not allowed him to hurt her or treat her badly, and she was sensible of that. Everything else had been an exercise in living together by wit and by guile, and they had survived it. They would survive a lot more, she thought. He would learn that she was not like Lydia.

411

He would learn how much she loved him.

She ran her hands lovingly over the deep-etched lines around his mouth, and as he spoke, she laid her fingers on his lips to feel the movement. "I used to watch you from the jail cell window," he said in a haunted voice. "I really do believe, Lizzie, I meant to take you with me from the start."

They were ready to go as the sun rose fully over the mountain. Galt was going to fire the house. "We'll go out in a blaze of glory," he said grimly. "We'll never come back. The damned silver will melt in the heat and flow into the ashes and no one will be able to recoup it ever."

He threw a match into the barn onto a pile of straw and it blazed up with a whomp of heat. He tossed in another and another, and Elizabeth lit the lamp that came from her bedroom in Martha's house, and he threw it in a galvanic arc into the roof of the house. It crashed, and the flame slithered down the tar paper and caught the wood plank that secured it to the roof.

"They'll think we died inside," he said, his rich voice expressionless, and he lit another match and tossed it in the door, and still another into a window.

And they watched as the flames gathered force and began licking their way up the wooden walls and pole supports of the interior of the house. They watched until the whole house and barn were ablaze, and then Galt took her arm and led her to the horse and wagon he had moved outside the barnyard, well away from the heat of the fire.

He hitched up the horse, climbed up on his side, and took the reins. He slanted a look at her. "I love you, Lizzie." He hadn't intended to say that, but it was the start of their beginning, their true beginning. He reached for her and covered her mouth with his, and the sweetest taste, the sweetest love, rushed through him in a shower of sparks, hot enough to rival the flames burning through the timbers of the structures behind him.

"I think," she whispered, "I never meant to let you go."

He smiled that seductive smile that crinkled his eyes, the

one she loved so much. "We have nothing, Lizzie, no supplies, no money . . ."

"Oh—I forgot to tell you—I still have my knife—"

"Lizzie . . ."

"And a *little* of that money I—um—earned in Rim City . . ."

"I do love you, Lizzie." God, it was so easy to say . . . to her.

"—and I have *you,*" she finished softly, lovingly, reaching for him.

Galt snapped the reins, and as the roof of the house collapsed behind them, as if to punctuate the end of their life in Greenfields, the wagon pulled out of the yard.

Twenty-Seven

Two weeks later, after the devastating fire that had apparently taken the lives of Galt Saunders and Elizabeth Barnett, Martha Healey and her son trekked out to the graveyard in the dead of the night, shovels in hand, and confident that no one knew of their complicity and their deceit, they began digging up the grave of Edgar Healey.

<u>FREE</u> Preview Each Month and $ave

Zebra has made arrangements for you to preview 4 brand new HEARTFIRE novels each month...FREE for 10 days. You'll get them as soon as they are published. If you are not delighted with any of them, just return them with no questions asked. But if you decide these are everything we said they are, you'll pay just $3.25 each—a total of $13.00 (a $15.00 value). **That's a $2.00 saving each month off the regular price.** Plus there is NO shipping or handling charge. These are delivered right to your door absolutely free! There is no obligation and there is no minimum number of books to buy.

TO GET YOUR
FIRST MONTH'S PREVIEW...
Mail the Coupon Below!

Mail to:

 HEARTFIRE Home Subscription Service, Inc.
120 Brighton Road
P.O. Box 5214
Clifton, NJ 07015-5214

YES! I want to subscribe to Zebra's HEARTFIRE Home Subscription Service. Please send me my first month's books to preview free for ten days. I understand that if I am not pleased I may return them and owe nothing, but if I keep them I will pay just $3.25 each; a total of $13.00. That is a savings of $2.00 each month off the cover price. There are no shipping, handling or other hidden charges and there is no minimum number of books I must buy. I can cancel this subscription at any time with no questions asked.

NAME _____

ADDRESS _____ APT. NO. _____

CITY _____ STATE _____ ZIP _____

SIGNATURE (if under 18, parent or guardian must sign)
Terms and prices are subject to change.

2522

TURN TO CATHERINE CREEL — THE REAL THING — FOR THE FINEST IN HEART-SOARING ROMANCE!

CAPTIVE FLAME (2401, $3.95)

Meghan Kearney was grateful to American Devlin Montague for rescuing her from the gang of Bahamian cutthroats. But soon the handsome yet arrogant island planter insisted she serve his baser needs — and Meghan wondered if she'd merely traded one kind of imprisonment for another!

TEXAS SPITFIRE (2225, $3.95)

If fiery Dallas Brown failed to marry overbearing Ross Kincaid, she would lose her family inheritance. But though Dallas saw Kincaid as a low-down, shifty opportunist, the strong-willed beauty could not deny that he made her pulse race with an inexplicable flaming desire!

SCOUNDREL'S BRIDE (2062, $3.95)

Though filled with disgust for the seamen overrunning her island home, innocent Hillary Reynolds was overwhelmed by the tanned, masculine physique of dashing Ryan Gallagher. Until, in a moment of wild abandon, she offered herself like a purring tiger to his passionate, insistent caress!

Available wherever paperbacks are sold, or order direct from the Publisher. Send cover price plus 50¢ per copy for mailing and handling to Zebra Books, Dept. 2522, 475 Park Avenue South, New York, N.Y. 10016. Residents of New York, New Jersey and Pennsylvania must include sales tax. DO NOT SEND CASH.